"I have not read a book that has left me so broken in a long time. Ms. Jay makes you FEEL the hurt, the love, the terror of war. I have so much to say but nothing I say could do this book justice ... just read it."

—Sandra Hind, *NetGalley Reviewer*

"Jay's ... account is impressively ambitious, offering a sprawling view of the wages of war from three distinct perspectives. She ingeniously braids them into a coherent narrative tapestry, and along the way, she realistically describes the human degradation experienced by prisoners in the Nazi camps..."

—*Kirkus Reviews 2019*

"Karla M. Jay's novel *When We Were Brave* employs a dramatic triangle to create a highly-emotional, epic story of World War II, one that is as vivid as it is highly personal. Here is a moving, riveting tale that shows you how things once were—and how similar those times can feel to our own."

—Scott Lasser – Author of *Say Nice Things About Detroit*, Screenwriter for HBO's *True Detective Series*

"Historically accurate account of WWII, full of terror, sadness, hope, & vindication!"

—Doug Cook

"Combining excellent historical research with a compelling storyline, the hard work of author Karla M. Jay really pays off ... As the plot threads and connections slowly come together, the conclusion marks the realities of war and sticks in your mind for a long time after."

—*Readers Favorite Review*

"Jay demonstrates a mastery of emotion and landscape. The scenes are visceral, the dialogue is sharp and believable, and the narrators are immediately engrossing. For history enthusiasts, the level of detail, cultural accuracy, and research feels immersive. The world of the past spills out naturally, drawing readers into the relationships between these characters.

When We Were Brave is a vivid portrait of a time and place with characters who are immediately recognizable."

—*Self-Publishing Review*

"When We Were Brave … portrays all the horror, grief, inhumanity, and bravery found in a young Jewish boy, a disenchanted SS officer, and a German-American family."

—Barb, Blogger, *I'm Hooked on Books*

"One of the best WWII books I have read."

—Kelly Long, *NetGalley Reviewer*

"With complex characters and intricate plotting, Jay delivers a heart-wrenching, engrossing historical read."

—*The Prairies Book Review*

"The author's ability to weave these three heartbreaking stories together is breathtaking."

—Rachel F

WHEN WE
WERE BRAVE

— Karla M. Jay —

This is a work of fiction. All the characters, organizations, and events portrayed in the novel are either products of the author's imagination or used fictitiously.

WHEN WE WERE BRAVE

Printed in the United States of America
Book Circle Press

Cover designed by Julia Hardy

ISBN: 9780578477077

This book is dedicated to my mother-in-law
Marjorie Hardy Welker
who rode a train with German POWs
on an ordinary day so long ago

The opposite of bravery is not cowardice but conformity.
~ Robert Anthony

One does evil enough when one does nothing good.
~ German Proverb

WHEN WE WERE BRAVE

Karla M. Jay

-1-

WILHELM FALK

Avellino, Italy - November 11, 1943

SS officer, Sturmbannführer Wilhelm Falk kicked away the broken glass crunching under his boots in the shoemaker's second-story apartment, the shards making faint clinking sounds as they struck the fireplace bricks. He studied the three dead German soldiers who'd never return home. The place Hitler claimed they fought to protect. Not fighting to defend the "Fatherland," a vague term that didn't motivate troops. The Führer, known to be more masterful and cunning, instilled fear on a personal level. He targeted the soldier's family—the potential violation of his wife, the death of his children.

Early on, Falk believed that call to duty. But that was before he experienced the death camps. Nothing he saw there was even remotely connected to protecting his wife and children. He tried to bury the visions of skeletal, fellow human beings no more than a whisper away from death, of the beatings, and of chimneys pumping out foul smoke, but the memories always clawed their way to the forefront of his mind. Despair had filled his days and ghosts haunted his sleep until Falk knew he must do something or die trying.

The family who owned the cobbler's shop must have fled before the Germans took over the town. Depleted furnishings suggested the wood fueled the large fireplace through two bitter winters. Bookshelves lay broken apart. A few unburned books were spewed into dark corners. A lopsided antique dollhouse sat under the table, its small porcelain doll family strewn across the floor as fragmented as the rest of Hitler's empire.

Falk breathed a sigh of relief he'd found no other bodies in the attached rooms. He shook away an all-too-recent memory from inside a house near Warsaw. A man and woman were deceased in the kitchen, shot in the head, but the scent of death also emanated from the dining area. Two young boys were found dead, locked inside the center compartment of a hutch. What the parents must have hoped would keep their children safe resulted in an agonizing death. The bloody marks on the inside of the cupboard revealed the boys had tried to escape. The gruesome scene struck him in the gut as he thought of his two young sons.

Now by the look of this home, the three German soldiers had been taken by surprise by the British. Two shot dead at the dining table, their congealed meal still in front of them, while the third sat slumped against a wall, a broken coffee cup next to him. This soldier was shot while standing, and the blood-smeared wallpaper behind him marked his slide to the floor. Falk moved closer to the man, and with a squinted eye, studied him. A sculpted nose on a chiseled face, thick blond hair, and he seemed close to Falk's 5'10" height. Hard to be sure in that hunched position. But the soldier was the closest to what he'd been looking for in the last hour as he combed through buildings, turning over dozens of Wehrmacht corpses shot by the British when they reclaimed the Italian city.

Falk had nearly run out of time in his search and his head pounded from worrying he might fail. Although the loud thunder of the British bombers had stopped, the second wave of ground troops would soon arrive to check the buildings for any Germans they may have missed a few hours earlier. When the generals heard of the loss of another military line, they would be furious, but he no longer cared about the Wehrmacht's feelings as he wrestled with his own. The horrific things he'd seen. The things he'd done. But mostly the guilt from the things he hadn't done.

He reached for the stiff soldier's shirt and began unbuttoning and removing his uniform. Then he removed the soldier's identification papers and set them aside. The pulling and pushing on the corpse's rigid limbs to undress him soon had him breathing hard. His shaky fingers fumbled with the buttons on his own long coat as he shed his officer's uniform. The mix of exertion and fear slowed him down, chewing away at the precious minutes he had left. Falk set aside his weapon belt and quickly dressed in the infantry soldier's pants, shirt, and boots. Then he knelt and strained once again to outfit the dead man in his SS major's uniform. When finished, he glanced at the soldier and a shock zipped through him. The soldier's build and facial features were more similar to his own than he expected, and it was as if he were looking at a dead version of himself.

Which would be sooner rather than later if he were caught there.

Falk took off his signet ring and carefully removed the cyanide pill hidden inside. He pocketed the small tablet—insurance in case his plan failed. He reached for the soldier's cold hand and broke the rigor-curled finger, the snap resonating through his own hand before he slid on the ring. He removed his own gold Swiss watch and paused, turning it over to read the engraved inscription: *Wilhelm, My Love, My Life, My Hero. Ilse.* His chest tightened. Would his wife have the same sentiment today if she learned what he was doing? His sons. Would they be ashamed he was about to defect, or would they understand his sacrifice? He strapped the watch onto the dead man's hairy wrist and then stood and buttoned the enlisted infantryman's uniform. It was made of inferior quality wool and the original olive color faded to a greenish khaki. But it fit, and the blood on the chest of the jacket would be easy enough to explain. What soldier hadn't dragged a bleeding companion to safety?

He reached for his gun belt and unclipped his Walther P38, the aged leather crackling as he pulled out the weapon. His hand shook slightly with the knowledge there would be no turning back once he *killed* himself. SS-Sturmbannführer Wilhelm Falk would no longer exist, the only option left to him. Until a week ago, he managed to keep secrets from his fellow SS officers, secrets that would have gotten him shot. Then, at an undisclosed postbox in Brussels, he was caught checking his mail, and on that day, he'd talked his way out of it. No big deal. Many officers claimed a mistress, so he fabricated one with blonde curls and a flirty walk. The SS officer laughed and patted him on the back. But suspicion swirled like thick smoke among the highest-ranking officers and Falk hadn't missed the hard glint of distrust behind the hearty laughter, and he'd been right. Soon after, he was ordered to arrive in Berlin at his earliest convenience. With his new plan, Officer Falk would be "too dead" to report to Goering or the rest of Hitler's favorites.

He listened for footsteps from the hastily abandoned street below. Although he believed he was now alone in this part of the city, he wasn't a hundred percent sure. No other sounds reached him except for a loose wire scratching against the outside wall and the faint hiss of radio static in the distance.

Turning back to the dead soldier, he leveled the gun at the man's face and pulled the trigger. He felt the blast's reverberation in his back teeth and cringed as the sound echoed off the walls. The bullet hit its mark, obliterating the corpse's ashen-colored skin, leaving a mess for the burial corps— the "cold meat specialists."

His gun felt heavier than usual as he set it next to the soldier's hand. But more weight had not been added to the gun. The heaviness was mental. Desperation and remorse had drained the strength from him for months. With his nerves strung tight like old piano wires, ready to snap with any additional tension, he hadn't slept more than a few hours a night. He needed the brutalities he witnessed over the last fifteen months to stop playing through his mind. If his plan failed, the cyanide pill would put a prompt end to his nightmares.

Through the broken window, he gazed in the direction of the building across the street and then focused on one pair of work trousers hanging from the clothesline. A pant leg pinned by a wooden clip to the line while the other leg flapped against the wrought-iron balcony. If ever there was an image of abandonment, this would be it.

The last glass shard in the window threw a spotlight on the scene at Falk's feet—an impeccably dressed SS officer with no face. At that moment, he spotted the dead man's *soldbuch* on the floor, identification papers he needed or risk being shot.

He opened the leather-bound packet. He just became Klaus Stern, a low-ranking soldier. If he chased down Klaus's 10th Army Division in time, he'd be captured by the unrelenting British 8th Army that had the Germans pinned down. His new identity sheered two years off his thirty-two. Ironic.

What he wouldn't give to erase the last two years of his life, knowing what he knew now.

Again, he listened for noises outside. The distant stipple of gunfire confirmed the Wehrmacht soldiers still held the subterranean complexes beneath the medieval walls. The stone fortifications were the last bastion of defense to hold the Volturno Line before Hitler grudgingly moved another pushpin northward on the map of Italy.

Set high on a butte, the walled village of Avellino overlooked valleys in three directions. Unless the weary Germans found the resolve to climb over the soaring Partenio Mountains at their backs, they were trapped. Falk imagined the disillusionment the soldiers must be feeling. Hitler declared their fighting force remained as unbreakable as Krupp steel. But the harsh reality was that American and British troops had been cutting through their steel for six months in Africa and now Italy, slicing away at the dream of promised world domination. In the beginning, he believed there was a need to fight to save his country from Russian rule as witnessed in the Great War. But rage consumed him knowing Hitler created a secret war within this fight to "purify" the country and the entire continent, of different races. As a shocked observer at the death camps, Falk did nothing to stop the killings. One dead SS officer would have changed nothing. His inaction caused deep-seated guilt and nearly drove him to suicide several times, but that pain was ultimately the catalyst for defecting. He had a plan of action, a reason to live—to try to put a permanent stop to the exterminations.

The British 8th Army and American 5th Army had powered through Avellino earlier that morning, their growling vehicles cutting a wide swath through the cobblestone streets. Falk should have been on a train to Berlin as ordered but instead arrived without suspicion to "supervise" the war effort in Italy, a bonus his rank afforded him. He'd chosen Avellino because it appeared to be the next to fall to the Allies as they streamed through the central part of Italy, taking German POWs faster than they could ship them off continent. Earlier this day, he hid in the stone rubble of a 14th-century church, its majestic clock tower gutted, while he waited for the Allied forces to leave town. The clock's mechanisms hung upside down and continued to orchestrate time but in the wrong direction. The months and years ahead for the town's citizens were going to be hell. How would the ragged townspeople rearrange their broken village from piles of rocks and wooden beams into the shapes of buildings, into some semblance of life before the war?

It wouldn't be long before the bomb shelter doors creaked open and the residents stumbled into the daylight, praying for the best, expecting the worst. Falk studied the destruction in the shoe shop. Would this family return, start over, feel as if they were lucky? Perhaps if all the family members survived.

Falk drew in a deep breath, hoping to energize the fist-sized exhaustion coursing through him. The war had ground him down until sharp rage was the only motivation prodding him from one day to the next. He reached for that anger now as he slid the soldier's Luger into the holster on his own waist, and picked up a small backpack beside the man. He crossed to the door where only the top hinge held it in place, the splintered frame evidence the Tommies had not been invited in for a glass of local wine.

Falk slowly crept down the stairwell and stepped into the street, assuming his new role as a foot soldier, somewhat road-weary and rumpled. He walked over bits of wood and stone scattered atop the cobblestones. Everything about the scene suggested the village occupants left in haste. A scarf fluttering where it hooked on a fence post. A wooden tobacco pipe on the sidewalk near an overturned green metal table. A child's leather shoe lying in the gutter.

The residents hid in bunkers or cemetery crypts. When they emerged, the city dignitaries' first job would be to catalog the deceased civilians while the British dealt with noting the dead soldiers on both sides of the war. SS Officer Falk would be on the list sent to the Wehrmacht.

The sky boiled with battleship-grey clouds. The cold wind carried smoke and he wrinkled his nose at the odor of something burning that shouldn't be on fire. He hoped it would rain, not to put out the flames, but to give him a measure of cover as he chased down Stern's division.

As he peered down a trash-strewn alley, a sound caught his attention. A dog urinated against the wall. The mangy animal sniffed the air in Falk's direction and then, deciding Falk wasn't a threat, turned its thin body and trotted away down a wrecked path between crooked buildings. The streets were empty as Falk crept along block by block. A wooden sign declared the small stone building to his right as the post office, and his hands itched for a moment to enter the intact structure and jot down a quick letter to Ilse and his two boys. At ages eleven and nine, they were already asking questions about this war, and trading Heil Hitler salutes with their friends. The last time he'd written to them was two weeks ago while in Ferrazzano. The peace of that steepled town, which overlooked broad rows of plush vineyards, had been crushed in one afternoon marked by explosions and gunfire. In his letter to Ilse, he told her it was time to take the boys and get on the next train to her sister's in the Netherlands as they'd discussed. Once he finished delivering information to the Americans, something Ilse knew nothing about, he'd meet them in Holland. He'd fold his wife in his arms, shake his boys' hands, and make new family memories, although doing any of those things seemed far away at the moment.

His thoughts spun back through the years to when Hans and Dietrich were roly-poly fat. Now, at ages eleven and nine, they stood lean and tall when he embraced them. It was late summer when he last saw them. Both showed musical talent like Ilse, but wished to be soldiers like him. They'd clomped about in his jackboots on the patio behind their home near Düsseldorf, dressed in short pants and button-down shirts, pretending to give orders. Talking with deep voices and trying to sound serious.

"I don't sound like that, do I?"

She ignored him, lost in the pleasure of a cigarette he brought home. They sat at the edge of their sloping lawn as summer's heat hung onto the countryside.

He asked again.

When she replied, her voice was lazy and content. "You have a serious side, Wilhelm. It's why you're in a top position."

She meant her words to compliment, but they cut through him. Men in his top position were acting as if they'd made a pact with the devil. The fairytales this war espoused were that the SS were the elite, the chosen, the righteous. Nearly every month since signing up, he wanted to commit an act of irrational bravery, like hunting down Hitler and putting a bullet through his immoral heart. But it seemed a futile dream. While dozens had already tried, the Führer's protection squad numbered close to a thousand, and none succeeded. Falk kept his wife sheltered from the truths of what he'd seen but secretly seethed and wept more times as a grown man than as a knobby-kneed child.

"I suppose I've changed."

Wilhelm studied his property. Late summer was his favorite season at home. Fat grapes hung heavy on the arbor, and the garden was a tangle of vines cradling squash and pumpkins. The aroma of flowers mingled with the earthy green threads from the nearby forest, creating a scent that unwound his tangled nerves. If only he didn't have to leave.

He hadn't shared any of the horrors with Ilse. The images of Jews who'd become haunted-eyed skeletons. The burial pits layered twenty feet deep with bodies and dirt. Gleeful soldiers, trading necklaces and wallets mined from the stacks of luggage left near the trains. The piles and piles of empty shoes.

There were no words for such atrocities and to speak too openly about them would mean death or imprisonment for himself and his family. He'd been spun into a web he hadn't recognized until he was wrapped, layer upon layer, within its deadly circle.

Hans ran past their chairs, *bang-banging* a wooden gun at his brother. He wore his father's field-grey uniform coat, a garment crafted to make onlookers shudder with fear for their lives.

Falk took a long pull from his mug of Schwarzbier, welcoming the sharp bitter taste after months of watered-down beer. The boys wheeled around the yard, their arms outstretched, pretending to be airplanes on attack, and his chest tightened. What would happen to his children, his wife, if he never came back? Or worse, what if Hitler's henchmen came for them?

He leaned in closer, memorizing her scent while meeting her light-blue eyes with his own. "Promise me that if the day comes when I ask you to take the boys to Eindhoven, you will leave immediately."

Her eyebrows rose then drew together. "But the Netherlands is in no better shape than Germany, Wilhelm."

"Ilse. This most likely won't happen. But, if I ask, I must know that you are there with your relatives, not here." Growing up, Ilse's family summered in the Netherlands just across the German border.

She was silent for a moment then spoke. "Of course, darling. We'll go. But I hope it doesn't come to that."

"Me, too." He relaxed, but a worry tugged at him. "And don't believe everything you read." He spoke those words louder than intended.

Tears welled in her eyes as if she understood what he meant her to know. Had she? Right away, he regretted the firmness in his tone. Her voice trembled. "What is going on, Wilhelm?"

He slowly shook his head, fighting the words on his lips and the tremble in his chest. Should he tell her everything? The ghastly secrets kept behind barbed wire, the camps with so many unspeakable crimes? Forcing himself not to look away, he'd memorized every last detail in order to report them later. He had protected her from the horrors he'd seen, and she seemed content to have him home every two months, more when he was in the area. Their marriage was built on honesty, but the danger of her slipping and telling a friend what he'd learned about the extermination program would put her in immediate danger, and she'd be questioned. It was better that she never learned any details concerning his plans. "There's something I have to do. People may question my loyalty for a short time...until the truth comes out. You are an intelligent woman...please recognize the truth when you hear it."

Doves wheeled from Avellino's cathedral roof, startling him back to the present. He didn't want to leave the images of his family behind just yet, but the babble of voices reached him—townspeople returning from safe havens to assess their new reality. That prompted him to get moving. Getting hacked to death by angry citizens wasn't his plan. He needed to find the ragtag Wehrmacht 10th Army and surrender with them. He stuck to the alleys and small streets and headed toward the final battles at the edge of the city in order to slip into Klaus Stern's unit.

Becoming a POW and getting to the United States was his last hope to tell the world about the death camps.

He'd used his position as an SS inspection officer to travel and mail letters—while in each new city—to European clergy and Danish and Swiss political resistance groups, notifying them about the hidden truths of the "work camps." He prayed someone would rise up and stop Hitler's "acts of cleansing."

No one had.

His plan to surrender with the Wehrmacht soldiers could leave him in a hopeless situation with no option for escape. But with evil at his back and the possibility of disaster dead ahead, he chose the future.

-2-

IZAAK TAUBER

Amsterdam, Netherlands - November 11, 1943

"Almost," Izaak whispered, drawing the word out as he swiveled his hips slightly to the right, then to the left and back to the right again. The challenge? Line up the nail dangling from the string pinned to the back of his trousers with the opening of the empty milk bottle. This would be the moment his friends cheered him on if he still had friends. His leather-soled shoes made scraping sounds on the cement patio as he quickly shifted his feet. And his breath puffed out in the cold evening air, forming little see-through clouds that hung in front of his mouth for a second before dashing off to the sidelines. *You've got this.*

"Come on, Izaak!" Mama loud-whispered this, standing close to him, so she didn't have to yell since yelling was against the hiding rules. "Ten seconds!" she counted down from the timepiece Papa left behind.

Izaak was the Spijkerpoepen champ in his old neighborhood, beating Guus van Groot's record by two seconds. He hadn't played the game in over a month since his eighth birthday party, but needed to practice if he were to stay at the top, right?

"Five seconds!"

The happy tone in Mama's voice reminded him he needed to try to make her laugh more often. Papa's favorite saying ran through his head: *A man's true wealth is the good he does in this world.* Although Izaak repeated this motto three times a day during prayer, he knew he was on the poorer side of wealth because he hadn't cheered up anyone in weeks, including himself. Being funny was hard when every day was a new worry and another day without Papa.

With a *clink*, the spike hit the edge of the bottle balanced on the ground. Izaak's neck started to ache as he twisted around to try to angle the dangling nail into the right position. "Come on," he growled as he watched the nail turn and spin and then center above the bottle's opening. "Time?"

"Thirty-nine. Forty. Forty-one..."

Izaak dropped his hips a few centimeters and *ding!* The spike dropped in.

"Forty-two seconds!" Mama stuck the watch in her outer coat pocket and clapped. "You did it, darling."

Izaak slumped onto the cold cement as a surge of warm pride filled him. Although Mama was a nice audience, he couldn't wait to tell Guus about his new time. He picked up the milk bottle, pulled out the string and nail, and felt his smile disappear. The empty container reminded him of how he felt inside. He swallowed hard and fought his jittery chin as he tried not to cry, his throat aching from the effort.

The Germans had taken everyone away.

In his school journal, he wrote down the dates of every sad happening, although he wasn't allowed to go to school now. He wanted to be like Papa, who kept a daily agenda, saying "a full day meant a happy life." Izaak's dates started a year earlier when the Germans came for the Jewish families, who earlier that year were forced to wear a yellow star. That frightening night was filled with gunshots and screaming, and the neighbors who tried to hide were killed. More people than he could count were forced on board the Number 8 streetcar. As the train came and left throughout the night, he heard the screech of brakes and then the rattle of wheels—over and over again, coming and going. He nestled between his parents in their bed, worrying his family would be next. After all, Papa was Jewish. Izaak became so upset to the point his stomach hurt until he threw up. And, although Papa said they were safe, Mama cried, and his papa's jaw tightened as he offered a prayer for protection.

The kidnapping of the Jews left their neighborhood hollowed-out. The favorite bakeries and stores the Jewish families owned were closed. The only Jewish families left behind had a mama or papa from another religion, like his parents. Mama was raised Catholic, making Izaak half and half, a Mischling. It was all confusing to him, but he knew the Germans wanted to own all of Europe, and they were picky about who lived near them. Now that the Germans lived in the Netherlands, they wanted the Jews out.

The next date in his journal was three months ago, August 18. Instead of just asking for help from the papas left at home, the Germans blocked off their neighborhood that evening as the sun was setting. The soldiers yelled through loudspeakers that all the men needed to line up in the streets. His family was eating dinner at the time. Mama dropped a serving spoon on a plate. The clattering sounded extra loud in the sudden silence. Had he heard correctly? Izaak's heart pounded because when people were ordered to line up, they were usually shot. Weeks earlier, on the way back from his art lesson, he and Papa turned the corner into Munt Square where a group of twelve people stood against the old town wall, crying and holding each other. As the soldiers raised their guns, Papa yanked him backward. When the gunfire rang out, the roar from the blasts bounced off the buildings and pounded into his ears. He and Papa ran as others ducked into houses not wanting to be seen. Later, Papa learned the two families were accused of stealing food coupons. This seemed so unfair since everyone was starving. Papa said, "We believe things will remain the same in wartime, but we shouldn't count on fairness to be one of them."

That August evening, with the windows open, the abrupt announcement came again, the fresh summer breeze rustling through the elm trees ruined by the words. Papa and Mama slowly stood and looked at each other without saying a word, which made the moment scarier. Izaak's throat tightened and his heart pounded in his ears. Had the Germans learned Papa was only pretending to be Catholic? And why did all the men need to line up? Maybe this was just a document check. The Germans loved their paperwork. Izaak might be getting upset for no reason. They would return to eating the boiled potatoes, and Papa would say the soldiers were drunk and acting mean as they liked to do.

He believed his hopeful story until he noticed Mama's hands. They shook when she reached for Papa. Papa pulled Mama and him into his arms, and they stayed that way while Izaak prayed the Germans would take away the other men and move on. *Please, God. Please, God, not Papa.*

But God lived far away, and Izaak's prayer hadn't reached Him in time because someone pounded on their front door and then banged their door knocker over and over again. The soldiers weren't leaving.

"I'll go see what they want," Papa said, his voice deeper than usual. He kissed Izaak and then Mama. "I love you both, and I'll see you soon."

Izaak's legs wouldn't stop trembling as he watched through the window, the lace curtains pulled back. Papa stopped outside their front door and touched the praying hands door knocker he'd bought at a church sale in Haarlem. Mama made fun of the hand's size, and Papa declared they must be the hands of God. He made a ritual of touching them each time he came home or left, saying they brought him luck, and Izaak hoped that was true now more than ever. Papa climbed into the open back of a military vehicle with dozens of other men. A soldier yelled, and the truck jerked to life and sped off.

The Germans were getting away with doing horrible things, and Izaak had no idea when it would stop. His stomach hurt most days because he wondered if Mama would be next. What would he do without her? He could never have believed Papa would be gone this long. As an engineer, Papa used to be gone overnight when he traveled far away for a project, but never away for months like now.

Izaak was sure the Germans chose Papa because he would do a good job building whatever they needed. It was hard to know when he'd be home.

When an SS officer showed up a week after Papa left and announced he would be staying at their house, Mama's eyes got huge like a trapped rabbit. She showed the officer to the guest room above Izaak's bedroom and hurried back to the kitchen and slumped against the wall, her face white.

"Who is he, Mama?"

"I don't know." Mama started to put together dinner but tugged on her apron and seemed to forget what she was doing from minute to minute.

Why was she so nervous? "Should we be afraid?" Izaak whispered, although the man was still upstairs.

"No, not afraid. But we shouldn't tell the soldier anything about our family, Izaak. We have no choice but to host him, but we should stay out of his way." Which turned out to be easy. Izaak had seen many SS men shoot people for no reason, but this man was different. He seemed lost in his thoughts and spent most of his time in his room. Izaak lay in his bed and listened to the footsteps above him as the officer paced the floor with his boots on, often for hours. When the man wasn't yelling out in the middle of the night, he often talked to himself. Izaak wished he understood German then he'd know what the man was saying. And one morning, without them knowing, the man was up and gone. He left a thank-you note written in Dutch, thanking Mama for her kindness the past week. He also left a small bag of ginger candy. "For your proper son."

Izaak shared the extra-special treat with his friends but kept most of it for Papa's return. Each night after dinner when Papa enjoyed his pipe, he'd ask Izaak to talk about his day. Papa always moved a hard piece of candy side to side with his tongue. The soft *clinking* on his teeth was a sound he missed. A sound he never thought he'd noticed before, but now it was high on the list of all the little things he wanted back.

A cold wind blew across the patio, and Izaak shivered. Mainly because he was chilly, but also because this is where he had to remember why he no longer saw Guus. The third date in Izaak's logbook, October 8, was just a month ago. The last image he had of Guus flashed in his head—a memory he tried to forget. Why did some part of his brain always hold on to sad thoughts? That day, he and Guus were horse-riding broom handles along the Herengracht Canal because all their bicycles were taken away by the Germans. Cort, the scissors' sharpener, sat in their kitchen and explained the Germans needed to steal the rubber from the tires because there wasn't any left to buy. Rabbi Feinstein taught that stealing was a sin no matter the reason or season. Apparently, the Germans had never heard of God's rules even though Papa said everyone shared the same God.

A military truck had stopped in front of Guus's large house, three doors down from Izaak's, and German soldiers poured out of it. While one soldier battered open Guus's front door with his rifle butt, another grabbed Guus from his broom handle just two meters away from Izaak and threw the stick in the canal.

"Leave me alone!" Guus had yelled as the German pulled him to the truck.

Izaak panicked and could hardly breathe. His short quick gasps sounded like a baby bird that fell out of its nest.

Guus's mother and three-year-old sister, Olivia, rushed onto their front steps, his mama's face as white as Witte Wieven. A ghost from a fable that told children to stay out of caves where the white witch lived.

And then the part that was worse than a scary witch story because it was really happening: The soldier picked up Guus by the arm and foot—Guus's eyes wide like a wild horse's—and threw him into the back of the truck like a trash bag.

Guus's mama screamed as the men grabbed Olivia and tossed her in the same way. Another soldier poked Mrs. Van Groot in the back with his gun barrel to force her inside the truck. Izaak ran home, his pants soaked in the front where he'd wet himself.

He squirmed, now remembering how ashamed he'd been.

"Izaak." Mama rubbed his back. He shook his head and once again was back on the patio, a Spijkerpoepen champ no longer lost in the bad thoughts. "Are you okay?"

He nodded and tucked his arms around his body, suddenly freezing. Then he smiled and studied Mama's expression. Even after all they'd been through, she was still pretty with her reddish-brown hair in contrast to Papa's dark curly hair. Paprika en Peper. Nicknames given to them by one of Mama's nurse friends. Izaak loved to draw although he was just learning. When he drew Mama's face, he always started with a heart shape. If she were deep in thought, he sketched her mouth with a smile on it because her thinking expression always looked happy. He added the deep dimple to her right cheek, the one Papa kissed first, but often teased he thought he might get lost inside. Mama always play-slapped him and giggled. Izaak missed hearing that sound, her laugh, like tiny bells jingling together. And he sure wasn't cheering her up at the moment. Her mouth was set in a straight line. It was her trying-to-be-happy face.

"I was just thinking"—he swallowed hard—"about Guus."

She stroked his smooth head, his Jewish curls sheared off to trick the Germans. "I know, love."

He secretly spied on the Van Groot house later that terrible afternoon

Guus's family was taken, but it sat empty. The windows remained dark rectangles even as evening fell. Surely, they would be brought back when they discovered the mistake. With Guus's papa away, his mama had taken in sewing from neighbors, and German officers sometimes dropped off their mending. The Germans liked a hard worker, and Mrs. Van Groot was that and more.

A week before they were thrown in the truck, Izaak had come looking for Guus to play marbles early one morning and found Guus's mama hurriedly packing stacks of fliers into a laundry basket. He'd startled her so much she clasped her hand over her chest and forgot how to talk for a moment. When she did, her voice shook. "Let's not tell anyone about this, Izaak." And he hadn't, although he didn't know why saying she had them would make her afraid. With all the radios gone, she must need them to let people know about her sewing skills. Although he never saw her hand out the pieces of paper.

"And I'm sad because I'm forgetting how Papa looks." He swallowed hard and blinked back tears as his mama rubbed his arm through his thin coat. The trash-filled area around the patio blurred, and he swiped at his eyes. They were told not to clean up the garbage or remove the broken birdhouse and rusted mower. It had to look as though nobody lived there if anyone searched the area. The problem was the terrible smell seeped into their rooms, a stinky mixture of spoiled meat and rotting vegetables that stuck in his nose and made his food taste worse than it already did.

And the last date in his journal? Twenty-nine nights ago—the night after Guus was thrown into the truck—Dr. Willem Schermerhorn visited them for the first time, telling them they had to leave their house immediately. That the Germans read through tax records and found Papa's donations to their local synagogue. Izaak and Mama scurried about while Dr. Schermerhorn urged them to go faster. While Mama packed jewelry and money, a few clothes and a photograph book, Izaak grabbed his drawing pad and pencils from the deep windowsill. This was his favorite drawing spot, a place where he could sit and create pictures. Sometimes drawing the fish peddlers along the water, or the boats on the canal. Sometimes, he drew so much he felt like he was in the pictures, hearing the shush of the water along the bottom of the boats and the captain barking orders.

One last thing he grabbed was Papa's pipe from the little table by Papa's favorite chair, knowing he would want it again. Unsure what was happening, or when he would return home, Izaak wanted to touch the praying hands on the front door one more time for good luck. But Dr. Schermerhorn rushed them out the back. "No one can know you left."

While hurrying, Izaak forgot to grab his journal, but the dates, along with the horrible images, he remembered.

Now Izaak and Mama lived in these two rooms in the back of an unused apartment building, waiting to get papers to leave the Netherlands. They were "onderduikers," or "under divers," Dr. Schermerhorn explained. They were hiding like other Jewish people, or in their case, half-Jewish people. He didn't know why everyone would let this happen, but it seemed the Germans answered to no one.

Mama opened her long coat wide like soft dove's wings and swaddled him inside. He wrapped his arms around her waist, losing himself in this safe place, her warmth moving through his cold hands and face. "Remember, Izaak... God is closest to those with broken hearts."

His heart cracked open enough right then, and he imagined God must be squeezed inside the coat between Mama and him.

She kissed the top of his head, her lips tickling him. Then she stepped away, and with two quick strokes, pushed invisible hair away from her eyes, a habit that said she had an idea.

"Let's go inside and look through photographs."

For him, the pictures of the fun times his family had before the Germans showed up left him empty. Like someone borrowed his feelings, wrung them out, and handed them back, pale and limp. But if looking through the photograph books made Mama smile, he would do it because that was his new goal.

An hour later after nightfall, a lantern shone a flickering yellow light on Mama's back as she stood at the small stained sink, washing their dinner bowls. Like Mama, he wore his coat with two layers of clothes underneath. The kitchen had a small stove they weren't allowed to use. No cooking, no warm water, no lights. He sat at the small drop-down table where he was drawing in the dim light, his stomach feeling funny from eating the chopped onion and tulip bulb sandwich. He knew when the flower bulbs showed up, they were out of food. Izaak tried not to think about it, but some days he knew he tasted dumplings and cheese when nothing was there but spit. He set down his pencil and cupped his cold hands, blowing heat onto his stiff fingers. "Mama?"

She half turned. "Yes, love?"

"Do you think Dr. Schermerhorn is coming back?" If Mama needed to go get food, she might be stopped, questioned, and then arrested for hiding from the Germans. The thought of something terrible happening to Mama, or being alone, made his throat hitch as he swallowed.

"He always keeps his promise, Izaak. He'll come when he feels it's safe."

"Do you think he would bring me a new pencil?" While he still had three sheets of sketch paper left, his last drawing pencil was worn until it was no bigger than his littlest finger.

"We can ask. But remember, Dr. Schermerhorn is in charge of many families like us."

"I know." He tucked his hands in his armpits.

Mama said the doctor received food from their very own Queen Wilhelmina. She moved to London with her family when the Germans arrived, but Mama heard the Royal Family was concerned for the people of the Netherlands. They sent money to Dr. Schermerhorn's big Bible group to help out.

"I'll bet he could get us apples." Izaak loved apples almost better than anything else, and everyone knew they kept people from being sick. Now that he hadn't eaten one for so long, it seemed to be all he could think about.

Someone rapped on the back door, and the sudden sound made Izaak's head snap up. They'd been found. Would he be tossed into a truck like Guus? His heart raced and he grabbed his crotch, worried he would lose control again. He didn't want to be like a baby, although Mama told him people of all ages can wet themselves when they're afraid. He wasn't so sure about that. Then the tapping turned into the secret code—three knocks, then four, and three again.

"It's okay, love." Mama slid the lock open, and Dr. Schermerhorn came inside with another man. Dr. Schermerhorn knew Mama from St. Mary's Hospital where she was a nurse. The doctor was tall and had to bend over to kiss Mama on each cheek. He removed his hat. His usually neat brown hair looked messy as if he'd just climbed out of bed.

"How are you holding up, Rachel?" His voice was rumbly, but he always spoke softly—a calming sound, like faraway thunder.

"We're good. Izaak is a brave boy, and his papa will be proud to hear that."

The doctor turned and tipped his head toward the man in the shadows. Much shorter than the doctor, he had wide shoulders, and Izaak bet he could lift a lion, an act he'd seen a strong man do at a circus. When the man stepped into the light to greet Mama, Izaak noticed the scars on his hand. He had big bushy eyebrows that hung low over his eyelids, making it hard to tell if the man was kind. "This is a friend of mine. We'll just call him Fritz."

"Hello." Mama smiled, but it wasn't one of her wide happy grins.

The first time the doctor met Izaak, he explained he belonged to a Bible study group. It had to be the biggest church group in the whole world because he overheard the doctor tell Mama 13,000 people were working together. And somehow the church was in the underground, an image Izaak tried to picture but never could. The doctor never looked dirty during the three times he'd been to their rooms, and although the doctor carried a Bible, he hadn't opened it. Until now.

He pulled out an envelope. "Izaak. I need to talk to your Mama about something." He tapped the envelope against his pant leg. "Could you go into the other room and show Fritz your drawings?"

"What a good idea," Mama said. Izaak didn't trust what was about to happen because when Mama tried to light a small lantern, the match shook back and forth. Once lit, she handed it to Fritz. "Izaak is a bit of a prodigy."

He wanted to ask what a prodigy was and why they didn't think being eight was old enough to hear the news. When he and Mama went to the Catholic Church hidden inside an apartment, they both listened to the British forbidden broadcast on the nuns' secret radio. He wouldn't go against an adult's request, so he didn't argue.

He slowly gathered his sketch pad and pencil and headed for the tiny area off the kitchen. It might have once been a pantry, but now it was his and Mama's sleeping area. Mama called it that because it wasn't a real room—just large enough to fit the mattress on the floor. The walls had empty nail holes, and Izaak wondered what kind of photographs or paintings once hung there. A broken light fixture on the wall sprouted wires as if a big bug pushed its feelers out of the hole and was stuck there. It scared him several times when he forgot they were there, and the wires brushed his arms.

Fritz followed and sat next to Izaak on the sagging mattress. A puff of moldy air rose when their weight squished it, and Izaak waved it away from his face. "It's stinky in here, huh?" He snuck a peek at the man, who was dressed in work pants and a heavy plaid coat.

"It's okay with me." The man held the light on his knees, and it brightened a big circle around them. The shadows on the man's face made him look angry, but his voice was kind. "I'd like to see what you've been drawing." He nudged Izaak with his shoulder like his papa would have done.

Izaak pulled out his recent pencil sketch. It showed his family standing next to each other with small drawings around the edges of the page. "This is us by the Zaanse Schans windmills." He moved his finger to another area on the paper. "These are the wooden shoes we learned how to make." He pointed to where he'd drawn a pair and was proud of the shading he'd managed on them—they almost looked real.

Mr. Fritz leaned closer. "Izaak. This astonishes me." He smiled and lines around his eyes crinkled. "Your mama said you were good, but this is more than I expected from a child."

His shoulders slumped because he didn't like being called a child. He liked it better when Mama called him her Little Man. "I'm in second grade at school now . . . I mean, if I went to school that's where I'd be. And I used to take art lessons."

"It shows. What are these other things?" Mr. Fritz pointed to three items sketched around the page.

One day Izaak hoped to draw like a real artist, with the items in front of each other, all together like in a painting.

"That's a burst of sunshine because it was a happy day. And these two are foods. A special goat cheese with salt crystals in it and a sweet almond cake." The thought of food made his stomach ache as though he had a bad sprain in there that wouldn't heal. That day trip to the windmills was the last outing his family took before the Germans forced Papa into the truck. That night, Izaak fell asleep on the ride home, safely tucked in the front seat between his mama and papa. Now his chin quivered and tears filled his eyes. "Are you going to get Papa back?"

"We're moving you to a safe place so your papa can join you."

"Really?" This was the best news ever! From the nuns' secret British radio broadcast, Mama and Izaak heard the Germans were slowly losing the war they started. Papa would come home! In the summer, they'd go to the Artis Royal Zoo, and wintertime meant they would ice skate on the frozen canals and warm up next to the bonfires in the park.

The nuns called the Germans "Barb Arians" that day, words that made his mama and the sisters laugh. Izaak didn't understand, but thought it meant they didn't follow any commandments, especially the "Thou Shall Not Kill" rule.

He rolled his tiny pencil back and forth across his leg and snuck another glance at the man. "Is my papa still building the wall?"

Dr. Schermerhorn explained that Papa and all the men taken away were making a giant cement fence called the Atlantic Wall, over 3,200 kilometers long. Hitler was afraid to let more outsiders into the Netherlands, so the wall started in France and would end all the way north in Norway. They received one note from Papa before they had to leave their house and go into hiding. Papa wrote he was sorry he might be away longer than expected because the wall was enormous. He reminded Izaak to say his prayers and take care of Mama. At night, under his soft quilt, he traced his papa's writing on the back of the note paper, his finger brushing over the slightly raised pen marks, his chest tight. He saved Papa's note in his journal, but it was still tucked under his mattress where he'd forgotten it.

"Your papa is now working in a camp, Izaak." The man dragged a hand over his thick hair.

Mr. Fritz seemed to know more about Papa than what he was saying. "But he'll be coming back soon, right?"

"We're working on that." The man paused and kept looking at him, so Izaak waited until he spoke again. "Do you know I have a secret name?"

What did this have to do with Papa? Izaak shook his head.

"I'm called the Wanderer."

Izaak remembered a fable about a knickerbocker, who traveled the world whenever he wanted, making knickers, or marbles as he called them. The man discovered a Japanese monster called an Oni. Izaak always wanted to be able to travel like that. "Do you get to go anywhere you want?"

"I do"—he nodded and then paused—"and tonight, Izaak, you and your mama are going with me."

-3-

HERBERT MÜLLER

Tulpehocken, Pennsylvania - November 11, 1943

Herbert Müller swept the cement floor around the millstones, the setting sun announcing he and his father, Otto, had outworked the day once again. "Pop. It's quitting time." His voice echoed across the main mill floor of the gristmill. The big stones sat silent after a day of rasping and groaning against each other. His father was in the workshop attached to the central floor tinkering with something he said was broken. Herbert leaned sideways with his hands pressed against his back, urging the stiff muscles there to loosen up. How his seventy-year-old father still worked the mill astounded him, but Otto was always quick to remind his son his grit was forged by surviving the Great War. He liked to add he had strong German blood pumping through his veins. Although Herbert shared that same bloodline, he was often outworked by his father, who rested only while asleep.

"Herbert!" Jutta's faint voice carried well over the flat field between the mill and the one-story wood-frame house Otto had built after immigrating to America in 1920. It had taken two years to scrape together the money for four ocean-liner tickets. Then a month on the boat, and then another month for his father's family to finally settle in central Pennsylvania. Now dotted with checkerboard farms spread out across the frosted fields.

Herbert stepped outside and raised a hand in the orange hue from the setting sun to show he'd heard his wife, and she raised hers in return. She was a marvelous cook. It would be a shame to let whatever she'd prepared grow cold.

Back inside, he found his father slapping the dust off his trousers, standing by the one-ton grinding stones. If Herbert wanted to know what he'd look like in another thirty-five years, he only needed to study his father. They had the same angular face and brown hair, although Otto's was shot through with silver. Otto was deceptively vigorous, despite the years marking his face and the bend in his back that kept him from holding himself to his five-eight height. His hands, twisted with arthritis, never stopped him from the demands of running the largest grinding mill outside Germantown.

"We need to get, a new weld, on this." Otto grabbed the damsel pole and wiggled it. On average, it shook three hundred pounds of dried corn a day through the hopper onto the grinding stones below.

"I'll weld it first thing in the morning, Pop." He laid his hand on his father's back and felt the bones there that muscle once covered. Age was wearing his father thin, but there was no way to convince the man of that. His father's motto was "The devil moves closer the less a man works." He let his hand remain there as they left the building. "I don't know about you, Pop, but I'm bushed." Herbert closed the mill door behind them.

A full moon hovered above the nearest hill and shrouded the Müller land and orchard in a silvery cold veil as a brisk wind brushed by. Their nearest neighbor's land abutted five acres to the north—another German family—but to the south were the Amish farms, one Irish family, and a few Swedes. "Europe West" he liked to call it. Herbert knew his and his children's lives were filled with many more opportunities here in contrast to life in Germany. Thankfully, his father saw the need to move the family after the First World War.

With a second war with Germany raging across Europe, he'd recently heard of local raids on German immigrant farms, families who hadn't been here long and were still assimilating, learning the language, fitting in. As Americans, he and his family would be safe. He and Jutta married in Pennsylvania, and their children were born in the upper bedroom of the farmhouse. American children, who attended an American school, and spoke only English, much to their grandfather's dismay.

The small white house with green shutters sat a hundred yards away on a knoll. Herbert could think of nowhere else he'd rather be.

They followed the paving stones in the direction of the back door, his father's boots scraping along the ground, moving slowly in the dim light, his vision not what it used to be.

"We had, a good week, son." Otto inhaled deeply, filling his lungs until his chest lifted. "Just smell that. Your mother, she loved the fall."

"And spring, and nighttime, and morning and the other seasons as well." He smiled. Everything made his mother happy when she was alive.

"Zat's about right." Otto chuckled and started forward again.

A wave of sadness coursed through Herbert at the thought of his father getting older and ultimately dying, too. His mother, Anni, died nine months ago of a massive stroke while picking peaches in the orchard. A blow to the family for sure. The matriarch remained vibrant at sixty-eight with her sometimes too-harsh honesty. She always made up for it with her deep family devotion and wanted nothing but to ensure her family's happiness. Otto seemed cut in half after her death even though surrounded by his loved ones. Herbert missed seeing his parents sitting close together outside on a warm summer evening, talking and laughing, often sharing a glass of lemonade.

He rubbed his achy right hip. His joint might as well be a barometer the way it signaled a storm's arrival. It also made him unfit to serve in the military. Herbert was turned away while Karl, two years older, fought in the Pacific with the U.S. Army Air Forces. Guilt about his 4-F status often rose to the surface, and he cursed his faulty leg length. But he stayed focused on the long hours grinding grain—food necessary for the troops. Or by taking his five-hour shifts in the watchtower on Pumpkin Hill, the tallest rise in the area, to help national security by watching for enemy planes. Yet he was embarrassed at the monthly Elks' meeting when it would be just him and the old guys, having a beer and planning community functions.

Caught in a brisk gust of wind, maple leaves raced past his feet. From inside the house, he heard the sound of crockery clacking against each other.

Dried twigs snapped behind him. In a blur, he felt something hit his midsection, and it sent him crashing to the side, face-first, to the frost-covered ground, his teeth nearly jarring loose as his jaws slammed together. "Hey!" Something gritty flew into his mouth and he spit out bits of dirt and wood. His mind spun. What the hell? He scrambled to his knees, found his footing and shook his head to clear his vision.

Two figures, one tall and one shorter, circled his father in the eerie moonlight, but Otto stood his ground. "*Schweine!*" he called out.

It wouldn't take a translator for the attackers to understand what they'd just been called. When they moved closer to Otto, Herbert raced toward them. "Leave him alone!"

The shorter one held up his hands like a boxer and turned toward Herbert, bouncing on the balls of his feet. He was backlit in the moonlight, so Herbert couldn't see his face.

The taller man spoke. "We're sending messages to Nazis."

"Nein! We are *not* Nazis," Otto said, straightening his spine.

Herbert panicked as his father took a bold step toward the tall attacker. Otto wouldn't back away from danger, and these men already demonstrated they meant to do harm. Herbert moved in front of his father while keeping the shorter one in sight. He raised his hands in a placating gesture. "Go inside, Pops." He needed to get the situation under control and not incite the men any further. He had Jutta and the children to worry about.

The taller man mocked Otto, using a fake sing-songy German accent. "Vee are citizenz, not goddamn Krauts." Then he sprang faster than Herbert could anticipate and shoved Otto with both hands.

"No!" Herbert lunged for his father and caught his arm, but Otto went down hard on one knee. He stepped in front of Otto hoping to shield him from further attack. "Knock it off!" he said as he helped Otto stand.

Clouds obscured the moon, and the temperature seemed to drop in the sudden darkness and destroy the illusion the moonbeam had offered warmth. The stench of cheap alcohol wafted off the men. With anger and booze fueling them, his thought to attempt reasoning with them disappeared. When the men spread out, his heart pounded faster. Other German immigrants who reported recent harassment, noted property damage, such as a broken window or hay bales set on fire, but no one was assaulted. These two seemed to have a different agenda.

Trying to keep both aggressors in sight with his father behind him, he backed him closer to the house. Otto limped, favoring the knee he just injured. How dare they attack an elderly person! A vein throbbed at Herbert's temple and his chest tightened with fear that the men weren't finished. "I'll call the sheriff if you don't leave." He forced calmness into his voice, but his words still rang with a tinge of panic.

The shorter one spoke. "You'll pay for being a German spy. Radioing messages, getting our fathers killed." The young men moved, and when the moonlight lit their faces, Herbert recognized them. A local pest and his sidekick, their eyes always hard with suspicion while they smoked outside the local five and dime store.

"You're trespassing, boys." Herbert's panic subsided. A couple drunk high school boys seemed less menacing. "It's time you left."

Harsh laughter came from the man-boy to his right. "Can't rightly dial a phone with broken arms."

Break his arms? Perhaps he'd misjudged how far they would go. He continued to nudge his father to the house and whispered, "Pop. Get inside and lock the door…and call the sheriff."

The two man-boys moved closer to them as the back door flew open, smacking the side of the house with a hollow *thunk*. His fifteen-year-old son, Alfred, stood backlit in the doorway with a rifle pointed at the attackers. Although his body had started to fill out his five-foot-nine frame, he still came across as wiry and too thin. "Get off our property!"

Herbert raised a cautionary hand to stop his son. Alfred had a lightning-fast temper, and confrontation was the perfect spark to set it off. He played nearly every high school sport, the best solution to helping him burn off his anger and remain an even-keeled kid. That is, until someone challenged him. Bringing a gun into this fight just made the situation worse.

"It's all right, son."

Alfred descended the steps, the cold wood protesting against his weight. "I said, leave." His voice rumbled.

The attackers turned their attention to Alfred. "You don't have it in you, Hitler Junior," the tall one said.

Oh, no! That kind of taunt would be hard for Alfred to overlook.

Ignoring the pain in his hip and side where there may have been a bruised rib, Herbert charged forward and swept the rifle out of Alfred's hands, set the stock on his shoulder, and aimed the barrel skyward with the swift, smooth actions of a seasoned hunter. He pulled the trigger, letting the rifle's blast freeze the anger-fueled scene before him. The attackers' eyes turned in his direction, and in the moonlight, he noticed the fear plastered on the cowards' faces.

Before they turned and ran, the short youth stopped long enough to yell over his shoulder, "The sheriff will hear about how you tried to shoot us."

Herbert snorted. As if the sheriff would ever believe that.

Moments later, an engine roared to life alongside the road. A truck pulled away, its headlights laying down yellow beams back toward Tulpehocken.

Herbert shouldered the rifle and turned to his father and son. "Never expected anything like that."

"We are called, Nazis now?" Otto let out a deep sigh and shook his head. "We have loyalty."

"A couple of drunk rabble-rousers is all." Herbert hoped that was true. Would others assume their German heritage meant they were in cahoots with Germany? He squeezed his father's arm. "Is your knee okay?"

"Ühm…only a bit zore." Otto rubbed his leg.

"They hurt you?" Alfred leaned closer to his grandfather, his face a mask of anger. "I'm going to kill them!"

"Kill who?" Jutta appeared on the stoop, hands wringing her apron. "What was that gunshot all about?" Her usual sweet voice wavered with worry. She was a small woman but made of the grit all farm wives had. Her hands were slight but calloused and always ready to pull her husband and children in for a warm embrace.

"No one's killing anybody, dear." He motioned Alfred and Otto to lead the way inside the house. He kissed Jutta on the cheek when he reached her. "A couple boys showed up shouting nonsense, but they're gone now." He needed to keep his family calm even though what just happened seemed preposterous. This was his family's community for over two decades. He thought back to three years earlier when the war broke out. Sure, the Alien Registration Act of 1940 required all German-born resident aliens, who still had German citizenship, to register with the federal government. His father and mother had complied along with forty percent of their county. So why now? Herbert and his family got along with everyone. Or so he thought.

The scent of pot roast and potatoes welcomed him inside the warm kitchen. This was his favorite room in the house. The deep enamel cast iron sink, with a side porcelain drainboard, was usually full of fresh vegetables. And he pictured the days Jutta used it as a bathtub when the children were babies. He remembered how he and his brother pounded in every nail along the white paneling on the walls when they helped build the house twenty years earlier. The stove and new electric icebox were avocado-colored, adding accent to the white background.

All eyes were on him, apparently waiting to hear what he would say. "A bit of a scuffle can't get in the way of a supper that smells this good." He pointed to the kitchen table where five places were set. "We'll talk about it later."

Herbert spotted Frieda cowering beside the china cabinet, her eyes stretched to their widest, extra dark against her fair complexion. She wore her long light-brown hair in pigtails. One arm was wrapped tightly around her side in a protective hug while, with the other hand, she twisted a braid around her finger, releasing it and turning again. The fear on her face made her look much younger than her thirteen years.

"Father?" Her voice trembled.

"We're fine, honey." He crossed the room and pulled her into an embrace. Her body trembled, and his throat tightened with emotion.

His little girl. Perhaps a bit naïve, she saw only the best in every situation, a miniature blueprint of her mother. She was a people-pleaser and often spent hours making a gift for anyone she thought might need cheering up. Ugliness and hate were emotions she hadn't been exposed to.

He walked her to the kitchen table and pulled out her chair. "Let's all sit."

Alfred remained standing, stiff with hostility, his fists opening and closing. "They beat up Grandfather." His face contorted and red splotches covered his neck. "They should be arrested."

"I was pushed down." Otto pulled out Jutta's chair, the wooden legs scraping on the black and white linoleum floor. After she took her seat, he sat in the one next to hers. "I am fine, Alfred."

Herbert walked over to his father and squeezed his shoulders. He was proud of Otto, never backing down when the attackers could have seriously injured him. "He'll need an ice bag and some arnica ointment on his knee"—he limped to his seat—"I'm going to need a helping of those, too, I think."

"You're hurt?" Jutta's eyes widened, searching his face. She tugged her left earlobe, a nervous habit he adored.

"My ribs. They might be sore for a day or two, but I'm in one piece." Herbert needed to stay positive, although he still bristled inside. He was still processing the series of events, ashamed he hadn't been more alert. And he felt guilty. He'd heard of neighbors being mistreated for their German heritage, but he hadn't asked about them. Fall was their busy time of year, and if he thought of them at all, he rationalized that perhaps the neighbors were doing something wrong. Now that his family was threatened, he wished he'd paid closer attention.

Herbert met Alfred's steady gaze. The boy wanted revenge, but Herbert wouldn't allow that. "Son. That was quick thinking with the rifle. It did the trick." He could only imagine what would have happened if Alfred had found a more serious situation outside. He'd like to think his son wouldn't shoot anyone, but he wasn't entirely sure. "Let's eat."

When everyone settled at the table, Herbert nodded to Otto. His father offered the prayers at mealtimes in his native tongue. Probably to hold to tradition, but some of it was to goad the children into learning German. As usual, Otto blessed the food, thanked God for all they had and asked for their health and safety. Then he added, "May these, foolhardy boys, be ashamed in the morning. Amen."

"Amen, Pops." Herbert studied the children, who were peeking at each other and their faces said they had no clue. Maybe he had done them a disservice not to insist the children learn German. He should have explained that language was a family treasure, much more meaningful than the heirlooms, family recipes, or old photos. And a bond perhaps to keep them united. It was never too late. He translated for the children.

"They won't feel ashamed." Alfred had his elbows on the table and his hands flat on the surface. It appeared as though he tried to pin his anger in place.

"Again, we'll discuss this after dinner, everyone." Herbert reached for the warm bread. "Let's not ruin this delicious meal."

They passed the plates and ate. Jutta reminded Frieda she'd need help finishing a baby quilt for their church donation corner. Herbert turned Alfred's attention to the weekend basketball game and their chances of beating the Lebanon Cedars. Although his son was the youngest on the Tulpehocken High School team, he was one of their top scorers.

"They won't know what hit them." Alfred made a fist and palmed it with his other hand.

Herbert drew in a long breath. He wished his son had mimed taking a basketball shot, but that wasn't how Alfred's mind worked. For him, every challenge was a battleground.

Jutta and Frieda cleared the table and returned with the Sweet Hubbard Squash Custard Pie made with his mother's recipe. When everyone had their serving, he cleared his throat. "Okay. Let's do this. It's Fact Time." This was a practice he and Jutta created when the children were younger. If a tough topic needed to be discussed, such as who broke the barn window or spilled honey on the couch, there would be no punishment for any fact or confession shared during Fact Time. All true statements were allowed. "Tell me what you're thinking."

"Calling the sheriff will do no good." Alfred's words sounded more like a growl. "The short one is his nephew."

"Ben's son?" Jutta's round eyes stretched extra-wide. Her eyebrows all but disappeared into her hairline.

Herbert now understood why the boys hadn't seemed frightened by his threat to call the sheriff.

Alfred nodded. "Glen Mason."

Color returned to Frieda's face. She swept her pigtails behind her shoulders. "My fact: His brother, Wallace, is in my class and last week the teacher caught him stealing lunch sacks out of our desks." Her eyes became thoughtful. "He must need food."

Everyone knew about Ben Mason. His wife and seven children barely survived in a shack off Wilson Lane, no more than two miles from the Müller home. Jutta's women's group took meals there twice a week ever since Ben died fighting in Italy a month ago.

"The boys say, we killed zeir fathers," Otto said. "Now... it makes sense."

Herbert nodded. Those boys were hurting, for sure. Who could they lash out at if not the locals who shared the enemy's heritage? "My fact is this: We will lock our doors at night."

Seriousness showed in Jutta's eyes, and Herbert tried to remember a time she ever appeared more worried. He added, "Just until this gets sorted out."

"I will make an extra sandwich for Frieda to take to Wallace," Jutta said.

"I'll get there early, and leave it in his desk, so he's not embarrassed." Frieda gave her pigtail a spin. Her kind-heartedness warmed Herbert.

"We'll try to be understanding," Herbert said. "Those boys can't see past their anger right now." He hoped he'd scared the young men enough to keep them away. Often, he was gone once or twice a week, taking orders from farmers or picking up supplies. If anyone watched his property, they'd know when his family was vulnerable. He pushed away the fear that harm would come to Jutta, his father, or the children.

"I'll meet with Pastor Huber in the morning. We need to warn other families that they might be targeted, and we should all come up with a plan." His family looked calmer, obviously trusting his words that this scare would be taken care of. If only he believed it. Something about how self-assured the boys seemed worried him.

"How about a game before bed?" Jutta collected the plates and set them in the sink.

"Let's play Dig," Frieda said. She had tied her pigtails together under her chin and was flipping the two hanging braids in the air, first with one hand and then the other.

"Is that supposed to be a beard?" Alfred squinted at his sister.

"Yes, it is"—she chuckled—"like you might have...someday."

Herbert smiled. His children were good friends and watched out for each other even with all the teasing. "Everyone else up for a game?"

After unanimous nods, Frieda retrieved the gameboard from the bookshelf. As she handed out the tiny hammers with their sticky ends and spread the tiles around, Herbert was surprised his father remained at the table. Not one to enjoy games in general, Dig was a word game and difficult for Otto to play in English.

"Not going to listen to the radio, Pop?"

"Tonight...no, staying here, is better." His deep devotion to the family, even though he didn't share the same hobbies, filled Herbert with peace. Otto's example was the blueprint he tried to follow as he raised his children. He sometimes worried when he worked too much that he wasn't measuring up to his father.

As Jutta shuffled the category cards, Herbert relaxed in his chair listening to the happy banter from the people he cherished most. He prayed he would always have the strength to fight anything that threatened his family.

—4—

Wilhelm Falk

Lake Laceno area, Italy - November 1943

F alk lowered himself next to a large rock and watched thousands of other soldiers fall like bags of sand into any open space along the shore of Lake Laceno. The surface of the water sparkled with sunlight, and the scent of wet weeds and water-soaked wood floated around them, while birds screeched overhead. The smells and sounds reminded him of fishing outside Düsseldorf with his boys. Barely old enough to hold fishing poles, Hans and Dietrich caught their first fish, declaring that day the best one ever. He promised them more but realized he'd failed miserably with that pledge. As they grew, he put in long hours managing Eastman Kodak Stuttgart, and then the war began and completely ripped him away.

A canteen with fresh water circulated. He accepted and drank deeply. They'd been walking for four hours, the day unusually warm for this late in the year. The British and American military hustled them along while the weather held. Spots floated in front of his eyes. He existed on meager rations twice a day, and his stomach growled. He'd had little sleep for three nights, and as he rubbed his eyes, he might as well have had a handful of sand thrown in them.

Falk, and what remained of Germany's 10th Division, crossed the perilous Monte Massico ridgeline the day before. Vineyards and olive groves terraced the steep side of the mountain, while the lower foothills were flecked with villages of tightly crowded stone houses, draped down the slopes. Now on the western side of the mountains, he was thankful for the wide valley and flat farmland in front of them as they marched to Naples, their final destination.

The first night after he surrendered, Falk stood along the inner perimeter of the filthy barbed-wire compound they were herded into. The wires. The guards in their brown uniforms. And the overcrowded area reminded him of the death camps spreading like leprosy across Europe's landmass. He blinked back the images of the sight and smell of dead and dying Jews and political dissenters. Then he turned his attention to the small group of infantrymen whispering to his left.

"We're probably going to be lined up and shot before the end of the day." The speaker was a wiry young man, thin-faced with eyes always darting about. If he'd been in Falk's division, he would have kept him running all day and all night until he stopped looking like a nervous girl.

"Don't be a fool." This man was broader and darker. He flicked a cigarette away. "Why would they line us up?"

"Because we did it to them," the shortest man in the group muttered.

Falk respected the civility with which the British and Americans were treating them. He knew firsthand military officers had killed Allied POWs because they were a bother to transport and feed.

He surveyed the lakeside, jam-packed with Hitler's Defense Force, confident he'd remain anonymous in the dirty mass of soldiers. Step one of his plan was nearly complete. Get captured. Done. Step two was totally out of his hands. Survive the ocean crossing to America without getting blown out of the water by one of his own military's U-boats. Step three was the vaguest part of his plan. Somehow talk his way out of a prison camp or wherever he was held and retrieve the documents he'd sent to his friend for safekeeping. Get an audience with someone who could stop Hitler—if even plausible. And step four? Was that where he returned to Ilse and the children guilt-free? That was his hope, but he doubted atonement would erase much guilt in the long run. In due time, he prayed he'd have peace knowing at least he'd tried.

The Führer's anger had to be at an all-time high as the tyrant's plans crumbled around him. Falk only met Hitler once. That was outside Bergen-Belsen where Hitler admonished the Sonderkommandos—work crews made up of Jewish inmates in charge of the gas chambers—to speed up exterminations. "To allow for new shipments soon to arrive."

Falk's hatred for the runty bastard had risen to new levels that day.

And "shipments"? As if each cattle car contained armaments or medicine, not devastated families forced to pay for their own deportations. The money went directly to the bogus program Heinrich Himmler called the resettlement work in the East. Falk didn't need to do the arithmetic to know that, even after German Railways took their portion, Himmler's henchmen earned millions of Reichsmarks since the transports began.

It was as if a moral lobotomy had been performed on the men closest to Hitler. Or, perhaps their sadistic tendencies were simply freed under his command. Regardless. Many of Hitler's closest comrades stepped across that line between good and evil. They separated family members with ease, without conscience. Turned a deaf ear to their pleas and cries. Then they grew impatient. Shooting the Jews one by one along trenches was a slow process. So they celebrated the decision to bring in roving extermination-by-gas trucks.

The man next to Falk startled him, nudging his boot against Falk's leg. The man's nose was flat, and he had full lips and a weak chin. "What division were you with?"

"Tenth army." Each POW received a large identification tag and was admonished to always wear it pinned on their outer clothing. Falk held it out from his chest, evidence of his new identity. "How about you?"

The man leaned in to study Falk's tag. A scowl creased the soldier's forehead. "Yeah. Me, too." He sat back, scrutinizing Falk. "Don't remember you."

"Too many of us." His heart beat faster as he made a show of pulling out the pack of cigarettes the real Klaus Stern carried in his pocket. He took his time with the matches, and after a long draw, handed the pack to the soldier. Maybe the offer of a smoke would get the guy off this interrogation kick.

The soldier tapped out a cigarette and accepted the matches, handing back the pack. "Thanks." He lit his smoke and took a deep pull. Then he scraped at his tongue with dirty fingers for loose tobacco pieces and flicked away something tiny.

"One notch above horse shit." Falk raised his hand holding the smoke. "But it's what we have."

The soldier inhaled deeply before he turned his attention back to Falk. "Still...I don't recognize you."

Christ. Dozens of divisions, all mingled together, and he ended up next to a soldier who happened to be in the same unit as Stern? "Barely came over from the Fifteenth Panzer Grenadier." Falk knew the commander of that Panzer Division and remembered it was stationed in Italy.

"Hunh." The soldier leveled a hard stare Falk's way. Then he pulled out the crackers the British distributed and took a bite. Crumbs fell onto his shirt and he brushed them away.

"I don't recognize you either," Falk said. "What's your name?"

"Hartmann." The soldier spat something to the side and leaned his head back against the rock. "Heard America's blown to bits. Maybe we'll get to see Canada."

Falk stubbed out his cigarette. That would be bad news for him. "No. We're going to America. Overheard it from the Brits."

"You understand English?"

"I understood New York City." Falk learned basic English when he was a teenager in the Association of Christian Students. Although greetings, food and clothing names wouldn't get him far in a real conversation.

Hartmann scratched at red welts on his arm. Falk had matching bites on his neck. Fleas and hunger were their two new enemies.

"New York is a mess," Hartmann said. "When the Führer wraps up Europe, we'll be in place to claim our cities, as promised. I'm taking Boston."

Falk's head pounded. He couldn't bear to listen to one more minute of this fanatical nonsense. Himmler and Goering pumped out propaganda about Germany's future ownership of the United States in a desperate attempt to bolster the troops' depleted morale. Hartmann was a committed Nazi and no amount of arguing would change his ideology.

He pointed to the soldier's boots. "Where'd you get those?" They were the newest style in British airmen wear, specialty boots that provided protection from the sub-zero temperatures. The Wehrmacht supplied nothing like those to its soldiers.

"Took them off a dead pilot in a snowbank in the Alps. Had to saw off his damn legs."

Falk slowly screwed the cap back on the canteen. "No shit?" If Hartmann was trying to shock him, he had a long way to go. This simpleton's brain would explode if he had glimpsed even a tiny portion of the misery and torture he had seen.

"Completely frozen onto his feet," Hartmann continued. "I heated his legs under the hood of the truck. Feet thawed out nicely and the boots came off real clean." Then he rocked his booted feet from side to side. "Heavy as hell though. Should have traded them for something lighter."

The guy was a fool. The boots came with a small hidden knife used to cut away the upper boot portion, leaving a regular, much lighter shoe underneath. Capture Escape Boots. They helped disguise a downed airman behind enemy lines who might find himself walking among the locals waiting for rescue. But Falk was in no mood to lighten the load of this pig-faced Nazi, so he didn't mention it. "Watch out. Some Tommy might believe you killed a comrade for the boots."

The Nazi scanned the field as if the British soldiers might be creeping up on him, and Falk chuckled inside. Hartmann was a deluded soldier who sooner or later would learn the truth about the leader he served. What Hitler was doing behind the cover of war had nothing to do with occupying all of Europe. Falk would not have believed Hitler's intent if he'd not personally seen it. At some level, he understood why his letters to dignitaries had gone unanswered. Who could comprehend such a massive extermination plan?

Hartmann pushed to his feet. "Good thinking, Stern. I'll lift a new pair of boots tonight. Someone's bound to die, right?" He stretched, and a crack sounded from his back. "Going to find a tree to squat behind." He turned to walk away and then stopped. "Stern. Just a warning. We've got anti-socialists among us."

He watched the Nazi wander off. If Hartmann only knew he'd been talking to one. In 1940, Falk had served nine months in Dachau prison for his outspokenness against Hitler. Two years later, he was forced to join the Wehrmacht. His prison time, those months away from Ilse and his sons, were pure hell. Purposefully denied letter exchanges, he worried his family could be punished because of him. Although they'd been left alone, the fear in Ilse's eyes lingered long after he returned. When he was released, the Army Chief of Staff, Generaloberst Ludwig Beck, a friend of Falk's father, convinced Falk to join the Action Group Zossen. The group comprised dozens of generals who planned a coup to replace Hitler if he started a war. Hitler continued to ignore their attempts to bring him to his senses after he overtook Poland in '39. But by 1940, Joseph Goebbels, the head of Public Enlightenment and Propaganda, had created the heroic image of Hitler as a towering genius. And Hitler believed his elevated status wholeheartedly, refusing to listen to the military experts around him. In '42, Falk was made to join the SS, and General Beck landed him a spot in the upper military ranks that were depleted by then. No one questioned him as they no longer had time to do background checks.

Falk ignored the conversations around him. He rolled onto his stomach and pulled out Stern's identification booklet and studied the 24 pages of dates and facts. Although already dismayed by his identity, he needed to be convincing if questioned. In order to surrender with a battle unit, he needed to find a look-alike soldier to trade places with, not someone with a re-markable military record. But some form of accomplishment on Stern's part would have been nice. Stern was assigned to units that fought at the edges of battles. Nothing notable there. His pay rate of 36 Reichsmarks a month wouldn't feed a family, which was good because Stern had only a wife. He'd earned no awards, had been on leave twice in two years, and had foot fun-gus. Falk wanted to shoot the dead man all over again for being such a loser.

"Hey." In his peripheral vision, he saw that the British pilot capture boots were back, planted not a foot from his face. Why couldn't the masses have swallowed up the annoying guy?

Falk sat up and tucked the booklet away. "Yeah?"

Hartmann ran a finger below his stubby nose and wiped the snot on his pant leg. "Think we can convince the Tommies to make a comfort stop?"

Falk slammed his hand on the ground before he pushed to his feet. Kidnapped women, numbering into the tens of thousands, were forced to work in the 500 brothels spread throughout the occupied countries to ser-vice the Wehrmacht. "Won't be any brothels left here."

"You ever have a Polish girl?" He smacked his fat lips together and grabbed his crotch. "They'll fight you, but it's worth the fuck."

He really hated this guy. When Goebbels proclaimed that lying to the country was necessary because the knowledge of the masses was restricted and their understanding feeble, this was the caliber of man the propaganda specialist described.

The move-out whistle spared Falk from punching Hartmann in the mouth. His arm actually ached as he refrained from busting apart that bloated smile. He grabbed his pack and quickly distanced himself from Hartmann and weaved to the front of his column. As British troops rumbled past them in Jeeps and tanks, moving to join the fight, he tolerated the jeers and catcalls of the conquerors. The soldier walking next to Falk dropped his head. "Shit," he muttered, apparently humiliated he'd been captured, while Falk was more ashamed of being part of the Wehrmacht in the first place.

He trudged on past train cars capsized beside the tracks, twisted and scarred by some hellish explosion. Ruined houses were everywhere, beams and bricks tumbled into charred heaps. At one point, he passed a POW dressed in woman's clothing, sporting a swollen lip and a black eye, stumbling along. An American guard served as an escort nearby. If this soldier—disguised as a housewife in order to defect—survived the night without being killed by one of their fellow Wehrmacht, it would be a small miracle. Defection meant death. Falk pushed ahead and tried not to look suspiciously empty-handed. While most prisoners carried duffel bags, small crates, or even suitcases from who knew where, Falk's tiny backpack held a small framed photo presumably of Stern's wife—an agreeable enough looking woman—some matches, and half a pack of those horseshit Eckstein cigarettes. He missed the Lucky Strikes he'd once found in a storehouse in France, but cigarettes of that quality were long gone.

When he reached the summit of a rocky field, he looked back searching for Hartmann. Good. Nowhere in sight. The POWs moved below him through the valley, like a long green and brown serpent, sluggish and endless.

Were any of the POWs in the group an SS officer like himself? It was possible. He couldn't be the only major who wanted out. After Hitler invaded Czechoslovakia and war was declared, the general's coup to dethrone Hitler lost momentum. They shifted their focus to fighting the British, leaving others to try to kill Hitler. Falk knew of twenty-two failed assassination plots, but there were probably twice as many. Getting close to Hitler was nearly impossible. Hundreds guarded him, all deeply devoted to their leader.

Hours wore on. He was thirsty, and his feet burned from several ruptured blisters. Hunger gnawed at his insides, but he dismissed it, recognizing he had no first-hand knowledge of what real hunger felt like. He'd watched starving Jews worked to death and done nothing more than take notes and snap a few quick photographs. He deserved to feel their pain. In the days before he'd made the decision to defect—when he was little more than a mental patient filled with alternating rage and regret—he'd nearly swallowed the cyanide pill. He'd written a letter to Ilse, begging for her understanding, explaining his disorientation, his guilt, the betrayal of everything good. The German people hung their trust, their lives, on what the military leaders sold them. The lies that the war was necessary to protect their families from the Russians.

He never mailed the letter, realizing the appeasement of his guilt shouldn't be a simple solution. A death by poison would be too quick, too easy.

The British guards announced their approach to Naples. The black cone of Vesuvius smoked gracefully on the right. The island of Capri rested serenely beyond the mouth of the bay. Naples spilled along the shore, fortified with walled battlements. Raised voices reached him before they arrived at the outskirts of the city. At the sight of the German POWs, an awaiting crowd turned into a riotous mob of screaming, hysterical people, throwing garbage and hurling insults and threats their way.

Up close, it became obvious why.

Although Naples was liberated a month earlier, the Wehrmacht relentlessly bombed it for three years. They attacked not only the harbor area to prevent Allied landings and sunk all the fishing boats, but they also destroyed municipal facilities and the beautiful complex of Santa Chiara. Thousands of citizens must have died. The main aqueduct bringing water to the city looked blown apart, and the city smelled as though the sewer lines were exposed.

Their guards moved closer, flanking the long line of POWs, waving back to the people who tried to hit the POWs with clubs or sticks.

Hundreds of dirty, ragged children braved the danger of being too close and cried to the British and American soldiers, begging for biscuits and sweets. Their thrusting hands plucked at the soldiers' clothing. "Pane. Biscotti." Falk had nothing to offer. His pockets were empty, save a lone cyanide pill. He watched their small heads droop when they realized the Wehrmacht soldiers were empty-handed. His insides twisted. This war was affecting even Europe's youngest, and he hated himself as he watched them slink away like mongrel dogs.

The guards prodded his group forward. Like an omen foretelling the future of the destroyed city, a huge ominous cloud obscured the ocean's western horizon as the men neared the camp. The storm moved closer and mist funnels broke from the bottoms of the clouds. Rain dropped in hazy trails and grew wider, weaving a hanging slate-colored blanket that floated toward them. Then the wind hit, whipping at his shirt, which became instantly plastered to his skin as the cold rain followed. The roar of the storm was so loud, it was hard to hear the guard's directions, but he followed the men in front who pushed in the direction of the large white building with a red-tiled roof. The hotel was transformed into a disarmament center. It sat on a flat hill above the port of Naples and was already packed full of earlier arrivals, leaving his group discarded outside. As Falk grabbed a tarp handed out by the guards, his hands shook—a combination of the cold and lack of food. He hunkered under it and soon three other POWs, without a word, joined him.

Once again, he was surrounded by razor wire fences, the ground of the enclosure trampled into a muddy arena. And in an instant, he was back in Auschwitz. The image of the boy with the strings floated before him. What happened to the child was the final act of brutality that snapped Falk in half. He was aware of his own instability by then and a giant timepiece seemed to tick in his head as to what he should do about the death camps. When the clock counted down the last minutes of the child's life, he knew he had to act.

He swiped tears away from his rain-splattered face. Exhaustion dulled his mind, but it was clear a stable part of him was now missing.

The process requiring that each POW show their identification papers was a slow one. To make matters more frustrating, a table beyond the checkpoint was filled with loaves of dark bread and large pots that emitted the aromatic scent of savory chicken and vegetables. The line inched slowly, but Falk's turn finally arrived.

After identifying himself as Klaus Stern, the inspector flipped through his *soldbuch* and handed it back. Falk had passed as Stern without a problem. Then he strode to the food, grabbed a bowl, and tried to hold it steady while an American soldier filled it with the steaming stew. He ate at an improvised table, no more than a board set across piled rocks. It didn't take long to devour the soup, and the meal and the meal proved to be just what he needed to regain his strength. He returned the bowl and wandered to his assigned area. This was his last night in Europe and it was a good feeling.

The rain was gone just as fast as it had arrived.

Once inside the enclosure, Falk chose the driest piece of ground he could find and rearranged a jumble of small rocks into a flat surface near a wellhead. With only his tiny backpack for a pillow, he lay down and buttoned his coat to his chin, cold but newly energized. He held out little hope of sleep. For months, his mind developed different plans every time he closed his eyes and tonight would be no different. Instead of reaching for sleep, he studied the sky.

A full moon climbed over the top of the hotel gables, illuminating the camp in an eerie silvery-blue light. The moonbeam briefly broke apart whenever a searchlight swept the compound. In those moments, the POWs looked like beached seals packed side by side, groaning, snoring, or rolling over searching for a more comfortable position.

Falk pictured Ilse, his sons. He prayed his plan would work and that she went to the Netherlands with the children. Then, when the letter of his "death" in Italy reached Düsseldorf, she wouldn't be there to receive it. By then, he'd have met with the U.S. government, perhaps with their specialty police force called the FBI. They'd get the American military involved in stopping Hitler's secret murders and his killing machine would grind to a halt. Falk would contact Ilse in the Netherlands before she ever heard he was "killed in action."

His mind rolled back to eighteen months ago when he was forced to join the war. He was trained along with other SS recruits at a facility called Hadamar, an asylum for persons with long-term afflictions or reduced mental capacity. Upon arrival, he learned the patients were long gone, euthanized in Nazi experiments. No one outside his elite group knew about the fifteen thousand harmless people the staff had gassed. The hospital became a practice facility for bigger operations planned in Poland. While there, he gathered more damning information about the Jewish extermination camps kept secret from the regular army and German citizens. But probably not all citizens. Dachau sat on the outskirts of Munich, so how blind could its residents be?

He stored the photos and notes in his postbox in Brussels until he amassed enough to send to America for safekeeping with his trusted friend, Theodore Graf. Until two weeks ago. Then, Falk was caught reading a return letter from Graf, the postmark clearly from the United States. He'd been on his way to meet fellow officers at the Rodenbach Brewery for a drink, a way not to appear isolated. Until that day, he'd managed not to shed light on his behind-the-scenes gathering of incriminating evidence as he traveled. He'd screwed up in Brussels by not watching his back. Days later, he received a summons to Berlin, a meeting from which no distrusted soldier returned. Even his father's friend, Generaloberst Ludwig Beck, and his Action Group Zossen with its dozens of discouraged generals, could not save his life if he were tried for treason.

For the first time since he abandoned his SS officer's uniform, Falk felt the tension melt from his shoulders. Surrounded by the musty odor of wet cloth, damp earth, and a salty sea breeze, he assessed his new situation. He'd slipped out of his SS skin and was now a regular soldier hidden among thousands. He was heading in the right direction. To the West, away from being recognized and certain death. And Ilse would have taken the boys to the Netherlands as he'd asked. He drew in a deep breath and studied the star-spattered night sky. Above all else, their safety gave him peace.

Plans, hurriedly thrown together two weeks ago as he fled Brussels, were coming together. In the end, this might be the biggest mistake, but it seemed better than continuing to do nothing.

—5—

IZAAK TAUBER

Amsterdam, Netherlands - December 1943

Izaak swallowed fast, and his heart pounded as he waited beside Mama inside their tiny kitchen. His stomach fluttered with excitement, but it was a scared feeling all at the same time. Fritz the Wanderer said he would be right back before he left, while he and Mama gathered their few things. Izaak put Papa's pipe inside his shirt and buttoned his coat. He wanted to know right where it was when he saw Papa again. He wasn't entirely sure where he and Mama were going, but he wasn't sad to leave the apartment behind.

Mama tied and untied the scarf around her neck, pulling it through her hands as she talked to Dr. Schermerhorn. "And after we reach the border?"

"Fritz knows the other members of the group, and they'll be ready." The doctor smiled and dropped his hand onto her once-beautiful blue coat that now hung wrong at the bottom. "You'll board the boat before morning."

A boat! When Izaak asked where they were going, Mama said she'd tell him later.

"You have your papers. I gave you the cash." Dr. Schermerhorn seemed as excited as Izaak. He walked around the room moving fast, putting a fist to his mouth and then quickly taking it away before he spoke again. "The organizers will notify me when you've arrived safely, and we'll work on connecting you with Saul again, or at least letting him know where you are."

Although they weren't going back to their beautiful house just yet, the underground Bible people were taking them someplace the Germans couldn't find them, but Papa could. This was what Izaak always asked God for during prayer time.

"Thank you," Mama said to Dr. Schermerhorn. She smiled down at Izaak and squeezed his hand three times. He pressed back, returning their secret *I Love You* signal.

A quick knock sounded on the door. "That's Fritz," Dr. Schermerhorn said. "You have to hurry but be very quiet." He gave each of them a quick hug. "Godspeed."

Again, Mama thanked her friend for everything and headed out the door. Izaak followed, lifting his suitcase as high as he could to keep it from scraping the stones as they crossed the patio. The gravel crunched under his feet, and he worried the neighbors could hear them. They followed Mr. Fritz alongside the house to the street. He pointed to the rear of an open-back truck and helped them climb into it. "Lie down," he whispered.

Izaak stretched out next to Mama, feeling like a log in a fireplace. Except it wasn't hot. It was snowing, and in the faint glow from a streetlamp, Mama's legs looked extra-long and white below her coat. She shivered as she pulled him close. He ducked his head in her armpit to avoid the huge snowflakes landing on his face.

Mr. Fritz looked serious. "Stay hidden until I let you out. Even if the truck stops, don't move." He covered them with a big piece of canvas. Moments later, something heavy was poured on top of them. Cans and bottles rattled as the objects settled around their bodies. It smelled like they were covered in garbage. The dark space suddenly seemed to run out of air.

"Mama, I can't breathe." Guus must have felt this scared after his family was thrown into the truck. Izaak didn't want to cry, but he knew tears were coming.

Mama shifted her shoulder, and the weight pressing on Izaak's side moved enough so he was no longer smashed. He snuggled closer to her as the truck's engine started. The vibration rumbled through the truck while it slowly moved along the street. It wasn't long before they were going faster. He tried to follow the truck's movements, but it seemed to make a turn on every block. Were they going in circles? He didn't want to end up back at the stinky apartment. "Do you think Mr. Fritz is lost?"

"No. He's making sure no one is following us, love." She kissed the top of his head. "Why don't you try to get some sleep? It could be a few hours before we get to our next stop."

The covering kept the snow off them, but it was still freezing. To take his mind off the cold, Izaak repeated Papa's favorite saying over and over in his head: *A man's true wealth is the good he does in this world.* Dr. Schermerhorn was doing good things, and Mr. Fritz must count himself wealthy since he helped people get away from the Germans. Izaak wanted to make Papa proud. He thought of the picture he could try to draw for Mama. Although he wasn't that good with getting people's faces right yet, he hoped to sketch Papa and get his smile just as he remembered it. The one he wore when he was about to do a funny thing like walking around in Mama's heels, teetering this way and that. Maybe at their next stop he could ask for a new drawing pencil.

The truck stopped suddenly, and he and Mama slid forward, slamming into the back of the cab. The garbage shifted on top of them. Izaak reached to rub his head where he hit it, but Mama pulled his hand back down.

"Don't move," she said right into his ear.

From the cab, Mr. Fritz cursed, and the gears ground against each other as if he had to shift extra hard. Then the truck started going backward.

"Oh!" Mama said. Her hands fumbled for him, and she pulled him closer, wrapping her legs over his. Her scared breathing came out in little gasps against his forehead.

Above the canvas, the wind made its edges snap up and down and bounce food and trash below and onto them. But inside Izaak's head, everything slowed down, and he couldn't sort out what he should think. If they were found, they'd be killed. Papa might never learn what happened to them. *Please, God, please, God, please, God, help us and help Fritz the Wanderer with whatever bad thing was happening on the road.*

His legs shook, but this time he knew it wasn't from the cold. And it was still nighttime. Even with his eyes extra wide, he couldn't see Mama's face. "Mama?"

"I know," she whispered. "We'll be fine. Remember, if the truck stops again, make no noise."

Two loud sounds came at once—glass breaking and a gunshot. Izaak's heart pounded in his ears when the truck spun around and around, the tires screaming under them until the vehicle rocked to another sudden stop.

Mama grabbed his hand and squeezed three times. He did the same.

Hurried footsteps slapped the ground around the truck, and men yelled in German. Izaak burrowed farther into Mama's coat. He worried the men might hear her pounding heart because it was pretty loud in his ear. What if they looked under the garbage? No one wanted to dig through rotten food, did they? Were Mama's legs sticking out below the covering? He didn't know if they were, but it was too late now. What he did know was that people in hiding got killed. Another sad thought crossed his mind. He'd told Papa he'd keep Mama safe. Now tears flowed and ran into his ear. They were trapped, so how could he keep her safe? They heard the truck's driver's side door open and something large and soft hit the ground. It was the same sound he'd heard after the people were shot in Munt Square. Fritz the Wanderer must be dead.

He squeezed his eyes to try to stop the tears. Not only was Mr. Fritz a nice man, but how would they now find their way to the safe place?

Two men spoke and it sounded like they were close by. The truck bed dropped down a few centimeters, as if they were leaning over the sides and looking in. He held his breath but couldn't stop shaking.

Garbage shifted above them. Any second, the killers would pull the canvas back and find them. He prayed harder. Maybe he and Mama could pretend to be dead. Or say they were Catholic. But the men would want to know why Catholics would ride in a truck under trash.

More garbage was pushed around and the men spoke again. The truck bed bounced back up, and the footsteps moved farther away. An engine started and that sound slowly disappeared.

"Izaak," Mama whispered, "we should wait just a few minutes before we move."

He wasn't sure he would be able to move. His body was stiff from the cold, and his legs felt like unbendable wood.

Time passed. An owl hooted close by, but no people sounds came from outside the cover. "I need you to be very brave, Izaak." Mama laid her hand on his cheek. "I think Mr. Fritz has been killed so we need to get away from here"—she swallowed—"If the truck won't run, we will have to walk...and it could be a long way. And it could be we will have to hide again."

He didn't want to believe this. He was tired of hiding, of waiting for the Bible people to bring food. Tired of whispering and secrets and never seeing Papa. The space under the canvas was suddenly too small, and he felt as though someone were pressing down on him. "There's not enough air, Mama."

She reached for the edge of the covering, pushed it up and away from them, and struggled to pull herself to her knees. Izaak followed her out of the opening until they stood knee-deep in trash, barely visible to each other, brushing off the food and garbage stuck on their clothes. Mama reached under the cover and pulled out their suitcases.

Izaak went first over the back end of the truck bed, and then Mama handed him the luggage before climbing down. "Stay back here for a minute, love." She walked along the driver's side of the truck and ducked down. Izaak studied the clear night sky. The snow had stopped, and the clouds were gone. Was Mr. Fritz sad right before he died about agreeing to help them? His chin quivered. He hoped Mr. Fritz didn't have a son at home waiting for him to come back. That would be the saddest of all.

He squinted at the dark sky. There were so many stars spattered against the black, it hurt his eyes to try to focus on them. Papa explained that heaven lay just beyond the hanging wall of stars, and the bright specks were people who had died. He wondered how long it would take Fritz the Wanderer to float to heaven and get a star.

"Meet me at the front of the truck"—she called over the roof from the driver's side door—"and don't come over here, okay?"

He was sad about their rescuer but glad he wouldn't see Mr. Fritz's dead body. He grabbed both suitcases and walked along the passenger side, the weeds soaking his pants and shoes. When he reached the front bumper, the glow from a broken headlamp lens lit up the area in front of the vehicle.

Mama knelt. She was in the weeds, using a stick to dig a hole. When it was a few centimeters deep, from her coat she pulled out the envelope Dr. Schermerhorn gave her and stuffed it in the hole. She stood and kicked dirt over it and then some stones.

Oh, no! Those were their important papers to get on the boat. "Mama? Won't we need them?"

She tugged her coat, smoothing it down. "Those papers were falsified for us. And someone must have told the authorities we had them, and that Mr. Fritz was helping us. Now it's dangerous for us to have them." She bent over and pulled him close. Her cheek against his felt wonderful. Then she whispered as if someone might be listening. "From now on we are us again, Rachel and Izaak Tauber, and we're Catholic. If anyone stops us, let me explain to them how we were going to visit relatives in Haarlem when our car broke down."

"Okay." This secret must have been what Dr. Schermerhorn and Mama had talked about while Izaak showed Mr. Fritz his drawings. He pointed to the wreck. The front of the truck was bent around a tree, the windshield in pieces, and one tire pointed the wrong way. The headlight shone past Mama into a field. "I guess we have to walk."

"We do." She rubbed his back.

He sniffed and swiped at his runny nose with his coat sleeve. Out in the darkness, past the lighted pasture, he pictured wild animals watching them. He shivered. If the Germans came back, he and Mama would have to hide, but with flat land around them, their only choice would be to run into the frightening black trees in the forest. "Where are we?"

Mama squinted into the darkness. "I'm thinking in the north since we were headed that way." She pulled her coat tighter. Her head turned to the left and then to the right, looking up and down the road. "I don't see any houses so we're away from any city." She checked her watch in the headlight. "Curfew will be over in a few hours, but we shouldn't get caught breaking it."

So much was going wrong, and he was tired and afraid. As he touched the pipe under his shirt, the promise he'd made to Papa to watch over Mama ran through his head. "I'm ready," he said, trying to sound brave. Then he reached for his suitcase and stumbled forward, his feet feeling like nothing more than blocks of ice as he lifted them one at a time. "I'm going to count how many steps it takes us to get to a town."

Mama swiped away invisible hair from her forehead. She picked up her luggage and drew in a long breath. "That sounds like a great plan."

When they were out of range of the truck's headlights, they entered a new world. The dark dome overhead reaching to the ground in every direction, sprinkled with stars filling the empty spaces. His insides soon stopped jittering.

Lucky for them, no cars were out, probably because of the curfew, or no one had extra petrol. He and Mama might as well be the only people alive, walking hand in hand as the leather soles of their shoes slapped the road surface. The odor of wet dirt carried by a sharp, cold breeze drifted off late fall fields. And ground fog hovered like sleeping ghosts in the bogs and ditches. It was like traveling inside the water globe Papa had on his desk. He felt safe for the first time in a long while.

–6–

HERBERT MÜLLER

Tulpehocken, Pennsylvania - December 1943

Herbert slept poorly, the pain in his ribs making every position in bed uncomfortable. Finally, he climbed out long before the sun urged the night upward and away. He found his father at the kitchen table. The weak light from a streetlamp through the front curtains accentuated the age lines on his father's face.

"You okay, Pop?"

"Fine, son." He rubbed the back of his neck. "Hm. Trying to think . . . who we, schould talk to, about last night."

"Me, too." He carefully pulled out his chair, not wanting to wake the rest of the house. "I thought about Pastor Huber and then remembered he's away for a week. How about Andel Smith?" The eighty-year-old came to mind as Herbert tossed and turned. Andel and his wife lived thirty minutes away and were active members in the Lancaster Liederkranz. A German Heritage Center that gathered local Germans together to enjoy traditional folk music and dancing.

Outside, the sun crept upward, pushing away the edges of night, and the room lightened to gray. What he saw in his father's face worried him. Otto did well to keep pace with Herbert each day in the mill. But the sag in his father's cheeks. The drooping upper eyelids, along with the deep creases above his brow. All signs Herbert once viewed as an honorable roadmap of his father's life. Now, seen through the heavy veil of worry in Herbert's mind, these were stark reminders of his father's advanced age. He swallowed hard, suppressing the emotion. He'd lose his father in the coming years, that was inevitable, but the idea was too much to think about right now.

"Andel...a good choice," Otto said, "especially since, we just saw him."

Herbert nodded, thinking back ten days to the Stiftungsfest fundraiser near Lancaster. He recalled the surprise on the children's faces when he and Jutta, after much cajoling, took to the dance floor with the other couples and showed off their Slap Dance, the Schuhplattler, skills. The next day, Herbert paid the price for the vigorous moves, his hip radiating with pain, but it was worth it. All the way home, the children talked about the food. The frankfurters, smoked and covered with mustard and horseradish, made the original Frankfurt, Germany, way. Potato pancakes, pickled beets, and Black Forest cake. The children might've been American-born, but it was nice to see them enjoying their heritage.

"Are you up for a drive, Pops?" Herbert pushed to his feet.

"Count me in."

Herbert helped his father into his winter coat and donned his own. He scribbled a note for Jutta, explaining where they were going and that they'd be back midmorning.

Andel Smith's one-story brick home sat on twenty-five acres outside the town of Lititz. A year ago, he'd switched out his crops from corn to hemp when the government initiated the Hemp for Victory campaign.

Andel's wife, Maria, offered a tray of coffee, biscuits, and peach jam. She was robustly built, with strong arms and a straight back. She wore her silver hair braided and twisted into a bun. The joints in her hands were enlarged, and her fingers were no longer straight, but her movements were delicate as she served them.

"Thank you," Herbert said. "How's the cannabis business, Andel?" He liked to tease the older man about growing the previously controlled drug.

"Lucrative." Andel chuckled. He had a shiny bald head with a body like a bear. Andel loved German dancing but graciously embarrassed himself weekly, tripping across the floor with his too-large feet. His gaze though, just chips of sapphire set in narrowed eyes, said he was nobody's fool. "I'm supplying any one of the forty-four processing mills, and until the Philippines open up again, and as long as the Navy needs rope, I'm in the hemp business." He turned to Otto. "You could convert your old mill. Get into fiber instead of grains."

Otto shook his head. "Nein. We will stay, with what we do. The war will not, last forever."

Herbert hoped that was true. They were well into the second year and he never thought it would go on this long. He scooted forward on the brown tweed armchair. The living room suited Andel's size. An overstuffed couch, two side chairs, a standing gramophone, and a wireless radio on the fireplace mantel. "About the war. We had some trouble last night at the house. We wondered if you've heard of other families being harassed."

Andel's face knotted. "What happened?"

"Some name-calling, accusations about helping Hitler, pushing." The anger returned as he thought of his family's vulnerability. "We're all fine, but I'm not sure who to report it to."

"One of the boys... is related to the sheriff," Otto said.

"I've heard that attacks are on the rise. Though I'm not sure how they're picking and choosing people." Andel spread jam on a biscuit. "There's a lot of us here."

"Once... you said something about problems... the First World War." Otto scratched his cheek. "We had not, moved here yet."

"Lordy. After Roosevelt denounced us and called us hyphenated Americans, we were in trouble. The government kept lists of about half a million German-Americans, and thousands went to jail."

So, the registration process Herbert's parents went through three years earlier had occurred before. He'd wondered about that. But thousands sent to jail? If his family were to be accused of spying or helping Germany, seems like it would have happened three years earlier, not now. He took this as a good sign—last night was a fluke.

"Ühm... who did you complain to, back then?" Otto asked.

"We had no one to complain to. When the president deems you

untrustworthy, well…" He raised his hands as if to say, What are you going to do?

"I remember we were offered the chance to prove our loyalty." Maria held her coffee cup in both hands, close to her chest.

"Yes, that's right"—he slapped his thighs—"We were forced, I mean *encouraged* to buy as many war bonds as we could, and it damn near wiped us out."

Herbert's family bought war bonds. Jutta's women's auxiliary club rolled bandages. And the children were involved in the "We're all in this together!" programs, collecting Hershey's wrapper foil, rubber bands, nylon stockings, brown paper bags, tin cans, and empty toothpaste tubes.

"You might want to change your names," Maria said. "We did."

Herbert's eyebrows rose. That was a surprise.

Andel smiled at his wife. "Yes, we did. Adalwolf and Mareike Schmidt didn't suit the neighbors, but Andel and Maria Smith did." He shook his head. "You could easily change to Miller."

Herbert knew times were different during WWI when the country was more anti-immigrant. But he would say, these days people understood a country's diversity was its strength. "I'm imagining all the legal paperwork to get our names changed. I don't think we need to go that far." He looked to Otto, who nodded.

"Back then, some German-Americans were arrested, and I remember a man in Illinois was killed, dragged out of jail and lynched." Andel leaned forward and stirred his coffee. The spoon made a high-pitched whirring sound against the porcelain cup.

Herbert never heard there were atrocities committed against Germans, although he knew of America's dark history when it came to the Negro population. "I think we're past all that," he said, wiping his sticky fingers on a napkin.

"I do, too." Andel reached for another biscuit, and his wife swatted his hand away. He chuckled and patted his large stomach. "You see how I am abused in my own home?"

"I am sure they see how starved you are, dear." Maria stood and collected the dishes.

Herbert took it as a sign they were finished and rose to his feet. "Thanks for your help." He pulled on his coat and helped his father with his. They walked out onto the front porch. The fields were pockmarked with dead hemp plants, the large leaves lay like brown layered skirts around the place where the harvested stems used to stand tall.

"Glad you figured out how to grow that stuff," he said, tipping his chin to point out the crops.

"If the medical community wins back the right to prescribe it again, I'll keep on growing it." Andel stuck out his hand and they all exchanged a handshake.

"One more bit of advice. Maybe keep to yourselves," Andel said, "and limit speaking German in public. This'll blow over."

"Let's hope so."

They turned toward their truck when Andel spoke again. "If you have more trouble, call the FBI. They have a division to protect your civil rights."

Herbert stored away the idea but hoped last evening's events were a one-time occurrence.

-7-

WILHELM FALK

Naples, Italy - December 1943

The coast of Italy slowly revealed itself under the gradual creep of morning light. The overpowering stench of mildew and smoke lingered in the camp as the POWs formed groups of twenty for interrogation. British officers and interpreters called each captive to a separate table outside the officers' makeshift tent. The interpreter at Falk's table was American, tall with dark wavy hair, clearly a well-fed youth. He stood beside two seated British officers.

"Papers, please," the interpreter asked in perfect German.

Falk held the officer's gaze as he reached into his uniform. The next moments were crucial to his plan. He handed over Klaus Stern's *soldbuch*. The army would tell Stern's wife her husband was a POW whisked off the continent until the war ended. Guilt flared in Falk's gut over this ruse, but it paled compared to the burden of remorse he harbored for the dark road his countrymen had chosen. Not all Germans, but too many. This downward spiral from decency and morality seemed unstoppable. Yet it was impossible to point to a specific circumstance when this terrible military endeavor was set in motion. Was it revenge over WWI, or had evil trailed humankind throughout history and waited for a man without integrity and a loud voice to rise again?

He had spent too much time hobbled by visions of starving children, those innocent youngsters instinctively crafting a game during a free moment at a train depot. Merely doing what children do, unaware that creative moment would be one of their last.

Perhaps it wasn't guilt Falk felt for Frau Stern. Sadness was more like it. The woman planned a life after the war with Klaus but now would spend her days wondering why her husband hadn't returned home. How would his own wife, Ilse, feel if she were informed he was captured and then never returned? Hope would slip away as the empty years dragged on. His sons growing up without a father. He said a silent prayer for the Stern family.

One British officer asked a question and the German-speaking American interpreted. "Do you have relatives in America, and if so, are you in touch with them?"

On his mother's side there was a very distant cousin somewhere in Arizona, but he was no longer his mother's son, now was he? Pastor Graf was also not a relative. "No."

The interpreter's breath carried the scent of sausage, reminding Falk that, although he was hungry, he fared better than the other POWs on the front lines. His status as an SS officer allowed him to enter a city and choose a sizable house or apartment in which to billet, an act which always felt wrong. The family, without recourse, invited him to join them for meals, often made from meager rations. He tried to be nonintrusive and often brought food or sweets if there were children in the house. But most times he was too emotionally unstable to be a good guest, wandering the house during all hours of the night, battling nightmares. He often snuck away before dawn to avoid seeing the tremendous relief on the homeowner's face.

The world could use a return to a habit of kindness, if there ever were such a time.

"Tell us how you came to be captured," said the interrogator.

Falk scratched at his short beard. He needed to convince them he was not a deserter because the Allies wanted to retain that type of soldier. A runaway who forgot what he was fighting for could be instrumental when embedded with allied forces. Although they were often used as laborers, a soldier knew valuable military strategy. He had no desire to stay behind.

"We were pinned to the hills in Avellino when our company commander called it defeat," he said. "Tenth Army Division."

The British officer took notes. Falk was ready for questions about his loyalty to Hitler's cause and whether he supported Nazism, when the two interrogators fell silent. They studied the picture of Stern inside the *soldbuch* and passed it back and forth, glancing at him and then the photo of Stern. Although Falk believed he was careful in handpicking Stern from the other dead soldiers, Stern wasn't a perfect match. He hoped all blond-haired, blue-eyed Germans looked similar to the British.

In rapid-fire German, one interviewer asked, "What is your height?"

"One point eight three meters."

"Where were you born?"

"Hamburg."

The translator looked bewildered at the speed of the questioning.

"Date of conscription?"

"Twelve, June, forty-one." Falk was pleased that, even under pressure, the time he took to memorize Stern's information paid off. It sounded like his own.

The officer slowly closed the identification booklet and handed it to Falk. He motioned for him to join the long line of POWs approved for shipment off the continent. Sagging in relief, he walked to the wire fencing and studied the enormous grey ships docked in the busy harbor below. He and the other prisoners were told ten ships would sail tonight to take advantage of the blackout conditions. To put as much distance as possible between their convoy and the treacherous German U-boats. His military may not have quality soldier boots, but their submarine division was deadly.

A salty wind rose off the water. Tall waves with deep troughs crashed against the rocky cliffs, sending spray impossibly high. Falk shoved his hands in his pockets, fists clenched, more from exhaustion than cold. The contempt for his country left him fatigued. Germany, a nation known worldwide for its art and culture, was now steeped in horrific crimes perpetrated under the orders of a dozen madmen. Add to that his personal guilt, and he felt drained. He'd watched the trains unload whole villages of people at the death camps, and did nothing.

But the moment that broke him was when he met the boy with the strings. After that day, Falk started taking photographs, gathered documents about the exterminations, and wrote down the camp officers' names. In order to get his parcel off continent, he visited a friend's canning factory.

He bought 4.5 kilograms of slab paraffin wax and a how-to book, explaining that Ilse canned more as the food supply became scarce. Falk sealed his documents, first in layers of wax paper, and then submerged it in melted paraffin. Once cooled, he packed the thick slab in a box containing the canning book, canning lids, and jar rings with a note to his trusted friend in America, Pastor Graf.

He pictured Theodore Graf, a clergyman he had not seen in four years. Graf was his mentor when Falk belonged to the German Association of Christian Students as a young man. This intense priest taught him passable English, eerily prophesying that perhaps there would come a day when English was a passport to better opportunities.

In the note, Falk told Graf he would find a wealth of knowledge in his exploration of the canning package. The postal department was on high alert for armaments, and as he hoped, his package with canning supplies reached Graf. Apparently, Falk communicated the dire situation facing the Jews quite well because Pastor Graf's return letter was full of disbelief about the horrors his country was perpetrating and asked what more he could do. That was the letter Falk was caught reading in the Brussels' post office.

He studied the harbor. A stone jetty in the shape of an exclamation mark pointed toward the U.S. Metal cables clanged against the sides of the ship's iron hull, and seagulls screeched, circling the fishermen's boats returning with their evening catch.

Falk worried about Pastor Graf's safety. Writing to someone in wartime Germany might land his friend in trouble. From the return address on Graf's letter, the pastor still lived in a small town in the state of New York, the place he immigrated to in '39.

He planned to meet Graf in America, and with the pastor's help, reach Washington, D.C. with the contents of his package. He'd give testimony as a witness to all he'd captured in the photos and notes. And then his plan had a fork in the road. If Ilse and his sons could be protected by the U.S. government, he'd move them out of Germany, possibly to the United States after the war. But if his actions as a traitor could put them in danger of imprisonment or death after he delivered his information, he would never let them know he was still alive. He'd swallow the cyanide pill, killing Wilhelm Falk once and for all, eliminating any chance his family would be harmed.

Squinting at the horizon, Falk studied the cobalt edge of the ocean where the water pressed against the sky. A blue line offering America on the other side, a place where sanity prevailed. A place for the telling. And, hopefully, a place to forgive himself for his silence, for hesitating too long, for the deaths of another hundred thousand.

-8-

IZAAK TAUBER

Alkmaar, Netherlands - December 1943

"Where is the hospital from here?" Mama asked the farmer, Mr. Luca, who picked them up along the road just before dawn. The man smelled like pigs, which made sense since he explained that's what he raised when he offered them a ride. His cheeks were pink, and his hands on the steering wheel were red and cracked. His big smile was missing several teeth.

Mr. Luca pulled his truck to a stop at the edge of Alkmaar. Izaak sat on the front seat between Mama and the farmer.

"Four blocks that way." Farmer Luca pointed to the right, where the red-roofed city began. The sun hadn't quite risen, and the storefronts were backlit by a soft purple that always painted the sky before the sun peeped over the edge of the world and streaked everything with yellow.

Izaak was glad to be in a town. His legs ached like they had bruises inside, and his hands stiffened into claws from gripping the suitcase handle for hours.

Mama pushed open the truck's door and stepped down. She helped Izaak out and leaned into the cab to speak to the farmer. "Thank you again."

"You are welcome. Enjoy your visit with your mother."

She lied to the farmer about needing to visit her sick mother in Alkmaar. Mama was raised in an orphanage by nuns after they found her wrapped in a blanket on the steps. She never knew her mother which really was sad when Izaak thought about it. But Mama prepared him for the lie. During their long walk last night, she'd explained that in the next few days they might have to do and say things that went against what they believed, until they found their way back to Amsterdam.

As Izaak pulled the suitcases from the truck bed, he spotted a giant windmill in the nearby field. The blades made a creaking noise as they slowly turned, and as far as he knew, they never stopped day after day unless the wind died. He might have to lie and say he wasn't Jewish, but inside, like the windmill, he'd never stop believing in everything Papa taught him about being Jewish.

"Let's find a church," Mama said. They followed a wide cobblestone street past the darkened windows of stores and shops. Benches painted in orange showed off their country's favorite color to honor the last name of the Royal Family, van Oranje-Nassau. The sky brightened and golden beams painted the underside of the charcoal clouds. When the ancient church came into view, they turned down the street leading to it.

"Will the church have a toilet?" Although Izaak had nothing to drink in a long time, he'd been nervous-peeing all night.

"It should, love."

A block later, they climbed the steps of the St. Laurenskerk, a massive tan building with slate roofs angled off each story. Mama pulled on the front door, but it didn't budge. "We'll go around back."

Now he really had to go. With his free hand, he clutched his crotch under his coat even though it wasn't polite and duck-walked alongside the church. Mama climbed the steps first and tugged on the handle. That door was also locked.

He bit down hard on his bottom lip. What if he wet himself again? He was horrified the first time it happened because eight-year-olds didn't do that.

"Be quick about it and pee over there." Mama pointed to a small area sided by three towering walls.

He hurriedly relieved himself, and while buttoning his pants, saw movement in a lower window. He hurried next to Mama. "Someone is inside."

Mama's face bunched together in her thinking-about-it look. She rubbed his neck as she studied the back door. "Let's see if someone can give us directions to the train station."

This was their real destination.

Mama tapped on the massive wooden door and they waited. Maybe the priest was hurrying about to get dressed since it was barely morning. He and Mama had eaten the last of the food Dr. Schermerhorn gave them before the farmer found them on his doorstep. Perhaps the priest had extra food.

The door opened a fraction of a meter. A man peered out. His black hair swept back from his forehead, and his eyes darted back and forth from Izaak to Mama. "May I help you?"

"We need directions to the train depot"—Mama smiled—"and perhaps a drink of water, if you could."

Izaak wanted to add how hungry they were but knew not to speak.

The priest opened the door wider, but didn't move back to allow them inside. He wore a long black coat with buttons from his neck to the floor. His white collar and cuffs looked yellowed, and the toes of his brown shoes were scuffed. He leaned forward and whispered, "This is not a good time." Then he stood taller and said in a louder voice, "Turn right on the street and take the next left. The train station is a half kilometer down." He had a stern expression.

"Yes…we will do that…and thank you, Father." Mama talked fast and reached for Izaak's hand as she took a step backward. She pulled him away, but he looked back one last time. He'd never known a priest not to be helpful. The man had stepped inside, but the door was still open as he spoke to someone. Izaak could see past his robes to a table set with food. His heart beat fast, and his ears started to ring when he spotted the field-grey coat with a black collar over the back of a chair. An SS officer was inside!

Now he tugged Mama along. They needed to get to the trains and fast. When they reached the street, he said, "Mama, there's a German officer in there."

"Oh"—she glanced at the church—"I guess I assumed as much from the priest's reaction. But we can't look panicked. We're just two people heading for the depot."

"Two Catholic people." Izaak tried to walk with easy, unhurried steps, but his movements felt strange. He'd become used to a quick pace, hurrying from one danger and away from another.

The town was waking up. One man walked a tiny dog, and another pushed a pipe organ to a street corner where it looked like he would set up. Izaak wished they could wait to watch the man dance and rattle his tin of coins in time to the music. He wanted to do normal things like that.

He breathed easier when the train station came into view. Once there, Mama would buy their tickets to Amsterdam. He replayed all that had happened since they'd left the back of the house the night before. It seemed like a week had passed since they climbed into the back of Mr. Fritz's truck, but it hadn't even been a full day.

"Excuse me, ma'am," a man spoke, directly behind them.

Mama stopped walking and turned. Two policemen stood there. Her hand tightened around Izaak's, and she pulled him closer. "Yes?"

"We need to see your identification," the taller officer said.

Izaak was proud to see that Mama's hand didn't shake as she set down her suitcase before handing over the papers. Just two Catholics catching a train, he repeated in his mind.

The men passed the pages back and forth and then handed them to her when the tall policeman rested his hands on his gun belt. Its leather crackled under the strain of the weight his heavy arms. Izaak didn't like the way the man stared at him.

"Where are you heading?"

The shorter policeman had a flabby rooster neck and tiny ears. When he smiled it looked wrong, like the mouth of the Big Bad Wolf in his storybook. That same wolf who turned out to be a big, bad liar.

"We are returning to Amsterdam." She dropped her hand to Izaak's back and rubbed it.

"Are you Jewish?" the taller man asked.

"You know as well as I do there are no Jewish people left in Amsterdam." Mama grabbed her luggage and smiled. "We really need to be going."

The taller policeman's eyes changed from friendly to angry. "Unless they have been in hiding."

This was bad. The men didn't believe their made-up story. Izaak's chin quivered and he willed himself not to cry.

"We found a dead man out in the countryside this morning, a known

Jew smuggler." The short policeman cupped his hands and blew into them. "We asked ourselves, Where is his cargo?"

Mama said nothing as she held the man's gaze.

"Where are you returning from?" The tall officer crossed his arms over his chest.

"From Hoorn," Mama said and scratched her nose. "We were only there one evening."

Izaak tried to smile as the tall officer turned his gaze his way, but his lips wouldn't stop twitching. He put his hands behind his back and pinched the skin between his thumb and finger to fight off his fear.

"And you arrived here by bus?" The tall man tilted his chin upwards.

"We did." Mama made a quick sniffing sound.

"Ah, there's the problem. There is no bus from Hoorn." The tall officer lowered his voice and spoke slowly. "Here's how we handle these…misunderstandings. We can shoot you both right here, right now, or…"—he drew the word out, and his voice rose higher—"you will volunteer to be transported to a work camp."

Mama's face turned white, and her lips trembled.

The short policeman unclipped his gun. "You need to decide."

Izaak's breath stuck in his throat. He buried his face in Mama's chest. His insides hurt because he didn't know how to protect her.

"We volunteer," Mama said above his head. Her shoulders sagged.

Izaak let out a long breath. They wouldn't be killed. And maybe this camp wouldn't be a terrible place. He and Mama had been hungry and tired for weeks. And hadn't Mr. Fritz told him Papa was at a work camp? Maybe they'd be taken to the same one.

How could it be that while they waited in an alley with the two policemen, life went on around them? It seemed wrong. A woman pinned clothes to a line strung between the buildings. Breakfast smells followed men out of their homes. Children skipped alongside their mothers heading to the center of the city. And he could tell people tried hard not to look their way.

A police van arrived. Once the back doors were opened, the tall policeman boosted Izaak inside and helped Mama. "Here." Then he handed them their suitcases.

The doors closed, and after a sharp rap on the metal side, the van drove off. Izaak scrambled onto a bench across from a lady with two boys. Both looked older than him. They tossed a small wooden ball back and forth between them. The van jerked and chugged forward, causing the younger boy to drop the ball. It rolled under the seat and hit Izaak's foot. He returned it to the boys.

Mama sat next to him and spoke to the woman. "Have you volunteered, as well?"

"If that's what we must call it." She smiled. "I'm Dahlia. These are my sons, Zev and Aharon."

Mama rubbed Izaak's head. "I'm Rachel, and this is Izaak."

The brothers studied Izaak before Aharon asked, "You want to play?"

He nodded, eager to do anything to forget they were prisoners.

"Where is your star?" Zev asked. He pointed to Izaak's unadorned coat. Zev's star was sewn to his brown jacket with the word JOOD in black lettering.

"We never got one because we went into hiding." Izaak unbuttoned his coat because he was suddenly hot in his many layers of clothes.

"We hid, too. In the brick factory oven," Zev said. He grabbed the ball from his brother and tossed it into the air with one hand and caught it with the other.

"From the bombs," Aharon said.

Izaak pictured his house and Mama bringing warm bread out of the oven. He wasn't sure he would fit inside any oven, and these boys were much bigger than he was. "How did you both crowd in there?"

Zev grabbed the ball from his brother and tossed it to Izaak. "The ovens are huge rooms that make thousands of bricks at a time. Hundreds of us were in there."

Izaak laughed. "Oh. I was imagining a big kitchen oven with large knobs on the front with a door that snapped upward and closed."

Zev laughed. "Like a monster's huge oven to cook people."

He pictured how that story would go and quickly brushed away those terrible thoughts.

The van wove through the streets and pitched them from side to side. Mama braced herself against the wall as she talked to Dahlia. "Where were you found?"

"We're from Haarlem. We'd been in a friend's basement, but I snuck back to our house to check the mail. I found a postcard from my sister who was taken away a few months ago. She's working on a farm in the east and said there was room for us there, as well. We packed and checked into the police station. I have to admit they've been accommodating so far."

Mama loosened the scarf she called Chanel from around her neck. She looked relaxed for the first time in a long while. She lowered her voice, but he clearly heard her. "What do you make of the rumors, that some circumstances for us are worse in Eastern Europe than just being deprived of freedoms?"

Izaak had overheard Papa and Mama whispering about this very same thing. That some place far away, the Germans were doing worse things than killing people. The confusing part is what could be worse than that?

"I think they're made-up stories." Dahlia tucked her short brown hair behind her ears and sighed. The dark circles under her eyes showed she didn't sleep very much.

"I hope so." Mama straightened her coat. "Two months ago, BBC reports claimed the Allies were winning back occupied countries. It seems the war is nearly over."

Izaak caught the ball and tossed it back to Zev. He was glad they were in a silent game of catch because this was important stuff the adults were sharing. As soon as the war ended, Papa would come home, he would go back to school, and they could return to happily being Jewish.

"Then all we have to do is wait it out," Dahlia said, "on this German work farm."

Tall apartment buildings flew by the one side window, creating multicolored flashes behind the leafless trees. Izaak wished they'd been invited to a farm.

"We are remanded to a work camp." Mama's mouth tightened. "Last I learned, my husband was sent to one."

Papa would be assigned to the construction team in his camp. Maybe he was in charge of making sure everyone had a house when they arrived. Perhaps he even built the house they would live in. That would be amazing.

Dahlia looked at Izaak and cut her eyes quickly back to Mama. Her mouth soured like she'd sucked on a lemon. "I have heard things about the work camps…about what the Germans expect."

"Work, I suppose," Mama said and laughed a little.

"That and the ability to demonstrate a talent…especially for a younger child to not be"—she glanced at Izaak again—"um, you understand, to not be worked too hard."

He didn't like Dahlia's look. It was like the time his mama found a hurt bird on the ground and said it would die.

"Where did you hear this?" Mama had her hands in her lap, clenched tight.

"An SS officer bragged to our protestant neighbor, who then told us."

"Before we were identified as Mischling, we had an officer in our home," Mama said. "I'm not sure I believe all he was muttering. He didn't seem very stable."

Izaak pictured the man. He'd looked uncomfortable, like his dark greyish uniform didn't fit him right. And he always talked to himself as he paced the room above Izaak's bedroom. His name was Falk, which meant "falcon" in German. Izaak remembered the soldier seemed more like a broken bird than a strong falcon when he stayed with them.

"I'm curious." Mama crossed her arms like she was freezing. "What age did they say was considered young?"

"Under twelve."

"Oh." Mama rubbed Izaak's back, and he saw worry lines on her forehead.

But he wasn't worried. He'd been told he was talented for his age. Maybe by drawing well, the camp leaders would treat him as if he were older than eight.

Their van pulled into Amsterdam's Centraal train station. The building could have been a palace, red and tan with gold in places and tall pointy tops like on the castles in Izaak's storybooks.

Izaak pressed his face against the van window and studied the shining trains with big wheels and massive engines. Which one would take them to their new house? This day had turned out to be half bad and half good. Poor Mr. Fritz was killed because he'd helped them and Izaak felt terrible about that. However, he and Mama were here, not dead but instead heading to a camp where his papa might very well be.

−9−

HERBERT MÜLLER

Tulpehocken, Pennsylvania - December 1943

At the sound of glass breaking, Herbert sprang from his bed. The clock showed 4:30 a.m. His heart hammered with fear that an intruder was in the house. He grabbed his rifle from the gun rack in the hallway, the linoleum cold and crackling under his feet as he headed into the living room.

Alfred stumbled from his room. "Dad? What is it?"

"I'm not sure." Herbert scanned the living room. One panel of the sheer curtains fluttered inward. The window behind it had a jagged opening like a giant mouth with razor-sharp teeth. Now that they kept their doors locked, he knew no one had come inside. As he flipped on the light, he noticed a grapefruit-sized white rock lay on the braided rug in the center of the room. Shards of glass created a gleaming trail from the floor. He set his gun against the wall and crossed the floor to pick up the rock.

"Nazis go home," he read. The letters were carefully painted in black. On the other side was a swastika.

Only a week had passed since the last incident. Apparently, the attack in the yard wasn't the end of the harassment. "Looks like they mean business, son."

"Let me go after them." Alfred's fist clenched and unclenched at his side. "They'll be the only car on the road right now."

"And what will you do?" His son, although quick-tempered, was no fighter. If Alfred caught up to them, they'd have to visit him in a hospital.

"I'd beat the tar out of them." His voice was a whispered growl. "Dad. We can't let these punks get away with this!"

He dropped his hand on Alfred's shoulder and squeezed. "No, we can't, but we'll take care of it the correct way. I'll call the FBI as soon as the sun comes up." He lifted his chin regarding the broken window. A brisk stream of autumn air circled the room. "Get some shoes on, and we'll cover that up."

He regretted waking the family, but nails didn't go through wood without hammering. The boards would have to do until he could get to town for glass. He quickly explained what happened and reassured them he'd keep watch until morning. Alfred and Frieda shuffled back to bed, and Jutta remained by his side. Otto pushed his fingers through his hair, his rumpled bedclothes hanging loose on his thin frame.

"We need...to have more care, son. Remember what Andel said. Twenty-five years ago, Cherman-Americans were killed. We know history, is repeated."

"You may be right." Herbert sighed and reached out to touch Jutta on the cheek. "Everyone try to get some sleep. I'm just going to stay up a bit longer."

Otto disappeared down the unlit hallway while Jutta reached for the colorful ripple-pattern afghan folded over the back of the chair. "I'll stay up with you."

"Are you sure, honey?"

"I can't leave you alone." She pulled him to the love seat, and once they were settled, draped the warm throw over them and snuggled closer.

Herbert's mind spun with all that was happening. He pinched the bridge of his nose and closed his eyes. What his father said was true. People were afraid, and as German-Americans, he and his family were the objects of that fear. But he worried more about his father. Otto had not become a citizen after immigrating. What would this mean for Otto if more people became fearful?

The next day, through the kitchen window, Herbert spotted the arrival of a black car as the family was finishing breakfast. It slid silently into the yard and parked under the line of bare maple trees. He threw the last splash of his coffee in the sink and waited for the two men in suits to knock on his door before opening it. As they entered, the crisp winter day pushed clean air and aftershave into his kitchen. "Good morning, men. Thank you for coming."

The badges and FBI IDs came out. The heavyset man with a jowly neck was Johnson, and the tall one with a beak-like nose was Gables.

"Jutta. Could we get the men some coffee?" He motioned to the table. "Children. Let's make some room, please."

Frieda and Alfred stood and cleared away their plates. They moved to the green loveseat next to the grandfather clock where Herbert and Jutta spent most of the night.

Each agent's hair was close-cropped, and they wore neatly-pressed suits from expensive material Herbert knew he could never afford.

After they were all seated, and Herbert made the introductions, the men accepted their coffee and stirred in cream. He leaned forward, his elbows on the table. "I'm not sure what you need to know in these types of harassment cases."

"Has anything happened since yesterday?" Gables asked. He pulled a notepad and pen out of his suit coat.

"No. We will get the window fixed today. But someone needs to put a stop to this trouble we've had. I'm worried that by alerting you, the people who did this will become angrier." He pointed to the rock on the floor beside Alfred's feet. "Hand that this way, son."

Alfred hefted the rock and walked the few steps to the table. Gables reached for it and moved it up and down in his hands as if weighing it. "That's a strong message." He handed it back to Alfred, who returned it to the floor with a thump. "Any idea who did this?"

Herbert didn't want to name names. Couldn't the FBI just spread the word that these acts were criminal?

"The sheriff's nephew, Glen Mason," Alfred said. "His brother steals food in school, according to Frieda."

"Their father was Ben Mason." Herbert slowly turned his coffee cup. "Killed a while back in Italy."

The agents looked at each other, but Herbert couldn't read their expressions. Did they already know about the Mason boys?

Johnson cleared his throat. "When you called yesterday, we checked to see if there were any other local complaints, and we found some."

"These same boys have been after other families?" Herbert turned to his father and raised his eyebrows. Otto was quieter than usual. Was he showing respect for men of authority, or was he afraid to speak with his heavy accent and choppy English?

"Not exactly." Gables flipped through his notes. "A neighbor reported your family a few weeks back for crimes against the United States. We believe that rumor circulated, which, no doubt, is what prompted the boys to pay you a visit."

"Crimes?" He threw his hands up in a what-gives gesture. If neighbors were talking behind their backs, his family could be in more trouble than he believed. "Who reported us?"

Alfred scrambled to his feet behind the agents. He loomed in the doorway leading to the parlor, his arms crossed, his eyes boiling with anger. Johnson turned to the sound and his gaze lingered too long on the boy, causing Herbert to feel uncomfortable.

Herbert sent Alfred a stern look. "Calm down."

Alfred dropped onto the loveseat.

"We're not at liberty to say who it was." Gables sat up straighter. "But we do have some questions."

Herbert hoped this would be short. He had repairs to complete in the mill and wanted to ride into town with Jutta, in case anyone tried to bother her. He often didn't help her with the Christmas shopping, but now they should do this together.

"Excuse me for a moment." Jutta stood and motioned Frieda and Alfred to their rooms. "Grab your school things." Then she spoke to the agents. "The children's bus will be here soon."

As the children left, Jutta handed each a sack lunch. Alfred yanked the door closed behind him hard enough to rattle the dishes in the hutch. Jutta offered a quick smile and reached to refill the coffee cups, but the agents waved it away.

"We'll get right to the government's concerns." Gables flipped the pages in the notebook.

The government's concerns? Herbert's anxiety level suddenly sparked, sending what felt like an electric shock through him. If the FBI sided with the false claims made by neighbors, clearing their name might take longer than expected. Otto held a spoon between both hands, flexing the normally unbendable utensil. Jutta cleared her throat and arched her eyebrows as she met Herbert's gaze.

"Now the government has concerns?" Herbert forced a short laugh. "I assume you mean concern for our safety."

"What is it you do here?" Johnson asked, ignoring Herbert's remark. "A neighbor said the mill business is a ruse to help fund Germany."

Herbert's body stiffened. He'd once suffered from the same temper as Alfred, but now restrained the quick anger and searched the two men's faces. He evened his tone and spoke carefully. "We run a mill business, grinding corn and wheat for roughly fifty customers." He swept a hand to indicate the rows and rows of cornfields the men must have passed on their way to his house. "I'm sure you noticed we sit in the middle of nothing but farms."

"We have orchards and sell apples and peaches to the stores in Tulpehocken," Jutta added. She unfolded a cloth napkin she'd pressed into a small square.

"We make money, to pay the bills. No money left...to send away," Otto said.

"Let's see." Gables scanned the page. Herbert looked at Johnson who seemed content to listen. "That is correct. You've not made any large withdrawals from your bank account."

What in the world? They checked with his bank? Gerry Hardin, the bank manager, was in Herbert's poker group. Would he now suspect him of crimes? Herbert scratched his hairline above his ear and found perspiration there. He'd expected help from these men not scrutiny. "Why are we under investigation? Someone attacked *us*. That's what we asked you to look into, not our finances."

"Let me continue," Gables said. "We also heard complaints that you've communicated through a shortwave radio to others who support Nazi idealism, you possess propaganda material, and you pass German messages along secret networks within your German community." He flipped the pad closed. "You can see our concern."

Secret networks within our German community? Were they mad? Their Lutheran Church was packed with Germans, and they attended sporadic folk festivals. But exactly as the other families spread out along the farming valley, everyone was so busy with their daily work, no one had enough time or energy to engage in secret meetings. He hoped the shock on his face was clear enough but for good measure, he shook his head. "We do none of those things. My children were born in America, Jutta and I are citizens, and although my father most often speaks German, he certainly is not conducting secret meetings. Your information is wrong."

Johnson turned to the elderly man. "Otto Müller. You immigrated here in 1920, but never became a citizen. You still have relatives near Frankfurt. How often are you in contact with them?"

Otto puffed out his chest. "I arrive 1920. My wife and I, work day to night, and rebuild the mill. We build the house...we have two boys to grow. Since the war, I am in no contact to Cherman family." He drew in a long breath. That was more English than Herbert ever heard his father speak.

"Pops always said he never found the time to gain citizenship," Herbert interjected. "After time passed, it didn't seem to matter. He's paid taxes and is dedicated to the United States."

"Citizenship doesn't matter?" Gable's voice held an edge of disdain.

"I mean after being here twenty plus years, he feels totally immersed in our American ideals."

"Hunh," Johnson said. "Do you take a German newspaper?"

"Yes," Otto said.

"A German club outside of Lancaster prints it," Jutta said. She tapped a knuckle against her low lip. "It doesn't come from Europe."

"Do you own a radio?" Gables scribbled on his pad.

"Yes. But it's simply a radio, unable to transmit anything," Herbert said. This line of questioning was going in the wrong direction, but he sensed that if he argued more, the FBI might think they were hiding something. "Glad to clear this up. I can see how people might get nervous during wartime. But we've fit into this community without problems all these years. It seems like you can take care of these rumors with a few well-placed phone calls."

"We will do that," Johnson said. The agents stood and shook hands all around. "Ma'am"—he nodded to Jutta—"thank you for the coffee."

"Our pleasure." Jutta smiled and stepped aside, allowing the men room to button their coats and walk to the door.

"You folks have a nice day," Gables called as he passed the stoop.

The tires sounded loud on the road's surface as the car drove away. Herbert turned to face his wife and father. "I think that went well." He pulled Jutta into an embrace. "Crazy though how these rumors have spiraled out of control."

"My Anni and I...should...have become citizens." Otto rubbed his neck. "However. I think today, not der time to apply." His smile showed the sarcasm in his statement.

"Yes, Pops, I'd hold off on that." He leaned sideways, stretching his hip. "Let's fix that arm on the grinding wheel and then, Jutta, you and I can head into town."

He pulled on a knit hat and his coat. He hadn't wanted Jutta or his father to worry, but wondered if his family was truly cleared of suspicion. In a panic, the government rounded up thousands of Japanese-Americans after Pearl Harbor. He knew of two German men from their Lutheran Church who were questioned by the FBI and sent to jail. Herbert just assumed they were doing something wrong. But what if they were doing nothing more than living their lives when someone made up a false story? He wished he knew which neighbor was afraid of his family. He'd make a point to visit and assure them nothing illegal was going on at his mill. Unless grinding corn for the troops was suddenly anti-American.

He stepped outside and waited for Otto, and scanned his family's land. His father accomplished so much after coming to America. Otto arrived with one hundred dollars, a few meager possessions, and a dream to create a safe place for Anni and him to raise their sons.

Wood smoke drifted through the apple orchard, a blue haze floating through the dry rattling leaves as they still clung to the branches. It was almost too cold to hang the washing outdoors, but Jutta would do it anyway. She remarked she loved the scent of a crisp winter day on the sheets, even if scented with a hint of smoke. The late fall landscape had taken on solemn, austere hues, but there were still brilliant flashes of color by the house. Orange chrysanthemums held their blooms against the cold nights, and purple ornamental cabbage leaves sprawled at the edge of the garden.

Otto exited the house, looking small in his flannel coat and wool hat.

Reflecting on their family's history and all that it represented—the American dream, hard work, a productive occupation—a lump formed in his throat. They stood to lose so much if the war circled any closer to them.

$-10-$

WILHELM FALK

Aboard the *Algonquin* - December 1943

F alk boarded the *Algonquin* soon after sunset, crossing a wobbly gangway, Stern's backpack slung over his shoulder. Before he stepped onto the main deck, the guards asked him to empty his pants pockets as they checked for mirrors, spoons, or anything else that could be used to signal an airplane. His cyanide pill remained in his shirt. A redheaded guard removed a button from his uniform and pocketed it—the Allies loved their souvenirs. He then nodded at Falk as if to say, See? You've lost your fight. Falk hoped that wasn't true since his fight was different than that of the other soldiers.

Two young privates, Eduard from Munich and Christoph from outside Berlin, pressed closer to Falk. If his sons were five years older, they would be these boys' ages, fourteen and sixteen respectively. Eduard's grandfather insisted he join the Wehrmacht by lying about his age to bring in more money for the family. The boy had sapphire eyes and large ears he needed to grow into. Christoph was brought up in the mandatory Hitler's Youth Program, and when he showed good marksman's skills during paramilitary training, they waived the age requirement and enlisted him. Burn scars from a childhood accident covered half his forehead, and his hairline receded on that side.

The ship's captain was French, and the crew American. The German noncommissioned officers were still in charge of keeping the POWs in line while answering to the Allied officers. POWs stood at attention, a ragtag mass of haggard men and boys, unshaven and smelly. In contrast, a well-groomed U.S. naval officer dressed in a double-breasted blue uniform, with three gold stripes on his cuffs, stood one level up on the bridge to address them. Graying sideburns poked from under his hat, his face narrow, hawkish, with thin lips.

"You are under the control of the United States Navy. We honor the Geneva Convention of 1929, so you will be treated humanely and protected under international law." Unlike his Wehrmacht.

The officer called out their onboard instructions, consisting of the rules they would follow while at sea: no spitting on the deck, no fighting, and if they died, they'd be buried at sea. He ended with a quick review of their daily schedule.

"You hear that, buddy?" The soldier beside Falk nudged him. Red flea bites covered the man's face and hands. The soldier growled, "Two meals a day. Shit. We should mutiny."

Falk took a step away. "I'll take all the food they offer. You heard them say they didn't expect this many of us."

"They're lying. We're probably the first group anyone rounded up." He scratched at his neck, tearing off scabs. "Everything I hear, we're winning on every front."

The guy was delusional, or deaf to the truth. All reports stated Germany was doing nothing but losing battle after battle.

"Yet here we are," Falk said. When a whistle blew, he turned away from the soldier and motioned to the young POWs. "Stay with me," he said before heading to the open hatch above the forward hold. The boy soldiers remained on his heels. A sailor handed him a putty-colored blanket and an orange life jacket, and pointed to the iron ladder, descending into the bowels of the ship. His footsteps on the metal ladder echoed off the interior walls, a hollow reverberation that moved through Falk's chest, and for the first time, he truly felt like a prisoner.

The lower compartment had poor lighting, but he made his way to a wall, backed against it, and slid down. Eduard and Christoph followed suit next to him. The hold filled with hundreds of men and soon there was no space. Then he waited. They were allowed to smoke, but in the confined space, only tempers flared, and few men lit up. He ignored the men around him and dozed. Soon, the ship rumbled to life and slowly began to move. The drumming of the powerful engines ramped up higher and became deafening, and he felt the vibrations rattle his back teeth. Maybe they would arrive safely in the United States, but at this rate, surely he would be deaf and on a soft-food diet.

They were told ten Liberty ships moved with them in close formation, flanked by dozens of destroyers, an aircraft carrier, and two frigates. The Liberty ship was nothing more than a freight hauler, defenseless if attacked. He learned that, when the United States entered the war in 1941, the British government asked for help to house German prisoners. The United States agreed, although it was not prepared. The big freighters were the only option to transport the overwhelming number of POWs.

The dark hold of the ship was nearly airless and soon awash with the sour stench of seasickness. The hastily assembled toilet overflowed, fouling each breath. Falk's thought always turned to the Jewish families— forced onto airless transports—who spent their last days with their families in worse conditions than this. He always thought of Ilse and the boys when he pictured those hapless victims. What if the tables had been turned? He and his family labeled and then rounded up due to propaganda and fear? Ripped from all they knew, starved, denigrated, and in the end, slated for death anyway?

Suddenly, the hatch opened. "Put on your life jackets. We've spotted U-boats." The hatch slammed shut and the POWs, with barely any room to move, scrambled into their vests.

Someone growled, "I don't want to die in the guts of this ship."

"I don't either," Eduard added. Christoph sounded like he was praying. These soldiers were merely children and had no idea what they were fighting for.

"We're fine," Falk said. He patted each boy on the leg.

"Hope so," Eduard replied. "Promised my mother I'd be back for her specialty goulash soon enough."

"You'll keep that promise," Falk said. But, as sentries' footsteps ran back and forth on the deck overhead, he wasn't so sure his words were true. Without warning, a nearby explosion and its shock waves reverberated through the metal hull, jarring his spine.

"Do our U-boat guys even know we're on this ship?" Christoph asked.

That was a good question. Falk imagined lying dead at the bottom of the ocean, and Ilse and his sons would never know what he tried to do. Eventually, they would hear he was shot in Italy, his face blown away. He would never reappear after the war to explain to her all the secrets he kept and how hard he worked under dangerous conditions to document the horrors. "We've got loads of protection out there. The Brits have been ahead of us in air patrol."

"You must rank higher than us," Eduard said. "We never learned stuff like that."

"I was in strategic planning." This was a lie. Falk never planned the war's direction but had designed his life to go in a new one. From what he saw in the troops within the last year, terror began to replace commitment as a means to keep men fighting on. *If you don't win, your wives will be raped, your children butchered.*

The ship rose and fell in the huge swells, and Falk drifted in and out of sleep. The captain said they'd be at sea three weeks, but the foul conditions could easily kill them well before they reached New York.

He and Ilse had spoken many times of sailing to New York or Boston on the *TS Bremen*, a German express liner, sleek and luxurious. They should have taken that trip. They thought they had time, but then Ilse became pregnant with Dietrich. How had eleven years gone by so quickly? He pictured the war ending, perhaps by summer. He'd hold his family tight, admire his sons' heights, kiss Ilse's soft lips. That is, if he were still alive.

Falk wished the Action Group Zossen and its dozens of generals had accomplished their coup to replace Hitler. But when the war escalated, they had no choice except to focus on the mechanics of fighting a war and drop their secret plans to kill the tyrant.

He reviewed his plan. After Pastor Graf received Falk's package, he wrote asking what he should do with the information. Should he take it to the authorities? In his original communication, Falk requested that the pastor not do anything with the contents of the package, but apparently his friend viewed enough of the documents and photographs to be alarmed and want to help. Now, with no way to reach Graf, Falk hoped the pastor did nothing more until he arrived.

Eduard shifted next to him. "Ass's gone numb."

"Stand for a while." Falk squeezed closer to Christoph to make room and then grabbed the boy's arm and pushed him upward. His guilt resurfaced. Jewish boys Eduard's age weren't immediately euthanized upon arriving at the extermination camps, but younger children like the boy with the strings, needed to have a purpose not to be immediately sent to the gas chambers. The echoes of wails from the little ones, torn from their parents at the station, ricocheted in the recesses of his mind. The horrors they suffered as their lives ended, completely unsheltered and defenseless and small. If his plan didn't work, and he chose his cyanide pill as a way out, he believed their cries would be the last sounds he heard.

Footsteps sounded above. The hatch was thrown open and groans of relief rose from the masses. It seemed to take forever, but once he climbed on deck, Falk breathed in the crisp night air as if he were a drowning man who finally pulled himself back to the water's surface. He turned to the young soldiers. "Has anything ever smelled this good?"

Christoph shook his head. "Never."

Above them the sky was black, shot through with stars. The other ships, nearly invisible in blackout conditions, flanked them like silent grey ghosts. The shush and splash of water, parted by the giant hulls, rolled across the dark surface.

"Fill your lungs, soldiers," a German noncommissioned officer yelled. "We'll be back below before sunrise."

Falk guided Christoph and Eduard to a long table with water kegs and cups. "Drink up. That foul liquid below can't be good for us."

Eduard drank deeply and then spoke. "Do you have children, Klaus?"

Falk looked around to see who the boy was talking to before he remembered he was Klaus. He quickly rattled off what he knew of Stern's information. "Just a wife." He added the lie, "But we'd like a family."

"You'll make a good father," Christoph said.

A small jolt raced through his chest. He wanted these boys out of danger, to be sent home now. But sent home to what? Would Germany ever be made right again, or was it too broken to be made whole?

"Thank you. Hopefully, my future children will grow up to be like you."

The smile on his face felt genuine. He was a good father or had been until 1942. His job as CEO of the film division of Eastman Kodak Stuttgart allowed him to be home many nights with Ilse and the boys. Then, he met the generals in the Hitler resistance, and they secured him the SS position, and in return, he thought he'd be helping them out, plotting to kill Hitler and ending the war.

He signaled the young soldiers to follow him. "Let's stretch our legs." They were all given an ample supply of cigarettes, and Falk lit one. The boys didn't follow suit. "You're smart. Use your smokes to trade for food when we get to camp." He inhaled and then exhaled slowly, the smoke ripped away by the breeze that rolled across the massive deck. "I'm not your commander, but here's my fatherly advice...be sure you write to your families from America. They'll be glad to know you're safe."

Eduard started to speak and then stopped. Finally, he asked, "Just exactly where will we be?"

Falk turned to the boy. "I don't know, but wherever it is...no one will be shooting at us."

-11-

IZAAK TAUBER

Amsterdam, Netherlands - December 1943

Izaak watched the German soldiers cross the cobblestone parking area before arriving at their van. Their image swayed for a second. He was so tired he'd fall asleep anywhere and hoped their train wasn't leaving right away. Centraal Station had food shops, and Mama still had money from Dr. Schermerhorn.

Mama squeezed his hand. "You're my brave boy, Izaak."

"I'm trying, Mama."

The guards separated Mama and Izaak from Dahlia and her sons. While two soldiers reviewed their papers, Izaak studied the men. A clean scent came from their uniforms as if recently laundered. He remembered his papa smelling this way after Mama brought in the laundry, all stiff and stand-uppy from drying on the line. The soldiers wore important buttons and medals on their coats and the shiniest boots. He bent over to see if his face would reflect back from the black boots, but Mama pulled him away and scowled at him.

The soldier smiled at him and then at his mama. "You made the right decision by volunteering." He flapped the note the policemen in Alkmaar gave Mama and handed back their important papers. "Did you receive a postcard from your family to join them?"

"No." Mama put the documents away in her brown shoulder purse and snapped the fold-over flap. "We've been unable to receive mail."

Izaak wondered if their mailbox was overflowing. They'd been away from home so long. All Mama's beautiful houseplants would be dead, and the turtle doves he fed in the winter must be staring through their kitchen window wondering what happened.

"True. Postmen can't be bothered to try to hunt you down."

Mama cleared her throat. "How will we know which train to take with so many options?"

The other soldier, with a skinny mustache and tiny eyes, answered. "You have one option." He pointed to the empty tracks. "It comes in there and goes to Westerbork Transit Camp. Platform eleven. From there the trains travel to the relocation towns. Show your papers, and you will get on the correct train." He motioned his chin in the direction of the busy platform. "You may purchase your tickets there. There's food on a cart outside, but you're not to enter the building. The train leaves in one hour."

The soldiers followed them as they got in line to pay for their tickets.

"One adult and one child to...to Westerbork."

Izaak studied the man in the ticket window. He wore a smart blue cap and blue uniform with a high collar. He also had a mustache that covered his upper lip. Izaak couldn't see what his mouth was doing, but his eyes looked as though he was smiling.

"One way or round trip?"

His mama's voice sounded funny when she said, "One way, sir." Mama slid money through the tiny window, and moments later, the man pushed the tickets to her. She tucked them into her coat pocket, took Izaak's hand, and followed the soldiers to a platform at the back of a long building.

"Wait here." One of the soldiers pointed to a crowd amassing near an empty railway line.

Izaak stood on tiptoe. Where were the food carts? He hoped the soldier wasn't lying. He was so hungry he'd eat beets right now, and he hated that vegetable.

Across the street, a big building was missing its top, and fast birds swooped and dived in and out of the metal arch that once held up the roof.

Mama had on her I-have-a-lot-to-think-about face as she looked around. She squeezed his hand and pulled him in a new direction. He liked the warmth of her gloves against his skin.

"This way." She'd spotted the food. Finally. They waited in a short line until they reached the wooden cart, but there wasn't much to choose from—brown bread, wilted carrots, and cheese. "We'd like some of each, please." The man didn't look at Mama and Izaak as he packed everything together in a brown bag. He set it on the cart and tapped on it.

"Leave two Reichsmarks there." The man stepped back and waited for Mama to count out the money.

They carried the sack to the corner of the platform and sat on a bench. Izaak bit into the hard bread and tore off a piece of cheese with his fingers before popping it in his mouth. His stomach growled, waiting impatiently for the food while he chewed.

There were more people on the platform than Izaak owned in marbles, and he owned two hundred. At least he had that many before he buried the sack behind the carriage house at home. He'd dig them up someday when they all returned.

Some minutes passed, and Mama rolled the top down on the bag. "We'll save the rest for later."

More and more people came to their platform. A woman, with hair going everywhere, walked by hand in hand with a small boy while lugging a large suitcase with the other. "Are we in the right place?" she asked Mama.

Izaak stared at the woman's very big stomach and imagined the baby inside. He knew all about babies. Mama helped get them out into the world from a secret opening before the mama's stomach popped open.

Mama read the information on the woman's tickets. "You're here. The train for Westerbork."

Just then, people started yelling from an open plaza behind them.

Izaak stood to see. A man was in a fight with the soldiers. His wife and children stood behind him. He was yelling they'd changed their minds about leaving and were going home.

The soldiers pointed their long guns at the man, forming a circle around him and his family. They would be killed if they didn't quiet down!

Mama grabbed his hand and pulled him into the crowd of people in long coats, all bumping against each other, and he could no longer see the plaza. Not long after, he heard five quick gunshots and felt sick to his stomach.

"Mama. Were those people…" He didn't finish the question because the terrified look on her face told him the answer. The family was dead.

A loud steam whistle blew, and a long black train pulled into the station. People swarmed forward when the doors opened. He moved up against Mama, his face pressed into her coat, their bodies touching. What if the train got too crowded before they boarded? How would they ever reach the work camp to try to find Papa? His heart beat faster as a scared feeling started in his legs, and he wasn't sure he'd be able to climb the steps. He closed his eyes and swayed in the crowd, slowly pushing toward the doors, breathing in Mama's familiar scent and letting her guide him.

Once there, he clambered up the metal stairs until he was inside the carriage, chose the first open bench, and slid across next to the window. Mama didn't sit right away but looked around, stretching her long birdlike neck as if trying to find someone—perhaps Dahlia. Finally, she put Izaak's suitcase on the floor beneath his feet before sitting beside him. "There you go, dear. Now your legs won't dangle for the whole ride."

Before long, the train sounded its whistle again and soon picked up speed. The world flew by the window. Rolling meadows, fields with tan stubble and piles of rocks, and whole villages with people doing normal things. The telephone wires along the tracks swooped up and down, hooked to the wooden poles along the way. The opa and oma in the seats across from him shared a cigarette, pointing to sights out the window and talking quietly. The opa brushed away ash where it fell on his pants.

The train sped into a tunnel, and Izaak snuggled closer to Mama as the world went black. Was this how dead people saw everything—black and dark and scary? When the train burst from the darkness, a row of trees lining the train tracks made the sun blink fast against his face, and he closed his eyes.

The wheels squealed, and Izaak startled awake. For a moment, he forgot they were on a train. It slowed as it pulled into the station, stopping next to the platform with a sign hung above long benches. Westerbork. Wherever that was. He tugged Mama's coat sleeve. "Is this the work camp?"

"I believe so, love. But we're still in the Netherlands."

"And Papa might be here."

She smiled down at him, but her eyes looked sad. "Dr. Schermerhorn said your father is much farther away. In Poland."

His shoulder slumped and he ducked his head. He didn't want to cry, but no one had mentioned "farther away" before this. With all the bombings, the Netherlands needed help rebuilding, so why would they send Papa to another country? It wasn't fair.

Mama lifted his chin and wiped tears from his face. "You're my courageous boy, Izaak. I know this is hard. I'm not promising anything, but maybe we can figure out how to transfer to Poland."

"Okay." He needed to remember his promise to watch over her and keep her happy like Papa always did.

Izaak and his mama carried their suitcases down the steps, bumping into people who juggled rolled blankets, shoulder packs, and small children. Everyone was nicely dressed, the men in suits and hats, and women in warm dresses with fancy scarves around their hair, or a hat with feathers or fruit. Mama's nice clothes were all in Amsterdam, but she was the prettiest anyway.

They walked through an open gate to a fenced-in area, and he stayed close to her side, trying not to let the suitcase bump the ground. He rose to his toes hoping to spot the houses they could live in.

"Oh, dear," Mama said as she peered ahead. A group of soldiers was dividing the group. Men and boys in one line, and women and girls in the other. "Izaak, I have to tell a lie so don't correct me."

Once there, Mama showed their identification papers.

Izaak's chest thumped hard inside his coat. He had no idea what Mama would say, but he sure didn't want to be separated from her. When a soldier pointed him to the men's line, he thought he'd never breathe again.

"My son is barely six"—Mama held his hand tighter—"Could we please stay together?"

The guard moved closer to Mama, his face red and bunched together. "What is your destination?"

"This camp." Izaak heard the nervousness in her voice. "But if possible, we'd like to go to Poland. If we could just wait for the train together."

The soldier flicked his chin and his mouth twisted into a crooked line. "You are asking to go to Poland? Is that right?"

"Yes."

He nodded and pointed to the women's line. "Take him with you. That special train leaves in five days."

Mama had done it. They were together, and in less than a week, they'd head to Poland to find Papa. He needed to keep track of all that had happened, so he could tell Papa when they saw him again. He spotted Zev and Aharon in the men's line. For once he was glad he was young. He silently repeated Papa's other saying: "We believe things will remain the same in wartime, but we shouldn't count on fairness to be one of them."

The train that brought them to camp backed away and left. While Izaak and Mama stood in line for registration, he felt some hope for the first time in a long time—maybe he *could* count on fairness again.

-12-

HERBERT MÜLLER

Tulpehocken, Pennsylvania - December 1943

Christmas hovered in the air, a mere week away. The FBI visit from the previous month was tucked at the back of Herbert's mind. The festive mood of the holiday season overcoming those few frightening moments. If the neighbors were wary, he hadn't noticed and was relieved no one had pitched any more rocks. The angry young men probably received a stiff warning about vandalism and heard the legal consequences of misguided hate.

Tonight, his family gathered around the advent wreath and lit the third white candle. The final candle would wait seven more days and be lit on Christmas Day while the holiday goose cooked. This evening, the scent of warm spices seized the kitchen as Frieda and Jutta baked *stollen*, ginger cookies, and marzipan chocolates in preparation for the holiday meal.

The lights in the dining room cast a warm, sheltered feeling as a snowstorm raged outside. The family sipped hot *glühwein* and ate roasted chestnuts.

"Play another, Pachelbel Hymn, bitte," Otto asked Jutta who sat at the piano.

Herbert sighed. If only Mother had lived longer. Christmas was her favorite holiday, and she'd be there beside Jutta on the piano bench.

Earlier in the evening, Alfred's girlfriend, Martha, a shy classmate with an eager smile and a face full of light freckles, arrived. Herbert suppressed a grin. His son and Martha sat side by side on the pale green high-backed sofa, holding the hymnal between them. An inch of space separated them from immodesty. Martha, the oldest daughter of an Irish farmer two miles away, was blessed with a lovely soprano voice. An added plus to Herbert's full-voiced, if sometimes off-key, family.

A loud banging on the front door startled them. Herbert shot a glance in that direction but could see no one beyond the curtains. Someone must be lost because who else would come out on such a wintry night? Jutta stopped playing, her hands frozen over the keys, as Herbert walked past and squeezed her shoulder. "It's fine."

He unlocked the door, revealing agents Gables and Johnson on the stoop. Snow covered their hats and coats, a curtain of white falling behind them.

The sobering looks on the agents' faces caused Herbert to worry. Had someone made new accusations against his family? Or had another family been attacked?

Jutta stepped to Herbert's side. At four foot ten inches, she straightened her back, a move he knew she reverted to whenever she was nervous. "Won't you enjoy a warm mug of *glühwein* with us? It will chase away the chill."

The FBI agents stepped inside and removed their hats, snow falling to the woven rag rug at their feet. Johnson unbuttoned his long coat. The scent of damp worsted material filled the room as he reached into his inside pocket and removed a sheaf of papers. "Please, everyone, take a seat."

Herbert stepped closer to Johnson and whispered near his ear. "We have company this evening. A neighbor's daughter is visiting. Could you just speak to me about whatever you have there?"

"You, your wife, and father need to take a chair, Mr. Müller," Johnson said.

Gables looked at Martha. "What is your last name?"

Martha remained silent, unsure of the situation.

Herbert said, "This young lady's father is Sean O'Leary, a dairy farmer on Stettler Road."

Johnson stepped forward and pointed to the telephone. "Miss. Call your father and have him come get you."

Alfred reached for Martha's hand. "You don't need to leave."

Herbert saw red flare in his son's neck and cheeks, and needed to rein in his temper. "It's okay, Martha. We have a small family matter to discuss." He turned to Alfred. "We'll have her over tomorrow, all right, son?"

Martha slowly stood and walked to the phone, lifted the mouthpiece from the hook, and dialed.

The agents declined offers of drink or food. They stood beside the china closet, a backdrop of a multicolored history full of Jutta's heirlooms and family collectibles. Vibrant against the agents' drab coats.

Soon, tires crunched on the deepening snow.

"I'm walking her out," Alfred said.

He stood and extended his hand to Martha who quietly said to Jutta, "Thank you for having me."

A moment later, he returned, a sour look on his face, and dropped into his chair. "Great. Her father is now suspicious of us—of me."

Frieda was seated but the adults remained standing. If the FBI had something to say, Herbert would hear it facing the men eye to eye.

"That's probably true." Johnson tapped the papers on the table and turned to his father. "Otto Müller, you are accused of being an enemy alien. You are under arrest."

Jutta gasped and her hands flew to her throat. Herbert thought his heart might have stopped. The ringing in his ears momentarily overcame the thudding of his heartbeat. "My father"—Herbert turned to Otto who looked smaller than usual, shrunken—"is no threat to anyone." Herbert waved his hands back and forth in front of him as if clearing away the situation. "What gives you the right?"

"President Roosevelt gives us the right under Executive Order Nine Zero Six Six." Gables crossed his arms. "This is best done peacefully, Mr. Müller. You should get your coat."

Herbert's face flushed with anger. The injustice of it all hit like a blow to his core. His parents came to America with so little and worked hard to make an abandoned gristmill operate again. He thought back to those evenings when they first arrived and how, for months, he and Karl worked alongside their father, building the house while the family slept in a tent. And now their patriotism was being questioned? Herbert crossed to stand beside his father, the worn flooring crackling under his footsteps.

"Is zere discussion, for zis?" Otto said, his accent thicker than usual.

"Yes." This seemed like a reasonable request to Herbert. "Could we meet with someone from the State Department first?" Who took someone away on a Friday evening in a blizzard? He swiped his hand through his hair. "What's the hurry?"

The agents' faces didn't change. Herbert might as well explain the process of grinding wheat for all the emotion they showed. Fear encircled him because he had no idea how to stop them from taking his father.

Gables pointed to the table. "No discussion but you will remain here while we go through the house. Our search won't take long."

Herbert stepped back and held up his hands. "This has gone far enough." A vein throbbed in his forehead. "I will say it again, slowly." He enunciated each of the next words. "We... are...Americans. We...have no loyalty...to Germany."

Johnson nodded. "Your father will get his chance to explain in front of the Immigration and Naturalization Service board."

A hot coal burned in Herbert's gut. They'd deliberately arrived on a Friday evening, so Otto could not get legal counsel. The stern looks on the men's faces told him nothing would change their minds tonight. His family huddled on one side of the kitchen table, their faces blanched, full of fear. The agents disappeared into the back rooms. They'd find nothing out of the ordinary. Modest furniture, a Philco radio, knickknacks, like a Hummel holding flowers. Would that make them an enemy of the state?

He signaled they should hold hands. "Let us pray." He didn't wait for Otto to offer the words. "Lord, may we be slow to anger and filled with patience. May we be ready to forgive ourselves and others. Not just this once, but as many times as it takes. And may Grandpa Otto be protected in these unsure times. Amen."

The prayer didn't alleviate any of his fears. His father was up there in years, and with high blood pressure and arthritis, jail was no place for him. He'd given the family a medical scare after Anni died. A dehydration problem that caused him to pass out, at the time appearing to be a heart attack.

Minutes later, Gables returned carrying their radio while Johnson lugged a typewriter.

Herbert stood and held out his hand, a halting gesture. He'd explained the radio was not two-way, but they were taking it anyway. It seemed like a spiteful move. And why the typewriter? Did the Feds think they were typing out secret messages to Hitler? He pointed to the machine. "Our children need that for their school studies."

"They must own paper and pencils," Johnson said, moving out of Herbert's way. He lifted his chin to Otto. "We'll come back for you."

Tears flowed down Jutta's cheeks, and she wiped them away as Herbert laid his hand on her back.

"Who do we appeal to?"—Herbert followed behind Johnson—"No one should be out on a night like this, especially my father."

Gables balanced the radio on the couch back as he reached for the door. "Your father will get his say when his case is heard." His mouth was set in a tight line as if he tried to contain his irritation.

Johnson leveled a flinty stare at Herbert. "You could keep defying us and find yourself in the same boat... same cell, I mean."

Thoughts circulated fruitlessly through Herbert's mind. Otto had done nothing wrong, except he stayed too busy and forgot to become a legal citizen. Sweat dampened his flannel shirt. He couldn't let his father go to jail, especially over a weekend. He pictured Otto alone, accused, unable to defend himself against shrewd questioning. If he went along, he could represent his father and get them both back home before Christmas Eve. His father's arrest was a mistake, and the government needed to hear as much. Jutta and the children could rely on church friends to watch over them while he was away.

"These ideas are crazy. I'll go along with my father."

"Are you calling President Roosevelt crazy?" Gables added an unsympathetic laugh.

"Yes," Alfred said, his voice agitated. His hands were fists again and red splotches broke across his cheeks. Jutta and Frieda held each other, their eyes wide.

"Son. No." Herbert shot Alfred the look he always gave the stubborn boy. Despite being taught not to talk back to his elders, Alfred was always too quick with his tongue. Alfred caught *the look* and at least appeared to be a little ashamed as he folded his arms and leaned against the doorway to the kitchen.

Then Herbert turned to Gables. "I respect the president, but the people interpreting his orders I'm not so sure of." That might piss them off, but he didn't care. The government hadn't come for Otto two years earlier when he'd registered with them. Now, they were checking names off an old list to try to find people they suspected of being enemy aliens. Trying to keep their jobs by fulfilling an arrest quota, perhaps.

Johnson and Gables exchanged looks. They said nothing, but their rigid stances said they were unhappy with him, and he was going to get his wish to accompany his father.

He wrapped Jutta and Frieda in a hug and met Alfred's gaze.

"Fact Time. I can't let Pops go alone. Alfred, you'll be safe here, so I'd recommend not flashing the gun around. We should be back Monday, as soon as we get in front of a magistrate, or whoever hears these cases."

"Oh, dear." Jutta tapped a knuckle to her lips and shook her head. "Herbert?"

His name on her lips asked so much. How could this be happening?

"We'll sort this out." He reached for Jutta's hand and clasped it between his. It felt like a trembling bird. He needed to remain calm, to appear logical and level-headed.

Gables fumbled under his coat and pulled out two sets of handcuffs. "Will we need these?"

Herbert stiffened. This was getting real. Otto beat him to an answer. "No." Otto appeared haggard but resolved, his fighting spirit surfacing. He turned to Herbert and in German said, "Sohn, bleib bei der Familie. Ich werde in Ordnung sein." *Son, stay with the family, I'll be fine.*

"Pops, I'm going, too." He pointed to the handcuffs. "See? They're counting on me." He walked to the closet and grabbed their coats and helped his father into his. With one last look at his huddled family, he said, "I love you. And kids...go with your mother when it's our shift in the watchtower."

Gables hefted the radio once again and cleared his throat. "No need. Your family no longer has the right to be there."

Anger boiled inside Herbert. That hadn't taken long. His family was already labeled as untrustworthy. They did more volunteering in this community than any other family. And not because they wanted accolades. They believed it was their responsibility as citizens to pull together.

Johnson nodded to the front door. "It's time."

Herbert crossed the floor, the tick of the grandfather clock sounding louder than usual. The pendulum swung side to side, ticking away the seconds that brought him closer to leaving his family. He opened the door and a blast of frigid air buffeted him. While holding his father's elbow, Herbert followed Gables out as they descended the snow-covered steps and crossed to the car. Johnson was last to exit, still carrying the typewriter.

Gables opened the rear door to the sedan. Herbert dropped into the seat and scooted over to make room for Otto, and then quickly brushed the snow from the seat that followed him inside. Once Otto was settled, Gables leaned in out of the storm. "Settle in. We have a long drive."

Panic seized Herbert. He'd never been in custody before and the confines of the back seat seemed to close in on him. Insecurity nailed him in place because he wasn't completely convinced the government would treat him and his father fairly. The sudden shock of being hauled away like criminals, while temporarily forfeiting their freedom, silently ripped at his insides. If this turned into more than a few days away, what would happen to his family?

Johnson slid into the driver's seat and turned on the wipers, which stalled for a few minutes, fighting the heavy snow accumulated there before gaining a regular momentum. Beyond the veil of thick flurries, the house glowed like a precious ember. He envisioned his family huddled inside, with Jutta crying, her emotions always so close to the edge. They'd be holding hands, trying to comfort each other. He swallowed a lump. Fear of the unknown moved in, and even in the cold, his hands felt sweaty. He'd never contemplated their safety before, the surety made up of everyday routines, his family's predictability, and the well-worn patterns which kept them together. Now, he wasn't sure what awaited Otto and him over the next few days.

The car passed the gristmill that loomed like a motionless apparition in the storm. He loved that building. Found comfort in its interior, with its combined scent of dried grains, the fresh grease on the wheels, and the burlaps sacks. Otto seemed to watch the building slip by. Was he remembering the long days of grinding seeds, the pleasure of changing unyielding grain into a useable food, feeding the troops, using the profits to buy more war bonds? Where had they gone wrong? The gristmill disappeared, and the countryside dissolved. Huge flakes hit the windshield, and the wipers barely cleaned a swath before the glass was covered again.

"Where are we heading?" Herbert leaned forward, his voice calm and measured, although still angry. He didn't like the feeling of being powerless, a victim with no immediate recourse.

"Into Reading tonight," Gables said, half turning in his seat. "From there you'll go to wherever we have room, not necessarily a camp."

A camp? What were they talking about?

"We've filled most of those with the Japanese." Johnson wiped his coat sleeve on the fogged side window, which squeaked as he cleared an oval shape.

"My understanding is we're going to be interviewed to clear this up." Herbert turned to his father. Otto's face looked pale, but his eyes were alert. Otto had served as a German guard in WWI at the POW camp in Merseburg, Germany. When he'd talk about it at all, he told frightening tales of beatings, forced labor, and the near-starvation of twenty thousand mixed- ethnicity soldiers. His father probably pictured himself in that devastating scenario when he heard the word "camp."

Herbert patted his father's leg and leaned closer to whisper, "Not gonna happen, Pops."

Otto offered a quick nod and a smile.

"You understand correctly," Gables said. He adjusted the heater vent in the deluxe sedan. "When you've cleared your names, you go home."

Herbert settled back against his seat. He should have been paying better attention to the anti-German fears. His unmarried brother, Karl, served in the Pacific theatre, flying with the Army Air Force there. He and Karl were better friends than brothers, having each other's backs during their younger years after arriving in the United States speaking no English. The family was fully vested in the news coming out of the Pacific. And although newsreels showed the American and British armies pushing the Germans northward from Italy's boot, Herbert couldn't explain what was happening in Germany and the surrounding countries. He would say as much when questioned. While he had sympathy for those suffering in Europe due to the war, he was ashamed his birth country had perpetrated the war in the first place.

The car crawled along the empty back road, cutting a path down the center to avoid a spin into the ditch. Herbert rubbed his numb fingers together. The car was heating up, but his hands seemed to have no warmth. He rested his head against the seatback, picturing his cozy home, the kids, and Jutta cleaning up the kitchen. They might fall asleep in his and Jutta's bed which they often did when he was away on hunting trips. Emotion filled him and tears pricked his eyes. His family was his past and his future, and although he tried to be a reasonable man, if it came to it, he'd fight like a caged tiger to keep them safe.

-13-

WILHELM FALK

Aboard the *Algonquin*, Atlantic Ocean - January 2, 1944

F alk pulled his jacket shut against the cold. The anemic winter sun did nothing to stave off the freezing temperature on deck even though it was late afternoon. It reached him in long stripes of lukewarm yellow beams, broken apart by stagnant clouds, which floated high above the ship. He tucked his meal card into his identification pack before sliding it back inside his coat. His card was punched each morning at nine and then again at three. The meals were small and often consisted of beans, but beans were better than nothing. At times, when the crew handed out front-line rations, he sucked on the bouillon cubes, didn't question the meat paste, and devoured the cookies. Yesterday, his rations contained two surprises—a bar of soap and small roll of toilet paper.

This was their fourteenth day at sea, zigzagging across the ocean. The aircraft carrier in their flotilla was conspicuously missing since the day of the U-boat scare. They never learned what happened. A week ago, an alarm sounded when a Luftwaffe plane buzzed the convoy. But it was quickly blown in half, the pieces corkscrewing into the sea. Beyond that, the crossing was quiet.

Now, Falk watched silvery sparkles of flying fish against the wide, rolling, green sea. In every direction, the icy water moved and churned with whitecaps showing their indifference to man and his ships. He rocked his head from side to side, stretching to loosen his tight neck muscles. Sleeping on the metal floor in the hull was doing a number on his back and neck. One more week. An army-issued cot in an American prison camp sounded like a luxury. He hadn't slept more than a few hours at a time these past days, or even weeks, and his fuzzy mind struggled to hold fast to the details as he replayed the next step of his plan. He patted his shirt pocket and fingered the cyanide pill. There would always be this option if he failed to reach the American officials. His *death* in Italy would be the final story told about him if unable to complete his goal. And millions more would die until the war ended.

Ilse and the boys most likely celebrated the traditions of Silvester two evenings ago in Eindhoven with her sister's family. Surely, the Germans in the Netherlands were allowed their New Year's Eve traditions with noise-makers, midnight soup, and walking from neighbor to neighbor's house. The children accepting sweets and the adults a shot of Schnapps. All to the rhythm of the Rummelpott drum. He was incomplete without his wife in his arms, his boys hugging his waist. Remembering them was so easy because he did it every moment of the day but missing them was the heart-ache that never went away.

A leisure area was roped off on deck. Sentries in crisp uniforms with machine guns patrolled it to keep the POWs well away from the control room and inner workings of the vessel. When he and the POWs were up top, guards seemed to be everywhere, and most proved to be friendly.

The German noncommissioned officers enforced discipline among their own. German soldiers were expected to salute their superiors and fol-low a chain of command. Just the day before, Falk was called out for not immediately saluting an officer. Lost in thought, he forgot he no longer outranked the men around him.

He'd hoped the Nazi ideology would have calmed down once they were all captive, but even joking about the Reich on board proved to be dangerous. One Nazi, with a scar dividing his right cheek nearly in half, put another POW in sickbay the night before for telling a joke. Falk hid his laughter and avoided repercussions, but the jokester's face wouldn't be recognizable to his family after the rearranging it sustained.

Falk circled the deck again as the sun sank lower, laying broken beams of light across the water's undulating surface. Men were lined up at the enclosed on-deck shower that pumped seawater. He washed earlier, but his clothes remained dirty. He envied the American guards in their crisp coats, caps, and shiny boots.

He searched for Eduard and Christoph and found them seated on deck, waiting for sundown and the ragtag concert to begin. Someone discovered a few musical instruments on board, and the last two nights running under a star-spattered sky, German military and folk songs floated out over the far-stretching waters.

For Falk, the upbeat songs brought back horrible memories of the death camps, the ruse of a lively band playing as the trains dislodged its victims while the scent of ash was in the air. The bored SS guards often toyed with the deportees, betting on who could tell the most outrageous lie:

"The men will stay to the right and will work in the fields and receive extra food."

"We very much need a woman's expertise in our kitchens. As you can smell, our current cooks seem to burn everything that goes into the ovens."

"Your young children will go to school. Please have them line up on the left for their room assignments."

Fury burned through Falk that day. The SS men entertained themselves by pointing the Jews to their deaths with false assurances. Although he never contributed, neither had he attempted to say anything to discourage the cruel lies, as that would lead to his end, too.

"Enjoy the music," he said to Eduard and Christoph. The German tunes turned his stomach. He chose to pace the deck. The dark, smelly hold below his only other option for escape. "I'm going to keep walking. I'll meet you later."

Falk backed away from the growing crowd and bumped into Hartmann, who was in the 10th Army with Klaus Stern. The POW still wore the British pilot's heavy boots he cooked off the airman's feet.

"Evening, Stern."

"Hartmann." Falk flicked his chin, intending to walk past him until the man grabbed his arm. "Hold up." Hartmann whistled and another soldier turned and headed their way.

Falk yanked his arm free. "What's up?"

"Give it a minute." He wore a smirk Falk couldn't read. A soldier arrived at Hartmann's side. A thick mustache overhung his lip, his beard scruffy like the rest of the POWs. Hartmann tapped the other soldier's chest. "Stern. You remember Ziegler, don't you? A fellow buddy from the Tenth?"

Falk shrugged, stalling. If they reported him for traveling under false papers, his plan to reach America would be over. He'd be sent to a prison for German officers. There, it would be his compatriots he needed to worry about when they found out he defected. The cyanide pill seemed to grow in his pocket, and he felt the weight of its purpose. "Like I told you. I'd barely joined the Tenth when it all went to hell."

Ziegler spoke. "See, that's where you're wrong. Stern and I drank beer together when we weren't looking for whores"—he jabbed at Falk's chest—"and although you look like him, you're not Stern."

Falk stepped back and raised his hands. "Let's just leave it at that." He turned, cursing his bad luck. Thousands captured, hundreds on board, and this man was Stern's whoring buddy.

"I think we should hear what some of the other men say." Hartmann's eyes said he was enjoying himself.

He would be ganged up on and although he might be able to say Hartmann was crazy, Ziegler had truth to corroborate his story.

Falk turned and darted to a sentry he knew spoke German. The soldier had a duty to protect the POWs and Falk needed to be convincing. Upon reaching the guard, he said, "Put me in solitary. Some men are trying to kill me for criticizing Hitler."

The sentry moved his rifle in front of him, at the ready, while he looked over Falk's shoulder. "Which men?"

Falk glanced back. Zeigler and Hartmann were closing in. He silently swore. Marshalling the fear of a doomed man with nothing to lose, he cocked his fist and punched the sentry in the face.

The other guards rushed him. Blows landed on his back and head, mixed with curses and shouts in both languages. But above it all, someone spoke the words he hoped for. "Take him to the brig."

Under guard, Falk was nudged along a narrow passageway toward a small cabin. He was limping and stumbled twice. "Lie down," said a sentry as he pointed to a cot. The sharp scents of antiseptics and rubbing alcohol filled the room. A medic, with a white gown over his uniform, pressed a cloth pad over the cut on Falk's right cheek where a guard with heavy boots kicked him. The relief to be off deck and away from his accusers proved so great, he hadn't registered his injuries until now.

In a mishmash of English and German, the doctor explained he needed to examine him. By the look of the instruments on the metal tray beside the bed, stitches were in Falk's future. Two armed sentries stood inside the door of the examination room. He clearly proved himself to be a danger. Perhaps he would be held in the brig until they reached the United States. He'd come too far to be caught as an SS officer in an enlisted man's clothes.

Falk gingerly unbuttoned his shirt and the doctor helped him pull it off and then set it on a chair. He gently pushed on Falk's abdomen and then asked him to move his arms and legs. When he touched his injured ribs on the right side, he jerked and gritted his teeth as razor-sharp pain tore through him there. His breath stuck in his lungs, and he didn't dare let it out for fear more movement would prolong the pain. He noticed a purple splotch bloom across his side.

"Broken," the doctor said and pulled a roll of adhesive wrap from a metal cabinet. He helped Falk sit up and then tightly wrapped his ribs, which felt like death by suffocation. Would he be able to inhale at all?

The doctor pointed to the cut on his cheek and once again helped him lie back. "Sewing time." An injection of morphine burned a cold path up Falk's arm, but the drug hadn't completely begun its job when the doctor cleaned his wound with alcohol and a cloth pad. His eyes watered and he clenched his jaws against the pain that shot through his whole head. The medic reached for items on a metal tray and soon dropped in eight stitches. Within minutes, it was all over.

"All fixed." The doctor moved on to another patient.

He'd be taken to the ship's brig now where he hoped for a cell of his own. The two guards helped him stand, handed him his shirt, and then walked him to a large sickbay, and not a jail cell. The room was dimly lit, crowded with evenly spaced beds with white curtains drawn around each. One guard motioned Falk to follow him to the back of the room. The other patients were German POWs, almost all with bandaged wounds.

The guard pulled aside a curtain. The rasp of the rings on the overhead rail was loud in the quiet room. Falk laid his clothes over the bedside chair and carefully rolled onto the bed. Even with the tape and morphine, his ribs made it difficult to breathe as he lowered himself to the pillow. The guard said in German, "Tomorrow you go in front of our master-at-arms to explain your actions on deck."

After the guard left, Falk floated in and out of shifting, drug–addled thoughts, detaching him from reality for minutes at a time.

Hitler. That tyrant was never far from his thoughts. What did other world leaders think of him? It seemed the dictator's atrocities only recently dawned on some of Germany's citizens, those who witnessed them firsthand. Hitler declared that everything decent people believed in was evil—the press, foreign trade, and world religions. Rational men must shake their heads. How had this man come to such power in a country known for culture, music, and art?

Hitler convinced people that lying for the better good of the country was not a sin. It was a necessity. Then he attacked religious traditions held for centuries. Years earlier, seven hundred leading churchmen were thrown out of the country or arrested. Many of those were now dead. Pastor Graf made the right decision to immigrate to the United States before the ruth-lessness began.

An injured POW moaned in the room. Footsteps hurried toward the sound. Falk drifted along on the winding road of images that brought him this far.

Before deciding to take advantage of the battle in Italy and fake his death, he had begun to quietly work against the Führer. He'd written to His Holy See, explaining the humiliation and degradation facing the nuns and priests. Falk hoped the letter—posted with no return address from a small town in Austria—would cause the pontiff to do something to protect the men and women of the cloth. Yet nothing came from the Vatican to sug-gest the pope spoke out. Hitler continued to proudly build his pagan master race, seemingly unabated.

Falk readjusted his pillow and sheet, their clean crispness a foreign fabric in stark contrast to life in the ship's hold, where luxury was using his boots for a pillow. He breathed in the linen's freshness, his mind conjuring up a summer day at home near Düsseldorf. His sons, Hans and Dietrich, were playing hide-and-seek in the clotheslines behind their home. Chasing each other, they enjoyed the feel of flapping layers of cotton dropping damp caresses on their sun-warmed arms and shoulders as they ducked under the sheets. He had done the same when he was a child.

The bandage on his face itched and he scratched the edge of it, his hand movement sluggish, his mind slow.

He had a hole in his heart without Ilse nearby, without his sons, and tears pricked the corners of his eyes. When they'd married, he told Ilse he wanted a half-dozen children, but was content with the two they were lucky enough to have. If he'd known there would come a time when he'd be away from them for months, he would have spent more time building model train sets with a child at each elbow, their heads nearly touching. He'd have played tin soldiers in the windowsills when they asked, thrown more balls, gone fishing all day instead of a few fleeting hours. His sons believed his officer status was admirable because they didn't know the true function of the Schutzstaffel. Built on a culture of violence and patriotism at all costs, they operated outside the bounds of morality and were the judge, jury, and executioner all in one, with the authority to kill anyone at their discretion.

It had to be the pain medication, but suddenly he was unsure of his plans. Would the information he delivered to Washington D.C. change anything? When Falk exposed the secret side of Hitler's war, he hoped to persuade the U.S. military where to strike. First on the list should be Hitler's hideouts, the Eagle's Nest overlooking Berchtesgaden valley and the alpine-style residence he called "The Berghof." The elite Nazis either lived or often visited there. Dropping heavy lead would solve many problems and make a quick end to the war. Falk was invited to the Eagle's Nest once but begged off, saying he had a terrible virus. Hitler's fear of germs undoubtedly worked in his favor that weekend. What if his efforts came to nothing?

A soldier coughed in the next bed and Falk opened his eyes, his heart racing. There were events that twisted life's course, and those involving the boy with the strings and Falk's decision to turn against the Wehrmacht were just that. A sudden lump formed in his throat. The world might be too broken to be made whole again. He'd been too late to help the child, a fact that shattered him. Once he delivered his facts in America and asked for help, would he find strength in his broken places, or remain a spent man eaten away from the inside out by guilt?

Someone shook Falk awake, and he startled upright, ready to fight, stifling a scream as his ribs ground against each other.

He'd fallen asleep at some point in the night.

The lights were on in the room and a wide-shouldered guard stood beside him with a tray of food. It must be morning. When Falk pushed back on the bed to sit, the man placed the metal tray on his lap. "Enjoy your meal."

"Thank you." Falk's mouth watered at the aromas of fried eggs and potatoes, food he hadn't tasted in a long while. Another unimaginable luxury—a Hershey's chocolate bar—was tucked beside the blue and white china plate. The coffee smelled like the real deal.

He carefully ate the food, hoping his empty stomach could keep it down. The chorus of utensils, clacking against plates in the room, signaled that many others were also well enough to feed themselves. Falk finished and the guard returned, offering a shaving kit and a mug of warm water. "Your meeting is in thirty minutes."

Falk got ready and was combing his hair when a fight broke out. A German POW landed a punch on an orderly's chin. Guards subdued and handcuffed him. He was still protesting his rights to have his war medals returned as he was dragged away.

After he buttoned his shirt, he patted the pocket, checking for his cyanide capsule. It was gone! Last evening, Falk laid the shirt over the chair, so it must have fallen out then. A quick death was his only option if everything went wrong with his plans, and he didn't like losing that choice. He patted the shirt pocket again. Not there. He carefully lowered to his knees and searched the floor beneath the chair. His fingers closed on the pill as the military escort entered the room.

"Did you lose something?" the older escort asked.

"No." He tucked the pill in his shirt pocket, glad not to explain why he had it in the first place. Enlisted men were not offered the opportunity for an easy out. Suicide was an option reserved for officers. "I'm ready," Falk said. He followed the men through the interior of the ship, carefully climbing a set of iron steps so as not to jar his ribs.

They arrived at a corridor that housed several security offices. The escorts led him into an ornate room and indicated he sit in a chair facing a large wooden desk. A replica of a sailing ship, with curved copper sails holding a naval clock, sat on its edge. The plush room smelled of rich leather, books, and boot polish.

A tall man in full military dress entered with a redheaded security guard. The guard stood just inside the closed door, rifle held in an at-ease position.

The officer wore wire-rimmed spectacles. His neatly clipped hair, shot through with gray, framed chiseled facial features that reminded him of some of Hitler's top men. As he sat in the leather chair behind the desk, the man introduced himself.

"I am Officer Fitzgerald, master-at-arms of the U.S. Navy. Petty Officer Dixon, who is at your back, is your interpreter."

Dixon relayed the information and Falk nodded. "I am Klaus Stern."

Fitzgerald asked for Stern's *soldbuch,* and Falk handed over the identification packet.

The officer reviewed the pages. "What was the problem on deck last evening?"

The guard translated, and Falk answered. "I don't adhere to the Nazi doctrine, and I laughed at a joke about Hitler..." It was best to go with a portion of the truth. "When several men threatened to kill me, I punched a guard to get taken away."

Fitzgerald wrote on a pad. "Do you believe those men are alone in these thoughts or are other men like-minded?"

"I believe half of the POWs on this ship still cling to the Nazi principles."

The officer seemed to consider those words. "These men who are devoted to Hitler...what do they believe will happen to them when they reach the United States?"

The brainwashed POWs were fools. Falk smiled. "They believe they are being sent there as part of a bigger Wehrmacht plan to defeat America on her own soil. And they'll welcome the Führer when he comes to rule."

Officer Fitzgerald listened to the translation and chuckled. His eyes crinkled at the sides. "I imagine they will be dismayed when they find themselves in prison camps until the war ends."

Falk nodded.

"If you are released back into the POW group, will you be safe?" He absently tapped his pen on the desk.

Falk shook his head. "I will be killed for treason." He needed to stay alert, pretending to be Stern was dangerous business, and he was off his game. His head was thumping, his mind fuzzy.

"We arrive in New York Harbor in two days. Until then, you will remain in sickbay," Fitzgerald said.

"Thank you, sir."

"I'd like to hear the Hitler joke."

"Hitler and Goering are standing on top the Berlin radio tower surveying the city below. Hitler says he wants to do something to put a smile on the Berliners' faces. Goering says, 'Then you should jump.'"

"Good one." Fitzgerald nodded and a tiny smile appeared on his lips. He pulled his spectacles to the tip of his nose and scrutinized Falk over them. "Don't make me regret this. If this is a ploy to get access to the ship for sabotage purposes, we will shoot you...You are dismissed."

At the entrance to sickbay, Dixon pulled Falk to a stop. "Remember. Special treatment or not, if you get out of line, we'll take you topside and let the Nazis deal with you."

"I'd expect exactly that." He'd kill himself long before that happened.

Falk remained in the doorway for a moment and turned to a commotion coming toward him in the hallway. A medic pushed a gurney while two doctors ran along, one on each side. The patient moaned and twisted on the mattress. Blood spread across the soldier's white undershirt, his uniform torn open. Falk stepped back, but clearly recognized the seriously injured POW. The scarred forehead, his barely-there beard. It was young Christoph.

-14-

IZAAK TAUBER

Westerbork Camp, Netherlands - January 1943

Izaak didn't like how he and Mama were pushed and shoved through the Westerbork Camp gates, but they had no choice as the guards hurried everyone inside. An older man, bent over and shaped like the crescent moon, approached Mama and said, "I am Abraham Schoenberg, the Campo of Westerbork. I heard you asking questions. I'm a Jew from Antwerp who came here for refuge. That, of course, has since changed and refuge is no longer what this camp is about." Then he cleared his throat. "We're a transition camp now." He lowered his voice. "Don't be in a hurry to board the trains going east. I will get you a job here for as long as I can."

Mama looked worried. "But my husband went to Poland, and we'd like to locate him."

Abraham moved closer. Izaak studied the man's thin face. He looked like a bird ready to peck at the ground. Why couldn't he stand up straight? Maybe this was the reason Mama always told him to mind his posture.

"I've worked here for two years," Abraham said. "The rumors from the east say conditions here are far better than where you could end up"—he looked Izaak's way—"especially with a young child. Besides, your husband will be held in a different part of the…um…work camp."

Sometimes being young worked in his favor, but he felt much older than eight after all he'd seen happen in the past few months. He would somehow prove he was more grown up when they got to their new place.

Mama looked around. "Surely Poland is better than this crowded camp."

The old man's face sagged as if he suddenly wore out. Older people needed to eat early and go to bed when the sun went down, or that's what Izaak's neighbors used to do. The sun was dropping fast now, so it was bedtime for the moon-shaped man. Izaak worried about night arriving before they were shown to their room to sleep. But where were the houses? This place looked like a huge campground with dirty streets between rows and rows of long sheds.

The moon-man looked at Mama and squished his eyebrows. "I pulled you aside because I recognize you, ma'am. You won't remember, but you helped deliver my son thirteen years ago. A difficult birth."

Mama shot him a wide smile. "What a nice surprise. Thank you for remembering me."

Izaak pictured a baby boy born with a bent-over back like Abraham's. That would be difficult.

"Are you still a maternity nurse?"

"Yes, until recently."

"Good. We have a hospital and maternity ward here. Tell them that when you get to the registration table." He moved away to talk to another group.

Izaak didn't want to be in this overcrowded camp. He tugged Mama's coat. "Are we staying here?"

She pulled him close. "Just for a few days. It wouldn't hurt to make a little money before we travel. Perhaps, we can pay for passage on an earlier train."

He trusted her to know what to do. They reached the interview barracks, a long white building that needed new paint. "Wait here, love." Mama pointed to a bench just inside the entryway. "I'll be back soon."

Mama walked into a huge room full of tables and typewriters. The noisy machines clicked and dinged, making it impossible to hear what she said to the two workers at the table. With nothing to do, he imagined how he would draw this room and the people. If he squinted, he saw a path through the middle of a human forest where people clustered in small groups around picnic tables. But no one was happy with what was offered at the tables because their faces were sad as they turned away.

Mama walked out and took his hand, and his pretend drawing vanished. It must be freezing inside the barracks because her face looked white and her hands felt cold, even through her gloves.

They moved to another line, still carrying their suitcases. "We were assigned a place to sleep, love." She squeezed his hand. "But it's not going to be nice."

"Should we pretend to be Catholic again?" The sun was gone, but a big moon shaped like Abraham showed up on the other side of the sky. He thought of Mr. Fritz being killed last night and their long walk. It seemed so long ago.

"No, we don't have to do that. But we have to share a room. There are just so many people here."

As they moved along the rows of barracks, he wrinkled his nose. Something smelled bad, like the open-pit toilets at the zoo. Those always scared him. Papa used to hold him on the seat, so he wouldn't disappear down the stinky hole, but that smell remained in his nose for hours.

He followed his mama, telling himself he would not complain no matter who else stayed in their assigned room. Then, he repeated Papa's favorite saying: "A man's true wealth is the good he does in this world." With each step, he let the words march through his head, determined to be that kind of person. He repeated the sentence twenty-four times before Mama said, "Here we are."

They passed so many long buildings. Surely, they'd left the stinky camp by now. Then he spotted tall wire fences around the outside of the barracks and a high tower with a big treehouse on top. He missed his treehouse in Amsterdam. This one looked like it was stuck on a tall wooden frame. Other children were here, including Zev and Aharon. Maybe they could all play in it tomorrow. It even had a light that moved a big beam back and forth along the ground, especially now that it was darker.

The long house chosen for them had the number 97 on the front. Once inside the door, they walked into the sleeping area—a stuffy, overcrowded room.

The building was made of wood, but the doors and windows didn't look as if they fit right. Someone built it too fast when they were making these big bedrooms. Papa would never allow this sloppy work when he had his company.

Izaak's heart beat faster. They weren't sharing a room with just a few people, but hundreds were crammed inside the building. And he didn't like bunk beds, but that's all they had along the walls, stacked three levels high. Once, he slept at Derek Van der Mullen's house before Derek couldn't play with him anymore, and Izaak was on the bottom bunk. He worried all night about being smashed into a people pancake if Derek's bed broke. He tugged his mama's arm. "We have to be on top."

They walked along the endless rows, looking for an opening on an upper bunk. The best they could find was on the middle level. Mama pushed their suitcases up into the space first and then motioned for him to climb the ladder. At the bed opening, he crawled onto a thin straw sack. Mama crawled in after. He held his breath because it smelled like someone had peed on this bed, maybe more than once. They had no closet, cupboard, or any other place to hang up their clothes, so they kept everything on the bed.

Izaak sat cross-legged and looked out from their shelf. Many of the other people looked back at them like the caged monkeys at the Artis Royal Zoo. Except, the zoo monkeys had an open space to live in, with lots of trees and houses. The people here were crowded onto the bunks, their eyes big, holding each other. His stomach hurt at the thought they had to stay here. He wanted to go back to hiding, back to the little pantry off the kitchen where he and Mama shared a mattress.

Mama unrolled a cloth, and they ate the last of the bread and shriveled carrots from the train station. She whispered, "There'll be breakfast in the morning. They have cooks and kitchens here. For now, we should just go to sleep."

He studied the other chimpanzees on the shelves, who were talking in quiet voices. "How many people are here, Mama?"

She didn't say anything at first, so she must have been counting them. But then she said, "More than enough."

Then she rubbed his back. "Close your eyes. It's been a long day."

The thin prickly mattress scratched his legs through his pants, and the pee smell made his eyes water. He'd never be able to sleep, but he lay down and curled up next to his mama, and she covered them with her long coat.

Mama asked him to be brave, and he could do that. She fell asleep as the people talked around them. His mind immediately turned to thoughts of Papa. He reached for his suitcase, and eased open the latch, and brought out the folded, pencil drawing of his family at the windmills he had shown Mr. Fritz. He turned it toward the dim light hanging in the center of the room. Then he ran his fingers over the pencil marks, tracing his papa's face. This was one of his best drawings yet. In this picture, Papa had a mustache, but often he shaved it off and then looked so different. Would Izaak recognize him when they met again? He put the drawing back in the suitcase and snuggled close to Mama. Before drifting off, he decided that no matter what his papa looked like, he would know him when he spoke his name. Papa had the best voice in the world.

At the end of their giant bedroom, one long trough ran down the middle of the white tiled area with lots of separate faucets, so people could wash and not bump each other. Izaak stood on a wooden stool to reach one of the sinks and scrubbed his face clean.

An awful thing about the camp was the one toilet for all of them. Because it was always too busy, he and Mama walked to the building called a latrine. And his first thoughts about the camp were correct: It was very smelly like the zoo toilet, but built even worse, with just a long board over an open ditch he hung his bottom over. And no privacy. He and Mama held up her coat for cover when they took turns.

The guard, who said they'd be here five days, was way off. For three weeks, they lived crowded together, still crammed onto the middle bunk. Every night, he dreamed of being crushed. No one mentioned when they would be allowed to leave, and it seemed Mama stopped asking the moon-man because he said it was too dangerous. Izaak's stomach felt sour inside every time he thought about Papa living in danger.

He and the other children were bored most of the time, but some days they explored the sections of the camp where they were allowed. It was set up like a small town. Although men and women couldn't be together at night, they saw each other every morning. In his nightly prayers, he asked that Papa be transferred to Westerbork. He didn't understand how the Germans made these decisions, but hoped God had some idea. Every morning, he rushed to the meeting place, his heart thumping, imagining Papa's face when he spotted him. But so far, Papa wasn't one of the arrivals.

And why the adults said going to another camp could be worse than this one, he didn't understand. They usually stopped talking when he was nearby. Many things were rotten about this camp, like the soup and bread they ate at every meal. The only good distraction was the camp tried to put together a school for ages one to nine, but even that wasn't enough to keep his mind off Papa.

The school was in the back section of a barracks and opened onto a playground. It had a sandbox, swing, and one seesaw. With so many children in the schoolroom, the teachers scheduled how many could be outside at one time. His favorite part of the day was to run around with boys his age, searching for sticks for sword fights and talking about the toys they would get when they arrived in their new towns. Those moments were more fun than he had for months. He asked his new friends if they'd ever met Guus, but no one had. With so many camps—he heard Abraham, the moon-shaped man, say there were over forty—it was hard to know where his friend was now.

Today, Mama was dressed in a blue smock. She worked with the babies at the camp hospital. Every day she walked him to school before heading to work.

Outside his school barrack, she kissed his head and smiled. "Let's go be valuable and useful, Izaak." The camp bosses were grumpy and made sure everyone had a job. Looking helpful and valuable was whispered about at night in their long bedroom, and everyone tried to follow this important instruction. People who broke the rules were sent to the other side of the camp. The part no one was allowed to visit.

The camp boss, Commandant Gemmeker, always looked cross. He hardly ever walked past the large locking gate into their side of the camp, but when he did, he carried a tiny dog that barked as if he hated all people.

Minutes after Izaak entered the school, rain started banging hard on the wooden roof. The teacher, Miss Ruby, hurried around to close the windows. She was pretty with a quick smile and warm hands that made Izaak melt when she rubbed his back. Before coming here, she worked in a school in Amsterdam for one year. Miss Ruby tried to create new things for them to do each day. One of his favorite activities so far was to roll small stones in a little paint to make colorful gifts for new arrivals.

This morning, Miss Ruby pushed her dark curly hair off her forehead and tightened the matching belt on her blue flowered dress. "Children, find a place to sit."

Izaak sat on the floor by Zev and Aharon and the older children. It wasn't that he didn't like babies because he often helped Miss Ruby rock them to sleep, but they couldn't listen well and often cried when important instructions were given.

She held her hands behind her back and smiled. "I found a nice surprise." She quickly pulled her hands around to show them what she held. "Look! Books! And since the weather won't let us go out today, we will have a long story time."

Izaak felt his face stretch into a wide grin. He missed books. Mama always read him a story before bed when he was younger, and when he started to read, they alternated reading a page each. Stories were like art. They took him to places he never saw and let him imagine dragons, magic treasure, and secret caves.

The children quieted down, and Miss Ruby opened the cover on the first book. It had big colorful pictures with a story about animals playing tricks on each other in the forest. The book was for younger children, but he soaked in how the artist had drawn the pictures.

The next book was about a boy who told a lie to help his opa get medicine for the sick oma. And the last book was about a snowstorm that trapped a family in a cabin in the mountains. Izaak and his mama were like the family in the story, working together to stay alive.

Some babies fell asleep. Miss Ruby let them stay on the floor and motioned the others to an area with a stack of paper and crayons. She whispered they should draw whatever was in their heads. Izaak's hand shook a little as he reached for a lovely new crayon. He'd been stuck with his stubby pencil for so long, he'd forgotten how beautiful color could be as he dragged the waxy tip across the page. Testing it out, leaving an impressive red streak in a long diagonal across the top of the page.

But what to draw? So many ideas flew through his mind as the girl beside him went right to work. She drew with a brown color, running her hand around in scribbly circles over and over, her face bunched together. "What are you drawing?"

She stopped and looked at it. "Don't know." Then she picked up a black crayon and went back to coloring over the brown lines.

Mama needed to smile again, so his decision was made. He chose a flesh color and carefully drew the lines from memory. He changed colors a few times but added tan and shades of brown, and then black for the hair. He gave the face a smile. When he studied the eyes, they looked a little surprised, but that seemed right. Mama would like it that way. Then he folded the paper several times until it fit in his pants pocket. He couldn't wait for tonight to show it to her.

The rain stopped by the time school ended, but he couldn't play in the streets because they were too muddy. What could he do while waiting for Mama? She wasn't finished working until sunset, and right now, it was still high above the treehouse towers.

"Want to explore?" It was Zev.

"Sure." Zev's twelve-year-old ideas were always interesting. "Where do you want to go?"

"I heard prisoners are locked away in factories over there," Zev whispered. He pointed to the side where no one was allowed.

Prisoners! That would be something to see. "Do you think they have chains on them?"

"Maybe," Zev said. "Or maybe ropes, and their feet are tied close together and they hop or walk like this." He demonstrated walking with tiny steps as if his ankles were stuck together.

They gave up trying to imagine what a prisoner could look like and decided to go find out for themselves. They snuck around buildings, staying close to the walls until they passed four treehouses with guards. Izaak was disappointed when he learned he couldn't play in any of the seven perches. The men with the guns up there made him nervous, until one day he waved to the guards and they waved back.

Izaak and Zev arrived on the other side of the camp, far away from their long barracks.

The buildings were bigger here and didn't have metal bars on them as he imagined. This spying was exciting, although he worried about what Mama would think if he got caught. He and Zev snuck around to the back of the building and found cracks between the wooden wallboards. They cupped their hands and peeked inside. Men and women talked to each other while they chopped open batteries with hammers and a sharp tool. They threw some of the parts from inside the batteries into one basket and the outer casing into another. The workers' faces were dirty, and they were dressed alike in wooden shoes and baggy grey clothes. Even the women wore pants. A strong smell leaked from the room, and Izaak stepped back and coughed. How could the people stand to be in there?

Loud clanging sounds came from the next long building. He and Zev scampered to it and peered in a low window. Men stood at long tables, flattening big metal pipes with hammers. The men weren't talking to each other, and he wondered if their heads hurt. The vibrations moved through his body with each blow of a hammer, dozens running up and down him every few seconds. He covered his ears and saw Zev do it, too.

Suddenly, they were grabbed from behind and nearly lifted off their feet as a man shouted at them in words he didn't understand. His heart pounded like a puppy running loose inside his chest, and he swallowed hard. The man pushed them to the ground and yelled again. Izaak ducked his head, hoping not to be hurt any further, and when he wasn't hit, he stood and straightened his shoulders. Zev scurried closer to him until their arms touched.

The man was dressed in a dark uniform decorated with medals and iron crosses. It was Commandant Gemmeker, the camp boss. His little dog wasn't with him, and his face was red and bunched together. His boots were shiny even though it was muddy outside, and he wore an armband with a red spider cross in the center. Izaak squeezed his eyes shut and tried not to cry. People who got in trouble were sent away. He might never see Mama again or might be stuck here on the bad side of camp hammering pipes.

The commandant studied them for a long time and then pointed to their side of the camp. He followed them as they walked through the mud this time. Izaak owned only one pair of shoes and ruining them would be another reason Mama would be angry. He knew better than to break a rule, and he shouldn't have listened to Zev.

At the gate, the commandant opened it and motioned them inside. Izaak was glad to see Abraham, the bent-over moon-man, hurry toward them. He was one of the nicest men in camp and someone Izaak trusted.

Gemmeker spoke to Abraham and laughed, but it was a mean sound.

Abraham nodded and kept his eyes down as he spoke to the commandant. He looked even older than usual, the skin on his face drooping around the edges of his mouth. Abraham scowled and said to Izaak and Zev, "Commandant Gemmeker says you're interested in working on the other side of the camp, along with the criminals."

Izaak shook his head. He knew it. He'd be a prisoner and Mama would never know what happened to him. The horrible smell in the battery room was still in his nose and the terrible noise from the other building muffled his hearing. He couldn't work there. He shrank away from the commandant. And even though lying was on the list of bad things to do, he said, "We got lost after school." His lips quivered. "We ran in the rain and didn't see where we were going."

Abraham spoke to Commandant Gemmeker in his language and then listened to the reply.

The moon-shaped man's shoulders drooped even lower as he faced Izaak and Zev. "The commandant says since you are so eager to leave the camp, you and your families will be scheduled on tomorrow's transport. I'm to add your names to the list." A long sigh escaped him. He nodded to Gemmeker, who turned and left. Abraham gently nudged Izaak and Zev in the direction of the hundreds of long houses. "I need to find your parents and give them the news. Are your papas here, or just your mamas?"

Both boys replied only their mamas.

Izaak's chest was beating in an excited way now. "But leaving sooner is good, right?"

Abraham didn't speak for a few moments. The only sound was mud squishing under their shoes. Izaak would need new clothes and shoes to travel. He hoped there was time to shop at the camp warehouse.

"Of course," Abraham said softly. "Good news."

Then Izaak got a bad feeling because Abraham's face did that thing where adults say one thing but mean something else. His forehead wrinkled and his eyes looked sad, but he tried to smile. Papa looked like this once. Said they couldn't go to the cinema anymore because all the movies were about war and not something Izaak should be watching. But Izaak's old friends still went to the neighborhood cinema. Papa's face looked like Abraham's did now as if his mouth got a squirt of lemon juice at the end of those words.

First, Abraham dropped off Zev at his mother's job in the stocking repair shop. Izaak didn't go inside, so he didn't know if Dahlia was happy or sad about the news. Abraham returned and took Izaak's hand. "Off to the hospital, to find your mama."

Abraham treated him and Mama extra nice because she'd delivered his son. Izaak asked the question stuck in his head since he first heard this. He imagined a rounded-back baby trying to sit up or walk. "Is your son okay? I mean, did he get...tall?"

"He's a big, healthy boy."

"Does he live here?"

"He went to Israel with his mother four years ago."

Izaak walked slower, liking the feel of Abraham's hand around his, warm and strong. He didn't want to reach the hospital too fast. "She might be busy right now delivering babies." He hoped Mama would be happy with the news about leaving and forgive him for breaking a camp rule.

"We'll check. There's lots of people working with her so maybe she'll be free." Then he pointed to the shops and storefronts. "We've become a regular town. Tailors, furniture makers, and bookbinders. I wish you could stay, Izaak." His voice was low, and he slowly shook his head.

"How long have you lived here?" Izaak asked, wondering how Abraham got his important job.

"Too long." Abraham stopped, and because he was a bent-over man, he could look Izaak right in the eyes. He used a serious tone. "The next part of your trip will be hard. It's a long way to where you are going." He cleared his throat. "Do you know how to sing or play a musical instrument?"

Izaak shook his head and laughed. "Mama said Papa and I sing the same...like sick mules."

Although this story usually made other people laugh, Abraham didn't even chuckle. Instead, he moved close enough that Izaak saw the small holes in the skin on his nose and dirt pieces in his eyebrows.

"What can you do? You need to be able to entertain adults."

Izaak remembered his new drawing and pulled it out of his pocket, unfolding it to show his grown-up friend. "I can draw people. That's my papa up-close."

Abraham studied the drawing. A small smile spread across his face. "Okay, then. When you arrive at the next stop, no matter how hard it was to get there, show this drawing to a soldier. Agree to sketch the important people in camp." He squeezed Izaak's shoulders and gave him a little shake. "Do it as soon as you get there, Izaak. Do you understand?"

"I will." Izaak was nervous because Abraham's voice trembled, but at the same time he was proud Abraham thought he was good enough to draw other people and make them happy. He smiled to himself, glad he chose to draw Papa today. And maybe it was a good decision for another reason. Maybe the men in the new place will recognize Papa from the drawing and take them right to him.

-15-

HERBERT MÜLLER

Reading, Pennsylvania - December 1943

Gables and Johnson said little to Herbert and Otto on the drive, which was fine with him. The more miles distancing him from his family, the angrier he became. His father, a man still grieving the loss of his wife, was no enemy to this country. Devoted to the family, Otto was a man with a heart of gold, and Herbert couldn't fathom why his elderly father was falsely accused of crimes. His mind hadn't kept pace as these recent events rushed at him. How could it be German-Americans were suddenly considered enemies of the country, his country? Where was the *We Welcome You to America* spirit his father and mother were offered?

He dug deep into his emotions searching for patience. Tomorrow, this would be over. The government would see he and Otto were no threat to America, but what would happen once he returned home? His family could face more retribution from the neighbors because of this unfounded hysteria.

Thousands of Japanese-Americans were already in internment camps, with the reasoning that Japan bombed the United States. They'd made a direct hit on the country. But were the Japanese families any different from his? He didn't believe so. They were a generation raised in America. Citizens with little in common with their country of origin and now labeled dangerous alien enemies.

The FBI turned into the parking lot of a high school. He'd expected a jail or an office building but not this. They must be having a pre-Christmas, Arrest-a-German Festival if a school was all they had left as a holding pen.

Pines loomed tall behind the rectangular two-story building. The deep shroud of snow gave it a Christmassy scene, except for the dozen black sedans parked side by side near the entrance.

On the way to the double doors, Herbert held Otto's arm as knee-high snow covered their shoes and pant legs. Inside, after stomping their feet to avoid slipping on the polished floor, the agents led them down a long hall, past classrooms with closed doors from where muffled voices could be heard.

They walked, their shoes squeaking on the linoleum, and stopped in front of a room with "Janitor" stenciled across the glass window.

Gables opened the door and gestured that Herbert and Otto should enter the small cluttered space.

Were they kidding? "You must have another room for us," Herbert said, his hands fisted at his side.

"We're working on it," Gables said. "The National Guard was bringing cots." He shoved his hands in his coat pockets and shrugged. "The storm, you know."

Wonderful. His comfortable bed, the warmth of Jutta's leg against his. Tonight would be a long night without those. In addition, a hard cot would do nothing for his father's achy bones.

"In you go," Johnson said. "Shouldn't be too long."

Herbert glared at the men as he let Otto enter the room first. He refused to dignify their actions with a response. When he had the opportunity to speak to a lawyer, which he hoped was tomorrow, he would argue the indignation of being held in a janitor's closet. "When do we get our hearing?"

"You'll be interviewed in the morning," Gables said as he closed the door.

With the click of the lock, overwhelming doubt surfaced. He had rights as a citizen but concerns about getting this all behind him and returning home. And he was worried about his father. With Roosevelt's order, labeling nonresident German immigrants as the enemy, Otto could be incarcerated until the war ended. A prospect he didn't want to consider.

"Things just get better and better, don't they, Pops?" Herbert turned a slow circle in the room. Shelving to one side contained cleaning supplies, rolls of paper towels, and light bulbs. A floor polisher, brooms, mops, and ladders nearly filled the rest of the room. How could they be treated this way? They weren't common criminals.

"We will... get through zis, son." He dragged his hand through his hair. "We have a chance, ühm, to prove... what we, are made of."

He found a clear space against the wall and helped Otto lower himself to the floor, and then sat next to him. Otto didn't have to prove what he was made of. In World War I, he'd gone without food for days on the Western Front, had hidden under dead soldiers for protection, and returned home at war's end to learn half his family and the town had died from influenza. The only test Herbert overcame was having a shorter leg. He had no clue what he was made of under extreme circumstances.

The windowless room smelled like damp rags, bleach, and mildew. The overhead light bulb shone garishly in their small confines but turning if off and sitting in the dark wasn't appealing. Cold from the cement wall soon crept into his back. The custodians must have set the temperature in the building just high enough, so the fuel oil wouldn't freeze over the holiday break but low enough to be uncomfortable without activity to stay warm.

"You warm enough, Pops?"

Otto nodded and patted the hard floor. "I thought... a pillow, would be nice for, the ühm backside."

"We'll write to management and complain about the accommodations."

Otto chuckled. But after a few moments, his face grew thoughtful. "Son... remember when... I took, zee, the custodian job... after we arrived?"

"I do. Vaguely." He must have been twelve and Karl fourteen, but he couldn't pull up images of his father cleaning an insurance building. "You worked nights, right?"

"Yup. The credit was, used up when we, roofed the house. The mill was running... but, we only had, a few customers. So I took the job, part-time."

"I don't remember helping you." His father worked twenty-hour days, between running the mill, building the house, and then taking a night shift.

"You boys did enough, by helping me build, the house... every day after school. I made sure that you did your studies." He breathed deeply.

"This scent, the cleaning products, reminds me to work towards a goal...no matter what the cost."

"I haven't told you enough, Pops. You've always been my hero." He often worried he fell short of his father's example. Otto worked hard yet found time to belong to the Elks Club, go on hunting trips, and play poker once a month. He worked and slept and worked harder. Life was easy for Herbert, thanks to his parents' sacrifices. He wrapped his coat tighter and thought of his family. Jutta and the children would be frantic wondering where they were taken. He'd call them first chance in the morning.

Voices in the hallway woke him. He'd dozed off. His watch showed 5:30 a.m. Six cold hours made him stiff as he tried to stand. Footsteps drew closer. "Might be the cavalry?" He pulled Otto to his feet as the door was unlocked.

Johnson stood there in a fresh black suit. He was blurry-eyed but clean-shaven. He motioned them into the hallway.

"We'll give you a few minutes in the washroom before you are questioned." Johnson motioned them down the hall to the school's lavatory. After using the toilet, Herbert walked to the sink and faced his reflection. He might be hopeful inside but looked like hell and as if he aged five years. He followed Otto's lead and splashed cold water on his face, sending a shiver through his already chilled body.

They walked along the main hallway, where Gables waited. "I know you're anxious to be interviewed, so you two are first up."

"Zank you," Otto said.

"We appreciate it," Herbert added. At this rate they'd be home for the noon meal. He'd make light of their time in the janitor's closet, they'd *tsk* and laugh, and life would get back to normal.

Johnson spoke to Herbert. "You're with me"—he pointed to the door stenciled *Principal*—"and your father will be across the hall."

He hadn't come all this way to be separated from his father. "I'd like us to stay together, if possible."

"It's not possible," Gables said. He touched Otto's elbow. "This way Mr. Müller." And directed him across the hall.

"I'm only here to support my father through this process," Herbert said. "His understanding of English is not always good, and I'd like to help." These were highly-charged times and he suspected they would press his father until he admitted some kind of infringement. Otto had once used extra gas coupons Herbert won in a poker game. Would that be a crime against the country? And why was Herbert being questioned? Not only was he a citizen but also volunteered to come last night. Anger rose inside. "I don't like how you're treating my father." He shot an obstinate glance at Johnson. "Feel free to write that down."

"Noted. The process will go faster this way." Johnson held the door as Herbert entered the principal's office. He'd been out of school seventeen years, but it still felt like a walk of shame.

The room was large with a desk to the left and a semicircle of chairs in front of it. A man in a tan suit stood behind one. A kerosene heater was positioned in an open area, fending off the cold. A woman sat at a desk in front of a typewriter, her eyes lowered, studying her hands in her lap as if they held an important message. Her unwillingness to make eye contact suggested she felt guilt for her involvement in such a farce. Or maybe, Herbert thought, he was reading it wrong, and she refused to meet the gaze of an enemy.

Johnson directed Herbert to a seat, and the man in the tan suit took the chair across from him. He wore his dark hair in a classic style—short on the sides and back, long on top, slick with pomade—shiny under the spotlight focused in Herbert's direction. Herbert raised his hand to shield his eyes. They burned from little sleep, and the room was already extra bright from the morning sun reflecting off the snowy white world outside.

"This is Detective Thorne," Johnson said, "a service officer with Immigration and Naturalization."

Perhaps this could work in their favor. What if this was a way to help Otto gain citizenship? As far as Herbert knew, Immigration and Naturalization investigated the background of those applying to immigrate, meaning they would find Otto crime-free during the twenty years he lived here. The positive twist renewed his plan to be out of here soon.

"Mr. Müller," Thorne said. His tone was stern and no-nonsense. "I expect our interview will take approximately twenty minutes. After that you'll be offered food and coffee. Are you ready to begin?"

Tension tightened his stomach. The unfamiliar feeling of being investigated as if he'd committed a crime destroyed his appetite. Thorne was too serious for what Herbert imagined the interview might entail. "Sure."

Thorne cleared his throat and spoke to the typist. "Are you ready, Lucille?"

She nodded.

Officer Thorne picked up a clipboard and pen. He asked Herbert to identify himself. Then said, "Tell us about your connections to Germany."

Unbelievable. It was as if Johnson hadn't explained he'd only come along to help his father. "Do you know I became a citizen in twenty-seven?"

"I see that noted here"—Thorne tapped his pen on the clipboard—"I'd like to hear about who you are in touch with in Germany."

The guy was cold and doing a great job of maintaining a frozen meat stare.

"I was born there and came here with my parents in 1920."

Thorne made a notation on his paper. "You are a member of an all-German club?"

"Yes. It's a social club. Like the Elks, the Masons or the Moose Lodge."

"What is the purpose of the club?"

"We listen to music we were raised with, eat German food, discuss who in the community needs help. Everyone's much too busy to plot the overthrow of the United States."

Johnson leaned closer, and his eyebrows drew together. "Cracks like that will put you in jail."

"There are over a million German-Americans in the U.S. If you plan to jail us all, you won't return home before summer."

The room fell silent as they studied him.

He needed to get a few things straight. After all, he had rights. "I should be allowed a phone call. I need to let my family know where I am."

Officer Thorne's mouth did something, but it was in no way a smile. "We sent someone to your house this morning with that information."

How had Jutta and the children taken the news that he and Otto were held in a high school? Jutta would have been stoic for the children's sake and hopefully they'd joked about it. Herbert always told them he was happy to leave high school behind because it was a painful experience for him, not academically but physically. The family had no car, and he and Karl, more often than not, ran the two miles to school because they'd slept in once again. His hip radiated pain all day at his desk, and then he had to run home.

Thorne read from a form on the clipboard. "Case number nine thousand four hundred and thirty-six. Herbert Müller, born 1909 in Stuttgart, Germany, to Otto and Anni Müller. Arrived 1920, with a brother, Karl, who currently fights in the Pacific. Anni is deceased. Herbert's wife, Jutta Weber, born in Schwerin, Germany, 1911. Parents deceased. Herbert and Jutta have living aunts and uncles in Germany and numerous cousins. Together, they accepted U.S. citizenship in 1927 and have two children who are citizens."

Thorne turned his gaze to Herbert. "Is that all correct?"

"Yes. Now that it's on record that we are citizens, I guess we're done here?" Taunting the man was wrong—he knew that. This was the kind of behavior he chastised Alfred for doing. But this questioning? It was all too surreal, and sarcastic remarks filled his head until he couldn't contain them all.

Thorne flipped the pages on the clipboard and pulled out a pen. "Your father was arrested for being an enemy alien. You decided to accompany him. Why?"

"Because we are innocent of any crime, and he shouldn't be here alone trying to explain that."

"When we are done this morning, you will be free to return home. For now. But, if you choose to be with him, we will have to arrest you." Thorne adjusted the front of his suitcoat. "I want to make that clear."

"Surely, he'll be freed once you've interrogated him." What kind of baloney had a neighbor fed the FBI to have them hold his father?

"Not just yet. He'll have a hearing before the Department of Justice. At that time, he may invite three witnesses to testify on his behalf. And yours if you are still here."

Lucille clacked away at the typewriter.

Herbert bit down on his tongue to keep himself from screaming. His only crime was his German heritage. He had no choice but to stay calm and made a show of nodding slowly. "Of course, sir. I'll make those phone calls now."

"The hearing isn't scheduled yet." Johnson adjusted the front crease of his pressed pants. "We have preliminary questions today."

His foggy brain tried to process the idea they intended to hold his father longer than just a day. He accepted he'd be arrested because there was no way he'd leave his father here, alone. "Then I will be staying, too." Jutta would understand his decision, and the minute he visited with a lawyer, he'd shared a few choice words about the State Department.

"In that case, I have a different set of questions for you," Thorne said, switching out papers on the clipboard. "How often do you associate with other German families?"

"Our Lutheran Church is ninety percent German."

Johnson spoke, annoyance riding high in his voice. "He didn't ask for a percentage."

"Weekly." Herbert kept his tone flat and dispassionate, but wondered at Johnson's sudden surliness. Must have missed his morning coffee.

"What is your attitude about your relatives in Germany?"

Herbert lifted his hands, and his coat sleeves slipped to his elbows. "I barely remember any of them, but to tell you the truth, I feel sorry for them. They could be here enjoying America's freedoms, like I am."

Thorne scowled, and Lucille's hands froze over the keys.

"You need to consider if wisecracking is such a good idea," Johnson said.

"I'm sure it's a terrible idea." Herbert rubbed his sore hip with his palm. "But I do feel sorry for all the people in Europe. I can't imagine a war raging in my backyard while I try to keep my family safe, the food deprivations. It must be awful."

"Is anyone in your family in contact with relatives in Germany?"

"No. My father and mother exchanged Christmas cards with a cousin before the war but nothing since." During mealtimes, his father often prayed for their relatives' safety. Otto had seen a war up-close, watched as people were slowly wrung out with fear, starvation, loss. With no word from Germany, he feared the worst.

"Do you speak German?"

"Yes, but I'm rusty. I arrived here at age eleven and was encouraged to learn English. My parents picked up on it fast, so we all spoke both languages at home, and English in the community."

"Why aren't you enlisted in the armed forces like your brother?"

"We drove to Philadelphia the day after the Japs struck Pearl Harbor. I have one short leg from birth. The military refused me."

Johnson leaned forward. "Do you have the paperwork proving you are unfit to serve?"

Heat flamed his cheeks. Herbert was on his feet before he knew he meant to stand. He would have gladly served.

The men jumped up, too, and Johnson pulled his firearm and pointed it at Herbert. "Sit down!"

His heart beat fast. Having a gun barrel pointed his way sent a ripple of shock through him. Still he had to make his point. "This is harassment!" Herbert pounded his fists on Lucille's desk. "I'll answer questions, but I will not be vilified. My family purchases war savings stamps through our children's school. Alfred belongs to the High School Victory Corps, preparing him to join the army when needed. We've collected over three tons of scrap paper for the war effort, single-handedly filling the truck several times a month and driving to the collection center when we have enough gas coupons." He slowly sat and took a long breath, but his heart hammered out a war cry in his chest. "You've accused the wrong family."

The other men were silent, and three sets of eyes studied him. Lucille reviewed her hands once again. The ticking of a clock on the wall near the American flag resounded in the quiet, seeming to move Herbert toward events he didn't understand. Sure, he'd be allowed to call in his neighbors to vouch for him, but at the moment, the questioning was not going in his favor. "I'd like to speak to a supervisor."

"President Roosevelt is my supervisor," Thorne said.

"Do you know this all started when we were assaulted by young men in the area?" Herbert fought to keep irritation out of his voice. He couldn't believe he was being treated like this. The room suddenly seemed smaller. Was it possible he had such little input in what the government planned to do? "You heard about that incident, right?"

Thorne cleared his throat. "Yes. Your son fired a shotgun to scare them away."

"I fired the gun." He shot Johnson a look. "You know the details of that night."

Johnson shrugged.

"Your son is how old?" Thorne pressed.

"Fifteen." Why the sudden change in questioning? Were they trying to make him drop his guard and trap him?

"What does he enjoy doing?"

"He plays basketball and is a whiz in mathematics. He'd like to be an accountant."

"The Victory Corps offers specialized training. Has he chosen a trade to study?"

"Radio code and mechanics." Herbert immediately regretted his answer. Clearly those skills could be interpreted as enemy activities. Why hadn't he simply said espionage? "But since you now have our radio, he'll have to find another trade."

Thorne looked thoughtful and then offered a tight smile. "Yes." He flipped through more papers on the clipboard and glanced at his watch. "We're done here. You'll be moved with your father to a converted shoe factory, where you will await your hearing. You may notify your family by post."

A shoe factory! This investigation was muddled at best. The FBI might as well be playing basketball with a tire. He shook his head. Perhaps he could request a bed for him and Otto on cow hides instead of sleeping on an assembly line.

The other men rose and Herbert stood. "I'd like to see my father, please." His throat was tight realizing Otto, as a noncitizen, may have gone through a tougher grilling.

He waited only five minutes before Otto joined him. "You okay, Pops?"

"Just tired." He looked small in his coat, and his shoulders sagged. "You probably know, that I am not, going home today."

"They told me"—he squeezed his father's arm—"I asked to stay with you, so they were kind enough to arrest me."

Otto vehemently shook his head. "No, son, go to Jutta, the family needs you there...to keep the place going."

"I won't argue. We're a team."

"The car is waiting," Gables said, buttoning his coat.

Otto shook his head but accepted Herbert's arm as they left the building. The air outside was crisp and refreshing with a mocking taste of freedom.

Johnson stood beside the open rear car door waiting for them, trying to light a cigarette. The match flared, but caught a strong wind and snuffed out. He turned his back to the gusts and bowed, protecting the flame.

Herbert eased Otto into the back seat and dropped in next to him. What a difference twelve hours made. He swallowed a lump of bitterness that threatened to choke him. When he'd arrived, he knew this was all a misunderstanding, and although coming here was annoying, he and his father would be heading home today. That hope was now dashed, splintered like a fragile family heirloom against a fireplace. America's freedoms were no longer his. The betrayal settled heavy around him.

Soon, they were on the move to the shoe factory. Why didn't the FBI call it what it was—a jail? He and his father would be jailed for an indefinite time. The thought cycled through his mind, but he couldn't get it to make sense. He closed his eyes against the brightness off the snow and planned what he needed to do. He was close to the deacons in his church. They'd watch over his family and help out if needed. A homecoming before Christmas would make that day extra special. But with only a mere five days between now and then, he needed to start writing letters the second his feet hit the factory floor.

He turned his head to the side and peeked at his father. Otto appeared to be asleep. Herbert was thankful his mother was not alive to see how their much-loved country was turning on her husband and its own citizens.

$-16-$

WILHELM FALK

New York Harbor - January 4, 1944

The thunder-grey skies were spitting early morning snow as the Liberty ship sailed into New York Harbor. Falk stood on a protected portion of the deck with other able-bodied prisoners from sickbay. During the last three days at sea, he searched for Christoph in the hospital rooms, but the boy must be in the critical care section, an area he couldn't enter. He asked an orderly about Christoph and was told it was none of his business. He tossed and turned most of last night, worried about the young soldier's condition and what happened.

The deck below him swarmed with hundreds of POWs also watching the New York City skyline glide into view. It was magnificent. The faces of the men around Falk changed from astonishment to dismay as the grand city rose tall, proud, and unharmed. They were just now realizing their leaders obviously lied. German air raids had not leveled the city. Footage of smoldering buildings shown to the Wehrmacht claimed to be what was left of New York City. Tens of thousands were reported killed here by nonstop Luftwaffe bombings.

Yet life appeared perfectly normal as motorcars and taxis drove along the roadways, and lights shone through the gloom. Himmler filmed bombed-out cities in Germany to make the propaganda films to bolster the slumping morale of the men on the front lines. Like everyone else in Germany, Falk lived under blackout orders since 1939. And although he expected to be impressed by a fully functioning New York, this twinkling city presented a scene right out of fairytales.

A foot soldier next to Falk coughed and spit on the deck. "This is all staged." He flicked his chin to the Statue of Liberty which grew larger by the minute. "We leveled the big bitch. They must have really scrambled to build a fake."

Falk crossed his arms and shrugged. "Looks real to me."

Other men spoke up. "I thought we bombed the hell out of this city."

"Maybe this isn't really New York."

"They didn't build a fake New York for us, you idiot."

The skyscrapers, with their lit windows, shone brightly in the overcast dawn, giving Falk fresh hope that this part of the world remained strong enough to defeat Germany.

As the ship glided past the towering statue, pale streaks of sunlight broke through the rolls of steely cotton above, illuminating the symbol of freedom for Americans.

While the other Liberty ships slipped into their assigned docks, the *Algonquin* came to port at one of the many huge concrete piers. Falk breathed deeply, taking in a strange mixture of saltwater, engine oil, rotting fish, and wet swollen wood. Overhead, seagulls circled, beating the salty air with their wings, their undulating screeches announcing the POWs' arrival.

Falk took his sons fishing many times to local lakes and rivers, but it hadn't been enough. Hans and Dietrich would hold only a sprinkling of memories of father-son trips if he never returned. When the war was over, he vowed to make sure his children appreciated everything life offered. If he accomplished his plan in America, he wanted his family to live outside Germany. He faced the facts. Once he turned on his country, he would remain a hunted man. Besides, once the war ended, what place would Germany hold in the world, with its largest cities reduced to piles of stone and debris? Germany might have to rebuild its glorious past from memory and faded photos.

The ship sprang to life, bells sounded, and calls went out for all hands on deck. The boatswain on the upper deck piped signals, sending groups of men to the ferries.

Two guards and a translator approached his group. "In about forty minutes you will be shuttled ashore. We suggest you return to sickbay and rest."

This was great news. Falk needed to avoid the main group of soldiers on the off chance he might meet up with Hartmann and Zeigler. Had Zeigler and Hartmann warned others about him? If they talked up his deception and passed it along, other POWs might be on the lookout for him. He didn't know how many prison camps there were, but he'd be surprised if he ran into these POWs again.

He followed the prisoners to sickbay. Many were on crutches, others in bloodied bandages, a few without visible wounds—shuffling, eyes vacant. *I get it comrade*, he wanted to say. *It's all too much.* The roar and rumble of the engines under his feet ceased, and the ship fell into an eerie quiet. For seventeen days, the steady vibration drowned out the ship's day-to-day noises. Now, conversation seemed especially loud. A phone ringing somewhere in the ship sounded close, and metal cables and hooks clanged loudly against the vessel's iron hull.

Thirty minutes later, the guards escorted the patients from sickbay to the lower decks down a series of stairs. In the jostling, Falk held his ribs close, but each downward step sent white-hot pain through his side.

Falk looked for Eduard. He and Christoph reminded him so much of his younger sons that he missed having them at his side. He couldn't help thinking how the young men's lives were just beginning and how he cared deeply that they make it home one day. He needed to know Christoph was fine. After failing to find Eduard in the crowd, he boarded a large ferry. The transport churned its way across the harbor as an icy wind blew off the water.

Once on land, the naval officer on their ferry made a show of transferring power to the Commanding General of the Port of Embarkation. The general stood tall on a raised platform, chest loaded with military hardware.

"You will be walking to Camp Shanks, four miles north of here," he said in passable German. "There you will remain until your transfer papers are processed, and you are assigned to a permanent work camp."

He was placed in a group of fifty and told to wait along the wharf. Again, each POW was questioned about where he was captured, his unit, and age. And there was a new question. "Do you possess any useful information you would like to exchange for special treatment?"

Falk hesitated. Part of him wanted to speak up, to say he possessed important information, shocking perhaps. But he remained silent. Until he did something right in this war, he was just another unworthy soldier, a guilty observer with a cyanide pill in his pocket if he didn't achieve his goals.

The man asked him again, this time louder.

"I have nothing to share."

The man motioned him to a waiting area encircled with barbed wire. For millions of people—dissidents, religious opponents, and entire ethnic populations—their last heavenward view was through twisted wire. His chest tightened, and he forced away images of the boy with the strings, of shuffling skeletons in striped clothing, of nauseating smoke and ash.

His group was given the go-ahead. They marched through New York City on designated streets, temporarily roped off from civilians. One of the guards, walking beside Falk's group, said in German, "Amazing, isn't it? Bet you don't have buildings like this in Germany."

"Even a chicken coop in Germany is bigger," said a man behind Falk.

The guard snorted. "Then, welcome to your new life at the bottom of the pecking order."

Falk rubbed under his nose to hide his smile. How long would it take the POWs to accept they were not the world's elite fighting corps they'd been led to believe? It was a long hard fall from the top and with no easy landing. He ignored the muttering of the men and studied the streets. No people were on the sidewalks the POWs were assigned to follow, but plenty of curtains were pulled aside as they passed through this predetermined area.

Every detail of normalcy jumped out at him. The intricate pattern of intact cast-iron fire escapes created shadows across a bakery window. Colorful pieces of laundry hung from lines stretched between balconies. Everywhere were electric signs, promoting carpenters, printers, Italian moving companies. On the cross streets, well away from the POW parade, food vendors' carts were parked with long lines of people snaking away from each one. Even at this distance, the scent of sausage and other roasted meats tore at his stomach. A person could know a city by studying its streets, and what Falk now knew was that New York City and possibly the rest of America, was largely unaffected by the war destroying his be-loved Europe—physically and morally.

An hour later, Falk crossed through the gates of Camp Shanks, shivering and stiff-legged. He and the other POWs learned that prior to becoming a camp, Shanks was a small town named Orangeburg. But a few months ago, the residents' homes, yards, and farms—approximately two thousand acres—were seized for the construction of the prison camp when Ellis Island filled up.

"Stay away from the fences," a guard told Falk's group. Apparently, not all citizens of Orangeburg left quietly. Recently, a POW, lured to the fence with the promise of food, was stabbed to death.

Falk entered a large building where he was told to strip. Men in medi-cal masks and protective goggles approached him. How strange he was considered toxic. A hospital orderly shouted in German above their com-plaints. "Spread your arms and legs when we get to you." He complied. A white powder was puffed onto his groin and under his arms and then above his head.

"What is this?" he asked, coughing.

"Delousing powder. D-D-T."

The workers sprinkled the powder on Falk's clothes and belongings. "For good measure."

Each German soldier was handed two string bags and an ID disk with a number. He slipped his cyanide pill inside his *soldbuch* when he saw the bags with clothing being loaded into a laundry bin. Falk's boots and *sol-dbuch* went into the other bag. As they moved toward the sounds of hissing steam and water splashing on tile, Falk's heart hammered. Scenes from the death camps flashed through his mind. The unsuspecting Jews followed these same types of orders: undress, hang your clothes on a hook, let's get you disinfected and off to your barracks.

Was this their captors' plan? Had the U.S. military already learned of the death camps and the showers, and this was their retaliation?

Falk tensed at the thought, although it would serve them right. But no shouts came from the line in front of him. It was just a shower. He hung his bag on the hook number matching his ID disk and then walked through the misty veil of welcoming steam. He grabbed a bar of soap from the holder and lathered quickly, the thick haze giving him a modicum of privacy. The hot water ran down his body, pure pleasure after weeks of bathing in cold seawater. As POWs continued to enter the shower, he was pushed along from spigot to spigot, like meat moving along a conveyor belt, and too soon, he was nudged free from the room. He strode down another hallway where a Negro soldier tossed each man a clean white towel.

"My God," the soldier next to him muttered into his towel. "More Negers?"

While a handful of Negroes fought in the Wehrmacht, most soldiers hadn't seen a colored man in years and believed them to be racially inferior.

"Keep your towels," the tall Negro said.

He and Ilse had good friends who fled to Barbados when Hitler came to power because of the color of their skin.

Falk wrapped his around his waist and walked to a row of chairs where he received a fast shave and haircut. He felt like a new man, reborn with soap, water, and a razor. While he stood in line for a medical examination, shouting broke out across from him. A POW was refusing to lift his arms for examination, loudly proclaiming enough inspection had been done.

Medical personnel held the man and forced his left arm above his head. About eight inches up from his elbow, on the underside of his arm, was the Waffen-SS tattoo. The black blood-group tattoo mark was just a single letter, the soldier's blood type, but it labeled him as an elite Nazi. A marking that would send him back to Europe to an SS prison. They dragged him away, German curses trailing behind him.

Falk hadn't recognized the SS soldier. Nor did the man seem to recognize him. That was luck. He turned back to his examiner.

"Raise your arms," the doctor said.

Falk slowly lifted his arms, his ribs screaming from bits of bone digging into nerves. He had no tattoos. Men like Falk, who came late into the

SS, weren't always given the blood-group marking. Even higher-ranking men like Dr. Mengele at Auschwitz was said not to have a mark.

The medic gently probed his head wound and said it was healing fine. He scribbled on a paper and handed it to Falk, saying he should be reexamined by the physician at his camp destination.

"With your injuries, you will not be sent on the westbound transports. Those trains take days to arrive. We'll keep you on the East Coast for now."

Exactly what Falk hoped to hear. Trying to find Troy, New York, and Pastor Graf would be hard enough from this coast. He didn't need to add the difficulty of navigating across the whole interior of the country.

Falk, still half-naked, was escorted to a group of three hundred in a large open room, waiting for their clothing bags. The group's mood was subdued. From now on, the POWs would be told where to go and what to do without recourse. What must have felt like failure to the other POWs, Falk celebrated as success. He'd made it to America.

When the bags finally arrived, his clothing had been miraculously washed and dried. He couldn't help it, but once he had his pants on, he pressed the shirt to his nose and breathed deeply. It was the scent of an open window on a spring day, of home, of love. The dull ache he carried when he thought about his family bloomed, and he fisted his hands in the shirt to hold back tears. He moved the cyanide pill into his shirt pocket, amazed he'd kept the poison safe this far.

Once dressed, he and his group crossed the camp to a dining hall, where under the watch of heavily armed soldiers, breakfast was served.

Each plate contained two pieces of toast, scrambled eggs, and a spoonful of brown paste, something none of them had ever seen, called peanut butter. Coffee was refilled as many times as a man asked. Falk focused on eating every bit of food offered, unsure when he might eat again.

After breakfast, he washed up, and in groups of one hundred, the prisoners were herded to the nearby train station.

Falk spotted Eduard in the group in front of him and hurried to catch up. "Hello," he said as he dropped his hand on the young man's shoulder.

Eduard turned then swatted away his hand. "I've been warned not to talk to you," he whispered.

Falk looked in both directions to see if they were being watched. "Who said that?"

"Who do you think? The Nazis. They're spreading the word that you're an American spy."

"You know that's not true."

The boy was clearly frightened—his eyes were huge, and his lips trembled.

"What happened to Christoph? I briefly saw him in sickbay."

Eduard stopped walking. "The night they hauled you off, he stuck up for you. Someone knifed him after the concert." His forehead was a twist of knotted skin. "He's dead." He leaned closer. "You might not be a spy, but there is something off about you. And I'm not about to get killed for it."

Falk remained stuck in place as the POWs flowed around and past him. A chill raced up his spine, and he tried to remember how to breathe. Christoph—barely sixteen, who never smoked—just recently forced into service. A high school swimmer. An only son. A boy who hoped to follow in his father's footsteps as a minister in his small hometown. Dead because Falk befriended him.

A guard prodded Falk forward. He had failed another child, and although Christoph wasn't as young as the boy with the strings, the pain that seared through him felt just the same. Thinking himself a father figure to the two young soldiers, he saw how wrong he was. He was no one's hero. The road blurred as he fought the sting of tears. At that moment, he knew he needed to try to remain invisible and solitary because the next time someone recognized him for the traitor he was, he would be as dead as Christoph.

Falk waited on the train platform, his hat pulled low over his face. He was notified his group was headed to the northeastern part of the country, to an area called New England to work as laborers for the wood pulp industry. He studied the other POWs in his group, relieved to see that Eduard, Zeigler, and Hartmann were not among the Germans being transported with him.

A long suburban train arrived with a dusty gush of cold air and screeching brakes. The group ahead of him boarded quickly. The doors *whooshed* shut and the train departed. Moments later, the next one arrived. Falk climbed aboard, surprised at the plush seating in the Pullman cars. He stowed his bag on the overhead shelf and slipped into a window seat and sat alone. The train quickly gained speed, racing past industrial areas, sometimes underground and sometimes on elevated tracks, transporting him northward.

He watched the winter countryside slide past his green velvet-draped window. The clacking of the wheels on the tracks nearly lulled him to sleep. He was tired on so many levels—physically, mentally. But he couldn't let his guard down. He hadn't yet figured out how to escape from the camp, and now that he was a marked man, the sooner he put distance between himself and the Nazis, the better.

Two hours later, they came to a halt at Percy Station outside the village of Sparks, New Hampshire. The POWs climbed off the train and Falk looked around. The station had a tiny platform with two curved-back wooden benches and a small building with a ticket window. Nothing more.

"Shit! The middle of nowhere," one man complained. Others grumbled their agreement.

Rolling hills surrounded the station and were covered with towering trees, the custodians of the mountainside. Bands of pale sun pushed through buffalos of clouds, pointing yellow fingers at the vastness around his new home. The drumming of woodpeckers in the distance meant the POWs would have company while working in the woods.

Many Germans wanted to be closer to a large city, but Falk couldn't have wished for a better place to settle into—then escape from.

Military vehicles arrived and the POWs climbed into canvas-covered truck beds. The bumpy ride in the back of the long bed over rutted dirt roads left Falk gasping and holding his still-tender ribs. A bullet wound would probably have hurt less. The forest peeled back revealing a cleared flat tract of land at the base of the hills. Sparks prison camp was surrounded by fencing and double rows of barbed wire. The black noses of machine guns stuck out from every angle of the four guard towers of the compound. Dozens of long wooden bunk houses filled the POW side of the complex, their stove pipes pushing out wood smoke that hovered along the rooflines.

He studied the fencing and tried to decide if he could climb the wire. With searchlights at the perimeters, it would be tricky. A double row of barbed fencing ran down the center of the camp, separating the POW side from the guards' barracks, the kitchen, and camp hospital.

Falk lined up with the other POWs and waited in the cold for the camp commander's welcome talk. He scraped his boots back and forth across the ground trying to maintain circulation in his cold feet. The commander couldn't be far away and must be making them wait, showing them who had the upper hand. Falk had no clue what to expect from an American POW camp. His experience with camp commanders was from watching the cruel SS officers run the concentration camps. Those commanders were hand-picked for their ability to torture and kill prisoners as easy as swatting a fly.

The frail sun lost its hold on the day, and an icy wind picked up. A Jeep pulled to a stop and a man in an army officer uniform stepped out. His hair was grayed at the temples, and there were burn scars across his neck and jawline.

A soldier beside the officer announced in German this was Major Dobbs, their camp commander.

Dobbs studied them for a few moments, and then in a voice much louder than suited his small frame, he spoke, and the soldier translated. "Sparks is a dangerous place." He pointed to the fences. "The wire boundary around the camp is not to keep you in as much as it serves to protect you from the local population."

Falk let that sink in because he hadn't factored hostile locals into his escape plans.

Dobbs continued. "The people who live in these mountains are half wild, avid hunters, rugged people who currently hate Germans. You've killed their fathers, brothers, and sons. If you were to escape into the surrounding forest, you would be shot by one of these gun-toting patriots."

He pointed to the hills in all directions. "There are bears out there, too. They often attack at night. My advice, and it's based on events that happened in camp these last five months, is to stay inside the wire unless you place little value on your life."

He continued. "Wake-up call is at six a.m. and roll call is at seven o'clock sharp. Your groups will be counted three times a day."

A successful escape meant understanding the camp's precautions, and right now, as he concentrated on the security procedures, he felt a noose tightening around his neck. The security was stricter than he'd imagined. If he didn't escape before the Nazis in the camp figured out he was a traitor, this whole plan was for nothing. Pastor Graf would be waiting to hear from him, not knowing what to do with the materials he sent.

"I assume we will have a productive time together." Then the major dismissed them. Each POW was handed a number corresponding to his assigned barracks.

Built out of lightweight construction materials, the buildings had large windows, unglazed glass, and shutters. Falk stepped inside building number three and chose a cot near one of the large stoves, betting he'd be glad for the warmth even though he wouldn't be staying long. Each camp bed had a towel, two blankets, and a pillow. He unfolded the blankets and moved the pillow to the head of the cot, his way of claiming it while he searched for the toilets.

The path between the barracks was a wooden walkway, slippery with snow and ice. He passed the POW kitchen and a large mess hall, and farther down the path, found the latrine. Twelve washbasins with mirrors filled one wall across the room from two rows of toilets with no dividers, no stalls. Dobbs announced there were two hundred and fifty POWs in camp. Vying for a toilet and sink might get difficult.

He washed at a sink. As more men filled the room, not only was German being spoken, but also Russian and Italian. If Falk were in charge, he would have separated them into groups based on their language. Housed together, the pressure of confinement aggravated by misunderstandings could easily lead to a disaster. But he was no longer a leader in charge of anyone.

Back in his barracks, the men played cards, or wrote letters using supplies stacked on a desk in the corner. Falk traded two packs of cigarettes for a pocket-sized English dictionary. He thumbed through it, surprised by how much of the language he remembered from his school days. He was determined to find someone with whom he could practice speaking English, knowing if he were to blend in, he needed to know more than a few broken phrases.

A POW entered the barracks. "The camp commander is making the rounds." Moments later, Major Dobbs entered with three guards and the translator. One guard called everyone to attention.

"You are here to work for the Brown Paper Company, squeezing all the pulpwood you can from these forests. You're required to cut a cord per person, per day, for which you will be paid eighty cents in camp scrip. Use that in the canteen." He unfolded a tan pair of army-issued pants and shirt and held them up, turning them back and forth. "You will wear these garments while on the job." The pants and shirts were prominently marked on the front and back with PW in white paint. "You will be escorted to and from the cutting sites by armed guards. Once again, you are safer in the camp than you are outside. Failed attempts at escape are posted on the wall in the mess hall if you get curious. Three of those men are dead. Another five are in the stockade on bread and water for sixty days."

More obstacles. Wearing marked clothing and armed guard escorts. Falk's mind spun through different scenarios, but without sleep, he struggled to form a clear path out of the camp. A day or two into the routine would help him make a decision.

Dobbs looked around the room. "Get some sleep. Your day starts before the sun rises."

The men left, and Falk carefully sank back onto his cot. He was in no shape to hack at a tree with an axe. His ribs would never heal that way, and he needed to be able to cover a lot of area when he escaped.

A group of men gathered at one end of the barracks. One called for quiet.

A beefy-chested POW with a bulldog face spoke. "I am Erich Braun, this barracks' controller. We were just told we are slave labor for the enemy."

Mumblings of agreement rippled through the crowd.

"Any of you who cooperate with the Americans, or if for any reason you are deemed insufficiently dedicated to Nazism, you will find yourself in front of our internal court. We will honor the Führer's vision of world dominance, even as we are held here. His ideology must prevail in our every action and thought."

He was disgusted. How anyone still followed Hitler's ideals shocked him.

Someone yelled "Heil, Hitler" and arms shot up in the gesture of respect. Falk faked a coughing spasm and held his ribs, keeping watch from the corner of his eye.

Braun approached a man who failed to salute. In fact, he had turned his back on the group. Braun spun him around, and without a second's warning, punched him in the nose. The cracking bones were heard throughout the barracks. The man grabbed his face as blood poured through his fingers.

Braun leaned into him. "Heil. Hitler," he growled, slow and clear. His arm shot out next to the man's head.

The soldier switched hands to cover his nose and slowly raised his bloody right hand. "Heil, mien Hitler."

Braun studied the soldier for a few minutes longer, and then turned to the others. "Sieg, heil!"

A chorus returned the victory acclamation while Falk raised his arm and mouthed nonsense words.

Braun returned to his cot, the closest to the front door.

Falk hid his English dictionary under his pillow, mulling over this new problem. With rabid Nazis in his barracks, the danger of being killed lurked within the wired enclosure as well as outside. He'd have to walk a fine line in order to survive long enough to escape.

-17-

IZAAK TAUBER

Aboard a train, Across Europe - January 1944

Izaak bounced up and down as he waited by the train tracks. They were finally leaving Westerbork. It was about time. Since he'd been caught yesterday on the wrong side of camp by Commandant Gemmeker time dragged by. He was tired of the crowded barracks and terrible food. They crawled down from their bunk bed early in the morning while it was dark. He made sure he tucked the drawing of Papa in his pants pocket. The other drawing of the windmill was in his small suitcase along with Papa's pipe. Although Mama said she was not angry he went exploring on the wrong side of camp, she became quiet after Abraham told her they were on the next transport. In fact, she said little all last night, and this morning looked as if she could sleep more.

They were at the toilets for one last time when a terrible thing happened. An oma had hanged herself by a belt hooked to the ceiling and swung there by the open pit. Her face was a weird color of blue and purple, colors he once loved but now were horrifying. Mama made him leave the toilets immediately, but not before people said the oma did this because she didn't want to go on the train.

What did she know that he and Mama weren't told?

He worried when he saw the large amount of people funneling to the tracks. Hopefully, he and Mama would get a seat. He got that jumpy stomach feeling, like when it was hard to know what might happen next. Finally, the train came into view. It looked like a long, scabby snake, cutting the camp in two, each end disappearing outside the fences.

Commandant Gemmeker stood on the platform, holding his little dog. His police friends in green uniforms were lined up at each train door. Abraham was also there and Izaak waved to him, but he didn't notice. He was busy talking to people, answering lots of questions.

Many passengers carried bread bags hanging from their shoulders, or a rolled blanket tied to their backs with a piece of rope. Some were skinny, wore dirty clothes, and didn't have suitcases. Where had they come from?

The mean barking dogs appeared, their thick black and grey fur bristling, leashed by soldiers carrying guns. A bus pulled to a stop alongside the big front gate. As soon as the doors opened, the soldiers yanked off the people, tugging jewelry from women and taking watches from the men's wrists.

Izaak clung to his mama's coat, his head pounding. Why were the police suddenly so mean? Guards rolled open the train's big doors. The bad sound of metal scraping on metal was loud for a second, but then protests from the first passengers to board were even louder, yelling there was no more room. He and Mama were pushed to an open door. It was black and dark inside like a monster's mouth, and the coach had no windows. It was a train car for cows. Guards threw bigger suitcases off the platform and yelled at the owners to get on the train without them. Izaak kept his suitcase close to him. A few steps before it was his and Mama's turn to climb into the open doorway, Abraham pulled them aside.

"This way," the moon-shaped man said. "You're on another car."

"Will we still be going to Poland?" Mama asked.

"Yes. But trust me, as my wife relied on you with her difficult birth. I hear these front cars will go on to a better place. Especially with a young boy in tow." As he pushed them along, he kept turning his head back and forth, looking as if he were doing something wrong and didn't want to get caught.

"Thank you for helping us," Mama said.

"May you travel in God's hands," Abraham said as he pointed to the front train car. Like the others, it had one small window. "When you get inside, move to the window or find a crack or an opening to stand near."

Izaak and his mama climbed into the car and moved to the back wall. The tiny window was so high on the wall, he would never be able to see out of it. His heart pounded as everyone squeezed in tighter and tighter. He now understood why people yelled about there being no more room.

Mama whispered, "Hold on to me, love." When they were packed against each other, the single door rolled shut. Instantly, people cried and shouted to be let off. Izaak wanted out, too. The air would run out. They would all die. His breath was hitching, and in the next moment, he was crying. Ashamed he wasn't braver, he was glad no one could see him in the dimness.

His mama stacked his smaller suitcase on top of her larger one and then picked him up and set him on top. She stood next to him, her arm around his shoulder. Most people had no place to sit.

The train made a growling noise and shook before it started to move. People fell against each other, and a man smashed Izaak against the wooden wall at his back.

"Sorry," the man said as he stood straight again.

They rode on for what seemed like forever. A man checked his pocket watch the guards hadn't discovered. In the little light pushing in from the window, the man announced, "Four hours."

Izaak tugged his mama's sleeve. "I have to go to the toilet."

The toilet was a bucket in one corner. He and Mama excused their way to that area, and people turned their backs for privacy, but it didn't matter much. The sounds and smells couldn't be kept private.

The train kept going and going. The cars jerked and jolted all the time and it was freezing inside. Izaak fell asleep, woke up, and then back to sleep. When someone spotted a town outside the window and the train slowed, passengers yelled, but the train didn't stop.

Mama lifted him so she could sit on the suitcases and then pulled him onto her lap. She fell asleep with her head banging against the wall.

"Eleven hours," someone announced.

Why wouldn't the train stop? Surely, they'd passed many towns with stations where they could have taken a break. Didn't the engineer need to rest? The mood in the train scared him. The longer they rode, the more often prayers for salvation were muttered—prayers for God to welcome them home. Were they all going to die? He asked Mama and she whispered they needed to stay strong, and they weren't going to die.

And then a woman screamed about her baby. A doctor moved in to help but shook his head. The baby was dead. Men prayed the Mourner's Kaddish as Izaak squeezed his eyes closed. The prayer would be worthless if he even peeked a tiny bit, a practice Papa taught him in synagogue.

"We will all get turns at the window," the doctor called out. "A chance at fresh air."

"We paid good money for our relocation," a man said. "This is not the way to treat paying passengers."

As they talked of letter-writing and sending formal complaints, Izaak swayed against his mama, but the train rattled on. It would run off the end of the world if they didn't stop soon.

Izaak continued to drift in and out of sleep.

Men announced the amount of time they were stuck inside, but it was said in days now—two, then three.

More people died, and the bodies were stacked in one corner.

"It's our turn, love," Izaak's mama said.

At first, he didn't understand what she was talking about. Was it their turn to go to heaven? He felt like that might happen. She tugged him to the window. Someone piled suitcases there, belonging to the people who weren't going to need them anymore. He climbed up and Mama stood close behind him, so both their faces caught the clean air through the tiny opening. In the daylight outside, the countryside flashed by with forests and snowy meadows. Small groups of pretty houses came and went. People drove cars. A boy walked a dog.

"It's like a movie, Mama." It was too unreal that outside their dark, horrible train, there were nice places with people doing things he once enjoyed.

"Breathe deeply," Mama said, "while you can."

All too soon, the doctor announced their time was up, and they returned to their spot.

"Do we have food?" Izaak's stomach hurt as if a tiger were scratching his insides.

She pulled him close. "Sorry, love. Try to sleep."

That was the easiest thing to do. He closed his eyes and remembered learning to ride his bike, his papa's smiling face, the way Papa laughed extra loud when Izaak did something funny. When they found each other, he would make Papa laugh again. And he would never complain when it was bath time. With those thoughts, he drifted off to the rumble and sway of the train.

It was night again when the train stopped. Izaak sounded out the word Będzin on the sign on the station wall. When the door rolled open, the German soldiers in their long grey coats yelled for the dead to be taken off. Mama looked scared, and although Izaak was, too, he wanted to be out of this car more than anything. He squeezed Mama's hand three times for I love you, and she squeezed back. He didn't trust that the doors wouldn't be rolled shut again. His heart pounded until he and Mama were allowed to exit.

When Izaak finally climbed down, his body swayed like tall grass in the wind, and Mama grabbed his arm and held him up. "Sorry, Mama," he mumbled. He wanted to be strong, but something was not right. His legs wobbled as if he were a boy made of pudding.

"Never apologize, Izaak. You're my brave boy, remember?" She put his suitcase on the ground in front of him. "I will hold you up if you can carry your case."

They shambled to a gate where soldiers in dark uniforms studied their papers. One soldier pointed them to another platform several tracks over.

He and Mama didn't talk as they shuffled in that direction, following the shoes and boots in front of them. Someone said something about food and Izaak's head snapped up. Just ahead of them was a table with buckets of water and stacks of bread and cheese. Everyone, including him and Mama, pushed forward, and forgetting their manners, grabbed handfuls of food. They drank from the ladles that hung off the sides of the buckets. Mama gave him two chunks of bread and then stuffed more into her pockets before she ate. "Just in case," she whispered.

Izaak was never allowed to grab food, or stuff it in his mouth, and his mama would never do that either. He sent a prayer to God, explaining that because they were so hungry to excuse their bad manners.

The terrible train that brought them here waited on the tracks, the engines still rumbling. Only the first six car doors were open. The other cars, lit by overhead lights in the station area, disappeared into the darkness, their doors closed. Ghostly-looking arms waved from the tiny windows while the guards stood below, ignoring the muffled calls.

"Oh, no! Not everyone is off," Izaak said. "We need to tell someone." He couldn't imagine how panicked the people must be waiting for the doors to open.

His mama cleared her throat and didn't answer right away. "We're not all going to the same places." She took his hand and pulled him to the platform where their group was told to go. They were directed to line up outside the toilets, not bothering with whether it was a boy's or girl's room. Buckets of water with soap waited on a bench with towels stained by people who already used them. The water was cold as Mama scrubbed his face, hands, and arms, but it felt good after all those days on the filthy train.

As they walked to the waiting train, he stalled in his tracks. He sensed he would die if he climbed aboard. The food in his stomach was acting up, and he swallowed hard to keep it down. "I don't want to go. Can we just sneak away and live here?"

"We're almost to the work camp, Izaak. Będzin is in Poland, and I overheard we are only a few hours away."

Hours? "I can't stand up that long. My body can't be as brave as I want it to be." His chin trembled. He was letting Papa down.

"Look. It's a passenger train." Mama pointed. "We will have seats."

They could sit? He hadn't noticed anything except the huge grime-covered wheels he knew could turn forever even as people right above them begged to get off. Suddenly, the long trip that almost killed them seemed worth it. Papa might be in the work camp, just a few more hours away.

-18-

HERBERT MÜLLER

Philadelphia, Pennsylvania - January 1944

Herbert and his father spent eleven frustrating nights in a Buster Brown shoe factory before they were finally granted their examination by the civilian hearing board in Philadelphia. His anger boiled just below the surface as the hours ticked by and no appointment was given. He and Otto missed Christmas and New Year's with his family, an overwhelming disappointment. They did allow a call on Christmas, and although Jutta said they were fine, her weary tone betrayed her fatigue. The children sounded falsely chipper, so he assumed they'd all made a pact not to share negative thoughts with him or Otto. He asked for Fact Time, but they only said, "I love you" and "I miss you." He tried to assure them this would soon be over, but he had his own moments of profound doubts the government was willing to move their cases along.

He had trouble sleeping, believing he'd been so wrong about his rights as a citizen. He worried about the mill and how his family managed the chores he usually handled, like shoveling coal into the cellar to feed the boiler. Alfred could do it, but it was a two-man job. Winter was a slow time for grinding, but he and Otto used those months to clean and fix the crushers, gearing up for the next harvest.

Gables and Johnson drove them to the courthouse in Philadelphia but weren't part of the questioning. He and his father were allowed to sit at the same table, facing four men on a raised platform. The panel must have been chosen because of their expertise in the areas of harassment, intimidation, and hostile questioning. During the hour, three witnesses came to vouch for them. A Jewish neighbor, a Polish man who ground his corn at their mill, and a storekeeper where Herbert's family bought dry goods. They each cited the Müllers' integrity and their devotion to the U.S., and each witness reported they never saw anything to suggest loyalty to Germany or Hitler.

Herbert nodded and smiled as their neighbors spoke, his mood lifting for the first time since their arrest. His moments of doubt gave birth to new certainties. This absurd situation was almost over.

Then the board of inquiry spent another hour posing questions mixed with insults, hoping to wear down Herbert and Otto's resolve.

"If the country were invaded by the Germans, would you be willing to defend it?"

"Yes, if the military would have me," Herbert said.

A question for both of them. "Do you participate in the Lend-Lease Act?"

"Yes," Herbert answered. "The government paid us to send two tons of feed grain for England in the past year." He smiled. "Would they pay German spies to do this?"

A man with heavy eyebrows said, "That doesn't clear you of suspicion."

"It should."

"It doesn't"—the man shuffled more papers—"Do you ever send money to Germany?"

"We do not," Otto answered.

One agent reached into his leather attaché case and pulled out a 10 x 12 glossy photo. A guard walked it to the polished wooden desk and slid it in front of Herbert. It was Alfred when he was about twelve.

"Is this your son, celebrating German-American day?"

The U.S. and German flags were both evident in the picture. "Yes. It's a popular event in many cities." Where had they found a photo of Alfred? This panel needed to leave his family out of it.

"Did he sing in the Kinderkor conducted by Kappelhoff?"

"Of course, he did." Herbert sighed, furious with these innuendos that everyday life was somehow a sign of treason. "Doris Day is Kappelhoff's daughter, and she sang in the Kor. Perhaps you will need to arrest America's sweetheart."

The agent's eyes flared. Silence enveloped the room. Then, "Did your son indoctrinate fellow students at his high school?"

"No." Alarms sounded in his head. Were they thinking of arresting Alfred?

"Were you in the Hitlerjugend?"

"Yes. It was a German Boy Scout troop back then." Herbert shifted in his hard chair. They seemed more focused on him, which he didn't mind, but it begged the question as to what they suspected Otto of doing.

They scribbled in their notebooks, and the questioning continued.

After the hearing, they were told to wait in a small room off the court for the board's decision. As hours ticked by, he became resentful. This seemed like a game to the government officials, a drawn-out process. Like a cat batting around mice, pulling them back then lifting a paw and giving them a little hope. He and Otto should be on their way home. The facts were so clear, witnesses vouched for them, and the government found no illegal activities.

The lead interviewer, a man with a broad neck and beefy hands, Officer Weber—ironically with a German surname—entered the room with two military police escorts. Herbert's hands began to sweat. Why the police presence? He and Otto stood to hear the verdict.

"The Alien Enemy Control Unit of the Department of Justice finds you, Herbert and Otto Müller to be a danger to the safety of Americans during wartime."

Otto swayed next to him, and Herbert grabbed his arm and helped him sit down. He wasn't doing so well himself. His legs shook as a feeling of disbelief washed over him, like a wave of instantaneous grief at the loss of his freedom.

"You are both remanded to the internment facility on Ellis Island until further examination of your cases," the interviewer added.

Their witnesses might as well have gone to watch an Athletics baseball game while in Philadelphia, instead of coming to the hearing. Herbert bit his tongue so he wouldn't swear, believing the review board had made up their minds before the interviews started. That all words of support from his neighbors meant nothing.

"Then we'll just appeal." Herbert needed time to get things in order at the mill, to make plans for when he would be gone. "Who is higher up than you to hear our request?"

Otto tugged at his sleeve, and Herbert leaned over. "This is where, we must part. You need to be home, with family. I am fine, to do zis alone."

"No. I'm not leaving you."

"What did he say?" Weber asked.

Herbert relayed his father's request.

"It's too late for that." Weber's eyes narrowed. "You're both internees. And to answer your question, you'll have an appeal opportunity in camp." He folded the document he carried. "The transport leaves immediately."

"I need to make a phone call." Herbert hated how his hands trembled. He stuffed them in his pockets. He needed to hear Jutta's calming voice, to tell her the disheartening news. People said sometimes you have to go through your worst, to arrive at your best. He didn't agree. He'd been at his absolute best when he was home taking care of his family and didn't need to experience a worst-case scenario.

"Once you get to Ellis Island, you will be afforded the same privileges as other prisoners." Weber and the police escorts left, their leather soles slapping on the polished floor in time with the word echoing through Herbert's head—prisoners, prisoners, prisoners.

-19-

WILHELM FALK

Sparks, New Hampshire - February 1944

After one week in camp, Falk continued to work on an escape plan. Security was tighter than he imagined, and his broken ribs hindered him from going into the forests. Like every morning, Falk now lined up on the open parade ground waiting to be counted. He stomped in place in the winter dawn. As the count crawled up and down the lines, he called out his number, his breath a visible puff that shot straight out and hung for seconds before dissipating. He cupped his hands around his mouth to hoard a piece of warm air.

The roll call continued.

The day seemed bleak and it didn't help that his feet ached. He scowled at his boots as if they were traitors, his feet almost frozen inside them in such a short time. The snow on the parade ground was trampled into brown slush, a swath of ugliness in the otherwise pristine view. From the eaves of the barracks to the mountains in the distance, the land was bleached white as far as he could see. He looked across the meadow, once again studying the village of Sparks. The tall church steeple and random columns of chimneys, spewing smoke, pointed the way to daily town life. The church bells rang each day at noon, and on Sunday's call to worship, the uplifting chimes mingled with the laughter of children. Those were the signs of normalcy that hurt Falk the most. A tranquil village with a covered bridge only five hundred meters away, its townspeople enjoying everyday activities so reminiscent of his days with Ilse and their sons before the war. He rarely looked toward the village. It was too painful of a reminder of what he'd lost.

When the captain's voice boomed for them to move out, it seemed to crack open the morning cold like fragile ice breaking on a pond, a sharp sound rippling across the camp.

The mess hall was stocked with plenty of food and strong coffee. Falk piled his plate with fried eggs, sausage, potatoes, and sweet bread. He avoided the Nazis from his barracks and ate breakfast with Jerry Schroeder, the guy with the broken nose. He and Jerry were assigned to the camp maintenance group, at least until their injuries healed. With Falk's company management skills, he could have offered an easy overhaul and new design for organizing the workings of the camp. But he was Klaus Stern, a sanitation engineer, relegated to fixing outdated plumbing and painting the interiors of the buildings.

He and Schroeder reported to the camp doctor, Birk Lauterbach, every few days to check on their health. Lauterbach reported Falk's medical assessment to the camp commanders and suggested how soon he could head out into the forests to start contributing to his share of pulpwood quotas. Lauterbach, in his mid-fifties but fit from playing tennis, spoke satisfactory German. He even shared that his grandparents, who emigrated from Munich, raised him. He seemed to hold no bitterness toward the POWs. Sometimes he'd offer a cigarette, or thick, brown bread with butter from the kitchen.

Dr. Lauterbach deemed Falk to be ready for work in the forest in two more days. In the meantime, he needed to continue modifying his plan to escape since he couldn't simply walk out of camp. With two belts of barbed wire ringing the compound, even if he got through the first one, the space between offered no place to hide. The lookouts in the four towers kept their guns tightly aimed on that inner ring. Of course, guards also patrolled the perimeter of the cutting areas, but the forest was a sizable place to watch.

Before setting off to the barracks to meet the plumbing crew, Falk stopped by the canteen for two Hershey's chocolate bars. He handed over the resin tokens used as currency. Then he pocketed the chocolate for now, as they would go in his secret food stash under his bed for the day he escaped.

The eight-man crew to which he was assigned was almost finished fitting pipes under a new shower building. The next job entailed fixing the shingles on the north-facing roofs that took the brunt of Canadian windstorms. By midday, his crew would be out from under the showers and up on the rooftops, grabbing not only fresh air but also a view of how the camp fit into its surroundings.

The morning passed, and they gathered in the mess hall for lunch. Each worker grabbed a paper sack from the food line and found a seat. Today, lunch consisted of a ham sandwich, a cookie, and a beer. The beer was a nice touch and surely came about when the camp kitchen assigned POWs to help cook. The Germans sold the kitchen commander on the idea the POWs required beer in their daily diet to remain docile.

Falk was halfway through his sandwich when a POW across the table, a dour man who rarely spoke, threw his arms in the air as if begging for mercy. The guards called him Adolf, a name they used for all Nazi support-ers, a guy Falk steered clear of in conversation.

The man muttered loudly an incoherent stream of consonants, inter-spersed with intelligible phrases, such as "line up" and "everyone out."

The guards' attention turned to him when he jumped to his feet and shouted, "I'm done and going home." He ran for the doors, but in an instant, was restrained by three guards who wrestled him outside. Dr. Lauterbach's lunch was about to be interrupted.

The room fell quiet as the POWs resumed eating. Falk could relate to the guy. Several times in the past year, he wanted to end it all to scrub his mind free of the guilt and misgivings. The need to tell someone the whole truth about the extermination camps kept him from suicide. That and his longing to see his family again.

A man at his table broke the silence. "Anybody know what that was about?"

Another with a hawkish face spoke, a guy who never participated in the Nazi songs and chants in the mess hall. When he moved, he walked like a man being dragged down by invisible forces, bent and struggling to move his youthful body from place to place. "Einsatzgruppen."

They all nodded, agreeing with his one-word response. Although there were rumors of what Hitler's Einsatzgruppen killing squads were involved in during the early years of the war, Falk doubted the other POWs knew the magnitude of what these roving slaughter teams did. He couldn't imagine what went through the soldiers' minds when they discovered the extra pay, drugs, and superior rations didn't always make up for machine-gunning hundreds of thousands of desperate men, women, and children because they were deemed racially inferior. Their screams and cries sounded no different than those of pure-blooded Germans.

Falk set his utensils on his plate. "Hard to come off the drugs."

The hawkish soldier said, "He was swallowing Pervitin like candy."

Falk worked hard to protect the one pill he smuggled in. How had the POW kept a large supply of pills from being undetected? He finished his lunch, took his sack to the trash, and waited near the door for the rest of the work crew. He watched a POW hand a letter to a guard to mail. He needed to write to Ilse. She should be in the Netherlands with their sons by now. Any information reaching Düsseldorf from Wehrmacht headquarters, notifying her Wilhelm was killed in Italy, hopefully would not have found its way to her. But just in case it had, his letter to her from Klaus Stern needed to be carefully worded to let her know he was still alive. In his last letter to her before he switched uniforms with Stern's corpse, he wrote, "Don't believe everything you hear." He prayed she remembered that in the coming months.

If he were lucky enough to be successful and not shipped back to Germany to be hanged, would he ever tell Ilse all he had done? She'd be shocked that his one and only killing was a German doctor, not the enemy.

He recalled his visit to Hadamar as a new SS officer in late '42. He'd arrived there with the pretense of needing to review the T-4 Program. Outside on the patio, recently cleared of snow, he talked with Dr. Heinrich Unger. Dr. Unger and others reviewed patient files in institutions across Germany, with the objective to determine which handicapped or mentally ill individuals should be flagged for elimination.

"I've supervised fourteen thousand 'undesirables' so far," Unger bragged.

"Are you feeling all right?" Unger asked Falk that day.

The sheer number of dead made him stumble in a moment of wooziness. Of course, he hadn't seen Auschwitz yet.

"I apologize. It might be the stench of the fog hanging over the facility."

Unger pointed to the gently falling ash. "They're prettier in death as ashes than they ever were in life, don't you think?"

Ashes? Falk clamped his lungs shut and avoided breathing in the remains of the condemned. His blood boiled, but he straightened his back.

"I'm fine." Steadying his beating heart and roiling stomach contents, he added, "I may have eaten a bad piece of fish in my travels." He cleared his throat. "Was everyone who lived here marked for extermination? Surely some had skills to offer the Reich."

"If a resident lived here, it was because they were flawed. We read all the files, and within a week, labeled each person with different-colored labels for one of three categories…kill, kill and remove their brain for research, kill and extract gold teeth."

This time, Falk turned to a snow-covered lawn and vomited the contents of his stomach. He retched long after, forcing the damning words from his head as if that were even possible. He hadn't seen the full horror of Hitler's plans until now. What had the generals talked him into? He couldn't take part in this immoral scheme, but he was trapped.

"Fucking British blockades," Unger said, his voice full of kindness. "Nothing but rotten food, making it nearly impossible to get a decent meal." He pointed to the medical offices and became more animated. "Come join us for a celebration. We have fine beer and wine."

"Celebration?" Falk asked, the word raw in his throat.

"Patient number fourteen thousand five reached the ovens last night. We think. We can't always keep an exact count."

Falk begged off. His body trembled to control his anger, but he simply said he needed to settle his digestive system. On the return drive to Limburg, the nearest town, his rage was nearly uncontrollable as he hurled his car along narrow roads, planning a dozen ways to kill Dr. Unger—all slow and painful.

Of course, he did none of what he first imagined, but when he returned a few weeks later, he brought Dutch Resistance letters he found in an abandoned house in Lititz. After forging Unger's name, he planted them in the doctor's briefcase. He waited at the edge of the woods until finally the doctor was dragged to the lawn. There, the SS shot him for harboring Jews, cutting short his protests of innocence.

Setting up Unger gave him a moment of satisfaction. But it would not stop the atrocities. After Hadamar, Falk set his sights on gathering information he could share with the world. He believed the world would listen and deal the death knell to Hitler's cleansing plans. So far, they hadn't. His trusted colleagues deemed his stories as exaggerated. Had his friends concluded he was merely another drugged SS officer?

Creating an army of evil had taken a few years to accomplish. His sons were coming close to recruitment age, and he needed them to be left out of the fight. Hitler's indoctrination into his hate club started early with the Hitler Youth, but the club did nothing but destroy innocent young minds. Hans and Dietrich looked up to him with his dark uniform, the brass and medals, the privilege. They would leap at the chance to follow in his footsteps, not knowing the emotional hell he'd traipsed through these last years to put a stop to it all. He prayed the war ended before the fisted power closed in around them. Before they were made to trade their play guns for the real thing.

$-20-$

IZAAK TAUBER

Płaszów, Poland - February 1944

"Nothing but farms out there, Mama!" Izaak pointed from one of the train's windows.

"I see that," she said.

The train ride proved to be the opposite of their last trip. No one died, but like Mama, the forty passengers looked nervous. Izaak's only experience with a work camp was the bad side of Westerbork, where he and Zev were caught peeking inside the long buildings. He didn't want to dress in grey clothes and break apart batteries. Maybe they'd get a job working outside.

He tried not to doze because, along the way, they passed some amazing sights. They crossed a deep wide valley on a skinny bridge. And when the ground dropped away on the sides of the train, Izaak's stomach fell, too, as he imagined they were flying across to the other side. They chugged past a slow parade of hundreds of people, mostly families pushing carts and carrying big bundles along a road. Everyone in the world was moving to new places.

And now, out the window, a circus train sat on the tracks next to them. The cars were painted in bright colors with animals drawn on the side. "A circus, Mama!" Horses poked their heads out of one car. "Do you think they will come to our new town?"

"From what I've heard, the work camps are away from towns and cities." Mama wrapped her arm around him. "But one day again...we'll all go see a circus."

When Mama made plans like this, the sick feeling in his stomach calmed down. He leaned into her embrace.

Farther on, the wheels under his feet slowed. The farms turned into open land then factories and warehouse buildings, and back to less pretty fields and rotting houses. When the train stopped, the pretty countryside was replaced by muddy fields and more barbed-wire fences.

The doors rolled open, and Mama grabbed his hand as the guards yelled for them to get out. They hurried down the steps with their suitcases as he tried to spot a friendly guard, like Abraham, someone who could help them. Instead, these guards had faces like stone.

"Is this Papa's camp, Mama?" It was hard not to turn an ankle on the road leading to the huge gate. Izaak watched his feet, careful to place each step in a solid indentation made in the frozen mud. Was Izaak following in one of Papa's footsteps? His pulse quickened as he stumbled, but he didn't fall. A man who fell moments ago was beaten by a guard with a rifle butt.

"It's a camp, Izaak, named Płaszów." She lowered her voice and it became kind of rough, like the old lady who used to live two houses down from them and liked to smoke smelly cigars that always made his eyes water. "But I don't know anything else."

Izaak lifted his eyes. The barracks sprawled forever inside tall rows of barbed fencing, making Westerbork seem tiny by comparison. Once through the gate, a terrible smell reached him, and he placed a gloved hand over his nose. The place smelled like a hundred open-pit toilets. A whispered message moved along the line in many languages. It hurried over Izaak's head, but Mama heard it because she was tall.

"Oh, dear," she said in a soft tone.

"What is it?" Izaak asked as he tugged Mama's arm.

When she didn't answer, Izaak squeezed her hand and asked again.

"This camp is very full," she said. "Over twenty thousand people. And, Izaak...we must follow the rules exactly as we are told."

"We always do that."

"But this time, love, we may not like what they ask us to do."

Izaak studied the guards' perches along the fences. The guns sticking out were huge with wide belts of bullets hanging off each. A spotlight swept back and forth, probably because the clouds were too thick to let in the sun.

"Women's side," a female guard yelled, pointing Izaak and his mama to the right.

They passed many long buildings until his group entered the one they were directed to. Just inside, a pinched-faced woman dressed in a dark dress, resembling the German guards' uniforms, yelled orders and pointed to a pile of striped rags in a corner.

"We need to change into other clothes, Izaak," Mama said. "This is one of the rules we won't like, but we have to do."

A woman with a shaved head handed out the ragged shirts, pants, and dresses. She leaned close. "The camp commandant is cruel. Stay away from him, especially if he is dressed in his white sweater and hat."

"What happens then?" Mama asked, accepting the garments handed her way.

"He stands on his balcony and shoots people for no reason . . . or he does worse."

Before Izaak could decide what was worse than getting shot, another woman guard grabbed at Izaak's suitcase. He held on tight. "My windmill drawing and Papa's pipe!" He couldn't lose the few things he owned that reminded him of Papa.

Mama pulled his fingers from the handle. "Please, Izaak." Her voice trembled. "We cannot argue with them."

The woman guard was bigger than most men. She smiled, but her eyes looked like a snake's. And as quick as a snake, she picked up Izaak and tossed him and the suitcase onto the pile of luggage.

He flew in slow motion, bracing for the pain he'd feel when he landed on the hard edges of the cases. His hearing had all but stopped, but in the background, he heard his mama's cry.

His heart raced as he tumbled onto the pile. Should he move or wait for the guard to tell him what to do? He swallowed a sob, afraid the guards would hurt Mama because of him.

Then Mama was at the edge of the cases and reaching for him. Her face was white, and her eyes were wide like a wild horse's. "Izaak." Her hands shook as she pulled him to his feet. "Never talk back." Her voice was broken, sounding like a cracked gramophone record.

The guard was back and kicked at Mama and said words that sounded like cursing. "Please," Mama said as she pushed him behind her. When the guard turned to yell at another prisoner, Mama scooped up the sets of clothes she'd been handed and prodded him to a changing area.

Izaak moved stiffly, anticipating another attack from behind, but it didn't come.

Mama handed him a set of striped pants and a shirt, both dirty and smelly. He fumbled with the buttons on his shirt, wondering what this meant. Once he shed his clothes, he would have nothing left that was his. His fingers fumbled with the buttons of the oversized ragged shirt. As he was taking off his pants, he felt the folded drawing of Papa in his pocket. He had to keep this. He sneaked a peek at the guards, and when no one was looking, switched the drawing into his shirt pocket. A wash of pride surged through him as if he'd saved Papa from destruction. According to Abraham, if he showed the guards his ability to draw, he and Mama might get better treatment.

He'd wait to do that. The guards here were yelling at everyone and he'd learned firsthand what could happen if he made a bad-tempered one angry.

"Let me fix your clothes," Mama said. She rolled up his pant legs, so they didn't drag on the ground and tore a strip off the bottom of her ragged dress to use as a belt around his waist.

Next, they were made to choose wooden shoes from a huge pile. Mama found the smallest pair for him, but even with his socks, they were too big. The guards yelled, "Schnell!" and poked their guns at people taking too long. His heart raced as one guard, with her hair braid wrapped like a snake on top her head, eyed Mama and began to move in her direction. "Hurry, Mama," he whispered. She shoved her feet into some shoes and a tingle of relief ran through him as the guard turned her attention elsewhere.

On his family's windmill trip, they tried on comfortable wooden Dutch shoes. The shoemakers in Poland needed to take lessons from the cobblers in his country because the shoes on his feet felt terrible.

The walk to the barracks seemed to take forever. He held up his pants and watched his feet because his clogs tried to slide off with each step. Suddenly, above the clomping of the wooden shoes on the frozen ground, a welcoming sound arose—birds chirping—and it sounded like a lot of them. Birds lived in trees. Maybe their barracks was near a forest, away from the crowded inner camp.

"Do you hear the birds, Mama?"

"It's just workers, love." She pointed to a road leading to a higher ridge. Hundreds of skinny people, in the same striped clothing, pushed squeaky wheelbarrows up and down the road.

"What are they doing?"

"I'm sure we will find out soon enough."

He hoped they could look for Papa right away. With twenty thousand people here, it might take a while, especially since Papa would live on the men's side of camp. He patted his shirt pocket with the drawing and vowed to protect it no matter what. His chin trembled and his chest ached. He should have been more careful hiding Papa's pipe, but how could he have known this camp was worse than Westerbork? He'd imagined a place where he and Mama worked in the fields, where the men built furniture and women made clothes. Płaszów was the opposite of the image he'd formed in his mind, and he held back tears of fear. But as prisoners, they were stuck here now. The one thing he could do was stick to his promise to Papa. He'd watch over Mama and try to be brave.

~21~

HERBERT MÜLLER

Ellis Island, New York Harbor - February 1944

Herbert and Otto boarded a train bound for New York City with other German-Americans, mostly men, but some traveled with their families. Why wives and children were arrested, he could only guess. Was it a preposterous accusation from a school teacher? Had the mailman delivered a Red Ryder secret decoder device with club instructions? Just before boarding the train, he'd received a letter from Jutta, and it wasn't great news. She wrote that many neighbors were treating them like criminals. Her women's volunteer club, a club she, herself, started, told her she was no longer needed. Her letter included an article from the local newspaper with a story applauding the raids on German families. Herbert's name was included on the list of men arrested for "deeds against the country." Alfred, Jutta wrote, visited all the mill's customers, trying to stave off losing business in the fall. But with ominous headlines fanning the flames of paranoia and hysteria, one by one, their customers begged off. It was clear Herbert would have to rebuild their clientele, and the sooner he returned home, the better. But with all that, he wouldn't want his family with him now, heading to an internment camp.

During the six hours of travel it took to reach the Essex Street Station in New York City, the train stopped twice. Once, to bring on more food and remove trash, and again, to pick up another hundred internees outside the city. En route, he and Otto walked the train aisle, meeting others with the same stories of being disgraced and unfairly arrested but many in worse situations.

"My wife is ill and cannot drive," a gaunt man from Hershey said. "Our son is making his way to our home from Colorado, but with the gas rationing, it will take days for him to reach her."

Someone had shot another man's draft horses for spite. "I will be hand-plowing if I cannot afford at least one new horse." The man looked as though he couldn't heft a bale of hay, let alone manage to turn a field harnessed to a plow.

Settled into the comfortable coach accommodations, Herbert flipped the pages on a book he wasn't really reading while Otto dozed. Two meals were offered, with the drink cart coming by every two hours, but Herbert's stomach twisted in knots because he feared for his family. Jutta tried to put a positive spin in her letter saying, even with the negative things happening to the family, they were watching out for each other and not worried. But he wasn't so sure they wouldn't be harmed. He and Otto needed to speed up the process as soon as they reached Ellis Island, if there were such a thing as making the wheels of government turn faster.

Leaving Jutta and the children unprotected was never his intention. What he assumed would be a long weekend just surpassed two weeks. He rode the ups and downs of anger and disbelief, but the inability to do anything to change their situation, was the most frustrating of all.

From Essex Street Station, surrounded by armed military personnel, Herbert, Otto, and the other detainees walked a short distance to the Ellis Island Ferry at Battery Park. It was a cold, dreary day, and several pedestrians stopped to watch. Who wouldn't be interested in a group of average-looking men and a few women and children escorted to the docks? The bleak frozen sky felt like a layer of lead overhead, a solid coffin encasing Herbert in heavy doubt about what it meant to be an American.

Once on the ferry, they churned through choppy swells to Ellis Island. Hundreds of men came into view, standing behind a fenced compound on the island, their faces showing no emotion. Herbert hoped to never know what it was like to watch the arrival of the next round of arrested Americans.

He and his father exited the ferry and trooped through a long tunnel on the north side of the island, arriving in an open-barracks hall with a sign reading Baggage and Dormitory Area. The room ran five hundred feet deep and fifty feet across. Twelve square brick pillars, evenly spaced near the center of the room, supported the tall ceiling. Large windows were set twelve feet apart with metal radiators below each. The walls were white-tiled from floor to chest height and the upper walls were painted green. He and Otto would bunk in the open dormitory area, while women and children were housed somewhere else on the property.

Two guards gave Herbert's group the grand tour. A communal bath area was just outside the dormitory. Dozens of sinks lined three walls, and the ten open bathtubs separated by brick partitions, were along another wall, set up so guards could see all the detainees from any spot in the room. So much for privacy. Except for the baths, the room, and even the locker room, were reminders of his high school days. But instead of men with whistles, these men carried guns.

A guard issued Herbert and Otto pairs of United States Army brogans, khaki socks, one tan shirt, a pair of pants, two sets of underwear, and a red plaid jacket, and were told to change.

The scent of starch and laundry products came off the clothes. "They are clean. It could be worse," Otto said. "Not necessary . . . to remove, the clothes from, the dead."

Otto hadn't told many people of his time in the trenches in WWI, but over the years, he shared enough with Herbert to describe the hell it was. Often the men's uniforms were so soiled from days of remaining dug in, or from crawling through ditches pooled with blood, feces, and urine. They abided by the agreement that if a soldier died, his uniform went to other brothers-in-arms who needed it more.

After Herbert and his father put their civilian garments in a bag and dressed in the required prison garb, the next task was to find a bed in the dormitory. Bunk beds, in sets of three, were suspended from the ceiling by chains and lined two walls. The individual beds near the radiators were already claimed. The huge room must be a beast to keep warm. They found two beds next to each other in the center aisle and unrolled the thin mattresses over the bed springs. Then he tucked his civilian clothes under the bed and helped his father. "Better than a shoe factory, I guess," he said. The cots in the factory were old and sagged in the center, leaving limited choices for a place to sleep. Otto hadn't complained, but each morning he struggled to stand erect, a sight that weighed heavy on Herbert. His own hip throbbed with pain until he got up and started moving. He could only imagine what his father felt. Otto should be home in his own bed and not subjected to these discomforts.

Moments later, a whistle sounded, and a guard yelled out, "You are ordered to stand."

A military man entered the room and hundreds of feet shuffled on the wooden floor as everyone stood. "I am Admiral Cahoon, in charge of this detention center." Cahoon wore his uniform with authority. His jawline was set hard, and his smooth chin hinted he enjoyed the luxury of shaving more than once a day.

"Although you will be housed and fed per military standards," he continued, "you will also receive three dollars a month in government scrip to purchase additional items from the store and canteen."

A month? Herbert would be tearing into someone if they were here more than a week.

"If you choose to perform maintenance jobs around the island, you will receive an additional ten cents an hour. When the national anthem plays, all internees will uncover their heads and stand at attention and face the music or the colors. If seated, upon the approach of an officer, you will rise, face toward him, and stand at attention until the officer orders otherwise."

The irony wasn't lost on him. He'd never gotten the chance to go through boot camp and follow a rigid military schedule, but here he was, following orders as a prisoner, not a soldier.

The admiral walked along the rows of beds, hands clasped behind him. "Some of you will be here a short period of time."

Herbert slid his foot over to tap Otto's. He met his father's gaze with one he hoped conveyed this would be their story. Otto nodded.

"Others may stay longer until they are cleared of their crimes. But all of you will adhere to the schedule established to maintain order on this island because we have six hundred new detainees moving through here each month. If you are romancing the idea of escape, two have tried and two have died, one by drowning and the other was cut in half by a boat propeller. That is a letter I do not want to write to your family. So, keep your noses clean, and your time in this transition camp will work out fine." He returned the guards' salutes as he left the room.

"Moving through here?" he said to Otto. "They act like we're in for the long haul."

"I do not, expect a fast review"—Otto shoved his hands in his pockets—"Delay seems, to be the plan to, ühm...wear us down."

They'd been told nothing of this possibility. Herbert's understanding was they would go home from here when their cases were settled, and not use this place as a jumping-off point to another unknown destination. And a transition camp? Different than the internment facility it was billed as. Anger welled up and broke through his usual ability to tamp it down. They were putting American citizens in prison camps as if the United States had an active war raging on its own soil. He couldn't remember a time when he felt so uncertain about what he should do to put their lives back together. This transpired so fast, and he was caught off-guard.

He'd fight to hang on to their dignity, recover his freedom, and return home if only he knew where to direct his fists. The false accusations came from neighbors, the FBI, and the Immigration Department. And they all passed the buck right to the top. Sounded as if he needed to punch Roosevelt in the nose to get someone to listen.

On the way back to the dormitory, he stopped his father in front of the small store. "Time to get busy and make something happen." He grabbed a pack of writing paper and a pen, buying them on credit not believing he'd be there long enough to earn enough to pay it back. He'd wire it to them when he returned home.

He wrote to Jutta, requesting she ask Rupert Jackowsky, their Polish neighbor who vouched for him, to help out on their property until they returned home. He wrote to D. Emmert Brumbaugh, a Republican state representative Otto knew quite well, and again to the Department of Justice, explaining the family's patriotism. His hand cramped around the pen as he forced his pent-up frustration onto the paper. The board of inquiry had nothing to accuse them of except they were born in Germany. He hoped the government would come to their senses and realize the blunder they'd made.

The evening meal started with a clanging bell, seemingly loud enough to be heard across the harbor. They ate in shifts in the Great Hall. Otto followed Herbert's lead and grabbed a metal tray and pushed it along the cafeteria line, collecting scoops of food until, at the end, they were handed a spoon and napkin.

"No forks?" Herbert asked the attendant.

"No." The attendant barely raised his eyes, but made a shooing motion for him to move along.

"So we can't murder each other," the man in front of Herbert said with a slight German accent, and tapped his tray with the spoon. He sported a short salt and pepper beard and combed-back hair to match. His face was kind and open, and he seemed content, lacking the bewildered look others had. He must have been a recent arrival.

Herbert studied the spoon, handle end up, thinking they might be surprised what an angry man could do. He thought of Alfred. Jutta wrote that their son struggled each day to restrain his frustration, and he had every reason to be angry. Martha refused to see him socially, and at basketball practice, bystanders harassed him with taunts. His teammates still rallied around him, but that alone couldn't mend his fifteen-year-old broken heart.

The man pointed Herbert and Otto to a table, and Otto found a seat next to Herbert. The clattering of hundreds of spoons, scraping against plates, made it nearly impossible to hear even though they all sat shoulder to shoulder. "Where did they bring you in from?" he asked the man.

"Near Albany. You?"

"Germantown, outside Philadelphia."

They chewed in silence as servicemen set pitchers of water on the table. Overhead, large American flags hung from poles along the balcony where guards stood, watching the room. Herbert poured water into his tin cup. "You just get here?"

"No." The old guy chuckled, a melodic sound coming from his throat. "Been here about six months."

Herbert dropped his spoon. "Six months, and no hearing?"

The man pointed his utensil to the ceiling and walls. "Here's what they didn't tell you, friend. This place satisfies the need to make Americans feel safe. The processing is barely moving along." He sipped his coffee. "I've only seen men leave in two ways. Because of sickness...or death."

Herbert's throat tightened at the possibility they could be stuck here until next summer. They could lose everything if he and Otto were gone that long.

"How has your family managed?" Herbert wiped his mouth on the paper napkin.

"Oh, I'm not married"—the man reached out his hand—"People call me Pastor Theodore."

"Herbert and Otto Müller." Being a pastor explained the man's calmness. He had no family business to lose. "We've left a busy gristmill and family behind. To hear we could be here longer than a week makes me pretty angry."

The pastor nodded. "I hear it all day. Hey. You should attend my sermons. I focus on staving off fear and staying strong. You're welcome to attend. Besides, being busy and filling in a few empty hours helps with the slow crawl of time."

"Thank you." Herbert pushed away his tray. He had nothing against attending a church service, but at the end of that Sunday, unless he and his father got a chance to appeal, they were no closer to going home. "I'm glad you've found a way to stay upbeat. I don't mean to be rude but getting back to my family is everything to me and my father."

"I completely understand. Unfortunately, your story mirrors most of the others here." The pastor stood and dropped his hand onto Herbert's shoulder. "I can only offer this...giving to others gets you outside of yourself and distracts you from your problems." He smiled. "I hope to see you Sunday."

Herbert believed in what the pastor was saying—the Müller family volunteered and reached out to many families in need—but the upbeat message irritated him. He and his father were wronged and separated from the people they loved. It was one thing to reach out to others when he had so much to give, but here, imprisoned with little recourse, Herbert was empty. Although it was probably spiritually wrong to think this way, he wanted to be on the receiving end this time and get the news they were free to go home.

-22-

WILHELM FALK

Sparks POW Camp, New Hampshire - March 1944

Large snowflakes fell around them as Falk and his group of twenty were nearly to the tree line where they would cut today. This was his third week working in the forest with this team. Today, as they hiked up the north face of the mountain, he was pain-free for the first time and no longer felt winded. The cutting area was too steep for the army vehicles, forcing the men to walk. Scrambling up the snow-packed slopes, carrying axes and two-man saws, was grueling and dangerous work.

Commander Dobb's mantra of cutting one cord per man per day was drilled into their heads and weary backs. Falk assumed the camp overseer must receive personal bonuses if he met the quotas for The Brown Paper Company.

The work area suffered from a fire at some point, leaving the spruce trees stunted and tangled, with bare branches sticking out of the snow, like blackened arms reaching toward the men. Falk's jacket was sweat-soaked from the climb, and he shivered from periodic chills but pushed on, half dizzy, yet keeping up with the others.

He was relieved to spend seven hours a day away from the tensions in camp. Ideological differences widened the gap between Nazi and anti-Nazi prisoners, making the camp a dangerous place. Racial purity was a heated topic, and one that couldn't be resolved. Anti-Nazis argued that, with the way Europe was settled, everyone has a mixed-race heritage. Nazis argued they descended from pure German stock. Arguments that Hitler was shortsighted ended in knife fights. Anti-Nazis claimed that building the

Atlantic Wall along the western seaboard of the Netherlands used valuable resources the military needed on the battlefront. Nazis argued the Wall was needed to protect the lands Germany had conquered.

Snitches gained favor from the Nazi loyalists in the form of extra smokes or canteen scrip. Early this morning, a Hitler supporter engaged Falk in a seemingly innocent conversation, trying to determine whether he was committed to the Führer's cause. Falk remained neutral, having seen what happened to Nazi traitors. Many suffered savage beatings, and others were often offered broken bottles as substitutes for razor blades to facilitate their *suicide*. An eighteen-year-old bled to death in the showers, a broken butter knife stuck in his back. An obvious suicide, the Nazis claimed.

With no reliable information from Germany reaching them, rumors and anxiety filled the POWs' days. Were their families safe? Who was winning the war? Would anything be left of their homeland when they returned?

Today, Falk's group reached the work area and was set to felling fir and hemlock identified with marks of red paint. He breathed in the scent of freshly chopped wood as axes and saws dropped tree after tree. He handled an axe across from Renke Novak. They swung in an alternating pattern, one *thunk* resounding after the other. Like all the other workers, Falk and Novak wore jackets and trousers emblazoned with the large letters PW stenciled on their pant legs and jacket backs.

"Got a letter from home," Renke said, his breath visible in the cold air.

Falk and Novak bonded over their anti-Nazi sentiments, but spoke of it only when they were far from the group or guards. Novak hailed from a small farming community outside Stuttgart and was married to a neighbor girl, who delivered a daughter he had yet to meet.

"How's your little girl?"

Renke showed the photograph of his two-year-old child to him and anyone who stood still. "Talking up a storm according to my wife." Then he raised his axe once again. The tree trunk cracked but didn't fall.

"That's good." Falk fondly recalled Hans talking early but Dietrich allowed his older brother to answer for him until Hans went off to school, leaving Dietrich no choice but to speak.

"The wife's not so good. Distraught." His words came with the rhythm of the axes' movements. "No milk. Meat. Electricity's unreliable."

"But your mail's getting through." This worried Falk. What if their neighbor was collecting their mail in Düsseldorf and decided to forward it to the Netherlands? The possibility hadn't occurred to him until now.

"You've heard nothing?" Renke asked.

Falk received the packages all the POWs obtained from the German Red Cross, but he hadn't written to Klaus Stern's wife yet because he didn't know where to begin. All he knew about Stern was he was married. Although if Hartmann could be believed, Stern forgot about his marriage vows when they went whoring. Many soldiers carried letters from home, but in the pockets of Stern's uniform, Falk only found packets of condoms, foot powder, and a woman's garter.

"I guess not every post office is in working order." Falk swung extra hard and the tree began to tip away from them. "Here she goes!"

"Timber!" Renke called out, the word the site boss insisted meant clear the hell away. The hollow thuds of axes, and the grunts of the laboring men, echoed through the trees.

Focusing on hard labor calmed Falk, leaving his mind free to plan his escape. Aboard ship, he'd never solved how he would escape camp once he arrived, but he didn't think it would take this long. The camp guards seemed less wary of the POWs with the passing of time. They'd become more casual during their patrols, especially in the woods. His barracks was no longer searched. But this harsh winter weather, coupled with rugged terrain, made each escape strategy he devised seem impossible when he planned the details.

As his frustration grew, he slept less, upset with the passage of time, which meant thousands more were murdered in the extermination camps. When he slept, he had a reoccurring nightmare. His sons stood on a dangerous cliff calling for him. He ran in their direction, his feet slipping on something spilled on the ground. He tried to climb the cliff, only to discover it was made of stacks of naked bodies that rolled under his scrambling feet. He made no progress to reach his sons. They would die. The eyes of the dead followed him. Condemning, accusing. He'd awake in a sweat and check his hands for the blood that should be there.

"Big bastard," Renke said, pointing to the next tree in their section, which snapped Falk's attention back to the forest. "One more to fill the quota."

"Let's do it." He flexed his cold fingers inside his gloves a few times before grabbing his axe.

Renke swung and made the first wedge cut.

This would be Falk's last quota of pulpwood. He'd wasted enough time planning. The next clear day, he'd wear his uniform under his POW clothes, carry his hoarded food, and disappear into the thickets and underbrush. While on the *Algonquin*, he tried to picture the United States, the cities, and houses. He planned to hide in dark alleys and abandoned buildings but hadn't envisioned vast tracts of unoccupied land. From scanning the area, he knew that beyond camp there were trees, lakes, and more mountains, which provided plenty of hiding places.

He still wrestled with his reasons for wanting to personally deliver the Nazi materials directly to representatives of the president of the United States. Why not ask Pastor Graf to pass them on? Was he trying to redeem himself for not intervening at the death camps, trying to be the hero who informed the world as to what Hitler was really doing? This is what made sense to him. By handing over photographs and documents—many signed by Hitler's hand—to the United States military, his firsthand accounts and explanations might carry more weight than if the government received the same documents from the pastor. Or anyone else without personal knowledge of the atrocities.

The storm grew in intensity, and the dark-brown tree trunks around him faded into a blurry backdrop. The clacking of boughs overhead meant the wind had a plan of its own and wouldn't be denied.

Without reason, the boy with the shoestrings in Auschwitz, pushed to the forefront of his thoughts. The child's eyes were unusual—one light brown and the other a piercing blue—both round and full of wonder. The stubble on his shaved head seemed to be the light-colored hair of a German child. When Falk first noticed the young boy handing out lengths of string on the arrival platform at Auschwitz, the child looked German, but Falk couldn't imagine a guard had brought his son into that hellish setting.

When he enquired, an SS officer said, "His grandparents were Jewish, but we like his Aryan looks. Besides, it calms the Jews. They see a healthy child the moment they get off the train. No arguments when we move their younger children off to the left, assuming their child will get a job like this boy."

The boy said his mother worked in the building nicknamed Canada. The workers there opened the suitcases and sorted the prisoner's belongings into huge piles of clothing, valuables, mementos, and toys. The clothing and toys were cleaned and shipped to stores throughout Germany, helping to alleviate shortages in the general population. Did the new owners feel the pain associated with each item? It was nonsense to think so, but he hoped some essence of each Jewish person was imbued in every article of clothing or piece of jewelry stolen from them. Falk was offered gold watches and rings with precious stones on many occasions. He begged off. "They should be saved for officers more notable," he would say.

When exhausted passengers reached the train platform, the boy pointed to the pair of shoes set in front of him and mimed tying the shoes together with a string he held. The simplest of deceits. *You will get both of your shoes back. Look, we have an orderly process.* To help paint an atmosphere of welcoming, the camp band, off to the side of the platform, attempted to play upbeat songs from the deportees' country of origin. The boy with the strings sang along in a clear voice when the songs were Czechoslovakian. If anyone noticed his stiff, unnatural posture, indicating his act was performed under duress, no one reacted. After the new arrivals were processed and the platform empty, the child spent hours carrying thousands of shoes—forty to fifty pairs at a time slung over his small shoulders—to his mother's building. Work shoes were thrown into a heap for the enslaved prisoners left alive.

Falk often spoke to the boy, as much as two people could speak in languages unfamiliar to the other. To keep up his healthy appearance, the child was fed somewhat better than many inmates and dressed in clean clothes. Still, Falk often slipped him a candy bar or a bread roll, whenever possible.

The child reminded him of his oldest son, Hans, at age seven, full of ideas and inventions he would work on when he grew up.

Falk made only four visits to Auschwitz, all devastating, but none as excruciating as his last, just five months ago. He planned to find the child and hire him and his mother on behalf of Herr Schindler's factory outside of Płaszów. Schindler operated an enamel goods factory seized from a Jewish owner, who was sent to the Kraków Ghetto. Falk knew Schindler was more than a factory owner, but never turned the man in. He would be in grave danger if his lie that Schindler asked to hire the boy and his mother was discovered. But he was willing to take that chance. Saving even one child would matter.

That rainy day in October, Falk arrived full of optimism for the one good deed he was about to do, only to find the boy with the strings replaced by a much older boy, handing out the dirty twine. No one knew—or was willing to say—what happened to the blond-haired boy with one brown and one blue eye. But on that day, he finally learned the boy's first name was Hiam.

The Sparks foreman blew a whistle, startling Falk back to the present. The workday ended. The blizzard won. Was this his chance to disappear into the curtain of white swirling around them? Although he didn't have his secret store of food, he had gone without food before. That wouldn't be the problem. He wore a jacket over one layer of clothes and his hands were already frozen in his gloves, so he knew he'd die within hours if he escaped today.

Knee-high snow made their trip back down the mountain difficult and hazardous. They reached the trucks and Jeeps, their transportation to and from camp. Falk stretched for the sidebar on the back of the truck bed but couldn't close his hand around it. He stepped back and let others board as he rubbed his thighs to warm his hands. Finally, he pulled himself up and crawled inside, and turned to help the others. The canvas flap at the rear sounded like a cracking whip as it snapped against itself until two MPs set down their machine guns to tie it shut. After the POWs were loaded inside, the guards retrieved their guns and then retreated to the Jeeps with the other guards. He hoped the guards' lack of concern about leaving an unattended rifle for a moment would soon work in his favor.

Falk was bumped and jostled against the other POWs on the rough logging road, but relished the reprieve from the cold. Once they entered camp, he stood shivering on the parade ground for the day's final count.

Which came up one short.

He groaned as the tally started again, and shifted his feet in place, thinking he might never walk again if he didn't get his feet warmed up soon.

After two additional checks, the guards determined who was missing. Falk knew the guy, a POW with a small head and mean little eyes, who always peered out from under a swath of blond hair. He'd worked like a piston engine, never stopping unless it was for a swallow of water. Obviously, he'd been in training, and his arm muscles had become massive from weeks in the forest.

Wehrmacht training indoctrinated them with the conviction that prisoners of war were bound by duty to attempt an escape. The bulletin board in the mess hall documented the faces and stories of the eight who tried and failed, but beady eyes was the first to flee since Falk arrived.

The POWs were ordered to their barracks and placed on lockdown. As Falk's group passed the watchtower closest to the town, a guard hand-cranked the Klaxon horn, its undulating wail loud enough to warn the villagers of Sparks a prisoner was on the loose. Would the residents panic or sigh, and realize another POW was tempting fate?

His jaws clamped tight, and he silently cursed. What bad timing. He was within a day of escaping. He'd worked on his English with a few friendly guards, who relaxed the rules of fraternization when they were in the forest. As a teenager, he spoke passable English prodded along by Pastor Graf who led their Christian Teen Group.

He sat on his cot, and the weight of disappointment rested heavy on his shoulders. They'd be closely supervised again. Each day his escape was delayed, 10,000 more men, women, and children were exterminated for no valid reason other than their audacity to exist.

Was he foolish to think he could do this without help? He had no way to contact Pastor Graf, with the censoring of the POWs' letters. If he explained to the camp commander why he was here, he doubted Dobbs would pat him on the back and say, "In that case, let me personally drive you to

Washington." He scrubbed his hands through his hair, knowing if he did that, he'd likely be traded to German high command for an American officer and summarily hanged or shot.

Disappearing into the forest wouldn't work. He needed a new plan.

By the next morning, Falk learned the locals were offered a fifteen-dollar bounty for the return of the missing prisoner of war, Harold Schmidt. The FBI, state police, and local sheriff departments in a fifty-mile radius joined the search. Although the storm ended, three feet of new snow hampered the hunt and surely affected Schmidt's progress.

Animated conversation in the showers went so far as to place bets on how long the solider would remain free. Some ventured that the POW was trying to return to Germany. Falk speculated the guy hoped to hide out and eventually blend into the large German population in the United States.

To discourage others against escape, the camp commander punished everyone. Their diet was changed to bread and water. Commander Dobbs immediately closed their canteen. Well before dawn, Falk and the others were rousted from their warm beds to assemble on the parade ground, shivering in the cold, while the guards searched their barracks.

An icy fog rolled in, and the lights in the village of Sparks were nearly lost in an eerie blur. The guards were stiff and formal again. All trust was gone. He counted off in the freezing darkness as the searchlight beams crisscrossed the area, making the frozen, white ground resemble a polished dance floor.

The prisoner count added up, and they returned to barracks just as the guards left, carrying full sacks.

Falk expected nothing less but felt deflated at the loss of his stash of food. His English dictionary was also gone. The other POWs complained of losing their hard-earned cigarettes and canteen purchases.

Confined to barracks, Falk couldn't put it off any longer. It looked suspicious that he wasn't communicating with his *wife*. But he had a problem writing to Frau Stern, the wife of the soldier he was impersonating.

From Stern's army papers, he learned Stern had a wife named Helga and no children were listed. He stared at the blank paper, completely baffled as to what to say. Had Helga had a child since this *soldbuch* was first issued? Did the Sterns live in a house or an apartment? Raise chickens? Have a sick relative? The letter would be censored for any information that might aid the enemy, adding another layer of difficulty. He finally arrived at a solution and wrote about being held in the United States and that he was in good health. Concluding with, he could only pray she and the family were safe and bearing up under the rationing and deprivations. He trusted her to be the brave woman he left behind when he enlisted. He signed it: *Your loving husband, Klaus.* He used the address from Stern's identification papers.

His mind turned to Ilse and their sons. If they were somehow notified of his death, his personal effects and medals most likely arrived in a cardboard box with the army's condolences. Imagining the pain and emptiness his wife and sons experienced if they received that news, gripped his heart. Would they be questioned by Reichsführer-SS Heinrich Himmler's men? Falk should have been in Berlin, reporting to Himmler or Hitler about his secret postbox when he *died* in Italy. He'd never told Ilse about any of his experiences in the extermination camps, and said nothing about gathering information to use against Hitler and the SS. She would be clueless as to what he had been doing. Had he protected his family enough?

With so many assassination attempts against the Führer, Himmler was stretched thin, trying to follow through with Hitler's genocide plan while protecting his leader. Hunting down a wayward SS officer's wife had to be at the bottom of Himmler's list. Or Falk hoped so. He couldn't live knowing Ilse and his sons were made to live in fear because of him.

A guard burst through their door and called everyone to attention.

"Prisoner Schmidt was located."

Murmurs spread through the barracks, and the men checked the clock on the wall to see if they won the capture lottery.

"At fourteen hundred hours, he was discovered ten miles from here." The guard slowly smiled. "Frozen to death."

Just as Falk imagined.

He needed a different way out of camp and couldn't spare the time to establish trust with the guards again—that had taken months. He jammed his thumbs into his temples and circled them, enjoying the pain as he pushed harder. He would get out even if he had to fake his death again.

-23-

IZAAK TAUBER

Płaszów Concentration Camp, Poland - March 1944

Izaak inched forward, towing the heavy cart he and three other boys had been assigned to. This had gone on for the last two weeks. The carts were filled with large, flat stones, and pulling them was nearly impossible. He imagined he and the other boys were old horses, so tired they couldn't tug the cart more than a few feet at a time, their horses' breaths puffing out in the frosty air.

Each boy had a rope looped across his chest, stretching behind him and attached to the wooden wagon. One wheel on the cart always tried to go the wrong way in the slushy snow, making the work that much harder.

Izaak wore two coats over his striped clothes. One to help fight the cold and one to stop the ropes from cutting into his skin. The boys didn't talk to each other. Ven from the Netherlands and Izaak spoke when they had energy, but the two other boys in their work group spoke different languages. When they all tried to talk to each other, they used sounds and their free hands to mime what they were trying to say.

The work was so hard. There was no time to talk. Breathing in and out without collapsing was about all he could do.

And falling down was bad.

Commandant Goeth was the mean man who ran the camp. It was true he liked to hurt everyone, from people who were extra tired to those just walking. Or working. Just last week, he stood on the porch of the grey house where he lived and used his rifle to shoot at another group of boys pulling sleds. They all died. And Goeth owned two tall dogs named Ralf and Rolf. They were fast, and Goeth liked to watch them chase people and bite their legs. When they couldn't walk any longer, they were loaded onto a bigger wagon and taken over a hill, crying and holding each other. Those people never came back.

He and the boys neared the grey house, and Izaak watched his feet. If he couldn't see Goeth, maybe the commandant wouldn't see him. The wagon moved faster now. Not only were the boys pulling harder, but also on this side of camp, the long paving stones fit together to make a slightly bumpy street in front of the officers' nice houses and important buildings.

Izaak kept his mind off the pain in his back and how hungry he was by trying to read the words on the headstones they walked over. Bogumił, Leszek, Ksawery. They were hard to sound out because they weren't in his language. When he found out the road was built from gravestones, he'd sobbed all the way back to where his mama worked. She hugged him quickly because hugs weren't allowed outside the barracks, and her lips trembled as she said, "Think about this. God can now see the names of the people who loved Him."

He and the boys walked quicker, and Izaak focused on the pretty Stars of David, or the Tzedakah boxes, carved into the upward-facing stones. Some had a photograph of a person in glass built right inside the marker. He silently apologized for walking on them.

An older boy said the bad men, who built this terrible camp, pushed over all the stones in the two old cemeteries until all the monuments and grave markers lay face down, or in broken piles. God would be confused as to who was who. Hundreds of adults, including Mama, had the job of digging the dead people out of the dirt and moving them to a bigger grave behind the rows of barracks, so the headstones could be used for streets on the guards' side of camp. He tried to picture a memorial, an enormous painting with everyone's picture on it, to remember those in the big grave. Izaak could help draw the people, although his drawing skills hadn't helped him and Mama so far. It was clear to him they were taken to the wrong camp, and he was too afraid to approach the guards with his drawing of Papa. There was no paper here, but whenever he got a chance, he drew in the snow with a stick, or scratched in the hard ground with a sharp stone. He drew each day to keep his mind off the fact Papa wasn't here according to the dozens of men he'd questioned. When he asked his mama how soon they would go to another work camp, she looked away and said she didn't know.

Izaak and the boys finally reached the end of the street. He could rest for a few minutes while men unloaded the gravestones from the cart. He leaned against the side of the cart and watched all the workers. Everyone had to have a job. Men and women were building more barracks for the people still coming. On top of the empty graves on the hill, workers built the latrines, bath houses, and a building to spray the germs off new arrivals.

All day long, the women prisoners pulled the squeaky-wheel carts filled with rocks uphill, the ones that sounded like birds. He was always sad when he watched the thirty-five scarecrow ladies roped to one another, staggering side by side dragging the carts. And if watching them wasn't awful enough, one day, Goeth shot one group, and they fell one at a time, unable to get away. He wet himself and held back tears until he saw Mama that night. She held him close and gave him good ideas to think about, so he could forget what he saw. When the bad pictures came into his head, she told him to sing songs, name all the people he remembered from Amsterdam, or paint something nice in his head. Her suggestions helped a little—sometimes—but not always.

Today, while he waited for the headstones to be unloaded, he tried to decide what picture to draw in his head since that was the distraction that worked best. The wagon was soon empty, and he and the other boys headed back to the tumbled-down cemetery to load more stones. As they passed through the different sections of camp, Izaak designed a nicer version of them in his mind. In the living quarters for men, he imagined small tables with board games and big glasses of water, fresh, not like the gloppy brown liquid scooped from two ponds in camp.

In the women's lodgings, he imagined brightly-colored curtains for the windows and flowerpots near the doors. For a moment, the picture in his head fuzzed out. He became dizzy and almost fell. This happened every day now, but he was afraid to tell Mama. She might not think he was still her strong little man, and he loved when she called him that.

They dragged the empty cart past the beautiful building called the Jewish Pre-Burial Hall. The top of the white building had three domes and looked like a small palace. Izaak used the eraser in his head to remove all the horses and pigs the guards let roam inside, including getting rid of the animals' piles of dung all over the pretty carpet and floors.

Near the railway station, skinny men shoveled snow from the tracks, working fast. A train sat ready to go, belching smoke, the rumble of the engine coming up through the ground, vibrating Izaak's legs. He and the boys slowed, watching the people climb the steps to enter the same awful cars he once rode.

"Where do you think they're going?" Ven asked and swiped at his nose, leaving a line of snot on his coat sleeve. He wore round spectacles that magnified his eyes like a bug.

The shorter boy in their work group, who spoke Polish, made chugging train sounds and showed his hands moving like a train and then quickly stopping. He pointed to his chest and then shook his head rapidly from side to side, which Izaak understood to mean, "I don't want to go."

Izaak wanted to leave. A train going anywhere was better than staying here. He squinted at the huge crowd of people on the platform waiting to board, happy for them, but disappointed it wasn't him and Mama leaving. Then, like magic, he spotted his friends Zev and Aharon, and their mama. If they received permission to leave, that meant he and Mama might be next. He wanted to yell out to them to say he would see them soon, but, at that moment, Commandant Goeth approached the train. The commandant must have a secret kitchen all to himself because his belly was big and round.

As soon as Goeth reached the loading area, the soldiers got pushy with their rifles and poked the families to climb aboard faster. One soldier carried a whip and cracked it at the back of their legs, but it was lucky that Izaak's friends were already aboard.

"When the trains go in that direction," Ven said, "I heard they're heading to a place called Auschwitz."

The name sounded like a tight sneeze—Auschwitz! "Is it better than this place?"

"I don't know but when people are chosen to leave, that's where most of them go."

If he stayed strong just a little while longer, surely he and Mama could get on the right train, maybe a train going there.

-24-

HERBERT MÜLLER

Ellis Island Internment Camp - March 1944

After a month, Herbert learned why so many men stayed outside and walked around the small property despite the cold. The frigid air was far better than the stale odor of six hundred nervous men, the overflowing toilets, and harsh cleaning chemicals. Besides, the rats, and roaches the size of mice, scuttled everywhere.

Inside, he and Otto often visited the "Library," a room with a dozen folding chairs and a table with boxes of books donated by the YMCA and International Red Cross. However, even there, some creature on the run to a darker corner crossed his foot. The majority of the books were printed in German, the volunteer groups assuming the internees were better versed in that language. While Otto read effortlessly, Herbert brushed up on his childhood language. He'd reread one of the titles, *Of Mice and Men*, twice now, empathizing with the main characters' dreams of owning their own land and settling down when tragedy strikes.

On Sundays, a chapel attached to the hospital offered alternating religious services in English and then in German. Herbert and his father attended the German service held by Pastor Theodore. The German hymns took him back to his childhood in Stuttgart. He and Karl were often impatient church-goers unless there was a hands-on project, like recreating Noah's Ark and the animals from sticks and clay.

Today, Herbert was fifty cents richer after finishing another five-hour shift, sweeping the halls and cleaning the toilets. His hip ached and his back spasmed, all for the ridiculous pay of ten cents an hour. The janitorial job served one purpose and one purpose only and that was to fill the frustrating hours as days dragged by with no date for their appeals.

He returned to the Immigration Hall and found Otto napping. Otto looked like a child curled on his side, his arms crossed and hands tucked in his armpits. His father's energy diminished each day they remained in custody, and it worried him. Otto blamed himself for their captivity. He lamented that he and Anni should have become American citizens. No matter how often Herbert reassured him they would be returning home together, Otto's face sagged and his eyes often glazed over.

He left his father's side and walked out the building through a side tunnel, his footsteps echoing off the tiled walls. He arrived in the fenced-in area and breathed deeply. A cold, salty breeze reached him from the sloshing waves hitting against the sides of the island. The New York skyline was lit in the midday light. Lady Liberty's shadow bridged the churning harbor waters, reaching Ellis Island a half mile away, and reminded Herbert of the liberties ripped away from him. Some mornings, he fought to stay immersed in daydreams of home. The patchwork quilt on his and Jutta's bed. The warm alcove near the stove, his favorite spot to sit and talk with her while she cooked.

The painful emptiness he carried without his wife and children went beyond what he experienced after his mother died, and he loved her beyond measure. When he closed his eyes, he saw his family. When he opened his eyes, reality mocked him. It was hard to be deprived of time together, and each day without them, left a void that had a weight of its own.

After he sent a flurry of letters to government officials, friends, and family, the Coast Guard commander restricted his letter writing. Now, he was only allowed two posts a week, both heavily censored according to what Jutta wrote in her single letter back to him. Words were either inked or snipped out. Who did the government hire to clip away his writing with tiny scissors? Or would it be razor blades? Seemed like a whole lot of wasted effort to edit his report on the mundane happenings on the island.

What unsettled him most was how worthless he felt, stuck in the internment camp while Jutta and the children tried to manage at home. A blizzard had dropped three feet of snow, and as Alfred tried to maneuver the tractor with the plow attached, he sheared off the downspout on one side of the house. Herbert applauded Alfred's effort since the boy had never driven the plow. But now water would pour off the eaves, and they'd have to navigate a flooded stretch of lawn, which would freeze into a hazardous skating rink just to get to the vegetable cellar.

Pastor Theodore walked up beside him at the wire.

"We enjoyed your sermon," Herbert said.

The pastor was a good orator and a better conversationalist. They'd met several times outside of church and now Herbert was always glad to spend time with him. Having a friend softened the ache of missing his family.

"I'm pleased." He looked around the open area. "Your father is not here?"

"I left him napping. Who can sleep well with the snoring and farting at night?"

The pastor chuckled and stroked his short beard. "When you talk from a pulpit you get used to the snoring part. Thank the heavens I don't get much of the latter." He had one eye that squinted when he talked. "If you want quiet, try the lavatories at three a.m. It's where I do my best thinking." Theodore turned and leaned back against the fence. "Any word from your family?"

Herbert smiled. "Yes. They're sending a rescue blimp with a long rope. Want to catch a lift?"

Theodore laughed and patted his large midsection. "They'll need a winch."

He had no family in America and was arrested after communicating with a friend in Germany who sent a package to him. His postman called the FBI.

"All kidding aside. My family has been granted permission to visit in a few weeks. I cannot tell you how far away that date seems."

Jutta wrote she had news but wanted to share it in person. She had written to many government bureaucrats, protesting Herbert's unfair arrest and asking for the officials' intervention. She would not have put their answers in writing. But it hardly mattered. Herbert lost all trust in the government being on his side.

"Wonderful news!" The pastor clasped his hands together. "I can't wait to meet them."

He and Otto were cautiously thrilled at the news, but aware the government could change its mind at any time.

"And you?" Herbert asked. "Any word on a new hearing?"

The man shook his head. "Same old excuses. There are a few thousand ahead of me. They are still investigating. Why don't I spend more time praying and less time talking."

Herbert chuckled. "I hear the same spiel, except for the praying part. No one's suggesting that."

Out on the water, two men in a small dingy were hauling in a full fishing net. The boat bobbed wildly, but the men rode it as if they were born to it.

"I've been meaning to ask." Herbert rubbed his hands together, hoping for warmth. "What happened in the library yesterday? Some guy tried to kill himself?"

"Overwhelmed, they said. I got there late, but he threatened to kill anyone who tried to stop him from opening an artery."

"Knife?"

"Fountain pen"—Theodore shook his head—"He's in the infirmary, heavily sedated."

"What set him off?" Herbert wanted to punch holes in walls, and he'd only been on the island a month.

"The government froze his assets. Apparently, a neighbor offered to buy his house, so his wife and four children could have rent money for an apartment. They moved out and found a scrubby little place on the bad side of Akron." He narrowed an eye. "The not-so-good neighbor then changed his mind and only offered a tenth of the price he promised for their home. Of course, there was no one to complain to. His wife had a nervous breakdown in the middle of city council chambers, where she took her complaint. After that, their children were whisked off to an orphanage. Until she *recovers*."

Herbert shook his head. "That's horrific." How did anyone recuperate from losses like that? His moods of nostalgia and melancholy came and went, a rollercoaster of emotions that surfaced in the unlikeliest of places.

He'd butter a piece of bread and study the slice as if he could discern where the grain was ground. Could it be from their mill? A slice of apple pie reminded him of the way his family made apple-picking season an adventure for themselves and the Haitian pickers they hired. South-of-the-border music. Tables loaded with food. The youngest dark-skinned children, playing on blankets in the shade with Alfred and Frieda years ago. The Haitian pickers often ran the risk of being deported if they broke the law. Wouldn't the workers be surprised to know their fellow employers were now under arrest and sitting in an internment camp?

"Someone's got to answer for that," Herbert said, "causing a wife to lose her mind. Sending the children to an orphanage. That's not the America we live in."

"I'm not so sure, Herbert." Theodore adjusted his collar. "But, let's hope our cases will soon be heard and we can get on with our lives." He straightened his back and looked to the other half of their island divided by tall wire fencing and protected by guards. "I'm going to head over there and watch what might turn into a pretty interesting show. Five thousand German P-O-Ws off Italy just docked. I heard the Nazis and anti-Nazi factions are already throwing fisticuffs. Might be free seats to a fight."

He'd heard German POWs were being shipped to the U.S. starting last year. A civil engineering camp near Hershey, Pennsylvania, was repurposed to hold two thousand prisoners. The farmer adjacent to Herbert's property used them as hired help under military police guard, reporting they were never a problem and proved themselves to be enthusiastic workers. Ironic that the locals accepted captured German soldiers to work among them, at times even inviting them for dinner with their families, but then turned their backs on their German-American neighbors.

"I'll take you up on your offer," Herbert said. "Military men fighting each other sounds intriguing. Mostly, I'm curious about what the enemy looks like, since I'm supposedly in cahoots with them."

"I'm in that same sinking boat." The two fell into step, weaving around men walking the perimeter. Like tigers in a zoo, the detainees followed the fence line, back and forth, back and forth. "And we'll have a better vantage point to spot your blimp."

"Absolutely. And I apologize." Herbert rested his hand of the man's back. "I never learned your full name."

"It's Graf. Pastor Theodore Graf."

-25-

WILHELM FALK

Sparks POW Camp, New Hampshire - March 1944

Another two weeks laced with guilt and anxiety, another hundred and fifty thousand souls lost, and Falk still had no opportunity to escape. Today, his group of thirty POWs finished clearing a path to the automatic weather station at the top of Mount Washington, a peak near Camp Sparks. They shoveled through banks of four meters of snow, trying not to get ripped from the side of the mountain by the gale force winds, to clear the way for the army vehicles to resupply fuel for the station.

He and the others rested against the railings on the front steps of the massive weather station, sucking in the thin cold air. Spots floated in and out of his vision from overexertion. As his sight cleared, he took in the beautiful view. Tree-covered mountains, all blanketed with snow, stretched below in every direction. The pristine mountain scene reminded him of many parts of Germany.

A guard next to him spoke. "Hold this." He couldn't have been more than twenty with a line of fuzz on his top lip. He handed his carbine rifle to Falk, and then pulled one hand from a glove to radio the army refueling trucks that the roads were now passable.

Was this a test? He was holding a loaded weapon. A buzzing in his head sent his senses to high alert. He'd dreamed of a moment like this when he would have the upper hand, a chance to get away.

The guard motioned for his gun, and Falk hesitated. Five guards were nearby and willing to kill him if need be. He handed the gun back. The young guard nodded to him then called out, "We're done here, men. Load up, we've got a special treat for you."

Falk headed for the truck, still reeling with disbelief he was trusted with a loaded gun. This could work in his favor if he were left alone with this young guard.

They returned to the vehicles and headed down the mountain, passing the refueling crew heading up. Forty minutes later, the trucks stopped at a log cabin-style building called the Casserole Café. Two guards went inside and returned with sack lunches. The POWs jumped down from the truck and accepted a sack. Falk found a place to lean on a split rail fence alongside the parking area. The storm was gone, and the sun was out. He dug through the bag and pulled out oven-warm bread with a thick piece of roast beef in between. A treat indeed.

As he chewed, Falk overheard a tall POW ask another, "The guards seem like regular fellows. Think if I ran into those woods, they'd shoot me?"

"You'd be dead before you reached the hedgerow," Falk said. He'd contemplated the same thing just moments earlier but changed his mind. He did not need new distrust to sprout as he was on his way out.

The POW who posed the question turned to Falk, an unpleasant look on his face. He had eyebrows that could say more with positioning than most men could utter with words.

"Piss off!" he snapped.

"You piss off," Falk said. "We've got it good so don't ruin it." He moved two meters away and lifted his face toward the sun, absorbing the warmth. And was in no hurry to climb back into the damp interior of the canvas-covered truck. He breathed in the unmistakable scent of new growth, pushing up through the fungal layers of last year's dead leaves, that floated on a breeze. Squirrels scurried between trees while somewhere up high, birds screeched opposing opinions before several took flight, pirouetting in the air. Their wings a whirr like the soft flapping of satin.

All too soon their time in the sun ended, and they were loaded and on the road. Once again in the trucks, the hour-long ride back to camp was quiet. When they arrived, the camp seemed busier than usual as they parked. In the middle of roll call, word circulated that a new group of POWs had checked in. The 999th Afrika Brigade—a force Falk knew well. Hitler emptied the prisons to create a fighting unit he believed would be undefeatable. But the 999th proved to be unreliable and ofttimes unmanageable. This boatload of criminals was bound to cause major problems.

Falk gathered his shaving kit and walked to the washroom. Claiming a sink at the end of a row. He stared at the haggard face in the mirror, his blond hair now a dull color. His comb collected more loose strands every day. At this rate, at war's end, Ilse would be welcoming back a bald husband with sunken eyes. Constantly agonizing over what he hadn't done to save Hiam was exhausting. And the guilt he felt a thousand times over for watching others suffer and not speaking up. The scales that balanced a righteous man against an evil one, tipped up and then down in his mind. He was a good husband, father, and company manager for Eastman Kodak, wasn't he? And he felt no shame for causing the death of the doctor at Hadamar. That guy deserved a slow death and not the quick bullet that ended his life outside the facility. Falk lay awake too many nights—often with his heart galloping in his chest—exhausted from hours in the woods but unable to sleep. Sometimes from remorse, other times by pangs of regret circumstances hadn't worked out differently. What started out as revenge for what he witnessed at Hadamar became a winding trail of gathering incriminatory documents to indict Hitler. His efforts, so far, seemed anemic as the Jewish exterminations continued.

He pulled out the hair from his comb and flicked it in the trash.

"Do I know you?" The soldier next to him stopped shaving, his face half lathered. "You look familiar."

Falk controlled his facial expression as he clearly recalled the day he threatened to kill this soldier. The man's name was Heichel, and he had raped a young German girl forced to deliver bread to the house where a dozen officers and enlisted men billeted. With close-set eyes over a bulbous nose, he was ugly on the outside, too. A boxer who couldn't keep his gloves up had a better face. Falk tucked his grooming items away and forced a little laugh.

"After a while, we all look alike, my friend."

Heichel narrowed his eyes as if trying hard to remember.

Falk turned to go, feeling the man's stare as he departed.

The rapist's presence just ratcheted up his urgency to escape. It wouldn't take Heichel long to remember Falk was the SS officer who had him imprisoned in the first place, before Hitler released him to the 999th.

The evening's final count complete, the men washed up and headed to supper. In the dining barracks, Heichel stood in a knot of the most devout Nazis who then—all at once—turned and looked Falk's way. He felt it in his gut. They planned to attack him tonight. Dying here after coming this far would not happen. He had a new scheme, but whether he could pull it off or not remained to be seen.

Dinner this night was traditional roasted pork, fried potatoes, and applesauce cake. Pork for dinner meant fatback lard sandwiches in the men's lunches tomorrow, a favorite of the POWs and guards alike. Falk had difficulty eating, though, knowing he might be dead within the next few hours.

He returned for another portion of potatoes and ate them while standing and set down his plate. He moved to the table with the coffeepots and cold-water dispensers. With a glance over his shoulder, he noticed the men and guards were all facedown over their meals, or busy talking. Except for beady-eyed Heichel, who glanced his way with a knowing sneer on his face. Falk leaned closer to the water dispenser and pulled a small bottle from his jacket pocket. Pretending to check the amount of water inside the container, he lifted the lid and poured the liquid from the bottle into the container. He then closed the lid and put away the bottle.

A POW nudged him from behind. "You getting water or what?"

Falk cleared his throat. "Think I'll go with coffee, after all."

Then he moved over to fill a coffee mug as the man took his place at the water dispenser. There was no turning back now. He headed to his seat and engineered a convincing stumble. Scalding coffee splashed onto his bare neck and inside his shirt. He gasped, dropping his cup and shouted curses to draw the guards' attention. Two approached him as he ripped away his shirt from the burned skin, gulping big breaths. His chest burned like hell and real tears welled in his eyes. The guards escorted him out of the mess hall to the camp hospital on the guards' side of the compound.

Dr. Birk Lauterbach sat outside the clinic, smoking in the darkness, the glowing tip of his cigarette the only giveaway he was there. Overhead, a few stars began to show, eternal lights that would remain long after he was dead, which Falk hoped he would not be within the next hour. The guards quickly explained what happened, and the doctor waved them inside.

Falk followed Lauterbach down a brightly lit hallway.

Once inside the exam room, Lauterbach pointed to his table. "Get your shirt off and let's take a look." He spoke to the guards. "Thanks, men. We're okay here." They left the room. Through the frosted glass window, Falk saw their silhouettes just outside door.

Falk gingerly climbed onto the table and took off his coffee-stained shirt. The doctor opened metal drawers, pulled out a roll of bandaging wrap, small scissors, and white adhesive tape, and set them on the counter. He opened a cupboard and spoke in German with his back to Falk. "I know the coffee is just a notch above piss, but that doesn't mean you should waste it."

He let out a pained laugh. "You figured out my plan to rid the camp of that foul liquid."

Lauterbach chuckled, still rummaging through the cupboards.

Falk studied the room. He had memorized the layout of the hospital when he was on maintenance detail. His group painted the interior and exterior while his broken ribs healed. It was then, when he painted the exam room, he easily slipped the bottle of Syrup of Ipecac into his sock. Later, he hid it in his shaving kit, thinking he'd drink it to get a trip to the hospital as part of an earlier plan to escape. Now it tainted the mess hall's water supply. His heart pounded as he waited for the medicine to kick in.

While the doctor covered the burns with an amber salve, they talked about the soccer match the POWs played the night before. As long as they remained inside the barbed wire, the camp commander didn't care how the men occupied themselves after their workday ended. With evening now holding on longer, the soccer matches were nightly events, the guards and camp staff wagering on the outcomes.

Lauterbach finished bandaging his chest, and Falk reached for his clothes. Loud noises erupted in the foyer. The guards disappeared from outside the door and their footsteps slapped the floor as they headed to the front entrance.

"Can I use the toilet before I head back?" Falk asked.

Semi-distracted, Lauterbach waved Falk toward the toilets in an attached room as he rushed in the direction of the commotion.

With the others out of sight, Falk hurried back to the exam room and opened Lauterbach's personal closet. He grabbed a set of clothes, shoes, and a hat. Wearing another man's clothes needed to work one more time. His hand hovered over the wallet, hesitating. The doctor always treated him well, more like a friend than a prisoner, and they developed a level of trust he appreciated.

Hiam flashed through his mind. If he were to make one wrong right, it would be to retrieve his information from Pastor Graf and reach Washington, D.C. He grabbed the money from the wallet.

Walking through the examination room, he snagged surgical gloves and a scalpel from a leather case. He ducked into the toilet, quickly changed into Lauterbach's clothing and shoes, and slipped the money and scalpel into his pockets. Then he bunched his prisoner pants and shirt and shoved them into two trash cans, and closed the lids. He opened the door. Listening.

Outside, men were shouting about being poisoned, and the sounds of vomiting came from every direction. He donned the hat and left the building through the back door. The lights from the guard towers had stopped roving and were focused on the area in front of the clinic, where POWs were sprawled on the ground, or on their hands and knees, heaving.

A small stab of guilt struck. Good soldiers depended on each other. They trusted each other implicitly and upheld the duty to care and bring each other safely home. His water sabotage killed no one, but from the sound of things, the POWs were miserable.

In the deep velvet of a moonless night, Falk saluted the lone guard at the main gate, a man clearly distracted by the turmoil. The guard returned the salute. "Goodnight, doctor."

Falk, in his practiced English accent, replied, "Goodnight," and then simply walked out of the prison camp, the ease of it astounding him.

Once in the staff parking area, he pulled on door handles until he found one open with keys hidden under the driver's seat. He slid into a black Ford and quickly closed the door to douse the dome light. Fumbling in the darkness, his hands shook, but eventually he put the key into the ignition. When he turned it, nothing happened. Panic slowly swelled in his chest as he felt around the dash. At last, his fingers found the safety feature of the starter button. Once pressed, the car's engine rumbled to life.

Falk pulled away from the lot and pointed the car down the road, headlamps off. Tasting freedom brought a disorienting strangeness. Moments later, the camp out of sight, he turned on the lights, focusing his full attention on driving—and driving fast.

How long before Lauterbach discovered his missing belongings? With so many sick men to attend to, it could be hours, unless someone searched the toilet area and found Falk's clothing. Then they might soon be on his trail.

From the map of the logging area, Falk knew Sparks POW Camp rested in the center of several hundred kilometers of heavily forested mountains shot through with several rivers. To the south, hundreds of lakes dotted the lower half of the state. He needed to wind through the lake region and head south by southwest to reach Pastor Graf's town. If he pushed through the night, he might stay ahead of the law. The good news was German POWs were no longer viewed as dangerous fugitives by the locals since no escapee had ever harmed anyone. Stories in the papers claimed people even invited hungry escapees into their homes and served them a home-cooked meal before calling law enforcement.

The dense forest pressed in from both sides. Its pitch-black walls blurred past the car as his headlight beams illuminated the dark macadam. He didn't see or hear another car. When law enforcement was alerted, this would all change. They would search the main highway, leading to Sparks, and then fan out from there. Eventually, he'd ditch the car but not until he got as much distance out of it as he could.

His sights were set on a mountainous lake area dotted with cabins. He hoped it was still too early for the residents to open them for the upcoming summer season. He leaned into the drive, eyes alert to any hint of light on the road in front or behind him.

His escape seemed almost magical, charmed even. Although his break-out played in his head for weeks, it always seemed fraught with immediate danger. But this spur-of-the-moment planning paid off, and he hoped this next part would go as smoothly. He lightly touched the burns on his chest. A small inconvenience in the larger scheme of things.

It would be a mistake, of course, to let down his guard. He stared at the curving road, mentally running through the days ahead, and wondering about the unknown hurdles he would surely encounter.

-26-

IZAAK TAUBER

Płaszów Concentration Camp - April 1944

O n the wide flat piece of ground called Roll Call Square, Izaak shiv-ered next to Mama. Every morning for two months, the women and children in their barracks lined up here, so camp bosses could count them. Today, his barracks' count was 158 people. They lived in one terrible room, eight to ten of them shoved onto the board bed with Mama and him. Yesterday, the count was 170 people, but some became ill and went away, while others died in their beds.

Izaak leaned against Mama's side. He was tired all the time. Instead of hauling rocks all day, why couldn't the camp bosses use the workers to get more food? Anybody could see there wasn't enough to go around. Every day, they had a piece of bread, a soup that tasted like water with garbage in it, and sometimes a small piece of cheese. His pants hardly stayed up, and his cloth belt wore out, so Mama found an old leather belt from a huge pile of clothes behind the hospital and poked it to make new holes. They never saw their suitcases again. He desperately wanted to retrieve Papa's pipe and the drawing of his family. He prayed every day, and if God only answered one prayer for him, he wanted it to be that they'd see Papa soon.

Now instead of being sent directly to work with their crews, they re-mained standing after the count. The cold pinched at his face like a mean bully. Then some whispering started. The lady in charge of their barracks said she heard new people were coming to live in their camp, from a town called Kraków Ghetto. The new barracks was already full, so where would they all live?

One by one, people in his group stopped talking. He ducked down to get a better view between the women in front of him. There, six men and two women were being shoved to an open area in front of them. Izaak couldn't believe it. They were nuns and priests. The men wore black robes and stiff white collars at the front of their necks, and the women were in long, black dresses and big, white hats that sat on their heads like paper airplanes. They looked scared, and Izaak didn't blame them. Behind the guards, Commandant Goeth stood, wearing his white hat, holding his rifle. Something bad was about to happen.

The guards yelled, and the church men and women started undressing.

His mama pulled him away and turned his head into her coat. "Think of our house and draw it in your head," she whispered.

She put her hands over his ears, and he was startled by how cold and rough they felt. Her hands used to be soft and warm, especially when she rubbed his back as he fell asleep.

He brought up the image of their kitchen, full of light blue dishes and lots of food. That made his stomach hurt, so he changed his mind and focused on Papa's study. The smell of sweet pipe tobacco, of worn books and new newspapers, and Papa's hair tonic. Sometimes, the dark red curtains were pulled shut and the room turned into a warm cocoon with soft carpet and a comfy couch. Izaak often fell asleep there while Papa worked on his building plans.

Mama's hands finally warmed his ears, but still the sound of crying came through. He peeked sideways. The Catholics were walking back and forth, completely naked, pushed along by the whips and guns. They looked pale and skinny without their big layers of clothes. A mean woman guard now wore a white bird hat on her head and acted as if it were hers, smiling and moving it around like she was a famous movie star. Then, as she raised her whip, Izaak squeezed his eyes shut and returned to his invisible drawing.

Shortly after, a whistle blew, loud enough to startle Izaak back to reality. Everyone was walking in a line past Commandant Goeth. He randomly stopped people, and through interpreters, asked questions. The Catholic people were nowhere in sight, but one of the white hats had rolled away and lay crumpled and dirty in the square like a dead bird. When Mama took his hand, hers shook.

He studied her face. It was tight with the worried look she wore while they were on the terrible train.

"What, Mama?" he whispered.

In a low voice, she answered, "New people are arriving. They're selecting who needs to leave camp to make room."

Izaak wanted to be picked. Papa was not here, and everything in this camp was wrong and cruel. The line moved closer. Goeth directed people in three directions: back to the work areas, to the train that went to Auschwitz, or to another train whose engine pointed in the opposite direction.

He prayed for the Auschwitz train. Dahlia, Zev, and Aharon were already there, and because it was the Germans' favorite place to send people, there was a good chance Papa was there as well.

An old couple in front of Mama walked as if their knees were rusted, like his papa's wheelbarrow after Izaak left it out in the rain. Goeth motioned them to the Auschwitz cars. He studied Izaak and his mama when their turn came. Then he spoke, and the man who spoke Dutch translated, "What percentage Jew are you?"

Mama replied in a small voice, "I am not Jewish, and my son is Mischling."

Goeth turned his eyes to Izaak. He squeezed his eyebrows together with the same look older people use when they didn't want young children around them. "How old is your son?"

"He's eight, but a hard worker."

The commandant made a snorting sound, like a horse.

Izaak grew afraid that being a hard worker was not enough to get on the trains. He needed to do something quick. He pulled the folded sketch of his papa, his only possession, from his shirt pocket where he carried it all the time. It was frayed and smudged. He opened it, and as he held it up, he noticed the pencil lines were smeared. His papa grew blurrier every day.

"I draw like this."

Goeth laughed at the translation and said something to a guard standing nearby. The guard leaned in to study the picture. His eyebrows rose like upside-down soup bowls, and he spoke to the commandant.

Seconds passed. The cold seemed to make Mama's whole body shake harder as they waited.

Finally, Goeth pointed to the train cars, the one with the engine pointing the opposite way Izaak wanted to go. "Artists go to Terezín," he said.

Izaak's weak legs moved faster than normal. Since they had nothing to collect from their barracks, he tugged Mama to the train. *Artists go to Terezín.* The mean commandant called him an artist. Would they ask him to draw portraits? He was getting better with those. Or maybe sketch pictures of people who were missing so they could be found? That would be hard to draw, with someone just telling him what a person looked like, but he would try. What mattered was they were leaving this horrible place.

Mama stumbled and dropped to her knees.

"Mama!"

She stayed there with her eyes shut. His throat closed. What happened to her? They had to get out of here, but he wasn't strong enough to help her stand. He shook her shoulder. It was small and bony, not soft like it used to be.

Slowly, she opened her eyes, and even now when she was the most tired, she still saved a smile for him. "I'm okay, love." Her voice was so soft he barely heard it.

He tugged her arm, and she stood. He needed to keep her happy, to get her excited about leaving. "The soldier saw my picture. He said I was an artist!" Then he waved the drawing in front of her eyes again even though she'd seen it a thousand times.

Mama nodded slowly as she steadied herself, one hand on his shoulder. "You are, sweet boy."

"We're going to a new place." Terezín didn't sound fancy at all and no one had talked about it like they talked about Auschwitz. "It must be better than this place if artists live there."

They boarded the train, once again standing because there were no seats. He fitted himself against Mama's side and wrapped his arms around her. This time when the guards closed the door, there weren't as many people in their car, and they found space on the floor to sit. He closed his eyes and thought of what it would be like to be a real artist. The moon-shaped man from Westerbork encouraged him to show his picture to guards to get special treatment, but it hadn't worked in all these months. He'd been angry with Abraham for giving him false hope. Maybe it hadn't been the right time until now. He and Mama were finally going to a place that had to be better. And always on his mind, a place where someone might know where Papa was.

-27-

HERBERT MÜLLER

Ellis Island, New York Harbor - April 1944

S taring through the barbed wire, Herbert huddled next to Otto, fending off a cold wind as they studied the ferry carrying Jutta and the children. Three months since his arrest, and he would finally hold his family close again. In eighteen years of marriage, he and Jutta were never apart for more than two days at a time, and those were when he went on annual hunting trips with the local sportsman lodge. When this was over, would he be accepted back into his community or still thought to be a criminal? And they might have to find a new church. It was hard to see the future through smeared hopes. All that mattered in the end was he had his family.

He and Otto hurried inside the complex to the visitation area.

And there they were, walking through the tunnel entryway. His smile faded when he noticed how tired they looked, even shell-shocked. Alfred's scowl deepened when guards searched them and their packages.

What did Jutta need to tell him? He hoped she'd found a way to appease the FBI's suspicions. Or perhaps she knew of other German-Americans who had already returned home.

Moments later, as they entered the grand hallway, he nearly ran to them, his hip shooting with pain he simply ignored. Otto was close behind. Herbert wrapped them in his arms, an embrace that needed to make up for their time apart but barely began to soothe his lonely heart. Otto moved in for his hug. Jutta and the children would notice Otto's decline, his stooped appearance, weaker voice.

Jutta stepped back to show him a basket of baked goods. Her eyes crinkled at the corners as she gave him that shy smile he fell for all those years ago.

"These will put meat back on your bones, Herbert. You are so thin now."

He hadn't told them about how overcrowded Ellis had become in the last month. Thanks to the FBI's frenetic arrests along the East Coast, the camp doubled in size. Food portions were cut, and he had already punched two new holes in his belt.

Herbert studied Alfred. How had his son grown taller in such a short time? Frieda twirled one of her braids, although they were shorter now, and she looked more grown up.

Guards patrolled the busy room, listening to conversations. Herbert caught one eyeing Frieda and his eyes flared with rage. How dare they ogle his young daughter? He stepped to her and pulled her close, shooting a challenging look back at the man.

"Creep," Alfred whispered. He'd also seen the guard's interest in Frieda. His face bunched with anger. He looked around and his gaze stalled on the barred windows. "This is a prison."

Herbert leaned closer and offered a reassuring but counterfeit smile. He didn't need Alfred creating a scene. He reached for his son's clenched fist and gently squeezed until he relaxed. The camp officials wouldn't hesitate to arrest another potential enemy of the United States. "Let's enjoy this time. We've missed you all so much."

Otto nodded and turned to Frieda. "You . . . more beautiful over time."

"Thank you, Grandfather." She blushed before hugging him again.

"Your studies good?" Otto asked Alfred.

"School is . . . stressful." Frustrated, he threw up his hands. "I'm not going to lie. Half of our friends won't talk to us."

Herbert studied his children. Frieda kept her arms wrapped tightly around her body while Alfred rubbed his thighs with his fists.

"Mary Parker passed around a note asking who thought I was a Nazi," Frieda said, her voice barely audible. "Half the class signed it." Her lips quivered.

Herbert's blood pounded in his ears. How dare others treat his American children this way! Was this what Jutta couldn't put in writing? His chest tightened. Frieda and Alfred were good students, kind and thoughtful young adults. Even though Alfred was a hothead, he was generous to a fault.

"Are the teachers aware of this?" Herbert bent closer.

"Mrs. Nagle tore it up and lectured the class on acceptance," Frieda said. "It's better now, so don't worry." She spun a braid around her finger.

"I'm sorry," Herbert said, sadness weighing heavy on his heart. His German lineage had cursed his children, and one look at his father, revealed Otto cycled through the same conclusion.

He turned to Alfred, eager to come up with a positive subject. "How's the basketball team looking? Are we in for a championship year?"

Alfred glanced at his mother, who ever so slightly shook her head, but Herbert caught the movement. "Okay. What aren't you telling me?"

She hesitated before speaking. "He was cut from the team. Some parents complained to Coach McCarthy. He told me he had no choice." She offered a tentative smile. "He'll try out next season... after you're all home."

"I'm not sure I want to." Alfred's eyes flared with anger.

Sports meant everything to him, and he was popular because he excelled in all of them. Had been popular.

"I'm sorry, son." Herbert scrubbed his hands over his face and then arranged it into what he trusted was an optimistic expression. It was then he noticed tiny wrinkles around Jutta's eyes he'd never seen before. She must not be sleeping any better than he was. "How are you holding up, dear?"

She took his hand and squeezed. "First, tell us what it is like here. We need to know you both are safe."

"We, are safe," Otto nodded. "And getting, closer to, our review date."

"True," Herbert added. "This place runs like a small community. A bit crowded but organized. The men and boys sleep in the Grand Hall you passed through, and the women and children are down another corridor in smaller rooms."

Jutta's forehead wrinkled. "Families have been arrested? Children, too?" Her voice was higher than usual. Flustered.

"Not arrested. Some choose to join their husbands and fathers if the appeal date drags on."

Jutta seemed to process that while Alfred asked, "Are you in danger?"

"No. We've heard of some petty theft or stealing from the canteen, but nothing dangerous."

There was still an undercurrent of secrecy from his wife and children. "Okay, family. Fact Time. What is it you came here to tell me?"

Jutta studied her hands before speaking. "Our bank account is frozen. But we'll get jobs until it's available again."

The floor seemed to shift under his feet. He shook away some momentary dizziness. Twelve thousand dollars and some change that he scrimped and saved for years to amass. "You've talked to Mr. Fassbinder at the bank? Remind him we supply wheat for his wife's bakery," he said. "I mean what's he thinking? It affects him, too, if he tries to put us out of business."

"It's the government, dear. Not Mr. Fassbinder."

Herbert was quiet for a moment. Otto's face had paled. His father's American dream, along with decades of hard work, was on the line. "There's two hundred dollars hidden in the mill. In the drill bit box."

"Thank you," Jutta whispered.

"We'll be all right, Father. I'm clearing snow," Alfred said, "and hauling water for the Jenkins family."

Frieda nodded. "I'm tending the Abrams' four children. We're making enough for food and bills."

"And we're working to get you back home, Herbert." Jutta smoothed her skirt, a nervous habit he never pointed out because he thought it endearing. "Civil rights lawyers offered to help defend you, but they're overwhelmed. There were ten thousand arrests...with more to come."

"Ten thousand?" Herbert let out a low whistle. Of course, the lawyers were busy. And what if this were just a way for lawyers to take advantage of people desperate for help? "Have you met these attorneys?"

Alfred spoke. "They came to the house. Word spreads fast."

"Do you think we can trust them?"

"They need four hundred dollars to get started," Jutta said.

No wonder the government froze their bank account. It limited his ability to obtain legal representation. The government was way ahead of him. He silently swore and straightened against all the disheartening news and then bent closer. "Contact any neighbors who are still speaking to us. See if they want to buy the tractor"—he turned to Alfred—"I'm sorry, son. That means you'll be shoveling by hand."

"I can do that." Alfred straightened his back, ready to prove himself.

"Sell my accordion," Otto said, "und Anni's antique dolls. They have value."

Jutta shook her head. "No. Those things mean too much to you, Pops. And, Herbert… you'll need the tractor when you get home. We're earning the money. I've already talked to some of the business owners in town. They'll pay me to clean their stores after-hours."

Herbert clenched his fists and pushed them together. Jutta would not be reduced to scrubbing floors. At his sudden movement, the guards stepped closer. He took in a long breath to calm down.

"You will do no such thing, Jutta. Sell these things as we've asked. They will mean nothing to us if we're never to come home again."

~28~

WILHELM FALK

Green Mountains, Vermont - May 1944

The southwestern Vermont forest Falk traveled through teemed with ancient oaks and towering pines. The living giants, with knotted arms, inspired a sense of awe. But most important, they provided good cover. The grasses and wild flowers in the sparse meadows were in full spring blush. Areas he avoided but enjoyed their scents from the edges of the woods.

With the anonymity of driving a common black Ford on the main road, Falk traveled over three hundred kilometers his first night. Before dawn, he ditched it over a long embankment near Whitingham, Vermont, and then covered it with branches. Nearby, he swam almost one kilometer through the frigid Harriman Reservoir, knowing that tracking dogs would lose his scent at the water's edge. He thanked the icy waters of the Baltic Sea of his youth for preparing him for the frigid swim. Not only in crossing the reservoir but also a half-dozen snowmelt rivers so far.

Today, he left an unoccupied cabin in the lower hills. While there, he'd restocked his stolen rucksack with food and fresh clothing before heading for the higher peaks. According to a map he found two days earlier in another cabin, the Green Mountains were the last rugged stretch before he would reach the eastern border of New York.

Lauterbach's clothing had long since been shed and buried. Today, he wore a workman's outfit—heavy boots and tan canvas coveralls. He wished he'd found clothing with green forest tones, but thieves couldn't be choosy. In his pack, he stowed blue trousers and a matching shirt. Something to change into when closer to civilization.

So far, he neither saw nor heard signs of a search. If they cared about capturing him, the FBI would try to figure out where Klaus Stern headed. They'd first check to see if Stern had family or other connections in the United States.

Once he left the forest, he guessed he had three, maybe four, days of traversing rural farm communities before reaching Pastor Graf. He smiled, imagining the reunion with his longtime friend. More than that, six long months after he'd traded uniforms with Stern, he could finally achieve his goal. He'd grab his package of information and have Graf drive him to Washington, D.C.

He climbed around a jumble of boulders and sat down to rest. Something stirred behind him, and the overhead orchestra of birdsongs suddenly stopped. He tensed. A large bird, possibly a crow, took to the sky in a flash of gunmetal black, turning in a slow circle, perhaps to better assess him. Then, catching a warm thermal, the bird rose and flew off.

The scent from the crushed leaves of wild basil reached his nose, making him hunger for Ilse's wild mushroom and basil soup. He missed her—and his sons—terribly.

Falk first noticed Ilse in 1930 when he was twenty. He was touring the Romanesque church ruins outside Bad Hersfeld and also attending the Lutheran World Convention at Eichhof Castle. Both his and Ilse's youth organizations were on a summer tour, and stopped to visit the spot where Martin Luther once preached as he traveled through Hessen in 1552.

A friend was taking Ilse's photograph against an ancient rock wall. The valley breezes lifted her light brown hair off her neck, and she held her hat with one hand to keep it from blowing away. She was laughing, an intoxicating sound.

He approached her friend and asked if he might take a photo of the two of them together. Shortly after, she gave him her name and phone number. She was seventeen and just graduated from school. A kind, yet spunky girl. Irresistible.

Six months later they married, and within a year, Hans was born. Two years later, she gave birth to Dietrich. They made big plans to travel around Europe, to show their sons different cultures. They even talked of someday seeing America.

When he delivered his information to the most powerful men in this country, he would ask that his family be allowed to immigrate to the United States. They'd understand that a man who committed treason must protect his family. Nazis would eagerly question or imprison family members, German heritage be damned, if they thought the family was somehow involved. He'd purposefully kept Ilse in the dark about all his plans.

He scanned the valley below. According to the map, he was looking at the northwestern corner of Massachusetts and the Taconic Ridge State Forest bridging the border into New York. Just past the forest lay Troy.

The trail to the valley below was precipitous, a rocky face with steep inclines. The mountains seemed to fulfill a purpose, laid out like a giant amphitheater. Here and there, ribbons of deep blue sliced the lush greenery, the high cascading waterfalls of clean snowmelt reaching the townsfolk below.

Falk usually traveled after dark, but tonight he'd find a place on the mountaintop to sleep and then pick his way down at first light. He backed off the rocky escarpment and followed a moss-carpeted trail into a dense stand of maples. The leafy canopy allowed only flashes of sunlight onto the spongy floor, the perfect cover from a spotter plane. He bent and ducked under crisscrossing branches, eventually discovering a perfect hiding spot. Covered and surrounded by heavy limbs, the natural enclosure was three meters long. Ferns spread a little over a meter in each direction. He made a bed under them where he would sleep, safely hidden away.

From the rucksack, he took out a pack of dried meat and a small jar of honey and ate it, dipping the meat into the sweet sticky goo.

The sky faded to twilight, and the brightest stars appeared between the branches. He crawled under the awning of ferns and leveled his bed. Then he lay on his back surrounded by funereal silence. Nothing stirred the underbrush, nothing buzzed, nothing sang.

Fireflies hovered like sparks from a campfire in the deep dusk, just chips of light that disappeared between blinks.

He closed his eyes, but sleep eluded him.

Tangled in dark emotions, he lay on his spongy bed ruminating about the complexity of the hatred he harbored. He loved the Germany where he grew up, but despised what it became. A country that took it upon itself to eradicate all races they considered inferior. A madman's decree. A singular decision that entire segments of the populace were no longer worthy to live. He had an enduring love for his homeland but had learned to hate her sons.

And it was funny how forms of hatred sprang into existence only after they were named. Eugenics. Ethnic cleansing. Extermination. Before, in other parts of the world, when he heard those words, sadly they were mere letters slung together around the tears and deaths of others.

Cruelty now stalked the European continent, camouflaged in military uniforms. Surely, the Devil raised his hand and asked, "Who is with me?" and thousands rushed to the cause. The part he couldn't wrap his head around was how any military personnel who saw what was really happening—and those numbers increased as the war lingered—could stomach the horrors. Why hadn't the generals remained organized and followed through with their desire to take out Hitler? This madness would all be over by now.

Images of Hiam invaded his thoughts.

Before the boy disappeared from the train platform, he caught the attention of Dr. Josef Mengele. Mengele's genetic interests were cited at every SS gathering. Himmler pinned great expectations on the outcomes of Mengele's experiments. The doctor used Auschwitz for his anthropological research on heredity. Daily, he met the trains and selected his favorite types of children—sets of twins his first choice. He housed them together, providing better food and living conditions. The children had a playground and activities. And Mengele, a handsome, meticulously dressed man, did not instill fear in them. When the doctor visited the children, he introduced himself as "Uncle Josef" and offered sweets. This was the best thing that happened to these children since they were torn from their homelands.

But deep down, Mengele was a coldhearted Jew-hater. He experimented on the twins, hoping to identify the elusive genetic doubling factor that one day could be used to replicate the perfect German.

When Falk returned to check on Hiam and found him gone, he threatened the prisoner assigned to care for Mengele's children. The prisoner, rather than take a bullet to his head, explained what happened to Hiam.

They brought the child to live with other selected children in Mengele's special dormitory because of his uniquely-colored eyes. He lived there for a good two months until Mengele injected dye and other chemicals into Hiam's eyes to see if they would change color. Hiam went blind, and having served his purpose, was shot to death.

Falk barely made it out of Auschwitz that day. His legs trembled uncontrollably as he imagined the pain Hiam suffered. It was all he could do not to pull his Walther and shoot every guard he passed. Instead, he vowed to get out of the Wehrmacht and do something to stop the brutality.

A hoot owl sounded in the distance and then something rustled nearby in the leaves. Something small. He stared up through a slit in the ferns to where silvery stars lit the clear night sky. At first, the enormity of his task overwhelmed him. He was one man, and not a wholly innocent one at that. But with the time he had left in the world, he wanted more than anything to know Mengele died a slow, horrible death, and that the exterminations had ended.

-29-

IZAAK TAUBER

Terezín Concentration Camp, Czechoslovakia - May 1944

M ama called their latest home in Terezín the Upper Fortress. Workers sometimes crossed the Ohre River to the Lower Fortress, but he didn't know much about that place. Fortress meant a safe place, and so far, this town seemed safe from mean men like Commandant Goeth but not protected from the fleas and lice which followed them there three weeks earlier.

Upon arrival, they were allowed to change out of the dirty, striped clothes into a clean set of used clothing. Izaak didn't know what had happened to the boy who used to wear the pants and shirt he now wore. To push away bad possibilities, he drew the boy in his head, imagining he had returned home. He decided he was a farmer's son and surrounded by sheep and cows which were at a white fence to greet him.

Terezín was a whole village hidden on top of the slight hill with a tall-steepled church. Long yellow-brick buildings with red roofs were neatly laid out along the wide streets lined with large trees, just getting their full summer leaves. The town had walls around it and a grassy moat, like in stories about castles and dragons. He counted over two hundred houses in the village. He and Mama lived in a part of the city renamed The Ghetto, in one of eleven soldier barracks. Theirs was named Dresden, a building so big it filled a whole block, with an open courtyard in the center where he played with other children.

They shared their room with thirty other people. This time there were no bunk beds, but mattresses laid out on the floor. A comfort he'd nearly forgotten about after all their nights on wooden-board beds. At night, rats scurried over him, but they never stopped to bite, so he stopped flinching every time he felt their tiny feet on his arms or head. The windows in the room opened to let in fresh air, another luxury.

Everyone had a job, but the effort was nothing like hauling headstones or reburying bodies. Izaak's job was to work in the vegetable gardens in the wide moat with other children under age ten. They pulled weeds and dug the dirt to make it soft for planting. Being outside was wonderful, and the matron in charge of his group made games out of the job, or created sing-along times even though they all spoke different languages.

Today, the long black trains were leaving with the children who didn't know where their mamas and papas were, like Abel who was Izaak's friend in his art class. Just before Abel climbed the steps into the windowless coach, he waved goodbye. He hoped Abel found his mama and papa at the next camp.

He'd finished work not long ago as the sun dropped behind the trees. After the train left, he returned to his room in Dresden and was surprised to find only six people there, not thirty. Suddenly, he was nervous. The town seemed extra quiet outside the window as he sat on their straw mattress and waited for Mama to come home from the hospital. She no longer helped deliver babies, mainly because not many women were pregnant anymore.

Mama looked tired as she entered their room, carrying a stack of clothes. She saw him and smiled. "Nice and clean for you." Her job in the hospital laundry room, the only building with hot water, let her wash the fleas and lice out of their clothes every day. Izaak pulled on clean pants and a shirt as she asked him about his day.

"Matron Maria took us for a walk around town before we worked in the gardens. She pointed out her city, a small speck on the horizon, and said it was called Prague."

His mama smiled. "I've heard it's beautiful."

"But the Germans got there, too. Matron Maria said they sent many families here to live."

Mama set the clothes next to their mattresses and pulled him close and hugged him. "We will hear many sad stories. But remember, we're here together, love, and that's what matters." Her hip bone dug into his head, but he didn't complain even though she wasn't as soft as she used to be.

An hour later, Izaak and Mama walked with their house group to the evening meal in a building that used to be a dress factory. Sewing machines were pushed into dark corners, along with rows of half-made cloth bodies balanced on metal poles. The headless forms frightened him as they lurked in the gloomy edges of the room. He hated the idea he was afraid of so many things that never bothered him before, like men in uniforms with lots of medals, or the sound of heavy boots walking fast. To take his mind off the headless bodies, he studied the items he carried—a food voucher, a bowl, and a spoon.

Long tables filled the center of the room and big pots of soup waited along one wall. In line, Mama talked to another Dutch woman named Cornelia. Everyone in Ghetto wore yellow stars, but they all talked differently. He and Mama learned which ladies spoke Dutch, so they had people to talk to.

Cornelia looked older than Mama. Her two daughters lived in the girls' house called Heim L410 because they were over age ten. Once again, Izaak was glad he was only eight and not separated from Mama.

"You've been here for months," Mama said to Cornelia. "Have you had any contact with the men in the Lower Fortress?"

There were more men? Only a few men worked in the Upper Fortress, but could it be that Papa was working down below? He tugged on Mama's dress. Why hadn't she mentioned this before?

"They're political prisoners"—Cornelia lowered her voice—"used in mining and other dangerous jobs."

Mama ignored Izaak's tugging. "But I heard there are professionals, men with skills and talents deliberately sent here."

Cornelia made a snorting noise and laughed, but her next words didn't seem all that funny. "Some of the best composers, artists, and tailors are here to entertain or work for the SS. It's like they had a spare-your-favorite-Jew day and brought them here."

"I've noticed," Mama said.

When they reached the food servers, Izaak accepted a slice of bread and a scoop of potato soup. It was hard to have to wait to spoon the few pieces of vegetables into his mouth. Hundreds of people ate together at long tables, but no one talked during this time. The room fell into an important silence like inside a synagogue, but here, eating replaced ritual prayers.

He wanted to know if his papa could be in the Lower Fortress. Maybe he was chosen on favorite-Jew day. Mama put down her spoon and Izaak tapped her arm to ask his question, but at that moment, the man in charge of the Council of Elders stood and banged a metal cup against a post. Everyone turned his way as he spoke.

Elder Eppstein was tall, and his head was not shaven like the other older boys and men.

"The council and I bring good news. The living conditions here are about to change. The commandant, SS-Sturmbannführer Karl Rahm, has ordered this Upper Fortress to be cleaned from top to bottom. Many great improvements will be made. We will all contribute to the beautification of this once great city. We need painters, people to plant flowers and shrubs, and men and boys to repair the buildings, add electricity, and get the plumbing working."

As the message was repeated in other languages, people looked at each other with surprised "could-it-be-true?" eyes. Izaak hoped the Germans weren't playing a cruel joke.

Then Elder Eppstein said something that made Izaak sit up straight.

"The commandant wants children's artwork on the walls, he wants a soccer field, a café, a store, and there will be concerts and plays. If you have talent in these areas, please report to me."

After living in two bad camps before this, he didn't trust this would really happen. The Germans never did anything nice to help the Jews. In fact, it seemed they spent a lot of time planning how to make their lives more miserable. Hopefully, he and Mama and the other people would get to stay when the town was all fixed up, and that it wasn't for Germans. He needed to be positive. Terezín was already so much better than Westerbork or Płaszów.

He'd volunteer to draw pictures. They'd shop at a real store. When he worked in the moat, he'd get brave and climb the grassy ramparts to have a peek at the Lower Fortress. Tomorrow, if he got a chance while in the gardens, he would wave like crazy to the men below. If his papa was there he would see Izaak and know where to find them.

-30-

HERBERT MÜLLER

Ellis Island, New York Harbor - May 1944

Herbert sealed his letter to the Acting Assistant Commissioner for Alien Control, asking that his and his father's reviews be expedited. He reiterated the facts of his case, pointing out he and his family were taxpaying Americans with no contact with Germans in Europe since the war broke out. He pleaded for a quick return to his home, emphasizing the valuable service his gristmill provided to the local farmers, and hence, the war effort.

After delivering the letter to the censorship office, he wandered the grounds. Someone owned a radio and music washed over the yard. Frank Sinatra, Tommy Dorsey, and the Mills Brothers ruled the airwaves. Their lyrics of innocent love and walks in the moonlight and, "Oh, What a Beautiful Morning," all made him irritable, feel empty inside. The most popular song was an oldie from Cole Porter. The men gathered in groups and sang "Don't Fence Me In," a song they all related to and somehow hoped would not be their fate much longer.

In Jutta's recent letter, she wrote his family saved thirty dollars to help with the additional two hundred a piece they needed to hire civil rights attorneys. Not that he was bitter. The fact they'd saved thirty dollars showed frugality on their part. But at that rate, they'd be working their odd jobs for another year, and in that time, the mill would close. They'd lose everything. He never showed Alfred how to work the massive grinding stones, or talked to him about the proper storage of grain and corn. Had never needed Jutta to deal with the books or finances, or learn how he negotiated prices each year with farmers. Jutta wrote they'd purchased several dozen chickens and were selling eggs, but that wouldn't even pay the property taxes.

He couldn't imagine he'd be here a year. Another month at most. If the headlines in the papers were believable, the Allies had the upper hand in Europe. Perhaps the war was nearly over. Until then, his own little war with his country dragged on. The wheels of justice barely turned, or were perhaps purposefully rusted in place.

A rainstorm that moved through earlier left brown water pouring into the gutters from the roofs. Herbert sidestepped the cigarette butts and other trash, floating in the stream alongside the buildings, and headed for the far fence where Pastor Graf stood.

"Herbert"—Graf stuck out his hand and smiled—"breathe deeply. Don't you just love how it smells after the rain?"

"I do." He returned Graf's smile. It would be nice to have a single grain of the pastor's ability to remain content while his future was being negotiated. "Any news of the world?"

"Hitler's still alive."

"That's unfortunate." It might be evil to wish someone dead, but the dictator's war had reached Herbert's living room, making it personal.

"But the Allies have won back most of Italy." Graf's eyes crinkled at the edges. The man looked like a Coca-Cola Santa Claus, with a hint of pink in his cheeks.

"So we hang on, waiting?"

Graf nodded. "A ferry left this morning with a large group of older men and women, who volunteered to repatriate to Germany. Sounded like they'd never become citizens. The commander announced it's an option for all of us."

"I'll stay. My family is pretty Americanized." Besides, where would they go in Germany? Their connections to relatives barely existed these last years.

"I imagine Germany is no place to be right now."

Later, he sat on a bench outside the infirmary. His father experienced a dizzy spell and asked to see a doctor. Otto appeared despondent these last few days, and Herbert blamed it on the ongoing melancholy over their stagnant situation. Daily, if not hourly, Herbert fought off the gloom of despair as he tried to keep his thoughts positive. Otto shouldered the unwarranted blame for what happened to them, for why they were here in the first place. Herbert pointed his daggers of blame to the justice department.

The doctor waved him into the examination room, and although the specialist's face was a mask of seriousness, Herbert wasn't ready for the medical diagnosis. "Your father had a slight heart attack."

Shock ripped through him as he processed the words. Otto needed to be transported to a real hospital. "When can he be transferred?" His lips were going numb as the blood drained from them.

"He'll be treated here, of course"—the doctor fiddled with his stethoscope—"We have good medical care."

"I have the medication, son." Otto sat on the examination table in his shorts and undershirt. He appeared weak and shrunken. His legs dangled over the side of the table, like thin white sticks, fragile, breakable.

Herbert moved to his side, his stomach jittery, worry blurring his thoughts. He reached for the bottle in Otto's hand and squinted to read the words. "What did they give you?" They knew nothing about his father's medical history.

"Nitroglycerin pills," the doctor said, "and we will monitor him overnight."

"My father needs to be home and done with all of these worries." Their situation came into sharp focus. It was bad enough they were prisoners for no good cause, but a critical health problem changed everything. The government's game of holding them as enemy suspects needed to end now.

"Surely he qualifies to be freed to seek proper care."

"Our care is no different than at any other civilian hospital." The doctor's nostrils flared, and his eyes closed to slits.

The taste in Herbert's mouth was sour. Arguing with one of the island's keeper of the keys would get him nowhere. He needed to get outside help. Then he turned his back to the doctor.

"Pops, I'll bring your shaving kit and bed clothes. And our playing cards. I plan on spending the night in your room."

He passed the doctor on the way out of the room.

"And no one is going to stop me."

His father slept through the night, but Herbert didn't fare as well. The folding wooden chair the hospital staff provided was impossible to do more than nod off in. Besides, every change in Otto's breathing threw Herbert into a raging panic. Had his father always snored and then suddenly stopped breathing, and after several long moments, breathe again?

Daylight brightened the window. He left Otto sitting in bed, eating a light breakfast of oatmeal and fruit Herbert had brought him and followed an MP through the corridors of the business building. He'd requested a meeting with Admiral Cahoon, and was shocked when a message arrived in Otto's room, saying Cahoon would receive him. Now he was getting somewhere. The doctor must have spoken to the upper Coast Guard brass about Otto's health.

"Wait here," the escort said, indicating the carpeted waiting area with three green leather upholstered chairs.

He sank into one, the padding nothing short of luxurious compared to the wooden slats he'd sat on all night. He rubbed his aching hip, the joint always a gauge of how rested he was, or as of late, how tired.

An interior door with a frosted-glass pane opened and the escort waited there. "The admiral will see you now." He motioned for Herbert to enter.

Herbert tried not to limp as he crossed the room, but today it took a few steps to get his joints functioning. The interior of the room was decorated with solid pieces of furniture, from large bookcases to a sizeable desk. A realistic oil portrait of President Roosevelt hung on the wall behind the desk, and the American flag was on a brass stand in the corner. A splash of patriotism in the confines of a yellow cinderblock room.

"Thank you for seeing me, sir." Herbert remained standing.

The admiral's dark hair was buzzed short, and his jowls spilled over the collar of his white shirt under his blue bedecked uniform. His face was neutral, a practiced look if Herbert had ever seen one. "Have a seat."

Herbert sat and waited as he studied the desktop. Besides the black phone on one corner, there was one other ornamental piece. A model of a Coast Guard cutter atop a goldtone pole on a wooden base. The inscription on the side of the base read, United States Lighthouse Service, 1790 to 1914.

Cahoon answered the question Herbert was about to ask. "The Lighthouse Service became the Coast Guard in 1915."

"I didn't know that." But he wasn't here for a history lesson. "If you don't mind, sir. I'd like to talk about my father. I'm sure you've heard he had a heart attack yesterday."

"I did"—he shifted his lower jaw side to side—"I was informed he is doing well."

"For the time being. He is frail, an old man." Herbert's throat tightened, and he quickly cleared it. "We plead with you to let us return home. When we are called for a rehearing, you know where to find us." His rehearsed words sounded like a sane request. Cahoon must understand that although he and Otto were scooped up in the enemy-alien net, not everyone in custody was guilty.

When Cahoon smiled, it was nothing more than a tight red line where his mouth had been. He planted his elbows on the desk and steepled his fingers in front of his mouth, studying Herbert over them.

Herbert wasn't going to beg any further. He'd stated his request, and he'd outwait the man's reply.

"The Duke of Wellington said, 'The whole art of war consists of guessing at what is on the other side of the hill.'" He dropped his hands to the desk. "He defeated Napoleon."

He didn't care if the duke defeated the Devil. "If this in any way relates to my family, sir, what do you see on the other side of the hill for us?"

Cahoon smiled wider this time, reducing his eyes to small slits with black pearls in the center. "I contacted the hearing board about your request to be reunited with your family."

Finally. He'd waited five long months to get them to answer anything.

"Well? What did they say?" If the man's answer included a history lesson, he would lose it.

"It was denied for both you and your father."

Denied? A wave of dizziness hit him as words failed. Cahoon's face registered no sympathy. Herbert shifted his gaze to view the painting of the president, the man who ruined his life with his executive order. Something in his chest dropped. Maybe he was having a heart attack. Did he even care? He might as well be dead for all the support he gave his family.

"You and your father will remain in this internment camp, and as stated before, you will each receive an impartial and just hearing. All alleged enemies are granted that, although it takes time."

Otto might not have time. "Could my father be released, and I will stay? It's pretty clear he's no danger to anyone."

"No. But to address your family's difficulties—"

"What difficulties are you talking about? What have you heard?"

In last week's letter, Jutta said someone spray-painted "Nazi" in five-foot-high letters on the side of the mill. Then, Alfred had a difficult time getting anyone to help paint over it until their Lutheran pastor and his son showed up.

"Your son was in a fight with some boys at school."

Alfred had finally lost control. Herbert wasn't surprised. "They've been harassing him and my daughter. How far can one kid get pushed before he pushes back?"

"When the sheriff came, your son threw a punch."

"That can't be right." Alfred knew better than to disrespect law enforcement no matter how angry he became. "Let me call home and talk to him."

"He's sitting in jail."

His world spiraled down into a pool of his worst fears. His son was jailed? "He's fifteen!" He pounded his fist on the desk. "And the sheriff's nephew is one of the boys who has been messing with my family and destroying our property."

"Your son's old enough." Cahoon looked at his expensive watch. "Boys his age have joined up and are off fighting."

"Not legally." Did the man seriously believe Alfred should go to war?

"No. But your son isn't exactly following the law either." He drew in a long breath. "Your family is in dire straits, Mr. Müller. Your bank accounts are frozen, and you will soon lose your assets."

Because of you and your cronies, he wanted to scream. "They have jobs."

"Well, we have an offer."

"I'm sure you do. You guys have everything worked out, whether it hurts a fellow American or not."

Cahoon cocked his eyebrow. "Your wife and children may secure your property with a trusted friend and then they can join you here on Ellis Island. You'll be together." He raised his hands as if to say, See? Isn't this a great idea? "There is a larger camp in Texas, Crystal City, that's more of a family camp. We would work on transferring you all there."

He tried to picture his family in this hellhole, or any other internment camp. Selfishly, he'd be with them again, which was everything he prayed for. But to take them away from a comfortable home to a crowded, often smelly, living arrangement? Unacceptable.

"The assault charges against your son will be dropped, and we will pay for your family's transportation."

With that, the rational part of his brain argued in favor of bringing them here. He had to get Alfred out of jail first and foremost. Who knew what havoc the angry boy might do there if he felt trapped? School was almost out for the year, and the children were reticent about attending anyway. There was a school on Ellis, and if they were here, he would at least know they were safe—and together. He was genuinely worried what more might occur if his family stayed in their home. "May I call my wife?"

The admiral nodded to the military escort. "Take Mr. Müller into the next office and let him make his call." He stood and absently ran his fingers over the outline of the fancy model ship. "You'll have five minutes."

Once in the adjoining office, Herbert tried to control the tremor in his finger and spun the phone dial, the guard standing just three feet away. He hadn't heard Jutta's voice in a month since their three-hour visit on the island. When she said hello, he felt his insides melt. God, he missed her!

"Herbert?" Her voice held disbelief. "Have you been released?"

"Honey. I just heard about Alfred. Is he still in jail?"

She was quiet and his heart beat faster. What else had happened? It was then he heard her quiet sobs. "He will be home tomorrow. We posted bail. Twelve dollars."

"That's great, Jutta." His grip on the phone tightened. He should be home helping Jutta through this field of landmines. "I got an offer today that I want to discuss with you." He explained that he and Otto still had no hearing date, but there was a bigger, hopefully better, camp in Texas they could all stay in until the war ended.

"You're saying we should just leave things?" She sounded composed but surprised.

He was stunned he was even thinking about this, but they'd be together and that felt like the right thing to do. "By all accounts, the war is winding down so I don't think this will be for long. It doesn't feel safe there anymore, and I'd rather have you all with me. I mean with us." He needed to tell her about Otto's health but would wait.

"Otto agrees, too?"

"Yes." A little lie since Otto had not heard the offer. "And the government will pay to get you here...What do you think?"

"We miss you so much." She choked on a sob. "And it's been hard here, Herbert. Everyone treats us like we've murdered someone. We might as well leave so they can rest easy."

He swallowed hard. They were coming. "Pack up the valuables and ask Pastor Huber to store them for us. Give the chickens to Mrs. Mason." She was the widow whose boys attacked Herbert and Otto six months earlier. He didn't know why he kept trying to prove he wasn't the enemy, but he hoped to return to Tulpehocken soon, definitely before September. If they returned home by then, they would be back in business for the fall harvest.

The guard tapped his watch and made a circling motion with his finger.

"Jutta, I'll get more details and call you back. I love you and tell the children I love and miss them."

"I will. And for better or worse, Herbert, we'll see this through."

He returned the receiver to the phone cradle and closed his eyes and pinched the bridge of his nose. Now, he needed to explain to his father why the family was joining them in prison.

-31-

WILHELM FALK

Green Mountains, Vermont - June 1944

The next morning, Falk opened his eyes to a slice of sunlight poking through the leafy mesh. When he sat up and stretched out the kinks in his back, a narrow vein of gold lit up the area around him.

Had he slept too late? He wanted to travel before first light, but his aching body demanded more sleep. He stood and listened to the sounds of the forest. The piping of songbirds and the chittering of squirrels split open the quiet as the forest came alive.

Parched, he stopped at a stream and filled a water jug, drinking deeply before heading to the tumble of boulders that marked the rugged trailhead to the valley. The descent would be challenging, but he was rested and ready.

The trees were sparse, and the rocky outcroppings provided little cover, so he pushed faster to get off the face of the mountain. He suspected Commander Dobbs's description of the New Hampshire citizens as "half-wild, avid hunters, rugged people who hated Germans" might be true of Vermonters, as well.

Using tree limbs to help hold his weight, he dropped to lower levels, often sliding on shale and loose rocks, sometimes easing over large logs and boulders on his backside.

After an hour, the forest thickened around him, and he discovered an authentic trail. He was still heading downhill, but covered more ground now that he could walk. He was making good time when a moving wall of pale white fog rolled in and just like that, he could see nothing. He swiped his arms in front of him, but it did little to clear a visual path. The fog seemed to glide with deadly intent, which was sure to be his fate if he tried to hike farther in whiteout conditions. He leaned against a tree, impatient to get moving again. He wished he had a cigarette, but those were long gone.

He focused on his upcoming reunion with Pastor Graf, a man he owed so much. Graf got him freed from prison in '40 when Falk and other social democrats spoke out against Hitler. Back then, Dachau was an unused gunpowder and munitions factory outside Munich, not yet a death camp. He loaded bullets for twelve hours a day, alongside other political prisoners.

At great peril to himself, Pastor Graf petitioned the government for his friend's release. Falk was an upstanding citizen, Graf argued, and a highly skilled manager at Eastman Kodak. As soon as he was safely home with Ilse and his sons, Graf immigrated to the United States under one of the few visas available at that time. Falk had known the pastor for over half of his thirty-four years and trusted him with his life.

A welcoming breeze moved through the forest, and the fog split into ribbons, carrying the scent of bogs and hay and farms. He was close to the valley now and to his reunion with his longtime friend. In the distance, the unmistakable buzz of chainsaws told him men worked nearby.

His heart jumped at the sound of breaking branches. Something large was coming toward him. The fog still slithered between the trees, leaving some areas clear and others obscured. He stopped and ducked behind an oak. All he had was Lauterbach's scalpel to fend off an attack. Not nearly enough protection if it were a bear.

More thrashing in the bushes and then an animal snorted. A deer burst from the woods to his right, charging down the trail ahead of him, the fog collapsing behind his disappearing hooves. He waited for a few moments, wondering what startled the animal. His own scent? After weeks in the forest, Falk figured he could wrinkle the nose of a Billy goat.

Sensing all was clear, he stepped from behind the tree back onto the path.

Immediately, the crack of a rifle sounded, and a white-hot pain shot through his shoulder and spun him to the ground.

Trying desperately to rein in the fear coursing through him, Falk crawled off the path using his one good arm. The wavering veils of fog made it almost impossible to find a place to hide. He spotted a huge moss-covered log and dragged himself in that direction.

Men's voices, out of breath, drew closer.

How had they found him? He'd come so far and covered his tracks so well.

Pulling himself up and over the log, he stifled a scream and dropped into the space behind. Lying flat, he couldn't see over the log and prayed his hiding spot would be sufficient.

A gunshot to the shoulder wouldn't end his plans. He could still make it to the valley. Trained to withstand pain, he reasoned if it proved to be too much, he still had the pain pills he stole from Dr. Lauterbach.

He just needed to stay hidden until the men moved on.

Then bad news arrived on the breeze. The sharp sound of a gun being cocked behind him.

Falk floated in and out, the fog of consciousness shifting to black then white. He and Ilse were in a hotel in Greece. The sun danced on the white ceiling above their bed, the sound of the ocean crashing on the rocks on the cliff below.

But, that couldn't be right. Why would his shoulder hurt so much?

Shoes squeaked on a floor.

The rattle of metal on metal, voices, antiseptic smells.

His heart thumped in his chest as reality crowded out his dreams. Suddenly, fully alert, memories returned in a rush. Flashes of being shot. Two English-speaking men hovering over him. The search party had found him. He'd failed. The forest moving above him as he was carried to a vehicle. Passing out, waking up, trying to remember to speak English.

The curtain slid to the side, and a young doctor studied him. "How is your pain?" he asked in German. He was a short man who wore black-framed glasses that magnified his eyes to twice their size.

They chose to speak to him in his native tongue? He must have spoken in German while in and out of consciousness. His ruse, pretending to be an American, was over.

"Where am I?" he asked in German.

"Where do you think you are?" The doctor reached for the stethoscope on the wall and draped it around his neck.

"In Vermont."

"You were shot in Vermont. Do you remember what happened?"

He nodded. "Some of it."

"You are a lucky man. A few more inches to the left, and we would not be having this talk." The doctor peeled up the corner of Falk's shoulder bandage and studied the wound. "It's looking better. You were in bad shape when you arrived here."

"Where is here?"

"A medical center"—the doctor reached for the stethoscope—"in Missouri." He positioned the device on the unbandaged area of Falk's chest to listen.

Falk's thundering heart must have been a deafening roar in the doctor's ears. Missouri? He was captured, and if his memory of a map of the United States served him, he was far from Troy, New York, his destination. He needed to ask for Pastor Graf. It was reasonable to ask for clergy after being shot, wasn't it?

The doctor stood back. "Are you a doctor?"

"No."

"You have no identification with you, but you were carrying a scalpel. And pills, including this one." The doctor held up a small vial containing his sole cyanide pill. His backup plan, if all else failed, was no longer an option. "Which is more than interesting."

Could it be they didn't suspect him of being an escapee? He'd try out that possibility. "I was on a day hike and didn't believe I needed identification." He would say no more about that, but he was curious about one thing. "The men who shot me . . . what were they doing out there?"

The doctor's eyebrows drew together, and he stared hard at Falk.

"Deer hunters." The doctor smiled. "They are in a little hot water since it is not deer season."

Falk had assumed wrong. They weren't tracking him. He drew in a breath, nodding, but his mind was spinning. "An accident then. And they helped me get to a hospital."

"Yes. First to one in Vermont, then you were transported here. Your mistake was wearing tan clothing in the woods, in the fog." The doctor clasped his hands behind his back. "I'm Doctor Roy Baker. How may I address you?"

"As the Foolish Man."

"With a scalpel." The doctor chuckled but was clearly unamused. "And a poison tablet.'

To end this questioning, he pretended pain suddenly gripped him, letting out a groan and panting hard for extra effect. "I have a friend." He laid out the next words with each labored breath. "A... pastor. Theodore... Graf. In Troy, New York."

The doctor pulled a pad and pen from his white coat and scribbled. "Who shall we say is asking to speak to him?"

"A friend from the old country." He groaned again.

"I'm going to give you a painkiller. Your heart rate is too rapid."

Falk closed his eyes and waited for the injection he didn't really want. He needed to stay alert and his pain level wasn't that high. There were sounds beyond the door but his room was quiet. He opened his eyes to see Dr. Baker holding the syringe, needle up, but motionless, studying his face.

The doctor pushed up his glasses. "There'll be more questions after we get you stable." He found a vein and pushed the plunger.

The fuzzy warmth moved up Falk's arm and filled his head.

"Sleep now. We'll get acquainted later."

The words *maybe we will and maybe we won't* floated through his head. He'd decide who he was pretending to be when the next round of questions came.

Voices roused Falk from sleep. Men's voices, talking fast, and drawing closer.

He tried to push himself to a sitting position, but unbearable agony ripped through his wounded shoulder. He managed to struggle upright as the door opened.

Expecting to greet his old friend, Theodore, Falk was unprepared for the four men who entered. Two men in military uniforms hung back, guarding the door while the other two approached his bedside. They wore dark business suits, white shirts, and fedoras. Simultaneously, they flashed badges, and the tallest man stated what Falk already assumed. "We are with the FBI." The man spoke perfect German. "I am Agent Klein, and this is Agent MacBride. I will be translating today."

He felt the heat of their attention. His seven-month struggle to reach Graf and reclaim his information came down to this. Was he about to be returned to Camp Sparks? Or worse, sent back to Europe? If he claimed to be Klaus Stern, it was unlikely he would ever connect with Graf. His only chance was to use the truth to explain what brought him here.

"We were called here to investigate a wounded German male without identification," Klein said. He was clean-shaven and smelled of expensive aftershave. "Let's start with who you are."

"My name is Wilhelm Falk. I was an officer in the German army. I defected to bring classified information to Washington, D.C."

He watched their faces knot as they looked to each other. One raised his eyebrows in surprise. They hadn't expected his honesty.

He continued. "You most likely have me listed as Klaus Stern, a prisoner of war escaped from Camp Sparks."

Klein pulled a notebook from his pocket, flipped through it, tapped his finger on a page and passed it to his partner.

"Then you were not just out for a walk?"

"It could be said I have been on a very long walk."

"To where?" MacBride asked.

He understood enough English to not need the question translated. "The circumstances are strange." He shifted some. "To meet up with my childhood friend, Theodore Graf. A pastor at a church in New York. He is expecting me."

"Expecting Falk or Stern?" Klein asked.

"Stern was a soldier killed in Italy. I took his identity to gain safe passage to the United States." He briefly told his story and the agents took notes, barely looking up as he spoke. This was a good sign. He had valuable information to share. "I'm worried too much time has passed. Every day, thousands die under Hitler's plan."

"What was *your plan* once you met up with Graf?"

"Months ago, I sent him photos and documents, and I laid out strategies for your country to take military action. I intended to have him drive me to your president's advisors, so I may explain what horrors are taking place." He studied their faces. They didn't appear excited about this tactic. "Please. Call Pastor Graf. He will bring you these documents."

The tall agent put away his notebook and nodded in the direction of the military police. "For now, you are under twenty-four-hour guard." He studied Falk. "And we already have the package you sent."

What? Graf had acted on his own and contacted the FBI? He had not been able to reply to the pastor's letter asking what he should do with the box of information he received. Falk had fled Brussels and headed to Italy to initiate his escape plan. He believed he would meet with the pastor within a month of sending the package, but nearly ten months passed.

"Then you know I am no threat. I would still like to meet with my friend back in New York."

"Theodore Graf won't be visiting you," the other FBI agent said. "Mr. Graf was arrested over a month ago for receiving military papers and for corresponding with the enemy." His face twisted into something resembling a smile. "Now you have cleared up a mystery for us. It was with you he was in contact."

The pastor was in jail because of him? Heavy disappointment settled in his chest. He'd imagined their face-to-face meeting so many times. It seemed impossible it wasn't going to happen. Falk needed to make this right. "He is guilty of nothing. Pastor Graf didn't ask to receive my documents. I am at fault. I will take his place in prison."

An FBI agent with a pencil-thin mustache laughed. "Just so you're aware, that won't be necessary. You are in the United States Medical Center for Federal Prisoners."

-32-

IZAAK TAUBER

Terezín Concentration Camp - June 1944

Izaak's new job was important. He recalled Papa's words about believing things will remain the same during wartime, but that he shouldn't count on fairness to be one of them. Well, fairness seemed to have circled back because his and Mama's lives were much improved, although nowhere near normal.

His new chore was to run messages from the Jewish Council and Paul Eppstein, who was in charge of making their new town beautiful, to each work area. He scampered past the new school and along the cobblestone streets under the big welcoming banner strung across the street. Mama said the words were in Danish because visitors from Denmark were arriving—the Danish International Red Cross. The group sounded important, and everyone was extra busy getting ready to show them their town. He liked the feel of how his legs were strong again, pumping under him, and he didn't get dizzy anymore. For weeks, they'd been served real food and not just soup. And he no longer sucked on a button to try to trick his stomach into believing it was full. It never worked very well anyway. His stomach was smarter than that button.

Despite missing Papa every day, he and Mama enjoyed the new town. Just last night, in the attic of the Magdeburg Barracks, they listened to a concert by a famous man, a composer. Gideon Klein, who used to perform in Prague and other big cities around Europe, walked to the piano and played as if showing off for a large audience. Even though there were only about fifty people sitting on the rough wooden benches. His hands flew over the keys, his face full of happiness. And the music crawled inside of Izaak, so much so, that his heart pounded and his stomach felt jumpy but in a good way. Later, as they left the building and he held Mama's hand, she said the music was by Chopin.

"It made me think of nice things," Izaak said.

"Me, too."

Today, he was headed to the freshly built café, a place where soon everyone would enjoy coffee. The town's rules changed quickly after the elders announced they were beautifying the walled city. People were no longer crowded in the houses. A school was built, so the children didn't have to learn in secret. And the old barracks, where women broke apart mica every day and got sick very fast, was turned into a dining hall. The servers wore white hats and pretty aprons.

The biggest change was everyone regained weight, and they didn't die while they worked.

Izaak's favorite change about this town was its art classes. They were taught by a real artist named Friedl Dicker-Brandeis. Mama said not to get too attached to the classes. She always worried everything would go bad again, but he trusted they were finally in a good camp this time. Mrs. Dicker-Brandeis wore her dark wavy hair tied back with a special pink ribbon. She explained she'd found it on the train ride from her home in Vienna to Terezín, and hoped to find the little girl who owned it. Izaak soaked in her admiration for his drawing ability, but she taught him many tricks, too, like how to see basic shapes in nature and sketch them with a few easy lines. The best part was all the paper and charcoal and paints she laid out in an open room in one of the barracks. Now their creations would decorate the Upper Fortress instead of secretly stowed inside her quarters.

As he ran along the streets, Izaak's skin was sticky with summertime sweat even though he wore a short-sleeved shirt and knickers. He studied the cheerful street signs and tried to remember the new names. His street, once called Q, was now named Heidelberg.

He turned the corner and slowed to a walking pace at the main square. This was his second favorite place. Grass shoots grew, creating a soft jade carpet in the center of the square. Protecting this lawn were rows of blooming rose bushes and newly painted benches. Until two weeks ago, a tall fence circling the beat-up grass kept anyone from using the park, and the bushes and flowers were all dead. He and the other people were never allowed near the church with the tall spire and big clock that stood nearby. Now he dragged his fingers along the pitted building blocks of the white cathedral just because he could. The church had a name above the tall double doors—MDCCCV. He couldn't sound it out, so it must be one of those other languages he didn't know.

On the road next to the square, workers pulled boards from the back of an open hearse and carried them to the center of the grassy area. Izaak tried to figure out what the men might be building there, but he'd wait and see.

He was always on the lookout for Papa in these groups of men. The man who helped rebuild the school said he thought he'd met a man named Tauber, who was here at one time. He nearly did flips, and Mama cried when she heard the news. Papa was handy with tools and a smart engineer, so Izaak wished he'd be brought back to rebuild the town.

Papa wasn't there today. Izaak took off running again, turning down two more streets before reaching the café. A man on a ladder attached a sign above the front door. This could only mean one thing—the Kaffeehaus would be open soon. He missed the taste of the sweetened coffee he and Papa used to enjoy after leaving the barbershop during their monthly appointments. The drink had more milk in it than coffee, but Izaak knew he looked grown-up sipping it from a fine china cup that matched Papa's. His head hurt from the memory, and he took big breaths to make it go away.

Inside the café, the waiting area contained plush chairs circled around a fancy table. There were also big vases filled with fresh flowers cut from the moat area. Izaak handed off the letter to the gentleman in charge of designing the building. "Thanks, little man," he said.

Izaak liked being called that, especially since he was almost nine. He no longer asked the men if they knew Saul Tauber since he'd already done that too much. The workers at every stop promised to let him know if they bumped into him.

The worker who called Izaak "little man" quit his hammering. "Do you have a part in the new opera?"

Brundibár was an opera just for children. Older boys and girls were talking about the parts they hoped to get, but Izaak hadn't been asked. "I don't think so."

One of the men, built like a skinny crowbar with a head stuck on, said, "I know the directors, Verdi and Franek. They need many younger children for the parts. I'll tell them about you."

"Thank you!" Happiness washed over him. He'd wanted to be in a play or concert ever since the town started holding secret shows in attics and cellars, but they didn't often need children. Mama said some of the musicians were very famous and once made more money than Izaak could even imagine. Here they played their secret shows in attics and earned half a kilogram of extra margarine a performance.

The older man saluted Izaak. "Thank you, Izaak Tauber."

The clock on the tall church steeple showed midmorning. Time for art class.

He walked into the barracks where Mevr. Dicker-Brandeis waited with a few children for everyone else to arrive. Wrapping her arms around him, the teacher gave him a big squeeze. "My favorite artist," she whispered in his ear. "May your day be full of energy and talent."

He hugged back extra hard, a smile stuck on his face. It was important to hug her each day. She explained that she and her husband hadn't had any children, so she needed the energy of young people around her to keep her happy and healthy.

When all forty children were gathered around eight tables, she held up postcards with colorful fronts. "These pictures were painted by an Austrian artist named Gustav Klimt. Each table will have a different painting that I want you to mimic in your own style, with either the watercolors or pencils."

There was a long table in the middle of the room covered with pencils, paintbrushes, watercolors, and paper. Izaak walked over and chose watercolors. He returned to his table and arranged his paints while Mevr. Dicker-Brandeis set the postcard in the center. "This is called Poppy Field." She smiled as she viewed the card. "It is one of my favorite places to turn to in my mind."

The painting was full of greens in the background with a vague outline of trees and fields. Orange and red splotches filled the foreground. The picture made Izaak's heart pound. What if he could someday create something this beautiful?

She let them paint any way they wanted and never criticized their artwork. Mama explained why Mevr. Dicker-Brandeis was so special. When she and her husband were told to leave their home, instead of filling her suitcase with clothes and jewelry, she reached her luggage weight limit with art supplies.

Her only rule, and this one made Izaak the happiest of all, was they could not draw anything from the camp. Their drawing needed to "move their minds to a different world."

Dipping into a brilliant green, Izaak dotted the background of his paper. A blue-green mixture came next. He disappeared into his work, smelling the fresh aroma from the field and the warmth of the summer sun on his back. The orange poppies brushed up against his legs, soft and fuzzy. Bees buzzed, a sound he used to be afraid of, but now it meant fresh air and freedom. He painted a house in the distance which was surrounded by apple trees, with a window and a door, barely showing through the branches and leaves. Then he walked to the house, and the fragrance of his mama's meat pie was strong on the breeze. He could almost taste the pastry filled with meat, cabbage, and sharp goat cheese. There would be lemonade. Then Papa would pat his full tummy, laughing about moving in with the hippos at the zoo.

Izaak painted layer after layer, each leading to something new.

At last, the sounds in the room brought him back to the class. He studied his painting and smiled. Someday, he and Mama and Papa would walk through a field just like this.

Mevr. Dicker-Brandeis leaned over him, placing her hands on the table, and rested her chin on top of his head. She sighed. "So beautiful, Izaak. You will be famous one day if"—her voice broke apart, as if she might be crying—"as you continue painting."

He turned and studied her face. It was squeezed tight, but she had no tears. She produced a smile and then took his painting to hang on a clothesline to dry. With hundreds of drawings and paintings stored inside this space, the room held an earthy odor of paint and wet paper. A wonderful scent so thick he tasted it in the back of his mouth, long after he returned to his barracks.

When everyone finished, Mevr. Dicker-Brandeis walked them to the room at the end of the building, where he and the other students washed their hands and arms. The mixture of colors from his hands ran together to make a beautiful river along the inside of the white sink and then down the drain—his escapist dream washed away for another day.

Izaak and six other children walked home together after art class. A man, leading the horse-drawn hearse filled with bread for the evening meal, stopped near him and his friends to watch the workers put up a new building in the town square. Izaak loved bread, but knew this same hearse took dead people to the Columbarium where the bodies got burned each morning. He tried not to think about the dead when he ate. He asked Mama why the dead were burned. She explained there was no room to bury all the deceased in their own graves, which was Jewish law, so the camp bosses suggested cremation.

"What's that going to be?" Izaak asked the hearse driver.

"A bandstand." The man raised his chin to the new construction as he picked his teeth with a small stick. "We'll have outside concerts now."

Music would make his mama happy. When she and Papa went to musical performances, they'd always come home cheerful and chatty about the wonderful evening.

"This really is turning into the best town," Izaak said.

The man bunched his face together and looked so sharply at Izaak that he quickly took a step away so angry germs wouldn't get on him. "We are all in a play, son. We just don't know how it ends yet."

The man slapped the horse on the rear and continued down the street.

A younger boy took Izaak's hand, tears running down his face.

"What's wrong?"

The boy's voice quivered. "That man."

Izaak understood what the child meant. The man's words sounded scary. He didn't really understand them, but the way the man spoke made Izaak suddenly afraid of their new life.

He squeezed the small hand in his. "Some people are never happy." Then he rubbed the boy's fuzzy head like his mama always rubbed his. Under the new town rules, they didn't need to have bald heads any longer. His mama and he were in a contest to see who could grow out their hair the fastest. He pulled the boy along and the other children followed.

"Do you like music?"

All the children nodded.

"Good. Because soon we will have music under the pretty moon instead of in the stinky attics."

He pictured nighttime concerts. The crickets. Stars sprinkled across the dark sky. Music floating all the way up to heaven for angels to enjoy.

The man with the hearse just had a bad attitude, probably because he didn't get to paint or do happy things. Instead, he just hauled around the dead and the bread. Mama said having a positive attitude would give Izaak great powers to overcome hard times.

And today was a positive day. He might get a part in the children's opera and that made him happy. In his thoughts, he ran away inside a sunlit Klimt poppy field like on the postcard. His arms outstretched. Twirling.

With all this good luck, he expected the war to end any day.

-33-

HERBERT MÜLLER

Ellis Island - June 1944

Within two weeks, Herbert's family relocated to Ellis Island, proving the government could move quickly when they so desired. Jutta and the children disembarked dressed in their Sunday best. His heart swelled as he held each of them, but with his elation came doubt—his family was officially in prison. All too soon they were escorted to the admissions office to be fingerprinted and photographed while he paced the hallway. Otto waited in the large dorm room, resting. He heeded the doctor's warning to avoid quick bouts of excitement for fear it could trigger another heart attack. His father wore out faster these days and was less alert. Although he notified the family of Otto's health issue and his recovery, they would surely notice the changes in him.

Jutta and Frieda exited the office first, escorted by a female Coast Guard officer. The woman was fresh-faced, young, with large oval eyes. "I'll show your wife and daughter to the other side of the island."

They were separating them? This wasn't right.

Frieda crossed her arms and hugged her sides as Jutta clasped her fists below her chin as if to keep her head propped up. "Herbert? I thought we were housed together."

"I was told as much." He turned to the officer. "We expected to be living in the family area. Where is that?"

"We don't have those accommodations here, but you can meet for an hour each day in the Great Hall."

Alfred joined them in the hallway, missing most of the conversation.

"Who can we meet each day?" He carried a folded set of army clothes that matched Herbert's.

He arrived on Ellis contrite and ashamed of his behavior in their hometown, and blamed himself for the family's move to the internment camp. Herbert assured him the transfer was to protect them from the growing dangers at home and wasn't based on his arrest. Alfred didn't need to bear any guilt when forces much greater, and at higher levels of the law, were the ones that conspired to run his family out of town.

"Us," Frieda said, twirling a pigtail. "Mother and I have to live in a different part of the camp."

"I had hoped to spend a lot of time with my father-in-law," Jutta said. "He's not well."

The female officer reached for Jutta's arm. "I have my orders. Right now, I am to show you to your separate room."

Had he been duped? Heat rose in his face. His family was here, yet they still couldn't be together. *Let's bait the German-Americans into convincing their relatives the internment camp was the answer.* He took Jutta by the arms and kissed her on the cheek. "Go. I'll get this straightened out." He hugged Frieda. "Get some rest, and we'll see you soon."

Moments later, Herbert stalked into the camp administrative offices and approached the director who organized this transfer.

"You told me that my entire family would be housed together if they joined me as volunteer internees."

"Separate quarters are all we have here. It's temporary," the director said. "Your family is slated for the Crystal City camp in Texas, but it's full right now." The man shrugged.

"This is unacceptable." His voice was tight and controlled, but he was close to shouting. "How long before they'll have room for us?"

"We have no way of knowing how many of your people we will be arresting."

The director turned and walked out of the meeting room, but Herbert remained standing. *Your people?* It was as if a veil fell over the eyes of everyone in the United States. He and other German-Americans somehow changed into something new, something their neighbors and government no longer recognized as belonging in America's melting pot. Granted, there was a slow burn toward these sentiments, but then a switch flipped, and all of a sudden, a class of Americans was considered outsiders, or untrustworthy. Former friends now viewed them through the wrong end of the telescope, diminishing them, making them look like small foreign objects.

He returned to his bed next to Alfred's and Otto's in the Grand Hall and relayed the director's message.

Alfred kicked at his bed springs. "You know what the Statue of Liberty is? A mocking lump of green metal!"

Herbert laid his arm around his son's shoulders. "We'll have a story to tell someday, won't we? It's unfair, it's unbelievable, but it's what we have at this moment, son. We can get through it if we stay calm."

Surprisingly, Alfred leaned into Herbert's embrace. Something his son had not done in years.

"Do you think Jutta, und meine granddaughter, will be okay?" Otto rubbed his eyes, waking up.

He nodded. "Sounds like they have a room to themselves. Better than our deal."

"Yeah. It is." Alfred dropped onto his army bed and scanned the big dormitory room. "You said we can take classes here?"

"You can. Even in the summer."

"Good," Alfred said. "Forget about accounting...I'm going to learn about the law."

Herbert's favorite part of the day was when he, Otto, and Alfred joined Jutta and Frieda each morning for one hour. For three weeks, they'd visited in the downstairs portion of the hall, huddled on wooden benches built for two. Otto was stronger now, energized by the family's attention and concern.

Most nights, Herbert had insomnia and silently paced the open room where more than three hundred men slept. Meal times were no better. The food barely went down his throat before it formed into a knot somewhere in his chest.

He hated the frown lines that appeared on Jutta's forehead. And still, their opportunity to transfer to the family camp in Texas hadn't come about. The children were resilient, thankfully naïve, but looked limp, tired. But they happily attended classes, which gave them time together. Alfred complained that his American History class was no more than a continuous lecture about how to be a good American citizen, and the evils of conspiring with the enemy.

Herbert protected them from the rumors that internees were being offered repatriation to Germany to help alleviate the overcrowding at the camp. What if it changed from an offer to a demand? They had only distant relatives in Germany, and he didn't believe a move would make his family better off. All of Europe was under rationing orders, and not just gas and sugar, as in the United States. The families who chose to go to Germany were in touch with extended families, willing to take them in even though most were forewarned about having to sleep on the floor, or in an attic, upon arrival. He and his family could find themselves in a woodshed, or on the street, without knowing what his relatives could provide.

And he tried to protect his family from the newest update about their home. The FBI had not only frozen their assets but also seized their property. His family had nothing left. There would be a county auction in two weeks. Once he broke the news to Otto, Jutta, and the children, he vowed he'd get the mill and house back one day. And insisted that the seizure and sale had to be unlawful. Herbert learned to hate the empty-handed mailman. Every day disappointed him more and more as no appeal date had been scheduled for him or Otto. He doubted the government actually moved cases through, especially if they had taken everything away from the internees. With the Japanese and German "enemies" locked away behind barbed wire, why do anything until the war was over?

"Time to go." Herbert had watched the clock for the last ten minutes until the last stroke before the visitation hour started. He helped his father stand.

Alfred was already on his feet. "What film do you think they got to watch last night?" The women's side had fewer *guests*, so Jutta and Frieda often were shown movies in the evening. It beat the male side of camp where cards, dice, and cussing were their only entertainment.

"*Tarzan, The Ape Man* is a good one," Herbert said. "But haven't they seen that one twice already?"

"I think so," Alfred said. "Mother said she was hoping for a Shirley Temple film."

Herbert spotted Jutta first and smiled. He raised his hand to wave and rose to his toes to try to spot Frieda. A man knows his wife's expressions, and in that moment, he knew something was terribly wrong. Her lips were pinched together as she stumbled to him, tears staining her face, struggling to hold back sobs.

He ran to her and hugged her tightly. "What's happened?"

"Frieda," she choked out.

Alfred darted to her side, and shortly after, Otto arrived out of breath. Alfred was wired, his nostrils flaring as he opened and closed his fists. "Where's Frieda?"

Herbert's heart leapt into his throat and he forgot how to breathe when he saw the fear in Jutta's eyes. Was his daughter ill? Or, God forbid, was it worse than that?

"Infirmary." She shook her head before she could speak again. "A maintenance volunteer... outside the showers... attacked her."

"Where is he?" Alfred turned his head to scan the room, his eyes boring into all the men.

He grabbed his son's arm to stop him from punching someone. He felt his breakfast rise. My God. Frieda was thirteen. "*How* is she injured?"

Jutta swallowed hard and gathered herself, and took a deep breath. "He stripped off her towel and was on top of her but didn't have time to... you know."

Otto dropped his head into his hands and let out a moan.

Herbert reached for Otto who appeared fine, just shocked. This type of startling news could kill his father!

"Can we see her?" he asked.

"The doctor said thirty minutes." Jutta brushed tears off her face.

Frieda. Herbert swallowed a sob and swore. His sweet, trusting little girl. Rescuer of baby birds. Always holding a soft spot for the underdog. Now this atrocious act, an incident he wouldn't be able to erase from her once-innocent mind. He pulled Jutta into a long embrace while she openly cried. Tears burned down his face, and he saw the same traces on Alfred's and Otto's. He regretted convincing Jutta they would be safe here. What was he thinking?

"Can you get us out of here, Herbert?" Jutta asked. "We didn't want to tell you, but it's not safe on our side. There are so many men around, supposedly workers, but…"

"I'll meet with the immigration commander." He looked deep into her eyes, as he thought of their only other option, since their transfer to Crystal City didn't seem to be on anyone's priority list. "I know for a fact the government will pay our way to Germany. Other families have already left." His mind spun around his indecision. He wasn't thinking straight. Arriving in Germany while the war raged? This might be just another terrible decision to follow the one that brought his family here.

"Will they send, us to family?" Otto asked.

"Yes." Herbert rubbed Jutta's arms to try to ease their trembling. "We would need someone to take us in."

"Your cousin, Elke, near Frankfurt," Otto said.

Herbert had no idea if Elke still lived there, or in what shape their lives were. He'd heard the saying, *War does not determine who is right—only who is left.* What if his cousin and her family were dead? "Let's talk about this."

"Fact Time," Alfred said, his voice deeper than Herbert had ever heard. "Frieda or Mother could be attacked again. We have to leave."

"The war could be over…when we reach Europe," Otto said.

"I like your hopefulness, Pops, but we don't know that for sure. Tell me what you think about going to Germany?"

"We have people, they will welcome us."

Herbert hoped that was a fact. He had to trust Otto's instinct there.

"We can't go home, but the family internment camp in Texas they promised might never have an opening."

Jutta raised her chin. "If we are all together again, I don't care where we go, but I want to leave here."

His family had spoken and surely Frieda would agree. With this dreadful turn of events, an idea he refuted just hours earlier seemed to be his family's future. He would volunteer them to repatriate to a country his children had never seen, and one he hadn't been to in over twenty years. In the end, he prayed this was the right decision.

Herbert moved through the crowded halls, trying to set his face to show an emotion other than anger, although he boiled inside. He wanted the last six months of his life back. He wanted to erase all that happened to his family, to erase Frieda's frightening experience. When he'd been allowed to briefly see her, he was at a loss for reassuring words as his daughter sobbed in his arms. She agreed with the choice to leave, to be anywhere but here. Jutta was now by her side in a separate room near the commander's office where they could stay until their ship sailed.

He left the building and wandered outside, heading to the fence, rubbing his achy hip. He listened to the water slap at the rocky edges of the island. Lost in thought, he startled when Pastor Theodore Graf touched his back.

Herbert shook his hand.

The pastor wore his white clerical garment, draped to the ankles and girdled with a rope. These once-clean vestments were stained and now loose-fitting. Curious he wore them today since he reserved them for when he was behind the pulpit. Usually, he dressed in the same military-issued clothes they all wore.

"How did your meeting go?" Herbert assumed Graf changed clothes for his interview with the review board.

"It's a story and a half," Graf said. "How are you, my friend?"

Herbert shook his head and relayed what happened to Frieda. A crush of sadness, built on raw guilt for bringing his family in the first place, still sat heavy in his chest.

"This is terrible news," Graf said. He dipped his head near Herbert and folded his hands. "I pray for peace for your family that surpasses all understanding at a time as this."

"Thank you, pastor. It's inconceivable, but we're relieved that it wasn't worse." He inhaled deeply. "We're going to be *repatriated* the day after tomorrow. I decided to take the offer of a free trip abroad to get away from here."

Graf lifted his eyebrows and offered a tight smile. "I also leave in two days. Perhaps, we are traveling together."

The pastor sounded less than enthusiastic. Herbert studied him and realized the pastor never answered the question concerning his interview. He was wary these days, and had become a seeker of signs, looking for the smallest bits of information that might hint to the future.

"And your interview?"

The pastor shook his head. "A group of eight showed. Three lawyers from the department's Enemy Alien Control Program, three men from the Special War Problems Division, and two others from the War Relocation Authority."

Herbert motioned to a long bench in the shade. The day waxed hotter and this seemed like a story that might take a while. "Sounds serious."

Graf sat, pulled out a cigarette, and offered Herbert one. He waved it away and waited for the pastor to get a good light. With the Hudson's breeze and his shaking hands, it took a while. The pastor was a rock-solid man, always undaunted, even after his arrest, even after the loss of his church when his congregation turned their backs on him. If the pastor was nervous, his news wasn't good.

The pastor forced out a long stream of smoke and crossed his legs at the ankles. Like the other men interned for months, his brown shoes were scuffed and ruined from rainwater and lack of a good polish.

"I guess the news is both good and bad," he said. "And, we got into a bigger discussion of what I know about the war. I told you my friend sent me those documents. A postal worker saw the European postage and suggested I be investigated. Just now they said my mistake was that I wrote back to him."

"Your friend is an SS officer, right?" Herbert knew only what he read in the newspapers, and these men were reportedly Hitler's vicious lapdogs. "Were you close?"

"Wilhelm Falk was a teenager in my youth group, the Association of Christian Students. He was an engaging young man, self-deprecating, eager to step up. Always on the side of charity"—he smiled—"He has a gracious wife with intoxicating intelligence and two young boys, though I suppose now they are nearly the age he was when I first met him."

"You must have been surprised to learn he was in the SS."

"I was. Falk did nine months in Dachau for speaking out against Hitler. My letters on his behalf got him released before I moved here in thirty-nine." Graf blew smoke rings that warped into ovals before disappearing. "I hadn't heard from him in nearly four years, and then he sent that package full of anti-Hitler information, so I'd say he's still the righteous guy I knew. The bible teaches 'Many are the plans in a person's heart, but it is the Lord's purpose that prevails.' Something happened after I immigrated that made him join, and then later go after Hitler's guards and the German army."

"He sounds like a decent man. Who knows what pressure he was under to join." He folded his arms. "And a brave guy. Did you see what he sent you before the FBI showed up?"

"I did." He shrugged. "I was curious. He wrapped everything in melted wax and disguised the package as a canning supply box. I had to know what was so secretive he went to such effort. There was a letter inside asking me to set everything aside until he could instruct me further."

"Have you heard from him?"

Graf slowly shook his head. "I wrote to the return address, a postbox in Brussels and asked how I could help him. That was last fall."

"Long time ago, now."

"If I hadn't written back to Falk and immediately turned over the documents to the FBI, then I'd still be in my church preaching. But by writing back...I wanted to be more helpful to Falk than just storing his documents."

"It seems so unfair." Herbert studied the pastor. "But the FBI has the information now. I guess that was your friend's end goal. So in a way he delivered his message...whatever he felt was so important."

"What he wanted the U.S. to know is that Hitler is murdering all the Jewish and ethnic people he can round up. He's created a well-oiled death machine over there."

Herbert recalled something he read in the back pages of the paper. "Around Thanksgiving, there was an article in the New York Times about the Nazis' attempt to keep secret their Jewish relocation camps. Then nothing else was reported."

"Falk's notes and photos show these camps. I think the national news is refusing to report it because it sounds too unbelievable." Graf offered a tense smile. "But, yes, the good news is the state department now has this evidence and may act on it."

"According to Falk, Hitler is killing civilians?" The U.S. government hadn't done everything right, but it wasn't killing its own. A seagull floated over Herbert's head and landed a few feet away. The bird cocked its head as if listening to their conversation.

"Hundreds of thousands were transported to the camps, but by Falk's estimate, ten thousand a day are put to death."

Ten thousand deaths a day? Times three hundred and sixty-five? Alfred could have done the calculation in an instant. More despairing news. He was already drained because of his family's catastrophe, but he ached with a new sorrow for the thousands of broken families in his home country.

Graf scrubbed over his face with his reddened fingers, closing his eyes and digging into them with his thumb and index finger bridging his nose.

The seagull took to the air, wheeling overhead on a warm current and floating without effort.

Graf dropped his cigarette and ground it into the dirt with the toe of his shoe.

"Falk suggested they bomb the railway lines leading into the camps. He drew out maps and made it clear where the prisoners were held versus where the guards live."

"Your friend will be a hero. He did this at great risk to himself."

Graf rested his hands on his legs as his face fought an expression of personal sorrow. The rattle of the surrounding fencing, as a basketball bounced off it, blended with birds screeching overhead. The warm day was ripe as a pungent rivulet of sewer stench rippled through the air. Graf wiped moisture from his eyes.

"Falk was killed in November in Italy."

"Oh, no." He let solemn silence fill the space between them. "I'm sorry. Did his men catch him gathering more evidence?"

"It doesn't sound like it. He was shot near the front lines although I'm not sure why he'd be that close to the fight"—Graf slapped his legs—"Our government was interested in him, of course, so they followed up. They asked if I knew where his wife and children might be, since a notice of his death was returned, undeliverable from their home near Düsseldorf."

"Where do you think they are?"

"His wife had a sister in Eindhoven, over the border into the Netherlands. He probably sent them there to keep them safe." Graf tilted his head and looked at Herbert with his customary squint. "And you know what? I didn't share the Netherlands' address with the review panel." Graf's voice was low, somber. "I want to be the one to tell Falk's wife her husband was a hero before he died."

Herbert tried to visualize the green pastoral images of Germany he remembered from his childhood, now sprouting large prison camps, imprisoning, even killing, thousands of its citizens. "It's hard to believe Germany has come to this."

Graf nodded. "I've been trying to work out how a nation agrees to annihilate their ethnic inhabitants and, in turn, have their citizens, cities, and monuments destroyed." Following a moment of silence, the pastor offered an ecclesiastical smile. "I suppose we will soon find out."

-34-

WILHELM FALK

United States Medical Center for Federal Prisoners
Springfield, Missouri - July 1944

F alk knew doctors were keeping him drugged. He surfaced for a few
blurry moments, and then slipped back into the pleasant void where
Ilse laughed while playing with the boys. Her voice high, filled with a
happy lilt. If he could just get closer and touch her, he'd know the war
had been no more than a nightmare. Hans and Dietrich appeared and raced
across the yard. They were strong runners for their ages. Then he was con-
scious again. If only the war would end, and he could hold them. The boys
would have grown. Perhaps they could outrun him now.

There were no pills with breakfast, and his mind felt clearer. His shoulder still ached, but pain no longer radiated down his arm. How long had he
been in this hospital? The nurses and guards spoke openly, but his muddled
mind was unable to translate. Each day, he asked to meet with someone of
importance, but the guards remained noncommittal. He needed to help free
Graf. Knowing the pastor sat in a prison weighed heavily on him. He carried enough guilt for what he didn't do while he served in the Wehrmacht,
and now, he had the added remorse of what he did do: he sent Graf the
package that led to his arrest.

The door opened and a nurse he nicknamed Red entered. Her carrot-
colored hair was styled into a neat bun below her white cap. Two uniformed
guards accompanied her, so something was up. One spoke in German. "You
will shower and dress. Your interview begins in one hour."

"With whom?"

"An attaché to President Roosevelt."

This was success. One of the last steps in his plan even if it now unfolded in a prison hospital.

The soldiers left and Red walked him to the showers at the end of the hall. She handed him off to a male orderly who supervised Falk as he turned his back to wash. Trickles of blood escaped from under his bandages, racing down his body in light-pink rivulets. He slowly lifted his aching arm, relieved it wasn't paralyzed.

Once dry, he returned to his room where Red changed the wet bandages and then helped him put on fresh clothing—a prison jumpsuit of sorts.

The guards returned, flanking him as they led him through a maze of green hallways and into another building, the linoleum older and yellowed nearest the wallboards. They climbed stairs to a door with COURTROOM stenciled across its glass. Once inside, he sat in a leather chair at a table facing a raised platform. Where five official-looking men in uniform, heavy with medals, regarded him from behind a long wooden table. He squinted against the brightness of the overhead lights and breathed in the scent of old floor wax.

Falk's heart thumped in his ears. The professional setting gave this meeting the weight of something real, something important enough for this caliber of men to gather.

A court clerk entered. She was a solid woman, her hair in tight blonde curls, with her stocky calves peeking from below the skirt of a crisp army uniform. She took a seat at a table below the five men, in front of her steno machine.

Another man entered and sat at the end of Falk's table. He was burly with ropey arms that led to huge, meaty hands. He had a lift to his eyes that made him appear as if he were surprised even when he wasn't.

"I will be your translator," he said in flawless German.

Falk nodded. "Danke."

The heavily decorated officer seated at the center of the five men, briefly shuffled papers and then spoke. "I am General William Donovan, head of the Office for the Coordination of Intelligence Information." He motioned to the other men at the table. "These men are trained in enemy affairs and answer to Army Chief of Staff George Marshall and the Joint Chiefs of Staff. We're here on behalf of President Roosevelt."

He nodded, pleased and somewhat overwhelmed. He'd pictured this moment for so long.

"I'm glad to meet with you." He adjusted his position to afford his sore shoulder and arm a more comfortable resting place.

"We're here to determine why and how you obtained official papers and photos of the Jewish extermination camps. We are also interested in other information you may have regarding Hitler and the Third Reich."

"Yes, sirs. I'm thrilled to share it, but we may be here for days."

Colonel Donovan smiled. "Not a problem, Officer Falk. However long you need." The colonel folded his hands in front of him on the table. "Let's start with you telling us about your military service."

He explained how he avoided serving the Reich for two years while working as the plant manager for Eastman Kodak Stuttgart, providing film for the war.

"In forty-two I was forced to join. My father's friend, Army Chief of the O-K-H General Staff, Generaloberst Ludwig Beck, got me an officer position in the Schutzstaffel."

The panel took notes as the translator repeated his story.

He began speaking of the camps, the dead bodies, the hatred and beliefs that led to slavery and murder. Now the American agents were still. Eyes downcast, heads nodding at times, at other times shaking in disbelief. Did they believe him? Would he believe such things if he hadn't seen them for himself?

He spoke of the gas chambers built to look like showers, and the rows of crematoriums constructed to deal with the thousands of dead bodies every day. One dark-haired agent sat with his hand over his mouth. Were the details making him sick? They should. Falk finished, his voice running out of energy as he searched his mind for what more he could share.

Donovan raised his pen in the air. "To whom did you report these atrocities?"

The question gave him pause. After his discoveries at the Hadamar hospital, he was on a fact-finding mission, gathering information as quickly as possible.

"I didn't tell anyone in the Wehrmacht."

"And why not?"

"I had to survive long enough to get the information *out*. It was a death sentence for anyone who spoke against Hitler, let alone as an officer in the *upper levels* of the Wehrmacht."

When he said Hitler's name, it was with the poisonous hatred he harbored for the monster.

"Surely others opposed him?"

"Dozens of men, even some senior officers, tried to murder Hitler. Last year it was General Hubert Lanz, Hitler's chief of staff." He took a deep breath. "They were all shot."

The generals studied him without speaking. The room's atmosphere was heavy with scrutiny, all directed his way.

Falk took a moment to gather his thoughts. He needed to convince them he tried to tell other world leaders, but no one would listen.

"To be killed like all others did not seem to be the answer. I wrote to clergy of all denominations, including the Holy See. Ambassadors from Sweden, Norway and Spain. In 1942 I wrote to Dr. Gerhart Riegner, the representative of the Jewish World Congress in Geneva. He assured me that he would alert the Jewish leaders in the United States. It seemed as if no country wanted to be involved. I began to take detailed notes and pictures, if I could, in the hope that one day the forces of the United States and Great Britain would stop the slaughter." Frustrated, he raised his hands. "I never thought it would take so long to be heard."

The colonel glanced at the papers in front of him. "Do you know Anastasy Vonsyatsky?"

"No."

"Do you believe that Jewish families could be considered fortunate because they were moved out of the German cities that were bombed to rubble? That being in a labor camp was a safer place for them?"

"With respect, sir, that is ridiculous!" Falk's words came out too loudly. "Operation Reinhard is no more than the thinnest of excuses to bring the Jewish and Roma populations to a place where they could be secretly and efficiently murdered." He pressed his hands onto the wooden seat to keep them from shaking. "Who is Vonsyatsky?"

"A Russian," Donovan said. "He's being held here as a German spy." His eyebrows rose in a questioning manner.

Falk bristled. They doubted his intentions, negating all he sacrificed. "If I were a spy, I would choose an easier way to the United States than I have just suffered."

One of Chief Marshall's associates asked, "Did your family know of your part in this extermination?"

His part in the extermination? He felt as if he were clubbed.

"I couldn't confide in anyone, not even family members. When I joined the SS, I became a munitions factory manager and not a part of the killing squads or Hitler's guards. My crime is that I observed mass murders in Auschwitz, Bergen-Belsen, and Sobibór and didn't intervene to stop them. But I never participated," he said, gritting his teeth. He never expected to be the one on trial. "Never. My task was to monitor the operations of chemical plants and munitions factories which meant that I traveled extensively. I risked my life often, by destroying shipments of Zyklon-B gas to be used in the extermination chambers."

"Explain that," Marshall said.

"I told them the gas was spoiled during transport. The railway crews buried the canisters because of my false report that the gas would not work."

Marshall's associate tapped his pencil on the table. "In your travels, you saw many disturbing things, you took notes, and shot photographs and developed them. What made you finally decide to desert and seek safer shores?"

Falk bristled at the insinuation. He was not a mere deserter. The brutal death of the boy with the strings flashed through his mind. It had been the final straw.

In measured tones, he said, "I had waited to see what the people I wrote to would do. When too much time passed, I knew it was up to me."

A man to the left of Donovan asked, "How did you receive mail without getting caught?"

"I kept a secret mailbox in Brussels, and I checked it whenever I could." He leaned forward, careful to cradle his arm. "I was caught when I received a letter from the United States from Theodore Graf. I was called to a meeting with Himmler and knew that this was the end for me. I went to Italy and changed clothes with a dead soldier who looked like me. Incidentally, Pastor Graf was not involved in my plans. I used the man. He was the only person I knew to send my information in America. Please allow him to return to his church."

"We will take that under consideration." Donovan pinched the bridge of his nose as he met Falk's gaze. "Are you trained as a military strategist?"

"I am not." Where was this going?

"So, if we assume the descriptions in your papers are correct, how do you believe the United States can halt the genocide"—the colonel steepled his fingers and rested his chin on them—"from a *plant supervisor's* point of view?"

He ignored the jab. Finally. His recommendations would be heard.

"If you give me a map, I can show you the layout of many of the extermination camps. The worst of the perpetrators live nearby, for example, Josef Mengele. If the military bombed their homes, you would cut off the head of the snakes. The remaining guards would flee, and the camps could be freed."

Murmurs rippled between the five men. Did they know of Mengele's medical experiments? Or, was this another of the top leader's best-kept secrets?

Donovan sat back in his chair, his face a mask of concentration as if struggling toward a decision. "Any more you'd like to add?"

"Stop bombing innocent civilians in German cities. I understand it frightens the population and puts pressure on the government, but it won't scare these men in power. You need to target the railway tracks leading to the camps and find the SS residences. I drew critical regions for you. American forces have German citizens fleeing, afraid that another hundred thousand of them could be burned to death, but these people are only citizens. They are not complicit in the mass murders." Ilse and his boys—his chest thudded—they had to be safe in the Netherlands, or this was his family he was talking about.

Donovan nodded. "We will take your ideas to Washington." He stood and the officers rose alongside him. The meeting was obviously at an end.

"Here's what we need from you, Herr Falk. Write down everything you have learned that wasn't already included in your notes. We'll reconvene tomorrow at eleven a.m."

"The United States will do what is essential?" He had persuaded them to act. This was all he wanted at the start of his journey. Relief flooded through him.

"Our orders are simply to interrogate you and to report back to the president. A decision like this will have to come from him, our commander in chief."

Falk stood as the panel members left the room. The guards returned to his side and escorted him back to his stark white room. He collapsed into the chair beside his bed. On a nearby writing table lay a notebook and pen. He stared into the distance for a moment. A warm wash of sunlight pushed into the room, leaving the pattern of the barred windows on the linoleum in front of his feet. And he dreaded revisiting the horrors they asked that he describe.

Hiam's face floated before his eyes without invitation, resurrecting his shame. Old questions resurfaced—issues he suppressed. What if he had tried harder? Could he have supplied the Polish resistance with inside information about safe passage out of Poland? Derailed a few trains? Should he have at least attempted that? These thoughts weren't new. He cycled through these options every moment during the eighteen months he wore the German uniform. But he was here now. He'd withstood deprivation, pain, and setbacks but hadn't lost focus. His cyanide pill was confiscated, but he no longer needed it. Now, as he reached his goal, the sun through the window felt like a celebration of finding himself in the place he fought so long to reach.

A fly buzzed against the window, skirting the edges in search of an opening. Then the tiny *tap tap* sound of its attempts to break through. He had been that fly. Now he'd found his opening.

He smoothed out the top page, determined to remember every sight, every indignity, even if it took all night.

-35-

IZAAK TAUBER

Terezín, Czechoslovakia - June 23, 1944

Izaak had forgotten how much fun it was to skip instead of walking everywhere. He hadn't been strong or happy enough to do this for a long time. Tomorrow was the day he and the other children rehearsed for, the day they would perform a play in front of the Danish International Red Cross. He wasn't sure who they were, but there was a lot of hustle and bustle in the town and they were almost ready to show off the nice city they made.

The Jewish Council gave everyone parts to perform throughout their city during the Red Cross visit. Izaak had three parts, all pretty easy to remember, and he was a fast runner, so he could dart down back alleys to get to his next scene. It was exciting, almost like being in a make-believe storybook. Although, something about what they were being asked to do, also seemed made-up.

Adults whispered in worried tones but stopped when he was nearby. And Mama was nervous, squeezing him extra tight each time they got near each other. He loved it but also worried because she acted as if she might not get the chance again one day. He wanted to believe everything was as celebratory as it seemed but sometimes wondered if this play was a one-time show. And when the curtain came down at the end, they'd go back to how it had been. But he pushed that thought away. It would be silly to go through so much effort to make the town nicer if it wasn't going to stay that way.

Mevr. Friedl Dicker-Brandeis moved their artwork into a clean building with lots of lights. She called it the showroom. "No more hiding your wonderful work in the barracks," she announced. Every inch of the walls was covered with their colorful paintings, and from a distance, the room looked like a beautiful quilt. The new sign on the building read Children's Art Gallery. Mama gave him an extra big squeeze when she saw that eight of his paintings were hung on the first wall people would walk past when they entered.

His friend Aden's family and other people from Denmark were moved into newly painted houses that came with an added surprise—now families could live together! Mamas and Papas and children all in the same house. When Izaak visited Aden at his new home, there were normal beds with linens and blankets, and even a small kitchen. This meant Aden and his family could eat at home and not in the warehouse. Most special of all, a toilet and shower were attached outside the house just for them.

Soon he and Mama would get a house all their own. Right now, they only had four other people in their room, but the old woman named Greta snored like a big, brown bear. And Izaak was sure she was the one passing gas every night.

In the last couple of weeks, men busily painted the rooms in the houses yellow or white, and women, including Mama, sewed blue curtains for the windows that faced the square. Izaak hoped they would get a house near the new playground and pool. So far, he and the other children were not allowed to play in either, but after tomorrow that would change.

And as if the town wasn't already so nice, they now had a school. Somehow the hospital patients were allowed to move someplace else. Probably, to a much better place because the old hospital smelled like broken toilets and rotten food. The whole building was fixed up and repainted with bright colors, and inside, there were rows of benches and desks and a new chalkboard. A small note on the door said the school was closed for vacation. It wouldn't be long before he and the other students could stop hiding in attics to learn. He'd be back in a real class with honest-to-goodness books. The only question was what grade he would be in since he'd missed most of second grade.

He waited in their room until his mama returned from work then they could walk together to the dining hall. She didn't seem as thrilled as he was about having menus made of pretty paper with typed words. The first night the menus appeared he held one up. "Look! They're like the ones in the restaurants we used to go to with Papa." She used her pretend smile, the look he'd seen on her face so many times since they left Amsterdam.

They needed to find Papa. He always made Mama laugh no matter how sad she was. He'd put on funny clothes or walked like a monkey, or used silly voices that made Mama giggle even when she tried not to.

Footsteps sounded on the stairs leading to their room. Mama turned the corner of the doorway. When she smiled this time, it was real. "Did you have a nice day, love?"

He told her about delivering messages to new buildings while she bandaged two fingers. Sewing curtains was prickly work. As they walked to the warehouse to eat, Izaak held her not-sore hand. "Soon we can eat at home like Aden's family. Won't that be nice?"

She was quiet for a few moments. "I suppose. But I don't really mind the long tables and all the company, Izaak. I find strength in these friendships."

After they sat down, her words ran through his head as he ate a stew loaded with chicken and potatoes. Mama and the other women talked and talked. He realized he did the same with his friends in art class. Maybe they didn't need a house of their own, after all, just lots of friends.

They finished and put their plates in the bins to be washed.

Mama rubbed his back. "Let's go see the new pavilion."

At the town square they sat on the lawn. Musicians were practicing one last time before the guests arrived in the morning.

The grass was soft, tickling the back of his legs when he straightened them to lie back and study the darkening sky. Once, he tried to mix paint the color of what happens between the blue of day and the black of night. But it wasn't just one color. Rose, purple, and blue moved in and out as night took over, changing again and again, but slowly. He doubted he could ever mix that shade just right.

Later, he awoke as Mama laid him on their mattress and snuggled in next to him. He didn't remember falling asleep, but that was the thing about the Sandman—he was tricky.

Mama softly ran her fingers around his cheek and chin. "You have been the bravest boy, Izaak." She trailed her fingers down his arms, a touch that always relaxed him. "And I want you to remember something. If there comes a day when we aren't together for a while, I'll need you to stay strong."

A hot feeling of worry shot through his body, and he was wide awake, sitting upright. "But we will always be together!"

Mama pulled him back to her side and held him close. "Maybe the Red Cross will see your talents and want to take you and the other children to a better town."

"I won't go with them." What was she thinking? "I will always stay with you."

"Of course, Izaak." She kissed his forehead.

He fought the urge to cry because she just called him brave and he wanted to live up to that name. "Besides, we're in a good place now. We need to stay and wait for our own house and for a swim in the pool, and I'll go to school here."

"Things are much better now, I know." She moved backward, so she could see his face. He knew she saw a few tears there. "Our lives might stay this way until the war is over, but...I need you to promise me that if it's God's will that we are separated, you will do everything you can to stay well and be strong until we meet again."

He didn't want to promise anything like that because promising might mean what she said could happen. After losing Papa, he couldn't lose Mama.

"Izaak?"

Tears fell, and he couldn't stop them. Now he was worried about this Red Cross group and what they had in mind for children. His mama seemed to know a secret about them. Suddenly, he didn't want them to come to their freshly scrubbed town. He hoped their train got lost.

She wrapped her arms around him and scooped him closer, whispering in his ear. "Remember when we talked about the stars?"

He nodded, holding real still, afraid they might be separated at any moment.

"God gives us all a light, and after we die, we carry it to heaven..."

she whispered. Izaak always liked this story. "And hang it in the dark sky, letting everyone below know we are safe, that we are watching, especially when times feel gloomy."

He shifted on the mattress and relaxed his death grip on Mama's hand. "Lots and lots of people are already there."

Mama nodded. "Watching over us."

"Do Catholics take lights to their heaven?" He wasn't sure what he understood about who belonged in God's group and who didn't.

She laughed for the first time in a long while. He loved the sound.

"We all have the same heaven, love." She fluffed the skinny pillow under his head even though it never changed the softness. "Let's get to sleep. You have important things to do tomorrow."

The next morning, he dressed in the new clothes he was given and kissed his mama goodbye. "Have fun with the babies," he called before dashing down the stairs.

Mama's part in the play was to work in the new infants' home. It had real cribs and clean blue baby blankets. The glass bottles and nipples arrived, so the babies didn't have to suck on rags dipped in milk. That was messy, and the babies often cried for more after they ate. Today, Mama wore a clean, white nurse's uniform, a lot like the one she wore in Amsterdam.

Izaak stopped by Aden's house, but no one was home. The family must have already left for the train station. He ran the rest of the way there, dodging Ghetto guards who were also dashing around to make sure everybody knew it was time for the big show.

The musicians were ready to play at the bandstand, and the café was full of people—some inside, some at tables out front. Izaak joined his fellow actors, the children who were there to meet the train. There was so much excitement in the air that it was hard to stand still. He spotted Aden, who nudged in next to him, and they admired each other's shiny shoes, clean trousers and shirts. Before this, Izaak only saw his friend in used-up clothes. Now he looked like someone to get to know all over again.

Commandant Rahm sat in the back seat of his polished black car, wait-ing like the rest of them. In just a moment, the train carrying the Red Cross would arrive.

And just like that, the ground rumbled under his feet. Dark smoke from the engine showed up first. Then the black engine, pulling passenger cars, slid into sight from around the last curve.

Time must have broken. After an extra-long screech, the train finally stopped and sat vibrating on the tracks for a longer period. His legs quiv-ered from the vibration or excitement. He couldn't tell which.

The steps on the passenger car unfolded. Soldiers in crisp-looking black uniforms came down first and then moved to the side to help two men and two women off the train. They were dressed in light-grey matching uniforms, suits for the men, dresses for the women. A white band encircled their arms with a red cross in the center. The same marking was on the little hats they wore. They looked important and kind, not at all like children-stealers. Mama would be relieved. He most certainly was.

Rahm, now out of his car, shook their hands, and then turned to in-troduce the Ghetto elder, Dr. Paul Eppstein, who said, "Welcome to Theresienstadt." This was the German name for Terezín, and they told all the actors to use it if addressed by the visitors.

Izaak's part was about to begin. The group followed Rahm, and when he passed close to the children, he offered them candy. They each took a piece, and all together said, "Thank you, Uncle Rahm."

He laughed, patting the back of one boy and tousling the hair of an-other. "You brighten my day, children."

Izaak was always afraid of the commandant. As an SS officer, he was dressed like the mean guards he came to distrust. Rahm never spoke to them before but since rehearsal, it now seemed the man learned to like children.

Then Rahm smiled once again before leading the Danish officials away. The Red Cross workers waved at Izaak's group as they walked by, and on command, the children offered their greeting in the Danish language they practiced. "Welcome to our town" or in the case of Izaak's line, "It's nice to have you here."

With a scout running ahead of the visitors, the orchestra was playing Verdi's *Marcha Triunfal de Aida* before the group reached the town square. This was Izaak's cue to get to his next station while Aden ran off to his family's house, where the officials would stop later. Aden and three other children from his country were lucky enough to be seen playing on their front lawn with a rocking horse and a tetherball pole.

Izaak dashed through the back streets and reached the main route ahead of the visitors. Here, bakers dressed in white smocks and white hats busily kneaded bread. A load of fresh vegetables arrived on a clean wagon, and hopefully from now on, the hearse would remain parked in the distant alley where it was now hidden.

On Market Street, which used to be D Street, a group of the prettiest girls in town stood in front of the newly opened market, ready with baskets of fresh fruit. Izaak's part was to pay for the produce as the Red Cross people passed by and then carry his sack away, humming. In his pocket were real Korunas, not the fake money The Bank of the Jewish Autonomy paid his mama.

The Red Cross tour in their town was expected to last five hours, perhaps six. The group would visit the infants' house, the children's art gallery, and the Jewish elder's office after reaching Market Street. Izaak sat on one of the many benches along the way. The man playing the part of a city banker was ready to smoke his cigar and hand out cigarettes at just the right time. The pharmacist was waiting to help an elderly couple into his shop. It was nice to feel important.

A girl from the store approached Izaak and handed him a large red apple. He hadn't seen anything like it in such a long time. Just the feel of the produce in his hand was unreal. The ripe fruit inside of a shiny red peel. Nothing smooshy or wrinkly about this one.

"Go ahead. Eat it," she said. She pointed to the interior of the market. "There's so much food in there, they won't miss a few apples. We've all had one."

"Thank you." He bit into the crisp fruit and it made a loud snapping noise, the sound bringing back wonderful memories. He'd eaten many apples and never thought about how special they were. The juice ran down his chin, and he wiped it away with his arm before taking another bite. When half was gone, he slipped the remaining portion inside his shirt, where it sat sticky against his skin, saving it for Mama.

It wasn't long before the scout hurried to the top of Market Street and gave the five-minute warning. Izaak walked a few steps away from the fruit market and stood in his place. His heart beat faster. The Red Cross visitors entered the street, and on cue, he walked to the market, pointing out fruits to the same girl who gave him the apple. She began loading everything he pointed to into a sack, and he paid her with gleaming coins, just as the officials passed behind him. The visitors laughed and talked with the officers like old friends. The Germans' faces were neighborly, so unlike their usual harsh and demanding looks. He lifted his sack of fruit and headed back the same way the visitors entered. His second performance was clearly a success, and the third act was the one he looked forward to most.

He stopped by their apartment and hid the fruit under their mattress. Mama would be so surprised when she found it. With hours to kill before his last act, he sat on their cushion and thought about what it must be like to be a famous artist like Joseph E. A. Spier. The Germans asked Mr. Spier, a Dutch artist, to paint eighteen different watercolors. They were made into booklets, souvenirs for the Red Cross officials. The paintings showed cheerful scenes from Terezín/Theresienstadt, joyful people going about their everyday activities like in today's play.

Izaak memorized Spier's paintings in the booklets. He hoped someday he could paint like that. Spier also had secret paintings showing the not-so-happy times. Back when the town was dirty, and Rahm wasn't nice. Those images showed crowded bunkhouses painted with drab colors. Workers pulling the hearse full of dead people. And families gathered in a shadowy room at night to listen to a single accordion player, whose skeletal face looked scary in the light from one flickering candle.

Izaak's final part in the play was to help hand out the beautiful booklets. He kept one under their mattress to show Papa when they were together again. He stood up and left the building, trying to think how he might spend the next few hours. Unlike Aden's house, Izaak's courtyard at the Dresden Barracks had no playground equipment, but there was a half-inflated ball he and the other boys liked to kick around. He walked to the courtyard to see if anyone was free to play.

There, he found a tight circle of people praying over a wooden box. It was the only kind of funeral allowed. From here, the family would carry the coffin to the crematorium to be burned. The ashes were then stored in The Columbarium, an underground building at the end of a long brick tunnel. Once, he ran a message to the Jewish worker in charge, Solomon, a pleasant man who spoke Dutch. Inside, there were thousands of boxes filling the shelves, and he must have looked scared because Solomon led him outside. "Remember, here the dead have a name, son. Their families will know where they rest, unlike other..."

He didn't finish the sentence but started again. "Each box in there has the person's name, birthdate, place they were born, and the day they died. About as much respect as they will get from the Germans."

He didn't want to think about the dead on such a memorable day. He left the courtyard, and walked through blocks of back alleys, past the old building where the sick and elderly now lived. An old musician, who often performed for them, walked slowly down the street, his cane tap-tapping the cobblestones. He seemed to be enjoying the warm band of sun brightening the narrow space way between the buildings.

On the outskirts of the city was his favorite spot, the gardens along the moat. He descended the stone steps, leaving the higher walls of the town behind. In the spring, the cherry trees bloomed all at once, as if one day they decided to dress up in pink skirts. The smell was so sweet it made him dizzy under their graceful limbs.

He walked through the orchard, remembering times he and Aden picked cherries, secretly eating them when the guards looked away. Later this summer, they would pick peaches, pears, and crunchy apples. He licked his lips—the taste of apple still clearly there.

Today, workers bent over long rows of lettuce and peas, filling baskets to be loaded onto a wagon. Two horses ate tall grass as they waited to pull the wagon back up the slope to town.

Izaak climbed to the upper edge of the moat. From here, he could see forever, so forever must be able to see him right back. He waved his arms at no one, imagining what he looked like at the top of this tall hill. Way below, he barely made out houses beside two lines of trees shading a road. Farther on was the Lower Fortress. He was too far away for anyone to see him, and he'd never seen anyone there. Just as he started to look away, he spotted tiny dots walking through the archway, leading from the fortress. Other dots carrying itty-bitty guns, walked alongside he assumed were prisoners.

His heart thumped in his ears. What if Papa was one of the prisoners? He would be so surprised to see his son. If he could just get a little closer, he could tell if one of them was him. Of course, he shouldn't go beyond the moat, but just this one time would be fine, and he was ready with an answer if anyone asked why he was down there. He slid over the side of the mounded hill and walked downward, tracing a path the workers took when they gathered hay for the horses. After twenty minutes of winding down the hillside and through fields of brush, he reached the road leading to the Lower Fortress. Now his clothes were dirty and not so new-looking, but he could clean them up before his third part in the play. He crouched in a dry ditch and watched the men working in the field, picking up big rocks.

Up close, the men were grimy and skinny like the men in Płaszów. They dug in the field and then staggered to load rocks into a big wagon. They didn't talk, but the silence was broken by the heavy *thunks* of rocks landing on each other.

Izaak shielded his eyes, squinting at the men, looking for Papa.

Suddenly, he was yanked to his feet from behind and dropped hard onto the dirt road.

He struggled to stand, rubbing a sore elbow, as an SS guard spun him around and yelled words Izaak didn't understand. Other men with guns soon surrounded him. The world swam in a blurry panic of yelling, mixed with his overwhelming fear—he was going to be killed. Mama would never know what happened to him. He wouldn't finish his part in the play. A man slapped him hard across the face, and as pain radiated through his head, he burst into tears. He held his arms over his head.

"I've come for hay to feed the horses," he said. He pointed to the large fortress. It seemed so far away now. Through his tears it blurred, looking pretend and toy-sized.

A big man dragged him to another soldier. Izaak's toes barely touched the ground as his legs cycled along the road.

"What are you doing here?" the guard asked in Dutch. This man had a droopy mustache and a deep scar across his forehead.

"I came for hay," Izaak said again, as he gulped the spit stuck in his throat.

The men discussed it over his head before the guard spoke again.

"You are lying. The workers come with a cart to collect the hay." He smiled a rotten smile. "Is your cart in your pocket?"

"No."

The men laughed.

Lying was a very bad thing, but he'd learned it was allowed if you were about to be killed.

The guards talked together.

Izaak decided to just tell the truth. "I'm on break from our special play in town. It's for the Red Cross. I'm looking for my papa and when I saw the men down h—" His voice quit on him, but his mouth still moved.

The guards studied him. They kept looking at the town on the hill, and Izaak wished he was still up there, looking down. The guard with the scar took him by the arm and led him along a road under the line of trees and toward the opening to the Lower Fortress. He tried to pull away, but the man was very strong.

"You'll be taken back tomorrow. After the Red Cross leaves."

"But I need to be there this afternoon. I have another part. Please let me go back."

"We can't." The guard stopped and scowled at Izaak. He leaned close and Izaak smelled cigarettes and onions. "You see... what we do down here is quite different than what happens up there. And the Red Cross doesn't need to learn that from a nosy child."

The SS guard prodded him over a stone bridge that crossed another moat. They entered a brick tunnel which opened onto a narrow courtyard, with long brick buildings on each side. Tall grass grew on top of the dirt piled on the roof of the one-story buildings. The guard pulled him to an open door along the building.

Izaak dug in his heels. It looked like a dark prison inside. "No," was all he could say before the guard pushed him into the empty room, where he slid across the rough cement floor.

"This is what you wanted, right? When the men come back from work, you'll go with them to their barracks. Search all you want for that papa of yours." The guard closed the wooden door and the click of the lock echoed in the cell.

The room smelled bad, and the stains on the floor in the corner were probably where other people gave up trying to hold their pee.

Izaak stood and leaned against the door. Maybe the guard was just teaching him a lesson and soon the door would fly open. The man would laugh and say, "Go on, now. Get back up to Theresienstadt, you little rascal."

He waited and waited. The sunbeam through the tiny window in the door moved across the floor and then started to climb the far wall.

And still the door didn't open.

-36-

HERBERT MÜLLER

Crossing the Atlantic - July 1944

Herbert set down the pen on the large wooden desk, studying his signature on the oath of secrecy. And prayed he made the right decision for his family even though he knew they had no choice but to leave for Germany immediately. His stomach twisted in a knot when his complaint about Frieda being attacked was shrugged off. The answer? "We are overcrowded and undermanned."

He'd learned two things about their repatriation. First, his family would be exchanged for "real American citizens" trapped in Europe. Second, anyone who volunteered for deportation to Germany had the legal right to return to the United States at some future date after the war. Those who did not agree had no such privilege. In spite of all that transpired, he most certainly wanted to return.

He rounded up his family. The first step was receiving typhoid shots and smallpox inoculations. Next, they were escorted to the small room where they'd all slept the night before. Each family member was allowed to pack only one suitcase. With no idea how long they would remain in Germany, they added blankets, sweaters, and overcoats—items Jutta thought to bring from their home.

The repatriation process required that Herbert have a precise destination such as an address for the family in Germany. He gave the last known address of his married cousin, Elke Dressler, in Wiesbaden. He sent off a hastily written letter announcing their imminent arrival at some unknown date in the near future. The letter was sure to be a shock. Americans showing up in Germany when everyone else was trying to get out.

With suitcases ready, they changed into their street clothes for the voyage. Thankfully, they wouldn't arrive looking like criminals in their military prison uniforms. Some good news was Pastor Graf would be on their Liberty ship, the *MS Gripsholm*. He was returning to Stuttgart.

"Looks like we're in this together," the pastor said.

When they boarded a ferry to take them to the ship, the day offered a brilliant blue sky with seagulls circling overhead, their harsh cries matching Herbert's frayed nerves. The events of the last few days, coupled with the dread of the unknown future, were taking their toll. But he knew his role. He'd stay positive while leading his family safely to Wiesbaden. A plea ran through his head. God, let that city still be standing. On board the Swedish luxury ship, the *MS Gripsholm*, they were shown to their cabins where they stowed their cases. He and Jutta would finally be together, the children in the next cabin adjoining theirs, and Otto's separate was room in the same hallway. His father's health improved with the decision to leave. Confinement agreed with none of them, and even though they couldn't be certain they wouldn't be sleeping in the barn with cows in a few weeks, the feeling of no longer being trapped encouraged them.

They returned to the immense deck and sat on benches, watching the ship fill with hundreds of deportees and just as many crates of Red Cross supplies.

"We aren't the only ones who were convinced to leave," Jutta said.

"I'm looking forward to meeting my cousins." Frieda's pigtails lifted in the breeze blowing across deck.

"Yeah. With our amazing German skills"—Alfred patted his sister on the back—"you and I'll be able to greet them and name a few foods."

"We should have listened to you, Grandpa," Frieda said. "Maybe we can practice with you on the way there."

"Good plan." Otto reached for her hand and held it. "Think, of what you want, to learn to say."

"I know," Alfred said. Then in a whiny falsetto voice he continued.

"Take us in, please. We are convicts on the run from America." Jutta laughed and Herbert couldn't help but smile.

The ship's engines rumbled to life. The vibration under Herbert's feet signaled there was no turning back. "We're off," he said, pushing as much excitement as he could into his tone. The ocean liner slid away from the concrete pier and performed a slow rotation until its bow pointed them toward Europe. A pod of dolphins raced alongside, drilling light grayish-blue tunnels through the black water.

His family fell silent. Frieda leaned into Jutta's embrace as the New York skyline and the Statue of Liberty were absorbed by the horizon. And just like that, they were at sea.

Memories spun through Herbert's head like playing cards flipping in the spokes of a bicycle wheel. Church picnics, community dances, a German community that loved Beethoven and Bach unapologetically. Wonderful evenings around the radio, with Jutta knitting or baking while wide-eyed children listened to the Lone Ranger and Gangbusters. He pictured Alfred's face in his favorite comic books, *Aquaman* and the *Green Arrow*. Frieda and her stamp collection. Her pen pals from Kansas and Nevada. Her musical ability.

Through it all, there were hard times, as well. Times that molded them, united them as a family. But none of it, neither the long work days in the mill and orchard alongside his father nor the time he almost lost Jutta to summer pneumonia, and not even the death of his mother, prepared him for this moment. The country he loved, and believed loved him back, was trading his family like livestock.

He cleared his throat. "Fact Time, family. Here's mine. Time passes by so quickly. I know this seems like the worst that could possibly happen. But together we will make it. Someday, perhaps sooner than we think, New York City will be growing before our eyes instead of shrinking. You wait. Uncle Sam will regain his sanity."

"I never want to see New York City again," Frieda stated.

Jutta brushed away a strand of hair caught against her eyelashes.

"My turn. It's easy to be angry right now." She'd caught a cold and developed a cough that gave her voice a froggy tone. "We've seen our neighbors' and the government's mistakes. But the world slowly spins no matter how angry we might be. Let's think of this as a journey and see where it takes us."

Her insights always sounded prayerful to Herbert. He felt as if he should add an Amen.

"My Anni...I wish was with us," Otto said. "We talked about, returning to Chermany one day...just not this way."

They waited for Alfred to share his thoughts. He remained sullen.

"Son?" Herbert said. "You get to have your say."

"You're not going to like it."

"You know the deal. All facts are accepted." He patted Alfred's leg. "Spit it out."

"We're going to be forgotten." Alfred's mouth twisted into a bitter line. "Maybe that's not a fact but we're already unwanted. Who's going to give a hoot about us coming back?"

Herbert felt an invisible fist holding and squeezing his heart. These same unvoiced fears swirled through his head each hour. He ruffled Alfred's hair and one more time forced cheerfulness into his voice. "I promise you, I will make sure we come home together."

Just after sundown, Herbert met Pastor Graf on deck. They leaned on the steel railing. The relaxing *shush* and *slosh* of the waves vibrated the side of the ship. A pink and orange horizon lay nearly lost in a low-lying bank of clouds while brilliant clusters of starlight formed directly overhead.

Graf lit a cigarette and inhaled deeply.

Although Graf was twenty years older, and they were raised 4,000 miles apart, they had more in common than Herbert shared with his friends in Tulpehocken.

"Who's waiting for you in Stuttgart?" He knew about the pastor's life in Troy, New York, but not much of the pastor's German family.

"I have a married sister and three nieces. About the ages of your children. Her husband is fighting, last she understood, somewhere in Northern Italy."

"You have no other family?"

Graf shrugged. "A brother, but I have heard nothing from him. Could be dead. My father died in France at the end of the Great War. My mother died of a lung infection two years before I immigrated to America." He held up the cigarette. "Would you like one? These supposedly make for healthy lungs."

"No thank you." Herbert smoked when he and Karl were younger, mainly because other teenagers were trying it. He quit when Jutta let him know she wouldn't kiss him if he continued.

"How old was your father when he died?"

"Forty-five. Too young." He blew out a long stream of smoke. "I still have his letters. I should say, they're in my desk back in Troy. My father called the war a great stupidity."

"I suppose the initial itch to fight for your country wears off when the shock of what war is really all about hits you in the face. My brother is fighting in the Pacific. I wonder what he will say when it's over, or when he learns we've been sent to Germany." Karl could be dead for all Herbert knew as his brother was stationed on an aircraft carrier, flying from one battle to the next.

"My father's last letter was right after the army reached a ceasefire agreement with the French, just before he died of pneumonia," Graf said. "He wrote of an image he believed he would never forget. A French and a German soldier were on their knees leaning against each other as if embracing. They'd pierced each other with bayonets and dropped like that to the ground, dying in each other's arms."

"Wow. The big shots moving the pieces around on the war board don't see that kind of thing, do they?" Darkness closed in and the red tip of Graf's cigarette glowed in the gloom.

"I emigrated to avoid this war. Just because I was clergy did not mean I wouldn't be called to fight when the pool of troops ran dry. Knowing what I know now about the Nazi plan, I never could have aided and abetted the Nazi cause while ministering to the troops. I fear I would do as Falk did. Take notes and try to tell the world, even if it meant I died."

"I guess we all would." He prayed he would never have to find out.

-37-

IZAAK TAUBER

Terezín, Czechoslovakia - Early July 1944

After hours passed and no one opened the prison door, Izaak cried himself to sleep on the dirty floor. He'd made a big mistake, one that might mean he would never see his mother or friends again.

He woke up hungry, and the sun was now higher on the wall. The day was ending. He missed the last act of the play, and more painful than that, he missed his mama. He didn't want their talk from the night before to be what was happening now, where he needed to stay strong until they met again. His face quivered and more tears fell. His nose dripped snot, but he didn't care. He'd never be strong without her.

Footsteps crunched on the stones outside. Someone fiddled with the door, and he trembled as the rusty hinges screeched as it opened. Would he be dragged out and shot? A mean-faced guard waited there and motioned him outside. He struggled to his feet and wiped his arm across his drippy nose. He stepped out into the fresh air of the evening and took in a long shaky breath. The guard said something he didn't understand, but four men in ragged grey clothes surrounded him.

One of the shabby men spoke in Dutch. "You'll stay in our barracks."

Izaak nodded because he couldn't talk. His mouth was so dry from crying out all his water.

The men led him to a long stone building. Once inside, he was in a room with wide wooden bunk beds like the terrible quarters in the last two camps.

He tried to be brave but broke down and cried again. One man from the group of four prisoners knelt in front of him. "I'll bet you're hungry." When he smiled, Izaak noticed the man's teeth were broken, but his eyes were kind.

Izaak nodded. He was starving. The half apple he'd eaten was long gone.

The man with the broken smile led him to the edge of a bed and handed him a tin cup. Inside was cool water. After the first sip, Izaak gulped the rest. Then the man offered a piece of bread. As he ate, he studied the room, hoping against hope his papa was one of the skinny men staring back.

When he finished the bread, an older boy with holes in his pants sat next to him. "I'm Nicklaus." He nudged Izaak on the shoulder. "Dutch, like you."

"If you're from Amsterdam, have you crossed paths with my papa? Saul Tauber?"

The boy laughed. "I'm from Aalsmeer. But it's near Amsterdam." He crossed his arms as if he suddenly caught a chill in the hot room. "What's your name?"

"Izaak."

"How old are you?"

"Eight...In July, I'll be nine."

"Well, Izaak. It is July. Now we can call you The Brave Nine-Year-Old Dutch Boy from the hill."

He was nine? He imagined by now—this birthday—he would be back at home already with his papa and mama, not alone in some dirty old camp. And these men thought he was brave? He'd done nothing but cry for hours and ruin everything.

"I think my papa could be here." His chest tightened as if a rope had wrapped around it. He unfolded the drawing and showed it to the men. When they handed it back, he was sad to see the pencil lines smeared more than the last time he looked. Papa was getting fuzzier and fuzzier.

The man with the broken smile spoke. "A message will go out with your papa's name, but not all of the men are back from their jobs." He shook his head. "None of us in this barracks know him."

Nicklaus's face brightened. He pulled three shiny stones from his pocket. "I have an idea. Let me teach you to juggle." The older boy deftly circled the pebbles in perfect arcs above his hands before catching and releasing each of them.

The stones orbited each other over and over, almost hypnotizing Izaak.

After a few minutes, Nicklaus handed two stones to him. "Start with these."

Everyone watched as Izaak flipped one pebble into the air. He caught it before realizing he forgot to toss the second one in the air. After chasing the stones across the wooden floor too many times, he handed them back. "I'll stick with drawing."

When the sun set, his stomach hurt, and he felt like the air had leaked out of his insides. He climbed onto the bunk and stretched out next to Nicklaus. An old man on the bunk above softly sang in another language. Izaak remembered that just this morning he greeted the Red Cross train. It felt like weeks ago. His eyes slowly closed, and he drifted off to sleep.

Sometime in the night, a hand touched his arm, and he bolted upright. It was dark. A shadow hovered over him. He tried to back away, but the bed was packed with people, and he was stuck out on the edge.

"No!" he said, but his voice was too full of fear and it came out like a mouse's squeak.

The man reached for him again. "It's okay." A hand pulled him to a sitting position as he tried to fight him off. Then the man gasped as if choking. "Izaak, is it you?"

Izaak said he would recognize Papa by his voice, and it was a good thing he did because the boney man, who scooped him up and squeezed him tight, felt nothing like Papa.

Someone lit a candle, and he came into focus.

"Papa?" Was he dreaming? Izaak returned the squeeze. They dropped onto the floor wrapped around each other, and Papa rocked him back and forth. This was the happiest day he could ever remember! He couldn't wait to tell Mama. They had done it! They were all together again. "I found you!" He traced Papa's face with his fingers and tried to match up the lines with those he'd drawn.

His papa was crying, and his face was twisted, making him look even more like a stranger. "Yes. You found me." He ran his hand through Izaak's hair, down his arms. "You've grown, my son."

"I'm nine now." Half of his birthday wish was granted. His mama and papa were here. Now they just had to get back to the Netherlands.

The other men in the barracks were awake now and moving around like shadowy ghosts, pouring out of the beds. Someone lit a lantern and more light filled the room. A man began clapping, slowly at first, and then everyone joined in. Soon the applause was thunderous. The smile on Izaak's face was stuck there, and every time he tried to relax, it popped back in place. There should be balloons and pony rides and celebration cakes!

Papa took his hand and pulled him from the floor. "We have to go to my barracks. I need to be there for morning roll call." He paused and looked around at his fellow prisoners. "Thank you for spreading the word that my little man was here."

He and Papa tiptoed hand in hand to a building five rows over. Papa's bed was made of boards like everyone else's, but a bed never felt so wonderful. Wrapped in Papa's arms, he asked, "Have you been here the whole time?"

Papa let out a sigh. "I helped build the Atlantic Wall with the other men from our neighborhood, but then they figured out I was Jewish." He ran his hand over Izaak's short hair again and pulled him closer, if that were even possible. "I was in another camp, but not for long, then I came here."

"Mama and I were in two camps before here, both very bad," Izaak said. "Terezín up the hill has been the best, and just this morning we showed off the town to important visitors from Denmark."

Papa didn't laugh as Izaak expected. Moments passed. Papa's body shook and something wet dropped onto Izaak's face. He'd made Papa sad.

"Don't cry. Mama will be so surprised when she sees you again."

Papa gasped for the second time this night. "Izaak. Are you saying your mama is..." His voice cracked, and he quickly cleared his throat. "Your mama is fine?"

"She is. We were in a play just this morning and she sews curtains and we live in a room in a house with an old lady who farts all night, but soon we will get our own place." He didn't know how that would work out since there were still so many people and only a limited number of houses. "At least, I think we will. And she is a nurse again working with babies."

Papa's body sagged. He let out a long breath. "This is a miracle, Izaak. An absolute God-blessed miracle."

"I've been repeating your nice thoughts, Papa. At least three times a day." He took a breath. "A man's true wealth…"

Papa joined in, saying, "is the good he does in this world." He smiled. "You remembered. I'm proud of you."

He liked hearing Papa's deep voice say the words again. He wasn't sure he'd done much good for anyone since Papa went away, but he had tried.

Papa began a quiet prayer Izaak remembered from synagogue, a prayer of thanks. With his papa's voice rumbling near his ear, he fell asleep.

The next morning, he was assigned to underwear duty. Not his favorite, but he got over feeling embarrassed about touching women's undergarments, so it wasn't about that. Heaps of clean clothes dumped from thousands of suitcases somehow made it to the Lower Fortress without their owners, and it made him sad. He knew the families who packed the cases were forced from their homes like him and Mama. And he suspected many were dead.

But he and Mama and Papa were still here. He needed to keep good thoughts running through his head. One at a time.

He kept glancing at Papa, trying to get used to his older, thinner face. Papa insisted Izaak share the stories of his and Mama's journey to Terezín. He wanted to know everything. It was hard to talk about terrible Płaszów, the headstone road, and cruel Commandant Goeth. But they talked about nice things, too. He and Papa stood outside their shelter each night, looking at the lights from the town above and talking to Mama.

A moon hung over the Upper Fortress this night. Izaak snuggled against his papa. "Papa?"

"Yes, son."

"I'm worried Mama thinks the Red Cross workers took me away. Or that I got hurt and can't get back to our barracks."

"The Red Cross workers are good people. If they ever took you, it would be to help you out, so never fear them." Papa kissed the top of Izaak's head. "We'll get a message to her as soon as possible and let her know you're here with me."

The next morning, he stood by as Papa approached Nicklaus, the juggling boy who helped carry wood to the Upper Fortress every day. He asked the boy to pass along a secret message to Mama about his and Izaak's whereabouts, with his added hope they would soon reunite.

After two days, Nicklaus motioned for Papa to come nearer. He reported Mama was so happy he was safe and that he and Izaak were together. She had nearly gone crazy with worry ever since Izaak disappeared. The Upper Fortress was still treating her well, and now a movie was being filmed about the town on the hill.

Izaak was jealous he wouldn't be in a real movie, and he couldn't stop the tears when he thought of being away from Mama but realized Papa needed him, too. Papa said he'd forgotten how to laugh until he saw him again.

His papa worked in the rebuilding department. Sometimes he built barbed-wire fences. But other times he did strange jobs like pile up broken cars and parts of buildings on roads to make it impossible to drive on them. He and his team dug out other roads and filled them with gravel. The job was to stop the Russians. Whoever they were, the Russians were sure not welcome here. This week, he was working with hundreds of other men, digging deep ditches, so army tanks would get stuck nose-down in them. Last night, he made Izaak laugh so hard by hanging over the side of their bunk, pretending to be a stuck tank. "Get my face out of this mud!" he mumbled into his hand. Izaak pulled on his legs, but his papa pretended to be too heavy to move. He was glad Papa was still funny because that made up for everything else that wasn't.

The food was terrible, and everyone smelled dirty. They drank thin coffee for breakfast and ate a small piece of bread. Lunch was a watery soup with no chunks of anything in it. At night, it was more soup. Once a week, they put their clothes in a huge washer and then hung them to dry. Everyone walked around in their dingy underwear, their bodies all pointy with no soft places.

The long factory room Izaak worked in had windows that opened, so the heat didn't cook them on these hot summer days like in the barracks. An attached area at the end of the warehouse held the luggage sent to Terezín from all over. Izaak and Malachi, a boy from Prague, used to sneak into the room and play hide and seek in all the bags and trunks, especially since some were big enough to climb into. It was exciting until the guards yelled at them one day, accusing them of stealing clothes.

Izaak carried the sorted stack of women's slips to the folding and packing table. There, men folded the clothes and packed them into bags, so they looked brand new. He carefully slid his pile next to a long row of folded clothes. "Where are these packages sent?"

A man with a crooked nose looked up from rolling leather belts into coils. "To the enemy," he said in a growly voice. "We Jews are useless. But our apparel is fine enough to clothe Germans." He tossed a belt into a bag.

Izaak couldn't figure out what was going on. This whole mess was one big war, but Germany was fighting everyone else in the world. They were going to be in a lot of trouble, taking people they didn't like and putting them in camps and killing them. But everyone would be scattered and have to find their way back home. He broke his marble bag once and his prized toys rolled in all directions down the street. Some fell into the sewer drains. Others were lost in the leaves and garbage along the curbs. He hadn't recovered half of them. That's what he imagined would happen when family members went looking for each other.

He was lucky. He knew where his family was.

Some men from their barracks made the move to the Upper Fortress, and Papa was trying to get transferred, too. The moment his mama and papa saw each other again after so long, they should have fireworks to go with it. Papa could pick her up and swing her around like he used to do every day when he came home from work. Mama would giggle and Izaak would pretend to hide because he knew Tickle Time was about to happen, and his papa was an expert tickler.

Back to the pile of clothes. Izaak now searched for women's hosiery. Because they were impossible to stack, he learned to roll them up instead.

He tried to prove he was the best worker in the group, the most helpful, if asked. Because if Papa got transferred to the Upper Fortress, he needed to go, too. Only yesterday, two brothers, fifteen and sixteen, were separated. One, who broke his arm, was sent on the train going west and the other sent to a different camp to work in the mica mines. They begged to stay together, but the SS officers beat them with clubs until they followed orders.

Izaak didn't want to, but he'd take a beating if anyone tried to separate him from Papa. He wasn't going to be without him again.

-38-

HERBERT MÜLLER

Aboard the *MS Gripsholm* - August 1944

The Swedish-built *MS Gripsholm* flew the yellow and blue flag of its country. The hull was painted white and lit with bright lights to broadcast its protected status, hopefully lowering the risk of taking a torpedo as they crossed the Atlantic.

It surprised Herbert how quickly his family settled into a routine. With the unknown ahead of them, their ability to adapt to their new surroundings was nice to see. They'd been at sea nearly three weeks, received their second dose of immunizations, and established a normal schedule. After breakfast, they'd walk the deck for an hour, weather permitting, and then settle into one of the community areas to play chess, marbles, dominoes, or the most popular game, Chinese Checkers.

Alfred joined other teenage boys in Ping-Pong, and Frieda was getting faster on a typewriter. The trip took on a vacation-like atmosphere, a relief from the tedium and fears of Ellis Island. Although he worried about Jutta as her cold deepened, now Otto seemed to be coming down with it.

He and Pastor Graf met each day to share news they picked up from other passengers. Today, Graf put his back to the wind and pulled his coat closed.

"I was thinking how expensive we are. All the money and effort to move us off American soil. Hope it's worth it to them."

Herbert watched the ocean, the clouds casting shadows like black islands bobbing on the surface. They morphed and changed shapes, their shadows rising and falling on the swells.

"I worry about that. What if the Germans decide we'd make good laborers? They must have work camps just like the United States has for the German P-O-Ws. What if the German government counterparts forget about reuniting us with our family?"

Graf's brow wrinkled. "I think we're too valuable to their exchange program for them to lose track of us."

"True. They have to help *more important* Americans return home." Had his government really bartered with the Germans, using his family as mere objects of trade? "Big money must have changed hands."

A loud announcement over the ship's speakers momentarily stopped their conversation. The passengers should gather their belongings for the arrival. Herbert stood.

"Let's meet up here and disembark together."

"Yes." Graf shook Herbert's hand. "See you soon."

As the *MS Gripsholm* moved into the Le Vieux Port of Marseille, France, Herbert's heart quickened. His family would be landing on the fringe of a recent battle. The war was up close and real.

Otto stayed in his room to rest until it was time to disembark but the rest of his family climbed topside again. From the ship's deck, they enjoyed a bird's-eye view of the harbor's entrance guarded by ancient stone forts on each side. The horseshoe-shaped port was a buzzing, picturesque waterfront lined with boutiques, restaurants, and cafés. The Allies had wrestled the city away from the Germans six days earlier. The streets were jam-packed, and people cheered while others danced, holding their hands in the air, fingers formed in a V for victory. Girls kissed soldiers. The bars' doors must have been flung open, because drunkenness seemed to prevail.

After ten minutes, Jutta sat on a bench and the children took seats beside her. She was weak from her near-constant coughing.

It might be a long wait before they were allowed to disembark.

Herbert turned to the pastor. "Does it make you nervous that we are so close to the war? A week ago, this place was probably lit up like the Fourth of July."

"We're here just in time. A celebration feels good," Graf said. Then his brow furrowed. "But I do have mixed feelings."

"Why?" Herbert asked. If only they could remain here, he'd be thrilled.

"I'm torn. America is winning and that is the good news, but my German friends and neighbors…What has happened to them these past years?" He set his mouth in a firm line. "I can't help but think this is how Wilhelm Falk's life ended. Fighting to hold a city, but in Italy, overpowered by the Allies."

"I'm sorry," Herbert said. "Of course, you're torn between two countries."

"I feel allegiant to both."

"When we get interviewed, I'm going to ask about staying here, rather than chasing the battle into Germany. Jutta and Otto need rest, and not this nonstop travel."

"Let me know how that goes." Graf smiled. "Flexibility does not seem to be in our itinerary."

Herbert turned to Jutta. "I'm going to wake up Pops and bring his bag up"—he kissed the top of her head—"Sit tight, and I'll be back."

He wound through the passengers, heading for the staterooms and tried to shake off a sense of impending doom. His family would be fine. He just needed to adopt Graf's positive attitude. They were guaranteed safe passage to Elke's house with protection by military escorts. They'd been treated well, coddled almost, compared to their time on Ellis Island. But something nagged at him.

He tapped on his father's door and waited. He was glad Otto took a nap before their situation turned crazy again. Except for the chest cold, the ocean crossing added color to his father's cheeks, and he walked taller, ready to take on whatever came next.

He knocked louder. "Pops." He leaned closer to the door. "Time to go. Let me grab your case."

When no sound came from beyond the door, he turned the knob and stepped inside. The interior cabin was dark, but that wasn't what caused him to stall. He and Otto slept side by side on their cots for months in the open dormitory area, and he knew every breathing pattern Otto made. From the short quiet breaths when he was barely falling asleep, to his rumbling snores in the middle of the night.

The room was too quiet. Before he reached his father's side, anguish moved through his chest knowing what he would find—his father was dead.

~39~

IZAAK TAUBER

Terezín, Czechoslovakia - September 1944

Izaak liked snuggling against Papa as they sat on their bunk even though Papa was all bones now when he squeezed him.

The prisoners crowded in the biggest barracks to listen to Mr. Eppstein and Mr. Gerron talk about the movie they filmed in the Upper Fortress. It sounded like a success, but for some reason, the day they finished the movie, the two men were sent to the Lower Fortress.

Was his mama in the movie, maybe sewing, or feeding babies? He would ask the men after the talk. The movie was called *The Führer Gives the Jews a Town,* and it took eleven days to film.

"I doubt we will see it," Gerron said. "Once the filming was over, things"—he seemed to look right at Izaak—"returned to normal."

Kurt Gerron was an actor in real life, so he would know how to make a good movie. Paul Eppstein remained the main contact in the Upper Fortress between Commandant Rahm and the prisoners. Last Izaak saw, the two men got along fine, so it was strange he was sent down here now. Gideon Klein, who set up all the concerts in the town's new bandstand was also here along with artist Unger Rita, who helped Mr. Spier provide the artwork for the souvenir booklets for the Red Cross. Maybe they were here to now beautify the Lower Fortress.

Mr. Eppstein wiped a line of sweat from his face. The inside of the barracks was always too hot in the afternoon. "We must hold strong. The Red Army is rumored to be closing in."

That red-colored army must be on the prisoners' side because the men nodded their heads and many smiled, while others prayed. Izaak didn't understand it all, but the Germans were afraid of the Reds and the Russians. He was glad something scared them. They'd done nothing but ruin everyone's lives and keep the prisoners scared all day, every day.

"Is the war almost over?" Izaak whispered as he played with his papa's ring finger, where there used to be a gold band.

"It is sounding more positive. The groups fighting the Germans are closing in on all sides."

So many times, in his head, Izaak sketched what it would be like when his family returned home. Now it might finally happen. His papa would touch the praying hands door knocker and make a wish for good luck. Mama would check out the kitchen and pull drawers open, amazed by the choices there. Sometimes in his drawing, he raced next door to see if Guus were home, or he and Papa would walk hand in hand along the canals and get ice cream.

With the Reds moving in, Izaak and Papa's jobs changed. Papa was now building coffins, this time for German soldiers. Izaak sprayed military uniforms with a white dye, so the German soldiers could wear them and hide out in a town called the Russian Front. The strong-smelling paint gave Izaak headaches that made him dizzy for hours after.

"The trains are running on full schedule again," Mr. Gerron said. "We all know what that means."

Most of the men were silent but others swore. Izaak didn't know what *full schedule* meant. He leaned in to ask Papa, who gently shushed him.

"Friedl Dicker-Brandeis agreed to go on the transport with most of the children. Her husband volunteered to board with her." Mr. Eppstein studied his hands. His face was sad, and his mouth jumped around as if something inside was fighting to get out.

His art teacher was gone. He hoped whatever town she and the children went to, she could start another art class. Of course, he would miss out on that. And what of the paintings and drawings that hung in the art gallery? Maybe Mama could find a way to send a few down to brighten up their brown and dirty barracks. He and Papa hadn't heard from her in the past week and that worried him, but Nicklaus blamed himself. With less people in the Upper Fortress, it was more dangerous now to exchange messages.

Paul Eppstein concluded his talk with a prayer, emphasizing atonement and repentance. This evening was the start of Yom Kippur. "And no need to fast the next twenty-four hours. The Germans have taken care of that for us."

That was for sure. Every day was a fasting day.

Just as the men were leaving for their barracks, two SS guards entered and motioned for Paul Eppstein to follow them outside. As Izaak and Papa were kneeling to pray for Mama, a gunshot sounded and then repeated two more times. The room went silent, and a man whispered Paul Eppstein's name.

Izaak knew the Jewish lecturer was dead. He was too sad and weak to feel any more emotion except anger. The Germans chose a Jewish holy day to kill a special man.

Papa pulled Izaak closer and said a prayer right into Izaak's ear about getting rid of their sins. It went on for a long time, but he didn't mind. He loved Papa's voice, and like most nights, it relaxed him and made him feel safe until he drifted off to sleep.

-40-

HERBERT MÜLLER

Marseille to Bregenz, Austria - September 1944

" **M**y father has died." The words sounded foreign coming from Herbert's lips, and they physically hurt as he spoke them. "We would like to remain here in France to mourn."

His family stood in a weeping huddle next to him in the internee processing tent. He'd had little time to internalize that Otto was gone. Once he'd notified the ship's communications officer that his father had passed, and a doctor declared his cause of death to be a heart attack, the man radioed to shore. Two sailors arrived to take Otto's remains to a local morgue. Jutta and the children and Pastor Graf were praying over Otto's silent form. The sailors brushed them aside, stating the rules of international waters forbid the body from remaining on the ship.

The shore officer in charge of their repatriation looked from Herbert and his family to the ship's manifest he held in his hands. He flipped a page and ran his finger down a list of names before stopping and putting a checkmark beside one. "Otto Müller, right?"

"Yes." Herbert choked back tears. His father, the man he worked alongside, his personal idol, was gone. He expected when he had a second to grieve, his pent-up sorrow would flow out of every pore and leave him a mournful husk of a man. For now, he had decisions to make and his family to help. "We need to figure out how to have him returned to the United States, so he can be buried beside my mother." Herbert had nothing to lose, unsure of how matters were handled.

"Request denied." The officer took off his wireframe glasses. "I am sorry for the tragic loss of your father." He looked to Jutta and the children. "My condolences to all of you. However, repatriation law says his remains must stay here and not be returned. Often, cremation is the best solution as funerals are costly and I am aware you have limited travel funds."

"I can pay for a funeral," Graf said, stepping beside Herbert. "Let them give Otto a proper burial."

"And who are you?" the officer asked.

"Theodore Graf. A pastor and friend of the family." Graf loomed large in his long cloak.

Herbert was awash with gratitude with Graf's kind offer. A burial could cost hundreds of dollars. But how would he ever repay him?

"Thank you, pastor." Jutta barely said the word pastor before she broke into a coughing fit. Alfred wrapped his arm across her back to help her stay upright.

"Even if we allowed you to pay," the officer said, "you wouldn't be around for the ceremony." He swept his hand at the five of them. "You are all on the next train to Austria. No exceptions." He motioned to the guards who approached Herbert and his family.

Herbert was stunned into silence as they were ushered outside and led to a long bench away from the other deportees. Keep the weeping family away from the already nervous passengers seemed to be the plan. And his family was inconsolable. They had to leave their father and grandfather—a selfless man—on the coast of France like a useless life raft. The sun was out, but gloom settled at the edges of Herbert's vision, and he wanted to crumble to the ground and give up. His father died never seeing justice, or getting an apology for the misery he'd been put through. Otto was no one's enemy. He was a giving, hardworking family man who longed for the freedoms America offered twenty years earlier. Every action was to benefit his wife, children, and grandchildren. And his family could do nothing to show their love and respect in turn.

The pastor stood. "They cannot keep us from honoring your loved one. Please stand and hold hands as I offer these words." In an extra loud oratorical voice Herbert never heard Graf use in church, he prayed as if daring the military officers to silence him. "Go forth, Christian soul, from this world in the name of God the Almighty Father, who created you, in the name of Jesus Christ, Son of the Living God, who suffered for you. In the name of the Holy Spirit, who was poured out upon you, we bid thee a speedy return to the arms of your Father." He paused then added, "Give us the strength to forgive others, and I pray also that You forgive those who are full of ignorance, and have caused great misery for so many. Amen."

Herbert echoed the closing word and was surprised to hear many deportees standing nearby do the same. He wiped tears from his eyes, his throat constricted. Jutta and the children wept in a tight circle. He clasped the pastor's hands in his.

"Thank you. Your words, and friendship, mean more than you will ever know."

Graf nodded and smiled. "Let's see if they arrest me for calling them ignorant. That's not standard Lutheran verbiage, as you know."

"It's the truth." Alfred wiped tears from his face.

"Yes," Graf said, "but it seems in the midst of war, so few recognize it."

An hour dragged by before the ship's passengers were processed, a desolate time when grief circled back and struck each member of his family randomly. Herbert struggled with the knowledge his father lay nearby in some building, the horrible image his body was perhaps left on a cold floor. The thought drove a deep ache through his chest. He would never see his father again. He was consumed with guilt for not recognizing that his father's cold might lead to a more serious medical condition.

Graf left their side for his interview, and Herbert began to worry when his family was told to line up and the pastor was not back yet. Had he gotten in trouble for his portside prayer after all? When Graf returned, he seemed subdued. When Herbert asked what took so long, Graf shrugged. "You know. More of the same questioning."

With the help of the communications officer, Herbert sent a telegram to his brother, Karl, in the Pacific informing him Pops was gone. A dull ache settled at the back of his eyes. Was his brother even alive? He needed Karl to come home safely at the end of the war. To help him start a new business even though all they knew was the trade—running a gristmill and operating orchards. But mainly, Herbert couldn't stand the thought of losing another loved one.

His family and Graf were put in a group of twenty-five and directed less than half a mile through backstreets to the two-story Marseille Saint-Charles Station. Inside, sunlight filtered through the peaked glass ceiling, painting slices of yellow streaks along the shiny steam engine. Herbert and Jutta took seats in the comfortable Pullman car behind the children while Graf sat across the aisle.

As the train wove northward, Herbert was glad to see his emotionally exhausted family doze off. He went through the motions of eating and getting off the train at the stops to stretch his legs. But as the miles accumulated behind the coach distancing him from Otto, he was overcome with a loss so powerful he prayed he could keep moving. He'd abandoned his father. Should he have insisted on meeting with the American Embassy while in France? This plagued him even though the military made it clear he had no rights as an enemy alien.

The journey to Bregenz, a border city in the westernmost side of Austria, should only have taken one day. But it turned into an overnight trip due to the seemingly endless delays spent waiting for troop trains to pass. Arriving just as the sun rose over Pfander Mountain, he spotted Bregenz. The town nestled between the soaring peaks and a huge lake below.

He crossed the aisle to sit beside Graf who was awake and studying the scenery. "Beautiful area."

"Reminds me of my childhood in Bavaria," Graf said, a wistful look in his eye. "We summered there, hiking, dressed in my Lederhosen, going from festival to festival."

Herbert vaguely remembered the short pants and suspenders that disappeared once his family immigrated. He didn't expect to have any fond memories of his childhood, yet they rushed in as he studied the view.

"Same here. We did an awful lot of car camping and fishing in Bavaria. It gave my mother a break, I think. My father was opposed to paying for a hotel, no matter how much my brother and I begged him. Pops owned a huge 1920 Opel we three could sleep in and that was good enough for him."

Pastor Graf laughed. "I sold my neighbor my Opel Olympia before I moved to America." He shook his head. "That gas guzzler was big enough to sleep half my congregation."

The train came to a stop, and Herbert gently nudged his children awake. Frieda's pigtails, which she redid each day, were frazzled with hair poking out, and Alfred's hair stuck up in the back. Jutta was up but looked dazed. "Are we here?" she asked, her voice froggy.

"Yes. Bregenz." Herbert kissed her on the head and pointed to the buildings outside the window.

"It's pretty," Frieda said. The dark circles under her eyes were pronounced against her fair complexion.

"Marseille seemed pretty at first"—Alfred rubbed his eyes with his fists—"Look how that turned out."

"It's not France's fault Grandpa died," Frieda said, her voice full of emotion.

"You're right," Alfred said, "but I'm going to keep blaming everyone until I stop being mad and sad . . . and that feels like a long way off."

Herbert was glad to hear his son express his feelings. It might tone down his anger.

Soon, they gathered on the wide platform. The heat from the train's engine, floating off the machine in waves, pushed against Herbert's back. Jutta and the children excused themselves to use the washroom. He stretched his aching leg while the pastor smoked.

"Your family will heal, Herbert." Graf blew a perfect smoke ring. "It's important to direct your thoughts away from hate or revenge, although that's easier to say than to do. I try to set my sights on helping someone else out of a difficult situation. Most times it works."

This was the part of the pastor's makeup he envied. Herbert may have been uncaring to think this, but he had what was left of his family to protect, and from what he saw around him, not many others were worse off than what they were going through. But he didn't want to sound disagreeable. "I'll try to remember that."

As soon as his family returned, the officers in charge pointed them to buses that drove them to the Unterstadt Rathaus, the Lower City Town Hall. Once inside, they were fed sausages, bread, and potatoes.

"Reminds me of Grandma's cooking," Frieda said.

"Her Schweinebraten," Alfred said. "That was the best."

Herbert nodded. "Mother made great roast pork."

Jutta started to speak but quickly grabbed her handkerchief, a deep cough shaking her entire body.

"I'll be back. I'm going to ask for medicine." Herbert left Graf with his family to finish their meals. He needed to get a cough suppressant for Jutta before they set off on the next part of their journey.

He waited in line at a makeshift tent before being called next to speak to the medical team. When it was his turn, he explained Jutta's ailment and asked for cough syrup.

"All we have is Alka-Seltzer and Absorbine Junior." The young man raised his shoulders in semi-defeat. "Nothing for a cold. Give her lots of fluids and it will pass. Probably."

He wanted to punch the guy, although he realized it wasn't the young man's fault. "I'll take the Absorbine Junior, if you don't mind." Perhaps it could act as a substitute for a mentholated chest rub and relieve Jutta's congestion. He returned to the Town Hall.

"Did they have anything?" Alfred asked. He hovered over his mother, helpless, as she gasped for air after a long bout of coughing.

He shook his head. "Nothing for a cough." He turned to Jutta and held out the tube of pain relief. "You could try this."

"That might work," Jutta said, her positive tone ever-present. She tucked it into her dress pocket.

"If you're all done eating, they say you can check to see when your train is ready," Pastor Graf said.

Jutta reached for Graf's hand. "We're so glad you're traveling with us." The cough overtook her again, and she turned and bent at the waist. When she finally stood, she wiped tears from her cheeks.

He studied his family and sadness overtook him. Although they stood ready to go, they were bedraggled with worry lines on their faces, and exhaustion was evident in their posture. They looked to him for confidence, which he was short on. His father's death was a turning point. He no longer believed repatriating to Germany was the best solution. An immediate transfer to Crystal City in Texas is what he should have insisted on. His goal, until they reached his cousin Elke's house, was not to infect his family with his own self-doubt.

The suitcases they so carefully packed would be sent to a large warehouse and arrive later when another transport became available. Combat troops and war materials had priority since passenger space on the trains was limited, and railway service was sporadic at best.

They pulled a few pieces of clothing from the cases and packed two potato sacks the military offered.

At check-in, Herbert learned they were going to spend a night in the pews of St. Gallus Kirche before heading into Germany. The Catholic Diocese opened their churches to refugees passing through and now to internees coming from America.

Four American guards led their group across town. Jutta squeezed Herbert's hand, and he squeezed back. Together they'd face whatever came their way.

Father Karl Wegner waited at the doors of the St. Gallus Kirche, welcoming them. He said in German, "Leave your luggage in a pew of your choice. The bishop of the parish and I will guard. You can sit outside, but come inside before dark."

Herbert translated for the children and they moved to a pew on one side. Graf walked away, already in a deep conversation with Father Wegner. Herbert couldn't help but notice the slump to the pastor's back. Some worry weighed on his friend, something more than he was sharing.

"I noticed a beautiful park behind the rectory," Jutta said. "Let's enjoy the fresh air a bit longer while we can."

A short while later after Jutta and the children went for a walk, Herbert and Graf sat on the church steps as the sun balanced on the edge of Lake Constance.

"I wanted to speak to you alone," Graf said. "You told me your mill and property were auctioned. What will you do when you return home?"

"I'll start another business, hopefully with my brother. Although I don't know much outside of grinding grain and running an orchard, I think we can come up with something."

Graf's mouth opened and then closed. Whatever he wanted to say about this situation, the words weren't forming. "And you are a hard worker. I've no doubt you'll land on your feet."

"Have you heard when you leave?" Herbert asked. Initially, they hoped to travel on the same transport, but ultimately, they were headed in different directions.

"Tonight," Graf said. "Your family?"

"We report at eight in the morning." Herbert's chest tightened. Tomorrow, they headed into Germany—into the war zone. He'd moved toward their unknown future in moment-by-moment steps. First weeks, then days, and now mere hours away. "We take the early train to Ulm. God willing, our luggage will follow soon after."

Graf rubbed his forehead and met Herbert's gaze. He stood and offered a piece of paper. "We talked about exchanging addresses. Here is my sister's."

Herbert dug out a note from his shirt pocket. "My cousin's. Please stay in touch."

"May God bless your family as you have blessed me these past nine months. You've lost much, in particular your father, but also the comforts of home. I pray you will be embraced by your German relatives."

Herbert stood, and with a heavy heart, grasped the pastor's hand with both of his. "You're a good friend, Theodore." Graf always bolstered his spirit. "Safe travels to you. I sincerely hope we'll meet again when this madness ends."

"Most certainly." Graf pulled a sealed envelope from his shirt and offered it to Herbert. "To help with your resettlement."

Herbert held up his hands. "If it's that money you keep trying to give us, we can't take it."

"I insist, since I have no family"—he winked—"I learned to play the horses at the Saratoga Race Track. Let's just say I've done well. I've already sent money to Wilhelm Falk's widow in the Netherlands, adding my deepest regrets concerning his death." He stood and straightened his shoulders as if preparing for battle. Then he glanced over Herbert's shoulder, and quickly leaned forward, and tucked the envelope in Herbert's coat pocket.

"I won't need it," he whispered.

"But, of course you wi—"

Without warning, two U.S. soldiers surrounded them. One dropped a hand on Graf's shoulder and said, "Your time is up. Hands behind your back." Graf complied, and another snapped on handcuffs.

Herbert jumped to his feet. "What are you doing?"

Graf offered a humble smile. "They let me say goodbye to you. Herbert, that was kindness enough." The pastor looked resigned.

"But, wait. What's happening?"

"I learned today that I'm being traded, but not as I believed. I'm going to a military P-O-W camp, to one run by the German army."

"America is handing you over to the Germans?"

"The camp is for persons the Germans would like more information from. I'm told I'll be mixed in with downed British and American pilots."

"What information do they want from you?" Herbert couldn't believe what he was hearing. The United States had not honored their agreement to reunite Graf with his sister. Did this mean he and his family might end up in prison and not in Wiesbaden?

The soldiers tugged Graf, but he stood his ground.

"They're interested in what Falk mailed to me before he was killed in Italy," he said. "In other words, does the United States know of Germany's horrific secrets playing out in Poland?"

"Enough!" The soldiers pulled Graf to the canvas-backed truck and helped him climb in. Herbert's heartbeat thudded in his ears as he watched the vehicle make a U-turn and bump its way down the cobblestone street, heading north to Germany. Graf's eyes were closed, more than likely in prayer as the truck faded from view.

Herbert's nails tore half-moons into his palms because he squeezed them so tightly. He sat down on the steps and closed his eyes fighting back the tears.

Graf was minding his own business, living the life he made for himself in America when, by none of his own doing, he received a package. A package from an SS officer who inadvertently turned him into a messenger.

And from what Herbert knew, the Germans always killed the messenger.

-41-

WILHELM FALK

Springfield, Missouri, Federal Prison Hospital - October 1944

It had been over three months since Falk was shot, and his frustration intensified with each passing day. Despite two weeks of questions and discussions about Auschwitz and the other extermination camps, Falk had no idea if his information was being taken into consideration to halt the mass killings. "We passed everything on to President Roosevelt, and the decision is up to him and the military generals" was as much as anyone would tell him.

When he pleaded for more information and stressed that every day thousands of lives were lost, the officials only hinted there were plans in the works.

He'd written out twenty-three pages of notes, mainly focusing on the horrors of Auschwitz, saying there were forty other camps like the one he described. He gave details of the geography, the management of the camp, and how the prisoners lived and died. He made sure to emphasize the locations of Mengele's and the SS officers' houses.

While adding notes about the inner workings of the camps, he wrote about the discharge forms completed for prisoners who were gassed, showing that death rates in the camp were dramatically underreported. And that female prisoners and their newborns were immediately sent to the gas chambers within hours of birth. He described the cruelty of the female camp guard, Irma Grese, referring to her as the prisoners did—"the Beautiful Beast." Always dressed in a clean dress with a high-waisted belt and wearing jackboots, she was strikingly beautiful. Periwinkle eyes. Every blonde hair in place. And although only nineteen, she planned extravagant ways to torture and kill the prisoners.

His interrogators asked if he tried to intervene to stop her from committing the crimes stated in the report. He answered he had not.

Falk was no longer in a hospital room. The previous week, he was deemed healthy enough to move into a small prison cell with a single bed, toilet, and sink, and an echoing loneliness. Other prisoners along the hallways talked to each other, but he remained silent, unsure what American felons might do to a man with a German accent.

He requested paper and pen to write to his wife to explain his circumstances.

The request was denied.

He became a man of action without a solid plan. Everything he wanted to accomplish was altered, which left him cycling through new possible outcomes.

Again, he was ushered to the courtroom by his usual guards and took his seat next to the same translator. They informed him the inquiry board's focus for this meeting was the sketches and information in the report about the layout of the gas chambers.

"Why didn't the prisoners fight when they exited the trains and saw that certain death lay ahead of them?" General Donovan asked. He remained formal throughout the questioning while Chief of Staff Marshall often loosened his tie as the hours and days ticked on. "Surely word got out about the gassings."

Falk gave a tiny shake of his head. "When the inmates heard rumors, their fears were quenched as they got out of trains. They saw groups of red brick buildings designed like hospitals or offices. The SS troops, who welcomed them, were unusually friendly. While new arrivals stepped out, the prisoners in the camp played swing melodies and popular ballads and provided a peaceful atmosphere."

"Did you try to persuade other SS officers that this was wrong?"— Marshall looked up from his notes—"That at the war's end these actions would be viewed as high crimes?"

"No." He was culpable of that and more. A bitter taste filled his mouth as if someone had shoved pennies down his throat. Suddenly dizzy, his heart pounded as they watched him. And now wracked with anguish renewed by failure, he forced the next statement. "When death is close, we value life the most. I don't know who said that, but I have seen it again and again in the actions of the skeletal prisoners who hung on against all odds. For me, the decision to not speak up twisted my guts, however I also did not want to die there. My death would have been a small hiccup in Hitler's extermination plans. It's going to take an army."

"Once you sent the package of information to Graf," Donovan asked, "did you consider sabotaging the Reich's actions?"

Falk glanced at the ornate ceiling. Sabotage may sound so easy to men separated from the horrors by time and distance, but to him—while he was there—his priority was to secretly gather information and try not to get killed.

He cleared his throat. "I have already mentioned that I have diverted several trains with Zyklon-B gas. I wrote other dignitaries in a postal campaign for a year, and that proved fruitless. I felt that my only remaining option was to send my collected information to someone in America, and I trusted Pastor Graf. I didn't know how I'd end up coming here. Actually, I wasn't sure if it would happen."

Donovan looked through his papers and pulled one free. He nodded to a guard who took the sheet from him and walked it to Falk and set it on the table.

He studied the mugshots of eight men with their names below the photos.

"Who are these men?" They had German names—Dasch, Burger, Heinck, Quirin, and four more.

"The League of Eight."

"Should I know these people?" Falk asked.

Marshall leaned forward and narrowed his eyes. "That's what we wonder. Two years ago, the men pictured at the top of the page landed on a beach near Long Island. The bottom four landed four days later, on Ponte Vedra Beach, Florida. All were German spies."

He was suddenly exhausted, frustration wearing him down.

"Why should I know spies? They would kill me in a blink of an eye for treason."

"Well," Marshall said, "both groups landed wearing complete or partial German uniforms, disguising themselves as prisoners of war in case they were caught." He studied Falk. "Exactly as you arrived in our country."

After all he had risked, how could they still suspect him of conspiring with the enemy? He looked to the side windows where fall had arrived under a cobalt-blue sky. The trees prepared for the worst to come. The last of their golden leaves had shaken free, leaving brown antlers, entwined, hard-looking. Falk returned his gaze to the council.

"I have nothing to gain as a spy when I reveal the things I've seen. I told you the truth. I even made suggestions on how to stop the killings. Yet, the United States does nothing." He felt heat in his face as he held back a rising flush of anger. "Did I make a mistake when I came to the most powerful country in the world?"

Donovan was silent, appearing to weigh his next words. "If we believed you were a spy, you would be sentenced to life in prison or executed like the men in those photos." He smiled. "We're grateful for your information." The colonel stood, signaling their meeting was over. The men at the table followed suit. "President Roosevelt's final assessment is all efforts and resources need to remain with the active front. Men and planes cannot be spared to cross enemy territory to liberate the camps. Defeating Germany as quickly as possible is the best solution and still our main goal."

Falk shot to his feet and slammed his palms on the table. "Then he condemns another million Jews to death."

When the colonel spoke again, his voice conveyed a note of regret. "It is regrettable, but war always comes with casualties. Tomorrow is your sentencing."

"Sentencing? Have I not provided any helpful information to your government?"

"Roosevelt is predisposed to leniency because of your cooperation," Donovan said. "This tribunal meets one more time before deciding."

"I can continue to offer cooperation. Embed me with your field staff. I have firsthand knowledge of the Reich's warehouses and meeting places."

"We may ask you for that type of assistance." The colonel gathered the files from the table and smiled. "But, probably not, as we are winning without your help."

"I did not know I was on trial all along." He held his breath, willing the colonel to refute his words. Had he believed they would award him a metal? Give him citizenship? No, but he also hadn't thought this far ahead. He envisioned the exchange of information, the army stepping up to help, but not what might come after.

When the colonel didn't answer, Falk said, "If one option is I remain in prison, you can send me back to the war."

The colonel nodded. "Actually, sending you back is one of the options."

–42–

IZAAK TAUBER

Terezín, Czechoslovakia, Upper Fortress - October 1944

The truck rumbled and bumped up the winding hill to the Upper Fortress. Izaak stood next to Papa in the crowded truck bed. His stomach was ajitter. He'd prayed long and hard for this day, and finally his family would be together again.

This morning, the guards told the prisoners in the long sheds they were moving to the Upper Fortress. Way before sunrise, the guards were shooting over and over again out by the back wall. Papa said they were hunting rabbits and squirrels, food the guards liked to eat.

There was a time when squirrel meat sounded disgusting, but today his mouth watered at the thought of any kind of meat.

"Stocking up for the winter to come," Papa added, in an extra cheery voice. The one he used when Izaak was five. Now at nine, he understood that tone was to distract him from the bad news the guards were killing more prisoners.

"We're almost there." Izaak strained to look over the sideboards. He couldn't wait to see the surprise on Mama's face when he led Papa into their barracks. He pointed out the gardens and orchards in the moat area. "This is where we get the best fruit ever. The apples should be ripe now."

"An apple sounds wonderful, although apple season has passed."

Izaak studied the trees and felt sad. The red fruit was all gone. Then he remembered the new stores and shops. "We can buy them at the market." He leaned close to his papa's ear. "Getting fruit there was one of my parts in the big town play."

"This was a good town for you and your mama." Papa gave him a tiny smile. "I'm glad."

"It's still nice. But now for all of us."

Papa wrapped an arm across his shoulders as they circled the last part of the outer wall. Everyone must have been busy working inside because only a few people were on the town's streets. As they neared the road by the town square, two men strained to pull the same wooden hearse the horses once pulled. Bodies filled the wagon, crisscrossed like limp puppets on top of each other. His friend, Aden, was on top. He didn't want to look but couldn't stop staring at the horrible sight. His friend had to be pretending or having a nap. When they got closer, he saw neither guess was true. Aden's body was twisted and draped over the pile in a way only a dead person could lay.

"No!" He pressed his face away into Papa's sweaty shirt. "That's my friend. He shouldn't be there! He had a nice house with good food. We just got new clothes and everything."

Papa held him while tears ran down his face. How could Aden be dead? Old people and sick people died. Then a bad thought jumped into his head.

"Are we going to die?"

"Hush, son"—he rubbed Izaak's back—"We're going to be fine. I'm here to make sure of that."

Izaak pressed his ear against Papa's chest where his heart galloped fast. He didn't want to stay here anymore. He didn't want to see his friend dead. Tears fell from his eyes and his throat pinched painfully tight. They should find Mama and beg to leave as soon as they could.

The truck jerked to a stop and guards approached. They looked tired and grumpy, not like when he lived here before. One SS soldier, who wore an enormous belt buckle with a swastika in the center and a skull with crossing bones on his hat, yelled at them. "Schnell!"

They hurried down from the truck and into a long line, leading into the Jewish Council building. He tugged at Papa's shirt.

"This will take so long. Ask if we can just go to our barracks." His throat hurt whenever he pictured Aden. He didn't want to be crying when Mama saw him since he was her brave boy. But she would probably cry after she screamed their names and hugged them so tight. After hours of hugging, he'd show Papa the art showroom and hope some of the paintings were still there. Papa would be surprised at what a good artist he was, now that he was a year older.

Papa squeezed his hand. "I'll try to find out what's going on, son."

A man behind them tapped Papa on the back. "Most of the people were taken away on transports. Lots of trains coming through. As recently as this morning. The only reason we're still here is to help clean up things before the Russians arrive."

-43-

HERBERT MÜLLER

Bregenz, Austria - October 1944

The next morning, on the truck's bench seat, Herbert sat numb with exhaustion. All night, his mind was consumed by what might happen to Pastor Graf. He studied the morning sun with renewed hope that a prisoner of war camp, which included military personnel from the U.S. and Great Britain, would follow the Geneva Convention and Graf would be housed, fed, and kept safe according to the international pact.

He woke his family from their makeshift beds on the wooden pews, encouraging them to gather the few sacks with their belongings. They, along with the other deportees, were going to the German border on the back of a flatbed truck. As they climbed onto the bench seats, the morning seemed too beautiful for what was about to transpire.

The sun inched higher and higher against the sweeping horizon as they left the church. They reached a high plateau, and sunlight sparkled across the vast expanse of Lake Constance.

A wind that swept across the other passengers beside him was laden with the scent of fear.

He shielded his eyes from the sun and studied the lake. The city of Bregenz cascaded in a series of terraces to the lake. Switzerland lay to the west, Germany to the north.

Jutta turned her face his way. "It's lovely," she whispered. She looked worn from the illness as if she could tip over at any moment, and her eyes lacked the sparkle that won his heart all those years ago.

He wrapped his arm around her shoulder and pulled her closer.

"How are you doing, dear?"

"Just a bit off-kilter." She leaned into him. "How has it come to this? Your father is left behind in France and today we head into Germany." A sigh escaped her lips. "I always say, 'If this is the worst that can happen.' I need to stop saying that."

He paused for a moment, staring at the vibrant lakeshore where fishermen were bringing in their predawn catches. His gaze dropped to his lap, and he picked at a stain on his trousers. When he raised his head, he added a sad smile. "I can't stop thinking about deserting Pops. Losing him is the worst, love." His father taught him to be strong, but would he be strong enough to accept Otto was no longer here? "In three days, we'll be in Wiesbaden and maybe regain some sense of a normal routine. The American Embassy knows where Otto is buried. We can have him moved to our family plot one day."

"But he was cremated." She wiped a tear that raced down her cheek. "He deserved the dignity of a coffin, of a burial plot. I don't want his death to be stuck in our heads as the blurry nightmare it was. His life was so rich."

He had no answer. His father's work boots would forever stand empty beside the mudroom door where he kicked them off each day he entered the house. His favorite chair would still hold his imprint, but his kind spirit would be missing.

The truck ground through the countryside and up and over a mountain ridge before dropping into the valley below. Alfred and Frieda dozed leaning against each other.

Not long after, they pulled into a hard-packed dirt parking area.

"Gather all of your things," a soldier said. "This border crossing goes one way for you."

Herbert felt the hair on his arms rise. He shook off the sudden fear and forced the last ounce of strength into his voice. "Under God's watchful gaze, here we go."

His family walked forward. He and Jutta hand in hand, and Frieda and Alfred with linked arms. Three guards led them along a once-paved road, weeds pushing up through a surface broken by years of war. His hip ached. The days of travelling settled into his joints, making his limp more pronounced. In the distance, two tall sets of gates rose, each separated by a hundred yards. Both stood open. Soldiers restrained four large German Shepherds. The animals barked and snapped, pulling hard at their leashes. High over the border hung a large sign:

Willkommen in Deutschland!

Beyond the far gate, a dozen people waited. *The more important Americans.*

A U.S. soldier pointed to the ground. "Stand here." He crossed to the center area, boots scraping noisily on the rough road. Greeting a German soldier, they exchanged salutes and inaudible words. Then each soldier motioned to the armed guards on both sides of the border to bring their groups of people forward.

Herbert expected to see tension as soldiers from differing sides of the war dealt with each other, but it was apparent they respected the orders from their superiors and carried them out without rancor.

The people selected to be exchanged for his group looked no different than his family. Men and women in their thirties and forties, mostly couples with a few children, looking weary and needing haircuts and a change of clothes. Was that surprise on the faces of the rescued Americans? They were probably told they were being exchanged for felons, enemy aliens, who were forced to return Germany where they belonged.

Silence fell. The liberated Americans dropped their gazes as they walked by him and his family, passing within arm's length. The noxious fumes from the idling military vehicles floated in the air, and he felt the rumble of the engines through the ground. He wanted to let the freed Americans know they could thank mass hysteria in the States for their liberty.

Alfred's face was a fearful shade of white as uncertainty reduced him to a trembling adolescent.

A German soldier, broad-shouldered with penetrating blue eyes, motioned the repatriates to the rear of a canvas-backed truck. "*Willkommen zurück*," he said.

Welcome back? This made him question how much the German

government even knew about Herbert's family and the others in this group. Could anyone really believe they were happy to be in Germany?

Their American military escorts remained on the Austrian side of the border. Two German soldiers pointed his family to a canvas-covered lorry. The guards weren't older than twenty. Herbert climbed into the truck and helped pull up Jutta and the children. One soldier, tall with unruly blond hair, clambered aboard and sat on the end of the bench seat closest to the door flap. "Tonight, you'll come to Ulm. Then in the morning, each of you will be escorted to the right trains to transport you to your destinations. The tickets are paid. You must show your papers at every stop."

He translated for his children. His face felt stiff, too serious, and he couldn't force a smile now if he tried.

"We have to follow the prescribed route. We'll be your military chaperones all the way," the soldier said.

At least they'd be protected. That was his biggest worry.

The vehicle bounced along, the flaps slapping loudly against the sides of the truck, the road noise muffling all conversation. Anguish and despair weighed heavily on him. He mourned his father's death and worried about Pastor Graf. Theodore loved living in America, invigorated by his Lutheran congregation. He kept his departed father's war letters in his desk in Troy, a desk that would be emptied and discarded if Graf never returned. He also was troubled about the full day they'd travel through enemy territory. Yes, they had military orders stating they were to be safely delivered to Wiesbaden, but with all that transpired in the last few days, he no longer trusted anything written on paper.

Hours later, the truck slowed. The soldier near the door spit out a toothpick and said, "You're entering Ulm where they have a curfew. You must stay in the hotel at all times. People on the streets at night are stopped and questioned, but when these local Germans hear English spoken, they shoot first fearing the enemy." He shrugged as if to say, What else could they assume?

Dusk seeped into the city as they exited the truck. Herbert studied the hotel facing them. It was dismal at best, the walls in need of paint, a rain gutter hanging loose.

A roaring sound drew closer, and the soldiers ordered them off the street. Two German motorcycles with sidecars thundered past. Movement in the five-story apartment building next to the hotel caught Herbert's eye. Behind the closed shutters, fingers parted the slats. Dozens of eyes peered out between the laths. Following the motorcycles, four trucks rolled by and then a single black Mercedes.

The soldiers snapped to attention, pointed their arms to the sky, and yelled, "Heil Hitler!"

That's when reality walked up and looked Herbert in the eye. Everyone he held dear was now in the middle of an active war zone, and the only way out was to cross through it.

The next day was cloudy and humid, the air heavy with foreboding. His leg ached as he and his family walked to the train station through the ruined side of Ulm, flanked by the two soldiers. The city seemed to be left with nothing but a scattering of dirty children and people too poor for a ticket to a safer town. He'd caught a few hours of sleep in the sagging bed in the run-down hotel, but his family slept deeply for nine hours. Jutta's cold improved, perhaps from the Absorbine Jr., but more likely from a good night's rest.

Eginhardt Stutz was the younger of their escorts, barely nineteen, the tall one with unkempt blond hair. This post was Stutz's first time away from the family farm near Munich. He returned this morning from bartering at the shops, carrying a sack with bread, cheese, and potato soup. The other soldier was Leopold Bosch, age twenty-two. He shared he was in the thick of the war until injured. Scars raked his left cheek and ended where his left ear used to be. The damaged tissue pulled his eye to the side, giving him a permanent squint.

They finished eating just as their escorts received the all-clear to travel northward.

"Is this part of Germany under attack?" Herbert asked the soldiers.

"The Allies flattened two large truck factories five months earlier. That same night, the Royal Air Force thundered back with over five hundred aircraft. The center of Ulm is gone. All the long-standing churches, castles, and even the hospital were bombed," Bosch said. "Every city is the same. Thousands of civilians are dying as the Allies try to break the soldiers' families."

Herbert didn't know whether to apologize or applaud. As they walked to the train depot, truckload after truckload of German citizens, refugees on their own soil, passed at regular intervals. Stutz hadn't exaggerated.

"Where are all these people going?" Frieda asked.

Herbert translated her question, and Bosch answered. "Many have to go to the countryside, away from the cities." Then he translated Bosch's words.

"And I thought our country treated us badly," Alfred said. "You'd think Germany would have old prisons like Ellis Island to let their people live in."

Frieda's face bunched together. "Don't say that name."

He knew his daughter managed her emotions well, and she seemed determined not to let the attack and near-rape bring her down.

Alfred dropped his arm around her shoulder and pulled her close. "Sorry, sis. Never again." He swiped a lone tear from her cheek.

Herbert prayed the Americans and British were concentrating on other parts of Germany now, far from Frankfurt. Wiesbaden, their future home, was just west of there.

A coal-fueled haze hung over the long lines of blackened tracks when they arrived at the railway station. "Head to the back of the station," Stutz said. There, a small unattached house faced the back entrance to the larger station. "The booking clerk is inside."

The escorts entered and signaled Herbert inside. A man in a railway uniform sat on the bare floorboards, smoking a pipe, and reading a newspaper. He didn't look up from his reading until Stutz cleared his throat. They spoke rapidly in German, words centered on the next train's arrival, and then he stood and crossed to a table and handed them a map. A stocky woman stood at a white chipped-enamel stove with a dour expression that said the arrival of another stray family was merely routine. She ignored Herbert as she set a pot of water to boil, the hum of gas and the *tick, tick, tick* of cold metal heating. She dropped in quartered potatoes, peels and all. The couple's furnishings were almost down to nothing. A table, one stool, a bed in the corner, and floor space where furniture once fit.

"The Frankfurt Express leaves in thirty minutes," Bosch said. "I'll get the tickets."

"Our suitcases are at the warehouse, Herbert," Jutta said. "How will we get those?"

As Bosch and Stutz looked from Herbert to Jutta, Herbert translated and added, "That's a good question, if we keep moving, our luggage will never catch up with us."

Bosch opened the map the booking clerk handed him and flattened it on the table. His finger poised over the lower left side of the paper and then stabbed the word Ulm. "From here we follow the railway line to Frankfurt." Then his finger traced another spur to Wiesbaden. "You take this branch, and your baggage will be delivered there."

"Danke," Herbert said, and Jutta nodded. Bosch and Stutz seemed to take seriously the task of delivering the Müllers to their temporary home. Again, he wondered what the United States government paid to repatriate his family.

Bosch counted out coins and bills and handed them to the ticket office clerk.

The stout woman offered them two tin cups of cool water.

"Thank you. This is more than generous," Herbert said.

They sat in a circle on the floor and passed the water. "Kind of like Duck Duck Goose," Alfred said.

"You're it," Frieda said, "especially if anyone gets a whiff of your socks. They'll be running from you."

Alfred laughed. "Wait until tonight. I'm sleeping with my feet in your face."

"That's the problem"—Frieda waved a hand below her nose—"You already do!"

Herbert smiled. It was nice to hear the children teasing each other.

Jutta chuckled. "I admit, a hot bath will suit us all."

"Soon," Herbert said. "This train and then another spur and we're there." His thoughts propelled him into the near future when they would enjoy just the most basic comforts. Hot water, a change of clothes, and no sound of gunfire in the distance. His family deserved that.

Back outside on the platform, Bosch offered Herbert a cigarette. He waved it away and then watched the soldier attempt to light his smoke, flicking his Zippo lighter several times, but it wouldn't flame. Stutz reached over with a match and saved him.

"We need to let you know," Stutz said, "the train carries munitions, possibly bombs. Smoking on board is not allowed." He made an explosion sound and then threw his hands apart, miming something blowing up.

Herbert raised his eyebrows. "We don't smoke. Besides, that's the last thing I would do."

"Should it blow, it's the last thing we would all do," Bosch said, seemingly proud of his gallows humor. A soldier's coping mechanism. "I'm out of cigarettes after this."

Jutta and then Frieda settled onto a bench to wait, and Alfred joined Herbert next to the soldiers. Herbert lifted his head to the late morning sun, his face warmed after a brief lashing from fall's colder breezes. The train's whistle sounded well before the engine slipped around the distant corner and glided into the station. Soldiers carrying rifles rode on top of the front coaches. The train stopped and the up-top guards stood. Their gun barrels flashed blue in the sunlight as they watched passengers exit from the six cars directly behind the engine. Then a few dozen people boarded the same passenger cars.

Bosch pointed to the second coach from the end. "This car." A white circle with the word "Verboten" in the center was painted near the door.

"Forbidden?" Herbert asked. "What is this about?"

"We don't want any locals in here. This car is for the deportees we oversee."

Alfred grabbed his mother's sack as well as his own. "Hopefully this one won't smell like old soup and dirty hair."

Jutta entered the car first. "Nice and clean," she said over her shoulder. They sat two by two in seats facing each other. Bosch and Stutz sat across the aisle. Twelve other internees and four guards climbed aboard. Herbert replayed all that transpired since the FBI first knocked on their door eleven months earlier. Wild rumors and nationalist fears sent his family's life spiraling in a direction he never could have predicted. He believed being an American citizen included safety and freedoms with that honor. His father said when he was in the war, the best way to find out if he could trust another man in his unit was to give him a try. Otto had been willing to give their relocation a try, and now Herbert needed to trust two young soldiers to do what they were paid to do.

He crossed his arms and settled into his seat. Graf's envelope crinkled inside his coat pocket. He decided not to open it, believing that doing so would mean he would never see the pastor again. Would the Nazis torture a man of the cloth for the information they hoped he had? The stories Graf told of the Nazi atrocities from his officer friend revealed no one was immune from their viciousness. Sorrow lay heavy on his heart, imagining the pain Graf might be subjected to while in custody.

Bosch checked his watch as the train jolted forward and then, after several jerks and starts, rolled smoothly. "Exactly on schedule. Two o'clock."

Herbert squeezed Jutta's hand. "We'll be with Elke's family before supper. Are you excited?"

"A little bit." The practiced enthusiasm she often pushed into her voice was not there. "I can only hope they have a mind for taking us in."

"They will, Mother," Frieda said. "If it were us, wouldn't we take in castaways?"

"Castaways," Alfred said, "more like throwaways." Other passengers turned at his angry words. He met their gazes with a defiant stare.

"Easy, son," Herbert said. "We are all in this together."

After a few moments, Alfred spoke again. "We would take in castaways. It's who we are." The train's wheels clacked out a regular rhythm, and the children soon fell asleep shoulder to shoulder. Herbert wrapped Jutta in his arms and pulled her to his chest. Her breathing slowed and deepened. He leaned his head back and closed his eyes. A dozen possibilities circled his mind, ranging from a warm welcome in Wiesbaden to being thrown out on the street. When the war ended, how soon before they were allowed to return home? He tried to envision who bought his property at the county auction. Someone with skills to run a gristmill? They might ruin the mechanisms without proper knowledge. It might be delusional, but he held on to a tiny seed of hope he'd save enough to buy it all back one day.

The train sounds were regular, reliable, calming. They were moving forward.

He doubted he'd shed the ill will he now harbored for his country. The empty stretch between the person he once was and the person he was today felt like a chasm he might never bridge. Once he returned home, he'd never again be the naïve man who trusted he had rights and liberties because some lessons can never be unlearned.

-44-

WILHELM FALK

Bern, Switzerland - November 1944

Falk sat in a red leather chair in a heavily carpeted office at the International Red Cross building in Bern, Switzerland. Right then, he ached knowing how close in proximity he was to Ilse and the boys in Wiesbaden. Less than five hours by train, and he could wrap himself around them, and breathe in their essence. But, seeing them was not part of the U.S. government's plan for him. He was released from Federal Prison for one reason only. To guide the Swiss Red Cross when they reached three German extermination camps. His knowledge of the layout of the camps and how to deal with the SS guards while speaking German made him an asset. After the Danish Jews reached safety, his usefulness would be reassessed. He'd either be sent out on another rescue mission or spend time in an American prison until the war ended.

His efforts to get the word out about the Final Solution kept him from being executed. The U.S. would not hand him over to his own army. As a final favor, he asked that he, along with Ilse and their sons, be given visas to move to the United States. Remaining in Germany meant he'd be looking over his shoulder for years, wondering if an SS comrade thought he should die for defecting and turning against Hitler. The officials refused to say whether they'd agree to his request.

Today, he was offered coffee and *pepparkakor* cookies, a pure luxury, while he read the headlines written by a New York Times correspondent in Geneva. A story published in September, three months ago. It was titled, "Inquiry Confirms Nazi Death Camp," and the subtitle read, "1,715,000

Jews Said to Have Been Put to Death by the Germans." A follow-up article on July 6 added more to the story. "Two Death Camps Liberated—Swiss Red Cross calls them Places of Horror."

Had his letter to Bishop Charles Morerod in Geneva been the catalyst for the Swiss to investigate? He hadn't held out much confidence for Sweden's help. That country was the least likely to get involved with investigating the extermination camps because their country continued to trade with Germany, accepting gold for tungsten, wood, sardines, and iron ore.

Switzerland's banks received German gold as well, depositing it with little interest in its source—a large portion taken from Jews. But now, the Swiss Red Cross decided to do something about the death camps after all. Wars were hell. This one was long, made up of hard, grinding days that evidently quashed man's nobler instincts. The neutral countries may have tried to stay impartial but couldn't pull it off in the long run. Men of integrity must have stopped questioning themselves and decided they could benefit from Germany's actions.

Germany. His country. With all its contributions made to the arts and literature, would it ever have an honorable place on the world stage again?

Now here he was in Switzerland. He flew into Bern on a military transport, bound in handcuffs. According to the FBI, he was still under arrest. But unofficially, he was now a member of the U.S. War Refugee Board, the group working through the International Red Cross to rescue prisoners from the camps and relocate them to neutral territory. Apparently, his knowledge of the camps made him too important to leave locked up in a federal prison. The FBI accused him of not trying to stop the atrocities, and he still suffered the burn of their accusations. "You took photos, wrote letters as people were processed like cattle. You did not speak up, you did not try to stop it." This was the truth that ate at him all along.

But now he was here, ready to do whatever he could to help correct his failures. He would use this undercover role to save as many as he could, even if it meant deviating from the Red Cross's plan if he had the chance. The Red Cross was not political, did not choose sides. But he had.

A senior official in the Swiss Red Cross, Swiss commander, Lt. Marc Nilsson, explained to Falk who they were working with on the German side. Only Nilsson was aware of his identity as a former SS officer and the reason he was included on these rescues. That the Red Cross was working with Himmler couldn't be more of a shock than if Nilsson had said Hitler surrendered. Once again, men in Hitler's circle were making deals to stop the dictator. Colonel Walter Schellenberg was Hitler's foreign intelligence chief, a high-ranking SS officer and Himmler's most trusted aide. Somehow, he convinced Himmler to negotiate with the Allies to collaborate in Jewish rescue operations in exchange for being spared execution at the war's end. Falk was eager to learn why Himmler was cooperating. Last he knew, Himmler was dangerous, erratic, and certainly not trustworthy.

The door opened and Jean-Marie Musy, a former president of Switzerland, entered. He was nearly bald with a graying mustache, but it was his eyes that commanded attention. Their intensity conveyed an unwavering confidence. Falk was told Musy now served on the Federal Council of Switzerland and was affiliated with the Christian Democratic People's Party of Switzerland.

"You are here to guide us," Musy said as he shook Falk's hand.

"I am." Falk paused. It was dangerous to be too transparent, but he needed to know what the Swiss knew about him. "You heard my story?"

Musy nodded and motioned they should sit. "You were ahead of your time. Many SS officers are now trying to reach agreements before the war ends."

He restrained an urge to lash out. Not once did he think about how his actions would lessen his side-line participation after the war. He wanted to get the word out and return to his family or die trying.

"I'm just here to save people...in any way I can."

Musy offered the smile of a hardened skeptic. "How well do you know Himmler?"

"I met him twice, both times at big SS meetings."

"Would he recognize you?"

"He could. But it's been almost two years."

Musy stroked his mustache. "We'll keep you hidden if he's around, but it's unlikely we'll see him."

"May I ask a question?"

"Certainly. We need to trust each other."

"How do *you* know Himmler?" Falk asked.

"General Walter Schellenberg, his assistant. Himmler is very afraid of the arrival of the Red Army and wants to find favor with the allies." He smiled. "Of course, we didn't talk to Eisenhower about any such deal, but Schellenberg and Himmler don't know that."

Falk was relieved to hear these two were not getting away with their crimes. Himmler developed the SS from a mere 290 men to a million strong, changing their initial duties as Hitler's personal bodyguards to a well-oiled killing machine. Being duped by the Allies was a fitting end to Himmler and Schellenberg's long reigns of terror.

"These men are the highest-ranking SS officers, only one level under Hitler. Why do you believe they can be trusted?"

Musy crossed his legs and straightened the crease in his pants. "Himmler has been swaying for over a year with the idea of killing Hitler or following him to the end. Schellenberg convinced him that his flirtation with these insidious ideas would leave him dangerously close to the discovery of his betrayal by his very own police and intelligence services. He is now committed to this resistance, even if it is to win favor to save his life."

"Himmler was the brain behind the creation and organization of the 'final solution' camps." Falk rubbed his forehead. He'd never liked Himmler. The man was the opposite of the Aryan image Himmler himself advocated. He was neither tall, nor strong. Blond or blue-eyed, and although married, he visited Lebensborn clinics in Norway as often as possible, planting his "pure" seed in Viking girls paid to bear children with uncontaminated bloodlines.

The notion Himmler offered his assistance to return Jewish prisoners to Denmark stung like thistles lodged in his throat. The man needed to be executed, not rewarded.

The door opened and Musy's son, Benoit, entered. Benoit was a member of the Swiss Air Force and a younger version of his father.

Benoit knew the financiers of this operation, Recha Sternbuch and her husband, Yitzchak. Falk learned the Sternbuchs were Orthodox Jews who accepted a devil's bargain of 1,000 Reichsmarks, payable to Hitler, to release one Jewish prisoner. Thus far, the Sternbuchs raised enough money to bring 1,200 prisoners to safety. A small drop in the wide ocean of death, but an enormous amount of money and a place to start.

"We are ready," Benoit said.

The Red Cross would travel to Czechoslovakia and Poland in twelve white hospital buses with the large Red Cross emblem on the side. The staff consisted of medics, drivers, and volunteers, of which Falk was one. The convoy needed to pack their own supplies and not rely on purchasing goods or petrol in hostile countries. Himmler signed the release documents at Hohenlychen, his office outside Berlin. The papers secured the freedom of the Jews, but after handing the papers over to the Red Cross, he demanded that his name not be associated with the rescue in any way. Neither in foreign announcements nor in the Swedish or Swiss newspapers. And Schellenberg needed to be similarly careful. His position as Hitler's foreign intelligence officer couldn't save him if rumors of treason reached the Führer.

Part of Falk's role was to help choose the three camps to rescue. The Red Cross picked Terezín in Czechoslovakia because of the sheer number of women and children they saw there on an earlier visit. Falk suggested Gross-Rosen, a large sub camp in Poland. Also, in Poland, he wanted Auschwitz. When they reached Auschwitz, he planned to do more than rescue prisoners. Not everyone received a second chance to do something good in life.

-45-

Izaak Tauber

Terezín, Czechoslovakia - November 1944

They didn't get to move into a house that day, or any day after Izaak and Papa returned to Terezín. The nice houses in town sat empty, and the new stores, cafes, and library were closed. All the hard work the people put in to build a pretty place didn't seem to matter now.

They slept in giant wooden tray beds in a room with holes in the walls. Cold fingers of winter crept in at night and sent shivers up and down Izaak's back. When Papa woke him this morning, there was an ice dagger hanging from one of the holes. Even the heat of fifty men stuffed into one long room couldn't keep it warm. The guards were nervous and angry, yelling at the workers but also at each other. This city was more terrible than when he and Mama first arrived.

Papa helped him put on his layers of clothes to prepare for another day of work. Each day without Mama felt as if dark shadows followed him around. Papa didn't speak much but neither did the other men. Mama and the rest of the women left for Auschwitz on the early trains the morning he and Papa arrived. He hoped Mama lived in the same camp with his art teacher and the other children in his class.

He and Papa tried to cheer up each other with invented games. They used stones for checkers, or caught a ball made from a tobacco pouch filled with sand. When Papa started looking sad, Izaak always said, "Bet I can throw the ball farther than you this time."

Every day, in the moat around the fortress, the Germans burned piles and piles of papers. Big trucks kept arriving with more papers and the fires burned into the night, creating flickering orange monsters that rose high above the moat. Papa said they were burning something called archives and records, documents they didn't want anyone to see.

The prisoners shuffled to the cafeteria and claimed their bowl of warm broth and piece of bread. Papa said a prayer that the food would keep them strong and that they would see Mama soon.

On the way to work, Izaak studied the pencil lead-colored sky above their heads just before the white prickles of hard snow stung his face. He knew snow came in many types. There was soft snow and quiet snow. Those were pretty flakes as big as butterflies. But this snow was the uncaring kind, and he assumed the Germans had a hand in the hateful weather since they controlled everything. He huddled next to Papa and the other workers, their backs bent as the group walked to the Columbarium where the boxes of ashes were stored. Once they were in the long tunnel and underground, they stood tall and shook the icy flakes off their clothing and swept their hands over their hair really fast as if trying to get spiders out.

Like each morning the past week, they lined up in a long human stripe that stretched into the brick tunnel. The front of the line started in the deepest part of the Columbarium near shelves loaded with the boxes of the dead. The back of the line was outside and down the hill all the way to the Elbe River. The men changed places throughout the day, taking turns being stuck outside in the cold.

The cardboard boxes started moving, passed from one person to the next. Each container with the dead person's name moved along the people chain until they reached the river where the ashes were dumped into the rushing water. Something else the Germans were trying to hide—how many people died here. This passing of the remains went on for a long time every day. Izaak tried to be strong like the men, but after hours of working, he had to rest against the wall behind Papa's legs because his body shook from being so hungry and tired. Moving the dead to the river was a quiet job, the only sounds coming from the men, like his papa, were muttered prayers as they passed along the boxes.

Izaak tried to picture the river with piles of ashes building along the shoreline. Would the ashes someday make a dam like he saw happen at a river when too much sand piled up? If the Germans were trying to clean up before the Russians arrived, it seemed like they should get in trouble anyway, especially if they plugged up the clean blue river.

A man at the head of the Columbarium line, and the one at the river, kept count of how many boxes moved down the line. Then they compared numbers and wrote it in a tiny book Elder Levisohn kept. He was a judge in a court before he came to Terezín. Last night, the number reached 11,380 boxes, a number Izaak tried to count to, but he was too tired to think that high. Elder Levisohn said there might be 6,000 more to go.

The boxes were lighter than Izaak expected, but he knew the person's soul was the heavy part that floated to heaven with a light and became a twinkling star.

Something was happening off to his right. A man cried out as if he hurt himself. A few moments later, the man pushed by them, heading for the tunnel's opening while hugging a box to his chest and crying, "Ruth," over and over again.

Papa grabbed the man's arm trying to stop him. "Hide it until we're done." Other men told him not to be foolish. But the man pulled away and kept moving.

Papa suddenly started saying a popular prayer, not too loud but enough that other workers soon joined in, and their mumbled words filled the tunnel. Izaak knew some Hebrew from synagogue and "King, eternity, and mercy" were repeated. He didn't know why they were suddenly praying but joined in. Before Papa finished speaking, *pop-pop* noises came from far away. No one needed to say it, but that man had been shot.

The prayer ended and the boxes moved along again.

Hours later, a guard's whistle blew. They were finished for the day. They shuffled back to the exit.

The sun was nearly down when they reached the outside air. An eerie orange glow shown on the sides of a long black train, stretching from the town square all the way out of town. Through the windows on the coach cars, Izaak noticed no one was inside and the cattle car doors were open.

He felt a burst of nervousness and tugged Papa's sleeve. "Do you think this train is for us?"

Papa nodded but seemed to be only half listening as he looked at the train. He sounded tired when he said, "Just might be."

-46-

HERBERT MÜLLER

Near Heidelberg, Germany - November 1944

Herbert's family and guards were over two hours into the trip when the soldiers on top of the coaches began shouting. The dozen or so deportees in their coach startled awake, eyes wide, and looked out the windows, their heads whipping from one side of the car to the other to see what was happening. A rush of footsteps from the soldiers on top slapped the metal roof as the train slowed. They stopped in the middle of nowhere. Airplanes roared overhead as loud explosions sounded close by. Shock waves thumped into the side of the train, rocking it. Jutta gasped and Alfred and Frieda flew against them. Herbert marshalled them onto the floor, his arms wrapped around them.

Stutz yelled, "Get out now!" He pulled Jutta to her feet and headed for the door.

"Hurry!" Bosch grabbed Frieda and waved Herbert and Alfred forward.

Another explosion slammed the train. They were nearly knocked off their feet as they hurried down the steps and began running. Herbert felt, more than heard, the concussion as the front of the train exploded into orange flames. He turned to view black smoke roiling upward from the gaping hole where the engine had been. Then, rising like vultures from behind a row of hills, three planes thundered toward them. The white star in a black circle on the side identified them as American. He and Stutz propelled Jutta by the arms while Bosch helped Alfred drag a stunned Frieda to the nearby woods. They reached the trees just as the aircraft dove. From less than a hundred feet above, the planes strafed the train, thousands of machine gun bullets ripping through what was left of the *Frankfurt Express*.

They all hunkered down in dense brush between the towering trees. Bosch and Stutz signaled them to stay, and the two young men rushed back to help other soldiers, scrambling to set up an anti-aircraft gun atop the riddled roof of the last car. The soldiers fumbled and yelled the need to hurry faster as the gun was readied. The train sat destroyed. The wounded were pulled out and away from the tracks and into nearby weeds. Many were covered in blood and their screams and moans created a full-blown horror show. The uninjured cowered in the forest and like him, no doubt prayed the planes would not return.

"We'll wait here," he said, his voice stiff with fear, his mouth dry. Frieda openly cried in Alfred's arms while Jutta's breath was hitching in and out, her eyes wide. "Stutz and Bosch said the front cars carried explosives. I think that's what the big blast was, but I can't be sure."

"That's our army shooting at us!" Alfred said, his hand on Frieda's back. "We have to let them know we're here."

"We can't go out there, son." He pictured Alfred rushing out to the field waving his undershirt tied to a stick. "The pilots were on a mission to attack our train. They aren't here to protect us."

They huddled together as the growl of aircraft returned. The fighter pilots seemed once again locked onto what was left of the train. Through the trees, Herbert watched as the German gunners swung the anti-aircraft gun around on the roof and fired. Two planes peeled off, but gunfire caught the third as the pilot continued shelling the coaches. The damaged aircraft wobbled over a line of trees and then spiraled out of sight. Is this what his brother, Karl, faced each day? Karl could be dead, meeting the same fate as this pilot. He watched with mixed emotions as flames and smoke rose into the air. The Americans manning the planes were indirectly fighting for his personal freedoms, those he once enjoyed. But these same flyboys almost killed his family. And they might yet succeed.

Should they move deeper into the woods, or stay where the guards could find them? If the other two planes returned, it was unsafe to be out in the open. But if the Allies arrived on foot, they'd search the woods for the enemy and could easily be spooked into shooting his family.

He peered around a tree to see soldiers clambering down from the top of the train. But before they hit the ground, the front cars blew up, throwing chunks of metal to the sides, like truck tires kicking up gravel. Then those cars ignited the ones behind them in succession.

Seconds of eerie quiet followed. A moment of time depleted of all sound. Then the crackle of fire and screams of the wounded filled the air.

"Oh, no!" Jutta whispered. "Our bags."

"It's okay." Herbert assembled his family. He patted his coat pocket. "I still have our identification papers and permission to travel." Graf or Otto would have offered a prayer at this point, and Herbert wished they were here. He conjured up his father's voice in his head, using sheer will to try to push away the fear in his core.

"Let's pray." They huddled together and clasped hands. "Lord, we come before you to offer a plea for our safety in this fearful moment. Give us the wisdom to know how to complete this journey and the strength to follow through. We are grateful for the blessings we have through our Savior, Jesus. In His name we pray, Amen."

"Amen." Jutta wiped her eyes.

They waited in the trees. Overhead, the autumn foliage fluttered in brilliant shades of orange, red, and yellow while on the forest floor lay a spongy padding of fallen leaves, accumulating unspoiled, earthy, and damp. The cheerful colors were out of place for what had just happened. The forest should be standing in shades of ash and black. A clear view of the train showed their coach continued to burn, the flames a wavering orange film in front of their eyes. "Verboten" still visible on the car.

In the grassy area separating the tracks from the forest, a few soldiers began the gruesome task of assessing the damage and moving bodies to a central location in the nearby field. Passengers from the other Pullman cars stumbled from the woods and approached the train. They must have been in shock because they walked closer to the flames than Herbert thought safe.

He turned to his family. They huddled near a large tree trunk, visibly trembling, most likely in utter disbelief as he was. He should have questioned why their passenger train needed armed military personnel on top. They were trapped in an active war zone, and moments ago, almost fried to death. He could no longer count on the assurance they'd have safe passage to Elke's. "Stay here while I find our escorts."

He crossed the field and called out, "Bosch, Stutz. Where are you?" He rounded the back of the last burning train car and tripped over a burned soldier. He reeled backward, blood pounding in his ears. It was Bosch whose eyes were open, staring at nothing. Three soldiers lay sprawled near him. This time filled with dread, he approached another set of boots. He recognized Stutz and tried to process why the young man's body lay at a ninety-degree angle. A few steps closer revealed he was nearly cut in half by flying debris.

Herbert sank to the ground and vomited, gagging long after he emptied his stomach.

Back in the forest, he buffered the horror show he witnessed.

"Stutz and Bosch are dead."

"Great. Now what are we going to do?" Alfred asked. He slapped at a low hanging branch.

"How do we find transportation?" Jutta rubbed her arms as if chilled even though she wore a coat over her sweater.

"I don't know. The trains are easy targets," Herbert said. The Allies couldn't know some of the coaches carried Americans. Like Stutz said, the goal was to put fear in the German citizens. Some of the bombings had to be payback for the terror Londoners faced.

"No more trains for me." Frieda pulled and held both pigtails at chest level, one in each hand, as if trying to keep her head attached.

"I agree. We'll stay away from the tracks." Herbert reached for the map the booking clerk gave them and opened it. "We're in the northern part of the Black Forest, and it looks to be full of valleys, farms, and trails." He folded the edges under to highlight where they were, just south of Frankfurt and to the east of Wiesbaden. "We are only sixty miles away and the weather seems to be holding." The day was warm, an early autumn temperature, and the horizon was free of storm clouds. He made eye contact with each of them. "Fact Time. We can travel fifteen miles a day on back roads. Pop into a village and buy food, or maybe a farmer will feed us. I believe we can do this. If so, in four days we will be there."

"We can do this," Alfred said. "It's not like we have any luggage or sacks left to haul."

"We'll pretend it's like our camping trips in the Poconos but with more walking," Frieda added.

"I'm totally for it." Jutta's eyes crinkled at the edges when she forced a smile. "Otherwise, these weeks have all been in vain."

"Maybe the U.S. wanted us to die over here?" Alfred swatted dead leaves from an overhead branch with a stick.

"I don't believe that, son"—he took the stick from Alfred—"Until this bombing, they've kept their promise of safe passage. And, they couldn't know your grandpa would die." His chest ached. Saying the words more often didn't lessen the howling emptiness inside.

He checked his watch. "Maybe four more hours of daylight. Everybody ready?"

His family nodded.

He motioned them to a deer path, away from the carnage. Cries and moans faded as they walked deeper into the forest headed north. Unspoken words, a plea, kept time with his steps. *Please, God. Shelter us. Protect us. Lead us.* His mind buzzed with worry. Above all, let this be the right decision.

-47-

WILHELM FALK

Red Cross train, Poland & Czechoslovakia - December 1, 1944

After twenty days of caravanning across Germany, Falk's sixty-person Red Cross group pulled into Grünberg, Poland. The trip seemed to drag on forever. Twice, the buses waited on the side of the road for the rumbling army to pass. Another day, they were interviewed by the Gestapo, and once forced to detour hundreds of kilometers around a valley with a blown bridge.

He kept to himself as much as possible without being rude. Because they ate their meals together, he embraced the new identity he was given, Walden Falcon. A volunteer from the Netherlands with the International Red Cross, who had knowledge of the extermination camps from previous visits. He lived so long as an imposter he hoped he remembered what it was like to be himself when this was all over. Falcon, a name he helped choose, was close enough to Falk to make the word roll off his tongue with ease. In his new identity, he was married to a florist who remained behind in Rotterdam. They had no children.

And every time he told that lie, images of Ilse and his sons slowly flickered through his mind, a silent turning of pictures of their lives before the war. Ilse knitting baby booties for Hans. Dietrich learning to ride a bicycle on a back road, falling, skinning his knees. He and Ilse racing off the end of a dock hand in hand at Lake Kaarster See, swimming back to catch the young boys as they jumped. Giggling on a warm summer's eve, trying to make love in silence on an unstable lounger while the boys slept in their bedroom overhead. Opening a note Ilse slipped into his lunch sack when he worked at Kodak. The memories all there.

Swiss commander, Lt. Marc Nilsson, approached Falk's seat. He was a tall man, clean-shaven with a slight stoop. He dropped into the seat next to Falk and spoke quietly in German. "Remember, I will shoot you with very little provocation. The list includes, if you were to leave the train without permission, or contact members of the Nazi party, or put our mission at risk with your actions."

"That's fair." Falk spoke the words the commander wanted to hear, but he no longer believed in fairness. "But let me ask. May I write a letter to my wife?" She and the boys would be safely in the Netherlands, in Eindhoven with relatives, but she'd be worried sick as to why she heard nothing from him in over a year. He last wrote from Italy before he switched uniforms with the dead Stern, telling her to leave Düsseldorf.

"You would put her in danger?" Nilsson's eyebrows drew together. "You said that the Wehrmacht informed your wife about your death in Italy. Mail is being screened. If the postmaster sees a letter from you, the woman could be interrogated"—he lifted his hands—"You know personally what that means."

Falk's anger blazed and he hid his clenched fist. Nilsson's statement assumed Falk tortured and killed women and children like other Schutzstaffel officers. He accepted he was guilty by association for plenty, but he never murdered civilians. He already explained he was Waffen-SS, the military branch tasked with supervising shipments and supplies. A talent his commanders believed he offered because of his CEO role with Eastman Kodak. The SS-Totenkopfverbände, the unit that vowed their loyalty to the Führer to the death, was in charge of running the concentration camps, while the Gestapo and their security service, the Sicherheitsdienst, looked for enemies of the state and killed them.

"My wife and sons are in the Netherlands. Ilse would not have received the military report that I died." He wanted Ilse to know he was alive, that he was trying to right so many wrongs before he came home. That he loved her and the boys. "I would send her a letter there."

"I have to say 'no.'" His mouth set in a stern line. "For now. This mission cannot be threatened by external contact."

"Understood."

Falk debated many times if he should reach out to Ilse or not. The Wehrmacht didn't have the address in the Netherlands, and Ilse would be careful not to explain why her SS officer husband asked her to hide out there. But *what if?* His heart would be torn to shreds if any harm came to them for his actions. Ilse was a strong woman. She'd wait out the war to hear from him again.

Nilsson stood and looked through the bus windshield and then back to Falk. "Let's do what we came here for and remember, you listen for trouble, you hear in German, but you only speak Dutch."

"Yes, sir."

He and Nilsson were the last men off the bus. Three nurses readied cots for the prisoners. Grünberg was a terraced town with a crumbling church known for the monk's century-old white wines. A sub-camp in the huge Gross-Rosen system, it housed Jews from several countries. However, the Jews to be freed—thanks to the Sternbuchs' ransom—were from Denmark and Sweden.

Like the hundreds of other camps in the Nazi network, Grünberg stood behind an overhead arch which declared, "Arbeit Macht Frei," although Falk knew work never made these captives free—death did. On the other side of the entrance were rows of wooden houses with wisps of smoke billowing above the shabby roofs.

Three female SS officers stood next to the gate. They'd be tough to fight. These were muscular women with fierce expressions who could knock a person back a step or two. They carried their large weapons as easily as Ilse carried a purse. "Not allowed. You cannot go in," one said. "We bring the selected guests to you."

Guests. Falk flinched at the cruelty behind the term. Apparently, evil knows no gender.

His group moved away from the gate and stood with their backs against the brick wall to stay warm, rubbing their arms and legs in the morning light. His heart thudded. The chance of bumping into a fellow SS officer here was slim but considering the SS guards were exchanged throughout the camp network, it wasn't an impossibility.

Herman Ott moved beside Falk. Ott was a dedicated medic, and he found him to be bright-eyed, sweaty, and talkative. The medic offered cigarettes. "Warm yourself while we wait."

Falk accepted and lit up.

Jonathan Bauer joined them and also accepted a light. He was the youngest member of the group and spoke five languages, shifting between them with little effort.

Ott exhaled, and the smoke hung in the frigid air before dissipating. "Must be hell in that place. According to our connection, many workers committed suicide here. Perhaps a few hundred."

"Seems extreme," Bauer said. "Why not pick up and leave when it is dark?"

Nilsson smiled. "The Red Army is coming closer and closer, and before they attack, there are rumors. The Russians torture or kill citizens in the cities and towns in each camp. Their logic is that the local population knew what was happening, so they are just as guilty."

A lump formed in Falk's throat. That described him.

Iron grated against iron as the gates slowly swung open. The female guards flanked a long line of prisoners, hobbling along, four abreast, all with the smell of neglect trailing off them.

The Red Cross team moved into action. Falk reached for a man so emaciated it was hard to discern his age. He could've been thirty or eighty. The man shuffled along, muttering what must have been a prayer. He nearly carried the man up the few steps into the white bus where a nurse took over. Then he turned back for another ragged skeleton. The sight made Falk sick to his stomach. These survivors were a testament to man's will to persevere against all odds, a fight to the end against unimaginable evil. To each person Falk helped up the two steps, he said, "You are safe."

The prisoners' eyes were wary. Recognizing danger and double meanings was probably the only reason they survived this long. They were given water, tea, and packets of soft-cooked potatoes. The workers were warned not to overfeed the famished prisoners because it would make them vomit.

Many survivors immediately fell asleep. One man, with a wasted arthritic claw, tugged on Falk's coat while he covered him with a blanket.

He asked a question Falk couldn't understand, so he motioned Bauer to his side and the man asked again. Bauer translated. "He wants to know where they are going."

Bauer told the man they were going to Switzerland after two more stops.

The man turned to the window, and after a few moments, released Falk's coat. He asked another question. Bauer said, "He wants to know if we are coming back for those left behind?"

Bauer answered the stricken man, and then explained to Falk. "I told him we hope so."

Falk knew there was no such hope for this camp. Today would be the only rescue mission.

The answer appeared to brighten the man's spirits, and his smile revealed missing teeth.

"His sons are still there," Bauer said.

Falk's head thumped and he swallowed hard. What horror to leave children behind in this pit of hell. In this man's case, the children must be dead, or they would be in this rescued group. This small glimmer of hope might be the only thing keeping the man alive, and Falk refused to take it away.

When everyone had settled in, Falk took a seat in the rear of the bus and rested his head against the windowpane. Freeing prisoners was one small step on his road to healing and making amends. It felt good. He wasn't sure he'd share the horror stories of these camps with Ilse whenever he was home again. It was a sight he'd never forget and visions she never should have to comprehend.

Outside, the snow-dusted cornfields slid past. Then a stone barn. And a field with a huddle of sheep whizzed by, all under a winter-blue sky. The rhythm of the wheels on the road finally felt like he moved closer to his personal goal. It was not a plan he shared with the Red Cross but was, nevertheless, urgent.

-48-

IZAAK TAUBER

Auschwitz, Poland - December 1944

For two weeks, Izaak had been handing out strings at the Auschwitz train platform. He slowly stepped on his raised wooden box as the second train arrived today. His legs were wobbly from hunger, and he shivered under his coat. He was tired of being hungry, cold, and feeling sick.

"Here it comes," George Brady said. He was a teenage saxophonist in the camp orchestra. He nodded in the direction of the hissing train that grew larger and larger under the bare-limbed trees. George sat on a wobbly chair with the other orchestra members, freezing in their thin suits borrowed from a stack of clothing in the sorting building.

George's sister, Hana, was in Friedl Dicker-Brandeis's art class with Izaak in Terezín. Izaak asked where their art teacher and the children now lived because in the two weeks since he and Papa arrived, none of them were around. George said they all went to the showers, but Izaak couldn't believe that because showers didn't take that long. He assumed George didn't have any better information than he did until he learned, soon after, what *the showers* meant. He cried that night squeezed in the long bed with Papa and eight other men. His friends and favorite teacher were all dead. How could someone like his teacher, who knew about beauty and the magic of using art to take a person to another place, be gone?

Moments ago, he asked George if Hana brought any of the drawings and paintings from their art studio with them. George said Mevr. Dicker Brandeis locked hundreds of them in two suitcases and hid them at Terezín. That was good. Auschwitz had no nice buildings to hang anything.

The train came to a complete stop in a whistling cloud of steam. Then the orchestra broke into *Dąbrowski Mazurka*, the national anthem of Poland. Smoke rolled from the huge engine's stack as if it couldn't leave fast enough. The guards pulled the doors to the side. Jewish workers took off the dead people first. They wore rags tied around their mouths and noses, so they wouldn't catch the Typhus germs going around. The dead were piled onto a cart and hauled away.

Then the other passengers climbed down, and although Izaak stood on the box there, the guards warned him to never talk to them. The passengers' faces were full of surprise when the music played. The guards spoke in kind voices and told them which lines they wanted them to join.

Acting as if he had zipped his mouth shut, he handed out the strings. Passengers could tie their shoes together and be able to find them later in the building called Canada. For the next half hour, he offered strings and pointed to where people should leave their shoes. When the last person was out of sight, the music stopped.

Then he threw as many pairs of shoes over his shoulders as he could carry. His record was sixty-five, but today forty-three pairs seemed extra heavy, banging against his front and back as he slogged along the snow-covered ground. He hoped to make only twenty trips from the platform to the storage building called Canada and then he'd be finished. The only good news was these back-and-forth trips gave him a chance to check out the women's side of the camp and try to find Mama. For days, he and his papa asked about her, but the workers who went to the women's side never came back with any news. Papa knew about camp Bergen-Belsen nearby. He was there a short time before transferring to Terezín and said Mama might be there.

Bad thoughts slithered around in Izaak's brain like wet snakes. His mother said if they got separated it wouldn't be forever, but after six months he feared he'd never see her again.

At night, when he was almost asleep, he could hear her voice, low and soothing in his head like a soft piece of cloth he could touch if scared. It was so hard not knowing how long the war would last, and if they'd have to live in more bad places before they went home.

An inmate and a man in a grey-green uniform with silver skulls on the collar were waiting for him on the platform when he returned for the last load of shoes. The man in uniform was handsome and smelled clean like soap. The inmate smelled dirty like everyone in Izaak's room.

The clean man leaned down and pulled out a drawing from behind his back. It was Izaak's long-ago drawing of Papa. He spoke, and then the dirty man translated. "He wants to know if you are the one who drew this picture."

Izaak nodded, not understanding where he dropped it, or how the man found it. Was he in trouble?

"I'm sorry," Izaak said, his tongue barely working. "I left it some place." He made sure not to look in the soldier's eyes. Looking right at a guard made them angry and sometimes they hurt the person who dared look at them.

The men talked again. The dirty prisoner asked Izaak if he could draw like that all the time.

Izaak bobbed his head. "I'm better now. I took art classes from a famous person."

The clean soldier stood tall and put his hand on Izaak's shoulder and spoke. The prisoner changed the words around for Izaak to understand. "How would you like to live in a nice house and draw all day?"

He couldn't believe his ears. The soldier smiled and raised his eyebrows as if to say, "It's true."

A house? Drawing?

Abraham from Camp Westerbork told him over a year ago that his drawing of Papa might help him somehow. Now it was happening.

"Can Papa live there, too?" Izaak watched him nervously. This offer was unexpected and maybe couldn't be trusted. What if this was a cruel joke? The guards played bad jokes all the time and people got hurt.

Another flurry of words. "What is your Papa's name? We'll find him and let him know where you are. He can come visit."

Izaak's heart beat fast. This man might be the one who could get his family all together again.

"Saul Tauber. And my mama is Rachel Tauber. I think she's here some place, too."

The clean soldier motioned to the prisoner to carry the last of the shoes and follow them. He handed Izaak his drawing. The sun lowered letting nighttime come, and the wind blew extra cold. Izaak tucked his free hand into his armpit and hugged the drawing to his chest as he followed alongside the men. He found new energy in his legs with this turn of fortune.

The soldier spoke again through the prisoner. "And what is your name?"

"Izaak. And I'm nine." He wanted the man to know he was not a baby. That he was old enough to learn new things.

They walked by a group of men pulling a loaded cart of wood. The men looked up as they passed, but Izaak didn't spot his papa there to tell him the good news. He wished he could see Papa's face when he heard he was chosen to practice art.

The clean soldier smiled and then said through the translator, "But you are so young to be this talented. We must see about this gift you have." His smile was friendly, much different than the other soldiers who worked there. "My name is Uncle Josef. I'm a doctor."

Suddenly, the man's smile made Izaak nervous. It was too wide as if he were trying hard to make him believe something that wasn't true. Or maybe it was the look in the man's eyes? Something was off, but he couldn't say what. He hugged the drawing closer. The big question he asked himself was what interest did a doctor have in art students anyway?

-49-

HERBERT MÜLLER

On the road near Heidelberg, Germany - January 1945

T he first night in the forest, Herbert and the family found a camp along-side a logging trail. They watched from the trees in case someone lived there, but on closer inspection, it was abandoned.

"Paratroopers were here." Herbert walked closer to read the lettering on an open chute. "Look. It was our guys." Old parachutes with serial stamp numbers and *Made in Manchester, Conn.* were put up to create five tents.

"This is cool." Alfred wandered around the camp. "They were hiding from the Germans."

Inside each tent lay a straw mattress, kept semi-dry from the elements, with one rudimentary wooden table and chair. In one direction, a trail led thirty feet to an outhouse, and in the other, was a natural spring with tin cups hanging in a tree. Knowing the U.S. military had been here made it feel safer, although he knew that hope carried no weight. The paratroopers may have been snuck out, but his family was still in a war zone and no rescue operation was on its way to save them.

They dragged four mattresses into one tent and slept until dawn. The morning sun dropped warm golden beams to the forest floor through openings in the trees and an earthy scent—damp and rich—surrounded them.

As much as they wanted to stay in the camp, they had no food and needed to push north. He rolled up a parachute, so they'd have a ready-made tent at their next stop. They followed tractor ruts through a yellowed vineyard on the side of a long slope and eventually entered the edge of a small town.

"Oh, dear Lord," Jutta said, pointing to the dead bodies stacked like cordwood outside the church. Perhaps a dozen adults and a child.

A sudden gust carried the stench of rotting bodies and they covered their noses.

"Don't look, children." He kept them moving away from the dead, searching for a store or market. On the main road in the center of town, they passed families bundled in rags, pushing handcarts, one with a gaunt elderly person riding on top. Panic crept into his chest. If this is how German citizens fared, what could he expect for his family?

Smoke pushed out of the chimney at a dismal store at the edge of town, just as snow began to fall. The inside of the town market was dim, its floor covered with warped and cracked linoleum. His family gravitated to the woodstove in the corner as he greeted the owner, a lean man with wire spectacles and full black beard. He wore a bloodied apron over a threadbare, once-white dress shirt. The man's face was set in a frown.

A young woman clomped in through a curtained-off doorway behind the counter. She wore blocky, heavy shoes and kept her eyes on his family. The man slipped one hand under the counter and left it there. If a gun, he didn't blame the storekeeper. Waves of hungry refugees passed through the town and desperation outweighed societal rules.

Herbert filled a basket with bread, a small piece of dried ham, a bag of black walnuts, matches, and a lighter. He paid for the supplies from the forty Reichsmarks, their relocation allowance Stutz handed him before the trip began. He had yet to open Graf's envelope, hoping to hand it back to the pastor one day, a plan that kept his worry at bay concerning his friend.

Back outside, they huddled under the roof on the side of the store and made haphazard sandwiches with the bread and ham.

"Chewy," Alfred said, over-emphasizing how hard it was to grind through the meat. "Are we sure it's not old shoe leather?"

Frieda looked like a chipmunk with her bite of sandwich pocketed in one cheek. "Better than garbage." She laughed less and was more direct and focused on facts ever since the train blew up.

"Garbage is way down my list." Jutta ate the bread separately from the meat. Her cold was nearly gone, and her strength returned. "But we won't have to root through cans just yet."

"I hope you're joking, Mother." Frieda's nose and cheeks were pink from the frigid weather.

"She's joking, love," Herbert said, "but this shoe-leather sandwich might be dinner and breakfast, as well."

The snowflakes thickened and softened the town's drabness. A burg drained of all its hustle and bustle by deprivation and death. As they headed back into the woods, Herbert felt trapped inside a snow globe, shaken by some unseen hand, keeping him off balance as he guided them to safety.

They walked all day, sticking to trails along creeks and paths through farmers' fields, sometimes walking back roads. They'd become more brave when it appeared no one paid attention to them. What was another four refugees in a country with thousands wandering around? When Herbert saw Jutta stagger, he said, "Let's find a place to sleep."

Hours earlier, the snow stopped, but a clear cold night awaited them. They approached a farmhouse with a barn and silo, a small affair.

"I'm going to ask about the barn," Herbert said. "We need to be inside tonight."

"Tell him we'll milk his cows," Alfred said and chuckled.

"Warm milk sounds good." Frieda rubbed her hands and stuck them in her armpits.

Jutta and Herbert waited on the stoop after he knocked. His heart raced when beyond the gauzy curtains he made out the outline of a figure carrying a rifle. "Let's leave. We'll ask at another place."

A man yanked open the door. He wore layers of clothing and a surprised look stamped on his face. With the rifle clenched in one hand, he held open the door with the stump of his other arm. "What do you need?" His voice was like phlegm over gravel.

"One night in your barn, away from the cold," Herbert said in German. "We have children with us."

He leaned to the side to see Frieda and Alfred who were just a few steps behind. "Yes. Like so many. Can you pay?"

"How much?" Herbert and his family were dressed in layers, but not like in the rags other people on the road wore. The farmer may have guessed they had some money with them.

"Fifteen Reichsmarks." He used his shoulder to hold the door and pointed his stump to the barn. "The upper loft on the right, if you want it."

The cost was exorbitant. It was dusk and a brisk wind swirled at Herbert's back. They could try to find another farm, but there was the risk of being shot in the dark. "My father already died during this . . . this trip to unite with our relatives." If he said forced deportation, the man might wonder what type of people they were that the United States needed to send them away. He pulled out ten Reichsmarks. "We have so little left."

Otto might have been right at home jawing with this farmer if he were here. This one-handed guy could have fought in World War I alongside him. He looked to be close enough in age.

The man took the ten. "The army seized my horses, but the blankets are still there. You must be on your way at sunrise."

He closed the door as Jutta was saying, "Thank you."

"Did we get it?" Alfred asked.

"Yes. The hayloft for one night." Herbert guided his family across the damp grass before rolling open the large barn door.

"Children," Jutta said, "grab a blanket before you climb up." She pointed to the large wool blankets folded on a bale of hay.

"They stink," Alfred said, quickly pulling one away from his nose, "like horses."

Herbert closed the door. "Let's just be thankful the man wasn't raising pigs."

Moments later, they all reached the loft after climbing a homemade ladder, the rungs spaced so far apart, Jutta and Frieda needed a hand.

The loft covered half the length of the barn. Baled hay was stacked five high along the outer walls, a semi-effective barrier against the cold.

"Kind of like a straw fort," Alfred said.

The children created separate nests for themselves a few feet apart.

They wrapped the blanket around their shoulders before dropping down onto their beds.

Herbert helped Jutta clear a space in the loose hay at their feet. She layered the bottom with one blanket and used the other to cover themselves.

Alfred whispered something, and Frieda laughed.

"What are you two going on about?" Jutta asked.

"I told her if I needed to get down during the night, I'd just use our stolen parachute."

"And I told him we'd be pulling him the rest of the way on a sled if he did that."

Herbert smiled. "Speaking of...we made great time today and we should be proud. I think if we push through, we might only have two more nights in barns."

"We're so close." Jutta snuggled up to his side and rested her head on his chest. She yawned. "It seems too good to be true."

As the children whispered back and forth, Herbert lay down and pulled Jutta next to him. "How are you doing?"

"It's crazy. But in this moment, in this barn somewhere lost in Germany, I've never felt safer."

"I know what you mean." The ache for home lived inside him, pushing him forward. One day they'd return. But family was everything. Nestled in the loft, he cleared his mind of the worries that plagued him every second. He set aside the scenarios of danger that seemed to wait around every corner and tried to memorize this moment when all was right.

At sunrise, Herbert stood on the lower floor brushing off bits of straw. Drab sunlight pushed through two filthy windows across from the loft. The rays exposing the dust and grain particles driven up from the old barn's stone floor. A pang of loss hit Herbert. It was one sight he saw a thousand times back in his gristmill. All he had, the life they lived, were now like this chaff, drifting up and down on the winds of fate. When he had freedom, he hadn't noticed. But with those days ripped away, hour by hour, it felt harder and harder to know what lay ahead, or when they would be free again.

Jutta reached the barn floor next to him, buttoning her coat around her. "Breakfast time."

Herbert kissed her cheek. They brushed off the top of a barrel and laid out the leftover bread and dried ham from yesterday. He cracked dozens of walnuts with pliers he found in a toolbox.

"Looks good," Jutta said.

"Mrs. Positive." He smiled. "It looks bleak, but I love your attitude."

She called the children from the loft. One of Frieda's braids was undone with hay stuck in her hair. Alfred rubbed his eyes with the palms of his hands and yawned wide enough to set an apple inside.

They prayed over the meal. Standing in a patch of sunlight, they ate the dark bread and ham and dug the meat from the walnut shells.

"We need to find more food today." Herbert rolled up the paper the ham was wrapped in and dropped it in the scrap barrel near a work bench.

"Let me fix your hair, Frieda." Jutta patted a hay bale.

Frieda sat as Jutta undid the other braid. She combed her fingers through the blonde locks and started weaving the strands when Frieda stopped her. "I think I want to leave it down. It will be warmer on my ears."

In that moment it hit him. She was no longer his little pigtailed girl. The near-rape on Ellis Island and the events tagging her as an unwanted American had changed her. She was wary now, not just a passive observer. Gone were her innocence and naiveté. A small part of Herbert died along with her childlike spirit.

"Is everyone ready?" Jutta asked.

They buttoned their coats and rolled open the barn door. The day was cold but clear as they headed to the road, passing the farmer's abandoned truck, hub deep in mud. Does it run? Or was there no petrol?

"How far today, Pops?" Alfred asked. He had just started calling him that and he liked it. It was what Herbert always called his father.

"I'm thinking fifteen miles…twenty-four kilometers. That gets us to the next working railway station. If we think it's safe, we'll be riding the rails the rest of the way."

"I never thought I'd envy hobos"—Frieda wrapped her scarf tighter—"But let's measure the distance in miles. It doesn't sound as far."

Alfred played along in a teasing tone. "When did you start thinking on your own?"

Frieda mock-punched him. "Maybe I'll turn out to be the accountant in the family, not you."

They reached a two-lane road and walked shoulder to shoulder, only moving to the roadside the few times a vehicle passed. No one stopped to help. Everyone seemed cocooned in their own trials.

The air was crisp. A bite of pine and wood smoke floated on the gentle breeze. Houses set back in the trees stayed hidden until curling white plumes from their chimneys gave them away. This part of the Bavarian countryside was still pristine. Snow-covered hills, hidden lakes, and narrow, winding roads. It was hard to tell the war was still on.

When no one was nearby, they sang songs, or played Ghost by forming a chain of letters that spelled words. Herbert was off his game. Jutta and the children were besting him, sticking him with no option but to add the final letter that made a real word.

Hours passed.

His stomach growled, but they'd seen no towns. Midday, they stepped out of the woods next to a dead-end train spur near the town of Pfungstadt.

"What's that sound?" Frieda asked.

"Birds, I think," Alfred said.

They all froze, and Herbert strained to decipher the raspy sound ahead.

"Someone's crying," Jutta said.

They walked quicker, following the train tracks around a corner discovering an open boxcar.

"It sounds like a crying baby," Jutta said, reaching the opening first. Her hand flew to her mouth. "Oh, no!" Jutta pushed the children back. "Don't look!"

The children turned away, puzzled but willing to listen to their mother.

Herbert moved to Jutta's side as she leaned into the boxcar. A woman lay naked from the waist down, blue and stiff. A baby was tucked inside her coat, its cry weak, raspy. He tried to move the mother, but she was frozen to the boxcar's floor. Another woman, a teenage boy, and a man inside the abandoned train car, all appeared shot. There was no answer as to where the people came from, or why they were killed. He needed to move his family out now.

"We need to find help for this child," Jutta said, pulling herself up into the car. She gently lifted the naked baby boy from his dead mother's arms. She opened her coat, settling the infant between her shirt and chest. "He's so cold." A visible shiver raced through her.

He helped Jutta to the ground as his gaze returned to the horrible sight in the car. The woman had obviously just given birth before the people were shot. Pure evil must roam the countryside.

When he looked to Jutta, he noticed the tiny head with blinking eyes that peered out from the top of her blouse. The infant had stopped crying.

"Oh, Herbert"—Jutta wept openly—"These poor people."

"I know." His throat clenched around the words. "But we can't help them, and we need to go." The hair on his arms stood up. Since someone was willing to shoot civilians, the killers most certainly wouldn't have a problem murdering four more.

Alfred walked to the open door and his face paled. "Good God. What is wrong with this world?"

Herbert pulled him away and made sure Frieda didn't see the dead. Her face was already three shades of pale he'd never seen before.

"We are about four miles from Pfungstadt," Herbert said. "We need to hurry to keep this baby alive."

The railroad tracks ended thirty feet behind the abandoned car, and the ground was cleared as far as he could see past that as if new tracks might one day be added. Footprints in the soft ground circled the coach and headed back the way he and his family had approached the tracks from the woods, following a small road on other side. No footprints extended past the train tracks on the open ground.

"We'll stay off the road." He pointed to the cleared area. "This goes in the right direction, but we're going to get our feet wet."

"It's fine," Frieda said. She leaned in to see the baby. "Boy or girl?"

"Boy." Jutta wiped her eyes with one hand. "He's so weak. Poor little guy." She touched his cheek.

"We were meant to come this way, don't you think?" Frieda asked.

"I do." Jutta kept her hand on top of the baby's head to warm him.

Herbert's heart pounded as they headed out. His eyes swept from the tree line to the grassy hill on their left. Someone could be hiding just inside the tree line, and he wouldn't see them until it was too late. *Please, God. Protect us.*

They made good time, although it was through hilly country. Arriving on a hill overlooking Pfungstadt, they regarded the town with its buildings constructed with pink, red, and white bricks that filled a tight-knit area. A river cut through the town, and up on the far hills, were felled walls and crumbled towers, ruins of the past.

They followed the main road into town and stopped the first person they met, a man carrying sticks tied to his back. In German, Herbert asked for directions to the hospital.

"Bombarded," he said. He directed them to the doctor's home, no more than three streets farther. The home was large with two chimneys and a closed-in porch.

Dr. Seidel was middle-aged, nearly bald, wearing casual slacks and a tan wool sweater. He didn't seem surprised to see four strangers at his door and invited them into the house. The closed-in porch spanned the front of the house and was semi-converted into an examination room with a padded table, several cots, shiny white drawers for supplies, and extra lighting overhead. With the hospital damaged, the doctor had transformed his home. Herbert explained the child's situation as Jutta lifted the baby from her shirt and handed him over. Herbert saw her hesitate. She didn't want to release the baby.

"Where is this train car?" Seidel asked. He held the infant as if he knew what he was doing and reached for a towel to swaddle him. His skin tone had turned from blue to a shade of pink.

Herbert hoped the baby would live a happy life. Someone needed to survive this war.

"The car was abandoned, maybe four miles back. The railway tracks ended there," Herbert said. The authorities would need to know, although the likelihood was the dead people were not from Pfungstadt or they wouldn't be hiding in a train car. Unless they were on Hitler's list of disposables. "If anyone wanted to drive me there, I could point it out."

"It will be better for me to call." Seidel smiled. "I don't know why you would be here in these dangerous times, and I don't want to be involved." He looked at the door as if someone may have followed them. "But thank you for saving this child."

He wanted to assure the doctor his family had done nothing wrong but arguing against false beliefs might make him sound as if he had something to hide. He took the high road. "Of course. We could never leave the child to die."

The doctor nodded. "You must let me get to my work." He looked toward the windows where dusk enveloped the day. "The city has a strict curfew and the suspicion is high. You can sleep in the maid's residence behind my house, but it is best to be out of town before anyone asks questions"—he shrugged—"Many will believe that you inform the allies. We had our share of bombings and death."

Herbert thanked him.

"There is very little food in there but feel free to eat." He turned and carried the baby through another door, closed it behind him, and called out a woman's name.

"He asked what we are doing here." Herbert translated the conversation for the children as they circled the property to the maid's residence.

Alfred scoffed. "You should have said we're sightseeing." He scooped a stick from the ground and threw it across the yard.

"And we don't like the sights we're seeing." Frieda wrapped her arms around her sides.

"I'm glad you didn't look in the train car, sis." He pulled her close. "Seriously."

"Me, too."

The maid's cottage had three rooms. The bedroom with two beds, a dresser, two kerosene lamps, a small kitchen with a table, and a washroom attached to an outside commode.

"This feels like a luxury," Jutta said.

The children took turns washing while Jutta opened the cupboards and pulled out a few boxes and two jars. Herbert secured the doors and checked the windows. The doctor's words of warning spooked him. He pictured the townsfolk arriving in the middle of the night with torches, a scene right out of Frankenstein.

Soon, they were seated around the tiny table. Jutta cooked cornmeal porridge, a side dish of pickled red cabbage and apples, and fried black bean cakes.

"Delicious," Herbert said. "I'm not sure how you did this with so little to work with." He offered a prayer, his chest swelling with emotion as he thanked God for guiding them this far. For keeping them safe in horrible situations. He prayed for the baby, for the dead on the train. He ended with the petition that they would arrive safely, and soon, at Elke's house.

Jutta smiled at the compliment given for the creative meal. The food didn't last long, but Herbert couldn't remember food tasting that good. Deprivation made the simplest joys seem miraculous. Running water, soap, towels. Beds with pillows.

They all cleaned up and soon were in bed.

Jutta turned down the lamp, but he took his time easing under the covers, the slide of sheets against his skin feeling foreign. He lowered his head into the pillow's concave caress. Then he squeezed Jutta's hand. "Has anything ever felt this good?"

"It hasn't." She chuckled then grew quiet. "What the doctor said, Herbert. Are we going to get out of this town safely?"

"He was nice to warn us that we aren't welcome." He took in a long slow breath, trying to melt the tension in his body. "But we'll leave first thing as suggested."

Jutta crawled closer and wrapped her arm across his chest. Within minutes, she was asleep. Sometime in the dark, Frieda woke up screaming. Herbert and Jutta clawed their way out of sleep to soothe her fears caused by a nightmare. Once she calmed down, Herbert couldn't fall back to sleep.

Should they creep out of town looking like thieves, or walk through as if they knew where they were heading? He'd seen the sign for the train station on the way to the doctor's house. Two blocks to the main street and then out of town a few more blocks. They should appear to be just four people out for a walk, no baggage, nothing to worry about. The railway map showed a direct line to Flörsheim am Main, and then a spur to Wiesbaden. He hoped Elke received his note explaining they were coming tomorrow evening. Would she be shocked or saddened there were more mouths to feed? Probably a little of both.

The horrible scene from the train flashed behind his closed lids. The dead appeared to be European, but his family could have suffered the same fate. His throat tightened. What stopped bandits from roaming through the devastated towns searching for vulnerable people?

Or had locals done that? He doubted it. The doctor said he'd make the call to authorities, but would he say Americans wandered into town carrying a baby?

One more day. They just needed a good, uninterrupted travel day and this traumatic journey would be over.

He listened to his family sleeping—a comforting sound—all that was necessary in his life. He missed Otto. Missed having another adult male with him, especially one who'd survived a war. And he'd really miss him when they returned to America. Whenever that was.

-50-

WILHELM FALK

Terezín, Czechoslovakia - January 1945

The walled city of Terezín sat high above the Ohre River like an early morning winter scene from a postcard. After the white buses pulled in, Falk and several other workers approached two SS guards who gave their papers a perfunctory glance.

"Propaganda town," Falk said to Ott after they moved past the inspection area. "They refurbished it for the Danish Red Cross visit seven months ago and they made a film here to show how the Jews were treated well." He scanned the streets of faded glory and imagined he heard the shuffling footsteps of the tens of thousands who passed through. The pretense that took place here was nothing more than a denial of history.

There was only so much a humanitarian group could do. Today, they would liberate the 300 people left in the city. Large fires burned along the bastions, the cloying smoke making it hard to breathe. He suspected it wasn't trash but piles of incriminating records.

They entered a town hall, where SS-Sturmbannführer Karl Rahm shook their hands and thanked them for coming. Every Nazi's attitude had shifted. With the Red Army on their doorstep, officers like Himmler, and now Rahm, offered complete cooperation, acting as if they were only minor cogs in Hitler's killing machine.

Falk prayed his information might help send every one of Hitler's men to a hangman's noose. For their involvement with the Jewish exterminations. These officers knew what they were doing. Their moral foundations obliterated the first time they unfairly beat a man, or harmed a child because a maniac said it was right.

Rahm led them to several large dining halls where prisoners waited. Falk and Bauer moved through the group together, reassuring the haggard men and a few women they were safe. "You're going home," Bauer said, but the resignation in the prisoners' eyes said they were not convinced they were liberated.

Hours later, they'd loaded the last of the white buses. Before leaving the fortress, the vehicles circled the town square, and Falk spotted a new pavilion in the center. What sliver of optimism had the Jews been given when music filled the night breeze? They may have believed the Germans came to their senses and stopped the abuse and killings. Then, the painful realization they'd been deceived, once again, because evil never showed mercy.

Falk's bus pulled away from the town. The solid white sky broke open, and twilight rays of orange and gold lit the Sudeten Mountains like a vision of hope. The sun set, and he and the Red Cross members worked throughout the night, assessing the health of each passenger, feeding them, and handing out blankets.

Just before dawn, he settled onto a seat next to Lt. Nilsson. Nilsson nodded when he made eye contact with a volunteer in the aisle, carrying a coffee tray. "Buy a drink for you?" he asked Falk.

"Certainly, a double." He accepted a cup and took a cautious sip. He stared at the roof. The lights from the bus behind them flashed across the shiny surface illuminating the bus' interior. He turned his gaze to the lieutenant who was already studying him. "How many of these rescue operations have you carried out?"

"This is just our second," Nilsson said.

"A thousand Reichsmarks per person. The Wehrmacht is doing really well."

"No money has yet been released. It is still in a Swiss bank." He took a swallow of the hot drink. "Musy and the Sternbuchs have no intention of paying Himmler, but he does not know it yet. To whom will he complain? Hitler? He would be dead before he tried to blame someone else."

"Good to hear. The Jews should not be bought like cattle." In a fair world, Himmler and Hitler, and men like Mengele, would have the tables turned on them, and they would waste away in prison.

Falk wanted this time to speak to Nilsson alone. He pulled out a small notebook and an envelope and handed them to Nilsson.

"Take this, please. Two nights ago, when I couldn't sleep, I listed Hitler's most committed men. Where they were. The programs they monitored."

Nilsson looked genuinely confused. "Why do you give it to me?"

"It should be in neutral hands. I'm sure there will be war trials. These men can have a sudden memory loss about their participation. This list should help clarify."

Nilsson tucked the book inside a jacket pocket. He read the address on the front of the envelope. "Who is Karl van der Beck?"

"My wife's family. Where she and my sons are. You said I couldn't contact Ilse. But if for some reason I don't come back, I hope she receives this. I need her to know I tried to do good in this wickedness."

Nilsson narrowed his gaze. "Why do you think you're not coming back?"

"This is war and the camp we're going to is one of the worst." Falk kept a neutral expression. His deepest wish was to return to Ilse and the boys, but what he planned to attempt in Auschwitz might set him on a different course.

Nilsson pulled out a flask and handed it to Falk who opened it. The pop of the small chained cork, the sound of life returning to normal, a shared drink with a friend, were the everyday activities he missed. Falk lifted the silver flask. "Here's to the end of the war."

They passed the flask back and forth until it was empty.

Falk let his head drop back against the seat, listening to the sleet hit the window like uncooked rice tossed against glass. With a pang of guilt, it occurred to him he hadn't thought about Ilse enough today. But soon, if granted the sweet justice of killing Mengele he prayed for, he'd return to his family to rebuild a life. And although he'd always face miles of guilt, he'd learn to be content in the garden behind their home and avoid the temptation of looking over the hedges wondering, *what if?*

The horizon glowed with light-pink hues, but dark clouds hung above them. He ran his hand over his eyes and turned to Nilsson. "I have a favor to ask."

Nilsson's eyebrows rose. "I cannot let you disappear."

"That's not it, it's about when we reach Auschwitz."

-51-

IZAAK TAUBER

Auschwitz, Poland - January 1945

Another boy who didn't speak Izaak's language now handed out the strings at the platform. Izaak missed the band's music and missed seeing Papa who must be wondering where he was. Uncle Josef let him and eleven other children live in a big dormitory room where they each had their own beds. Some of the children were twin brothers or sisters and others, although older than Izaak, were smaller as if someone shrunk them. Uncle Josef gave them real food to eat—goulash, chicken, potatoes—and not just soup, and there was an honest-to-goodness play yard. Uncle Josef always dressed up when he visited, not like a doctor at all. No white coat or hat. And he brought sweets. At first, Izaak saved half for Papa, but Papa didn't come.

The other children never saw their parents either. He would gladly go back to his days as a hungry shoestring boy if Papa were nearby. Something was wrong about being chosen as a special child by Uncle Josef. Maybe the candy was meant to trick him and the other children, but he couldn't figure out what the trick was.

Uncle Josef watched him sketch each day. The doctor had weird ideas about the right way to draw, though. He made him shut his eyes and sketch a wooden box from memory. Then he had him draw with his left hand, and one time he even drew while reciting the Dutch alphabet over and over. The doctor always took the drawings but never hung them up. This made him suspect the doctor was somehow lying about wanting to learn how he drew.

Earlier today, the doctor came into their room and took away two brothers, who looked exactly alike, to do "something special." When the boys arrived at Uncle Josef's a few days ago, they were dressed in striped rags like the rest of the people in camp. Then he found matching shirts and pants for them. He told the boys, "You'll get to see your mama and papa after." So he decided to try harder to be the doctor's favorite and be chosen for something special.

When the doctor wasn't around, the children had to stay in their room. Izaak practiced drawing the house his family lived in before the war, taking extra time with details. The deep windowsill where he liked to sketch that overlooked the canal. The praying hands knocker on the front door and Papa's office desk. Sketching was the only pastime that kept his stomach from feeling sick. He threw his worries into the drawings, using more black and grey hues than ever before. His pictures looked more realistic with fear thrown in. His art teacher in Amsterdam would be proud.

Carefully, he unfolded the worn-out drawing of Papa he made over a year ago. Papa was so fuzzy, and all the details of his face were blurred. He barely recognized him, so he needed to draw another one that showed a skinnier Papa.

He worried a lot about Papa since he hadn't seen him. They'd slept snuggled together ever since they arrived, and now that it was snowing, what was Papa doing? And Mama? Thousands of women lived on the other side of camp, all with shaved heads, ali in baggy, striped dresses, many with mismatched shoes. Through the fence, the women looked like ragged ghosts. He would have to hear Mama's voice to tell her apart from the others, but the guards shot people who approached the wire, so that wasn't an option.

He didn't know what to do. The longer he lived in Uncle Josef's dormitory, the more his insides shook. Although he should be honored that an important officer enjoyed his art, he wanted to find his parents more than he cared about showing off for the too-nice man. But as soon as the doctor returned, he planned to ask him if he could go back to his shoestring job, or be chosen for an outing so he could see his mama and papa. Until then, he drew and drew.

-52-

HERBERT MÜLLER

Pfungstadt, German - January 1945

Herbert woke his family just as the first wisps of dawn paraded outside. A good night's sleep reflected in his family's behavior. Jutta fed them another serving of porridge and then hummed as she cleaned the kitchen, leaving it as they found it, minus the food. The scowl melted from Alfred's brow, and he and Frieda were joking back and forth as they headed to the washroom.

They left the maid's quarters just as the horizon turned pink. When they passed Dr. Seidel's house, the baby's cry came from inside. "He's still with us," Jutta said.

As traumatic as yesterday's events were, Herbert's family shared the delight in knowing they'd saved a baby's life. How often could a person brag about that? One day his children would tell their children about all they'd survived.

He set his worries aside and focused on the straightest path out of town. The streets were hushed. A sense of reverence hung in the air, fused with the pungent scent of old wood smoke. The sound of their footsteps, slapping the cobblestone, echoed off the stone buildings as they reached the outskirts of town.

A field beside the road was pockmarked with deep holes. Charred metal, twisted and cooled into violent shapes, was strewn along the edge of the road. The spill of iridescent oil on the road shimmered with dawn's yellow and lavender tints. A splash of color set against the dullness of everything else around them.

"Train station's this way." He pointed to the signpost.

"Wiesbaden, here we come"—Jutta wrapped her arm around Frieda—"No more walking."

"Goodbye, blisters!" Alfred slapped his palms back and forth as if wiping away something unwanted.

At the station, two women and a teenage girl stood against the wall bundled in baggy brown coats, their one piece of luggage at their feet tied shut with a rope, their eyes wary.

The ticket window sign said closed, and the inside of the building was dark.

"Do you speak in German?" Herbert asked in that language, although their dark features negated the typical blonde-haired blue-eyed stereotype.

They looked to each other and squeezed closer together. The older-looking woman, with a blue scarf tied around her curly hair, shook her head.

Alfred cupped his hands at the window. "There's a man in there."

"The sign says it opens in thirty." Frieda tapped the words on the sign. "I can read that much in German."

A German military vehicle raced around the corner and stopped next to them. Exhaust billowed from the tailpipe as two soldiers stepped out with guns drawn. "Your identification," one demanded.

Herbert recognized their uniforms—the Gestapo, Germany's secret police. An icy chill raced up his back. His family moved closer to his side as he handed over their travel papers.

The soldier walked it to a man seated in the vehicle, and the men conferred. A massive man in a crisp uniform stepped from the truck. He had a determined but aging face. "Why would Americans be in Germany?" Then he slapped the jacket of papers against his palm.

"We return to live with relatives." A vein in Herbert's neck throbbed. "We take the train from here to Wiesbaden." He hoped to play on their empathy if the police had any. "We've been walking for days since the *Frankfurt Express* was blown up."

The large man nodded and spoke rapidly to the other policemen. He seemed to be seeking confirmation that what Herbert said about the train was true. "Get your tickets and be on your way."

"Danke." A warm wash of relief flowed through him. He'd come to associate trust as if being left holding a piece of crumpled paper. Even when smoothed out again, the creases remained permanent as was his new distrust of authority. "As soon as the station opens." He spread his arms and herded his family to a bench next to the ticket window.

The soldiers turned their attention to the huddle of women who kept their eyes downcast. They pointed their drawn guns and demanded identification, but the women didn't understand and made no move to comply. The large man reached for the youngest girl and began pulling her away from the two.

The older woman complained in a keening voice. The rapid words sounded Slavic.

Another soldier pushed her, and she stumbled to her knees. She raised her arm pleading to the man, her voice cracking with emotion.

Before Herbert could stop him, Alfred crossed to the woman, pulled her up, and then put himself between the women and the police, his arms stretched outward in a protective manner. The ladies' eyes were huge and shifting in all directions, trying to understand what was going on. "They've done nothing wrong," he said in English.

Herbert quickly translated and slowly approached Alfred. He had never been prouder or more scared at the same time. "Son. Let me talk to them."

Alfred didn't move from his protective stance as Herbert turned to the police.

"These women do not seem to be a threat. And they don't speak German." He raised his hands. Surely, they had real criminals to apprehend. How about whoever murdered the baby's relatives? "Shouting louder won't help them understand."

A cruel smile grew on the lips of the lead Gestapo. "Your American arrogance. You claim to know who threatens our country?" His chuckle was throaty and hoarse. "You and your son have to come with us."

They stepped forward and jabbed the guns into Herbert's and Alfred's sides, separating them from the women.

Alfred reached to push the gun away. Then time slowed down even though the events happened in an instant.

"Pleased don't!" Herbert yelled as one policeman raised his rifle.

The Gestapo officer clubbed Alfred in the head with the butt of his weapon. A spray of blood misted the air.

Jutta screamed and Frieda fell to her knees, her face buried in her hands.

Alfred made no sound as he crumpled as if he were a puppet cut loose from its strings. He lay sprawled on the ground in an unnatural position, legs and arms going in opposite directions.

Jutta rushed to Alfred but another policeman slung his rifle outward, blocking her.

"You will still come with us," the large policeman said.

Herbert's mind spun. Lights flashed in front of his eyes. His worst fear was coming true. He failed to keep his family safe and the painful realization made his whole body tremble.

The police seemed intent on taking him and Alfred with them. How could he leave Jutta and Frieda to travel alone? And now Alfred was seriously injured. His stomach roiled and he fought the urge to vomit.

The big officer nudged Herbert, keeping the gun leveled his way. "Move!"

He slowly took off his coat and handed it to Jutta.

"It's very important that you take this and keep it with you," he said firmly, his eyes drilling into hers. Pastor Graf's envelope, that Jutta knew nothing about, was tucked in the inside pocket.

She accepted the coat, all the while shaking her head back and forth as if trying to will away what was happening.

The two soldiers reached for Alfred's arms and legs. Herbert stepped in to help lift his son into the back of the military truck. Jutta's cries of "no, no, no" turned into a wailing sound as he climbed in to kneel next to Alfred.

"Take the train and get to Elke's." He tried to sound confident but deep down he knew he'd been wrong to trust again, to think the Gestapo would ever be on their side.

The foreign women scurried around the building, but the police no longer seemed interested in them. That should have given him a measure of satisfaction. His son had saved the frightened women from who knows what. But the cost to his family was too high. They would be separated and with Alfred seriously injured, he was stripped bare of any hope.

"I know you can do this. I love you both." The horror on Jutta's face nearly ripped him in half as she reached for Frieda, sobs wracking them both.

He turned his attention to Alfred who lay on his side, unmoving but breathing. Thank God. When the vehicle lurched ahead, it knocked him onto his sore hip, and he silently cursed. His last glimpse of his wife and daughter left him more terrified than ever. Jutta and Frieda huddled together, stranded in hostile territory. They needed to stay safe for only a short while longer, but fear gnawed at his gut. Back at the abandoned train car, he'd witnessed what could happen to defenseless travelers. And as he watched them shrink from view, it was hard to breathe. Terror that he'd never see them again overtook him. Turning his face away from the police, he let the tears flow.

They were to be transported to Laufen Castle, an internment camp for British soldiers captured off the Channel Islands. He was informed he'd feel right at home with the 120 American citizens also held there. It flashed through his mind that this prison might be where Pastor Graf was held. He could use a friend.

During the two-hour ride, he struggled with overwhelming anxiety about Jutta and Frieda on one side, his wounded son on the other. Once, a small tremor moved through Alfred's body and his eyes fluttered, a sign he hoped meant his son was coming around. But he remained unconscious. If Alfred didn't get good medical attention soon, he might never open his eyes again. Waves of hopelessness and futility raced through him. He had taken so much for granted. His parents, their sacrifice to get him and Karl to America, and then build a good life. The gristmill and the daily labor that fulfilled him at the close of each day. His children growing, learning, their unique personalities. Frieda kind and giving. Alfred always on the defense but deep down, kindhearted. For the first time, Alfred had not struck out in rash anger. He'd been clubbed for being reasonable, for protecting the women.

The truck slowed and then ground gears as it wound up the hill. Traveling over an aqueduct, a red-roof village unfurled in the valley below. Finally, the truck slowed at a fortified gate and then proceeded through before stopping in front of an ancient-looking square-shaped château. It felt surreal to be driven past the high walls, the wired fences. To lose his freedom once again.

A guard with a hardened face ordered them out of the truck.

"What about my son?" Herbert motioned to Alfred's limp body.

Medics were called, and they carried Alfred inside the damp, stone fortress on an army stretcher as he followed.

They took them to a small cell containing two metal beds covered with thin mattresses, a wash basin, and wooden chair. Alfred moaned when the medics moved him to the bed, but he didn't awaken.

When the Germans turned to leave, he raised his hand to halt them. "Wait! He needs help."

The men stopped outside the cell and pulled the bars closed. "Yes. Today ... or tomorrow." The metal clang reverberated in the stone hallway.

In the cells across the hall, he saw men tightly packed on bunk beds, who seemed slumped in their personal sorrows.

"Is there a hospital here?" Herbert called across the way. He was led to believe Alfred would get medical attention.

"There are medics here." In a cell diagonally across, a man with a full beard stood at the bars. He gripped the iron rods and leaned his face between them. "Welcome to ILAG Seven, the camp for everyone they scraped off the countryside and don't know what to do with."

"That sounds about right." He paced the floor next to Alfred's bed. The boy let out a tiny moan. Herbert dropped to the concrete floor, leaning close to him. "Son. Can you hear me?"

Alfred's eyes opened, mere slits with a dark pebble behind each. Then he was out again.

He sighed.

"What happened to your boy?"

"He was hit in the head. How do I get the medics to look at him right now?" Heat filled his head. They'd been sent into Germany under such dangerous conditions. When he left Ellis Island, his main concern, and he thought it to be crazy at best, was whether they might become laborers, or detained in a prison camp. The image of dodging bombs never entered his mind since he'd been guaranteed they would have safe passage. He drew in a long breath to calm his anger. Alfred needed a level-headed father once he awakened.

"There is a clinic here, but it's understaffed and overrun with wounded soldiers. You should be on the civilian side of the prison. Rumor has it the Red Cross is good about providing food and medical attention there."

"And what about here?"

"I'm not sure the Red Cross knows we exist."

Hours later, Alfred stirred. His head rested on Herbert's lap as he sat on the bed with his back to the wall.

"Where are we?" Alfred's voice was barely a croak.

"Praise God, son." Relief washed through him. "You're awake."

"Everything's blurry." Alfred's eyes opened wider and moved over Herbert's face and then to the mottled stone walls.

"I'm sorry. It should clear up when your head heals." He hoped he was right. "You have no idea how good it is to hear your voice."

Alfred tried to touch his head, but his hand wobbled, and it took several attempts before he found the injured area. "I don't remember anything."

"You tried to protect those women at the train station. Very brave, son." Herbert told him what happened after the Gestapo hit him. "We're in a German camp of sorts. Actually, a castle."

"Mother and Frieda?"

"They should have arrived in Wiesbaden by now, but we have no way to know." He swallowed a lump in his throat and sent a dozen prayers skyward that Jutta and Frieda were safe. Unmolested. Unharmed in any way.

Raised to believe every sacrifice has a reward and every failure has a second chance if God were in the equation. He sent prayers out of habit. But with all that happened, his belief in divine intervention wavered.

He stroked Alfred's matted hair and studied the wild cast in his eyes.

"I need you to drink some water, son." He lifted a tin cup and raised Alfred's head. Most of the water ran down his chin and shirt, but some made it down his throat. He pictured Alfred as a baby, spitting out pureed carrots as Jutta tried to keep the orange paste from flying everywhere.

Alfred moaned. "My head sure hurts." He seemed shrunken, a broken fifteen-year-old.

"I've asked for a doctor." A vein pounded in his neck. He could do nothing for Alfred. "We just have to wait a little longer." Alfred drifted back to sleep as he prayed he'd spoken the truth—"a little longer."

-53-

WILHELM FALK

Auschwitz, Poland - January 1945

The SS officer who met Falk's Red Cross caravan in Auschwitz had the look of a cobra. Guards had rotated in the year since Falk was there, which meant it was unlikely anyone would remember him. A guard stopped them outside the gate, reminding the volunteers the other prisoners must not learn about the purchase. An uprising was the last thing they wanted.

He didn't count on the barracks being so far from where they were instructed to park. If the freed prisoners were to walk to the buses, he had no legitimate way to get to the barracks, no possibility of putting his plan into action. Kill Mengele. Help load the prisoners on the bus. Do what the U.S. government asked until the end of the war. Return to his wife and boys.

The only complication was the first part. Lieutenant Nilsson denied his request for twenty minutes inside the camp unchaperoned.

Another guard, with bulging eyes, took the release papers and studied them. "Two hundred Jews. That's it. Only Danish and Dutch. We have them ready to go in twenty minutes." He made an impatient gesture before heading back along the tracks.

Falk needed an excuse to get into camp, so he walked to the lead bus and found Bauer.

"I don't trust these guards. How do we know they will give us the correct people?" Falk asked.

"Why do these guards seem different than in the other camps?"

"I've heard that this camp has the cruelest and most deceitful SS." He couldn't explain he'd visited here before and what he witnessed. "Is it okay if I supervise?"

Bauer studied Falk. "If Lieutenant Nilsson gives us the green light." The young man set off in search of the commander.

He needed to move fast because there was no approval from Nilsson coming his way. He moved into the tree line that paralleled the train tracks. Working his way toward the camp, he reached the far side of the train platform. When he glanced into the fenced-in areas, he was jarred by what he saw. The number of prisoners had multiplied since he was last here. No wonder the guards didn't let the Red Cross any closer. Skeletal bodies in filthy clothing filled the compound, nearly to overflowing. Many stood just behind the fence, watching him. Were they hopeful the man in a Red Cross uniform meant something positive? That their struggle to hang on one more day meant they'd won? He averted his eyes and hurried on, the sight heartbreaking and beyond the reach of what he could do. By killing Mengele, he'd save hundreds from extreme medical experiments ultimately ending in death, and make amends for Hiam's death.

He approached the main gate and showed his fake Red Cross papers, grateful for the official patches and insignia on his clothes. Assuming the guards had heard of the transfer, he patted his coat pocket and said, "I am here for children," in what he hoped sounded like broken German. A man's attempt to speak their language. He dropped his hand and pantomimed patting the heads of children. "For Himmler."

He held his breath as they conferred. These guards looked young, like Eduard and the now-dead Christoph, the young soldiers from the *Algonquin*.

They handed him the papers and stepped back. He walked through the gate and into the camp proper. The crematorium's chimneys billowed ferociously, and a sickening stench settled over the entire camp.

He kept his head down and headed straight for Mengele's research building. Ever since he'd been asked to assist the Red Cross, he fantasized about killing the doctor, and his heart hammered—now only steps away.

The door to the main facility was locked. Falk circled to the side and entered through the attached dormitory. At his back, he felt the eyes of a hundred ragged prisoners in striped clothing follow his movements. Once through the door, his vision quickly adjusted in the dim light. He counted twelve children, some on their beds, others at tables, reading or drawing. The room held nice furniture, and curtains hung on the window.

He pushed his finger to his lips. "Shhh."

Wide-eyed, the children watched him, but none so much as blinked as he walked past their beds. He took a big breath, and then with muscles strung tight and ready to spring, turned the knob and rushed through the next door into Mengele's private quarters. Within seconds, he took in the scene. No one was there. He searched the other adjoining rooms. The doctor wasn't in the building. He clenched his fists as disappointment settled like spikes in his chest. Where the hell was Mengele? He had limited time to hunt for him, or he'd be left behind when the buses pulled away.

Then he returned to the dormitory. Several children were lined up and watching him. "Where is the man who lives there?" he asked the children in German.

A dwarf child answered. "He left this morning. Are you here to take us for our meal?"

The innocents! These children lived in the lion's lair but had not yet seen the teeth of the beast. He had no choice but to scrap the first part of his plan and follow through with the second. He was here to get prisoners out of camp and onto the buses, so he might as well start by saving these twelve from the doctor's horror show.

"Yes. I am also a doctor." He pointed to the red cross on his sleeve. "We will go to some buses outside the camp where there is something for everyone to eat."

A small boy stepped forward and held out a drawing of a house. It was excellent. He said in Dutch, "It's for Uncle Josef. I have to stay."

How could he convince the boy without making a scene? He bent to study the picture and smiled. His ability to speak Dutch was rusty, but passable. He now thanked Ilse for all the times they spoke in her native tongue when the children were younger, impressing upon them the need to speak both parents' languages.

"Is this your home?" he asked.

The boy nodded. Falk looked at the home. It did look like the houses in the Netherlands, especially Amsterdam. He and Ilse stopped there many times after visiting her sister in Eindhoven. The details of the boy's drawing were so distinct. Then, suddenly, one small detail caught his eye—a praying hands door knocker.

The child was studying his face when Falk looked more closely at him. He had billeted at a house with a door knocker exactly like the one in the drawing, just after he first visited Auschwitz. Was it even possible this boy and his mother were the same people forced to take him in? He recalled he paced their upstairs floor all night, half out of his mind because of what he'd witnessed in the extermination camps.

He bent down. "Do you know me?" he whispered to the boy.

The boy slowly bobbed his head and started to back away. "You were a German soldier, and you gave me sweets."

"That's right. But we can forget that because I am now with the Red Cross."

"Uncle Josef is also doctor who still wears his good grey uniform as you once did."

"Yes, he does." He took the boy's drawing and then tucked it in his coat. Then he stood, disliking the feeling of being compared to Mengele. He reached for the boy's hand and thankfully the child accepted it. He said to the children in Dutch, "We have to leave now, take another person's hand and follow me, do not stop until we reach the buses where we have the food."

And then in German, "We have to go now. Take the hand of another and follow me. Do not stop until we reach the buses where we have the food."

Outside, the arctic air hit Falk and cleared his head. Mengele could be anywhere in the camp and watching them leave. He needed to get the children to the coaches as soon as possible before the madman discovered they were missing. He had no doubt Mengele would have them all shot to make a point.

-54-

HERBERT MÜLLER

Laufen (Civilian Internment Camp), Germany - January 1945

Eleven days, and Herbert had no word as to when he and Alfred would be allowed to leave the Laufen internment camp and travel to Wiesbaden. The camp housed hundreds of men deported from the Channel Islands of Jersey and Guernsey, and some American civilians caught in Europe when Germany declared war. Those were the unlucky ones not exchanged for repatriated Americans like he and his family. The prisoners all seemed to live in a stew of anxiety on the civilian side of the prison. The International Red Cross was as involved as they could be. But with all the chaos in Europe, their directive to protect all internees held by a warring nation was lackluster at best as the numbers ran into the millions.

Because of Article 79 of the Geneva Convention, the Red Cross was allowed to pass on information or enquiries about POWs. These letters were restricted to twenty-five words and had to be family news only.

Although Herbert couldn't tell Jutta where they were, he wrote to let her know they were safe and that Alfred was healing. That they missed them, loved them, and dreamed of their reunion. His letter was sent to the International Red Cross headquarters in Geneva where it would be forwarded to Elke's address. Jutta should have it by now. And he'd almost wept two days earlier when the Red Cross confirmed Jutta and Frieda made it to Elke's. With tens of thousands of letters being exchanged each month, they told him to be patient with receiving a reply from Wiesbaden. He could wait. His family was divided but fine. The Red Cross worked on their request to be reunited, but for now he and Alfred were coping.

To his knowledge, Pastor Graf was not in the castle prison. He asked the Red Cross to try to track down his friend. Although they said they would, they added there were hundreds of camps throughout Germany and Austria holding Americans and others deemed enemy aliens.

This morning, he woke up early, like always, picturing home. The bright kitchen where they spent most of their time in the evenings. Jutta at the piano. The children showing off their Charleston moves when they tired of performing Waltz and Foxtrot steps. Frieda practicing the saxophone. What he wouldn't give to hear that plaintive sound with its little bit of brassiness and occasional off-key squeaks. Otto snoring in a living room chair, the German paper open on his lap. The radio announcing a Philly's baseball game. He wanted it all back more than ever but without the emotional suffering. Now, held captive thousands of miles away in a dim and dank prison cell, his former life seemed like an illusion.

Herbert pulled himself back to reality and crossed to the small sink where he shaved, using an old razor and sliver of soap, the water a few degrees above freezing.

He glanced at Alfred's reflection in the mirror—breathing steady, deeply asleep. Alfred continued to improve but remained dizzy. He couldn't stand or navigate far without Herbert's support. The medics checked on him frequently, stating nothing but time would heal his injured head.

He dressed. His clothes were freshly laundered and slipped between the bars of their cell during the night. Laundry service was once a week, barbering offered twice a month, and emergency dental appointments were available.

Men in the other cells began to stir. The squeaky wheel on the breakfast cart announced its arrival. He learned that when men had time on their hands, time took on extreme importance. Their breakfast trays would arrive in exactly five minutes and forty seconds, but only if an inmate didn't disrupt the flow.

He crossed to Alfred's bed and rubbed his son's back. "Good morning."

Alfred mumbled something Herbert didn't catch but made Herbert smile. How many mornings had his son muttered, "Just five more minutes?" while cocooned under thick quilts, unwilling to crawl out on a cold winter morning even for buttermilk pancakes?

Herbert gently shook Alfred's shoulder again. "Breakfast time, son. Wake up."

The boy didn't move. It was then he recognized the smell of urine. He pulled back the blanket. His son's pants were soaked. His pulse quickened. Alfred's face was covered with a sheen of moisture. How could he be sweating in their cold cell? He touched his son's forehead and discovered he was burning up.

Herbert rushed to the cell bars. "Medic! Quickly! My son needs help!"

Immediately, he heard the sounds of booted guards rushing toward their cell. They slid to a halt. "What happened?"

"My son has a fever, and I can't wake him." Bile rose in his throat. His breath came in bursts. "Please. Get the doctor."

They peeked into the cell as if to verify what he said before jogging away. He knelt next to Alfred's bed and scooped him up, and gently rocked him. "Hang on, son. You're going to get better." He felt the heat of Alfred's body through his own clothes. "Remember, Mother and Frieda are waiting for us. We all love you."

Moments later, two German medics pulled to a stop in front of Herbert's cell with a small gurney. It seemed to take forever for them to unlock the door, the keys clanging against the iron bars. Once inside, they approached Alfred. "How long has he been like this?" one asked in heavily-accented English.

"He was fine last night." He gulped at air. "This is how I found him just now." He moved to the back wall and pressed himself against it to keep his legs from buckling. Pushing away horrible thoughts, in silence he prayed, *please, please, please, let him be okay.*

One worker stood. "He'll go to the infirmary. His fever is too high." They gently lifted Alfred, draped like a large limp doll, and carried him outside the cell to the gurney. They pulled a sheet over his midsection, covering his urine-soaked pants.

He started to follow, but the guard raised his gun. "No."

What were they saying? Of course, he would go with Alfred.

"If you have to, handcuff me. I need to be with him." He had to be there when Alfred woke up. "I'm a danger to no one."

"You'll be allowed to visit shortly."

"But—"

"No." The English-speaking guard hung back as Alfred was wheeled away, the rattle of the gurney on the uneven stone floor fading. "When he is stable, we will come for you."

Returning to the bed, he sat on the edge. "It's just a fever," he whispered. Many times, he and Jutta nursed the children through high temperatures, whooping cough, croup. Alfred's wound had healed. No infection bloomed—a miracle in their dirty environment. "It's just a fever." He paced the room, around and around, like a caged tiger, minutes ticking by.

Then, he heard footsteps approaching, someone running. He shot to his feet. One of the same medics stopped outside the cell, out of breath, a guard close behind. The guard fumbled to unlock the door. "You must hurry!"

"Why?"

"Your son is suffering an epileptic fit."

When the cell door opened, he ran as if Alfred's life depended on it. Pain shot through his hip, but he kept up, his heart racing and his vision blurred. An epileptic fit? He pictured Alfred thrashing about, his eyes wild, casting about searching for his father. He choked on the image. They turned down several corridors, passing the curious who stared from their cells.

The scent of antiseptic hit his nose before he reached the infirmary. An arched stone doorway led into a bigger room with curtained-off beds. "In here," the worker said, pointing to where three doctors were frantically working, shouting in German, one administering chest compressions.

He reached his son's side and saw him lying crooked on the hospital bed. His skin a sickly pale color, his eyes half-open rolled back in his head.

Medics rushed around the small space, shoving away a cart to get closer to Alfred. One pushed a tube down his throat, and then the doctor squeezed a rubber ball at the other end. Alfred's chest inflated and relaxed.

Tears sprang into Herbert's eyes. "Alfred," he choked. "Come on, son!"

Another medic thumped hard on his chest twice, and Alfred's legs flailed as he nearly fell off the table.

The doctor pumping the tube doubled his efforts. The air rushing inside the rubber ball made an empty, eerie sound.

Please, please, please, God. He willed Alfred to move, to cry out, anything. Why wasn't this working?

The seconds ticked on, but he hadn't revived.

One doctor stepped away, his face grim. "The seizure caused him to stop breathing."

Herbert stared incredulously as the other medics stopped working on his son.

"You have to keep trying!"

One of the medics spoke. "We are very sorry. He's gone."

"No!" The word resounded through the stone room. He threw himself on Alfred's body. Even though still warm, he lay as still and empty as a mannequin.

"No, no, no," he cried into Alfred's chest. All hope, every reason to fight on, fled from his pained soul as he slid to the tile floor. Every moment with his son since birth flashed through his mind. Remembering every coat he ever buttoned for Alfred—every shoe he tied, days catching a baseball, laboring over homework—fleeting images of a life suddenly gone, taking a huge part of Herbert with him.

He wished to die. It would be easier than telling Jutta and Frieda their son and big brother wasn't coming home.

-55-

WILHELM FALK

Auschwitz, Poland - January 1945

Heads turned as Falk and the children crossed the open area, but no one reacted. No gunshots rang out. So far, so good. They reached the train platform where so many had been deceived with false hope. He pulled the children along the tracks leading to the buses. Some of the youngsters slipped on the snow-packed ground, but all managed to stay upright. They just needed to clear the guards at the entrance.

"Falcon!" Bauer approached. He was already inside the gate and headed to him at a trot. "What are you doing?" he asked in Dutch, believing it to be Falk's first language. Worry and fear contorted his face.

"These children will be murdered in terrible ways. We have to take them."

The Dutch boy let out a gasp, having understood Falk's words. He looked down and saw tears welling in the child's eyes. Good Lord. The boy had had enough terror in his short life and didn't need more fear. He leaned close to the child. "You will be safe, I promise."

The gate was ten meters away, and the guards had turned in his direction, but he knew they didn't understand a word of their exchange.

Bauer studied the children. He leaned closer. "How do you know this?"

"Trust me, Bauer. We have to get through that gate. I've convinced the guards I have the right papers for fifteen and here there are twelve." His voice strained with his plea. He never felt so desperate to make something happen, and his nerves were overwrought. He'd find a way to convince Nilsson these children needed to be extricated from this camp, and as far away from Mengele's insanity as they could get.

Bauer sighed, aiming a quick look at the guards. He took the hands of two girls. "You will answer to the lieutenant."

Falk nodded. Relief surged through his body. They walked to the entrance. Thirty steps and they'd be through the gate. He set his face to expressionless, just doing his Red Cross job.

The boy from Amsterdam balked and pulled Falk to a stop a few feet from the guard station. The child looked behind him to the camp.

"My papa. And I think my mama is in a nearby camp."

Good Lord. His parents were likely dead. Mengele killed the parents of all his subjects. That way no one came looking when the child never returned. How would he convince the child to go on?

"It's okay," he said with a soothing voice. "At this moment, we just have to go to the buses."

The boy started forward. As they passed through the arch, the boy spoke to Falk again. "Do you remember my mama from when you stayed with us?"

"I do," Falk said.

Bauer moved next to him and asked in German, "How do you know this boy?"

"I'll explain later," Falk whispered.

The buses came into sight. The 200 rescued Jews—almost all on board—were moved from camp along a side road. Falk walked faster now, nearly dragging his two charges. Nearly home-free.

Then he heard Ilse call his name. A figment of his imagination in his exhausted state. A desire so deep to see her again that it sounded real. He took another step and heard her voice again, raspy but louder.

His breath stopped as he turned and faced the tattered group of prisoners at the fence.

Even with a shaven head and skeletal features, he recognized his once-beautiful wife. He blinked and stared. This was impossible. His heart raced wild and fast, and he almost stopped breathing. Why would Ilse be here? Then the answer screamed through his mind. It was because of him.

In a dreamlike state, he dropped the boy's hand and said to him, "Please, follow the other children." He gently nudged the boy to Bauer, and the boy grabbed the hand of a girl, his eyes as huge as plums.

The guards were now focused on the conversation.

"I have papers," he said in German, hoping to stall, and made a show of reaching into his coat pocket. Instead of authorization papers, he pulled out the child's drawing and handed it to him.

Then he spoke to Bauer in Dutch. "Bauer. You have to go now." Falk's legs were rubber, but he willed them to keep him upright. "I need to do something." His voice was robotic. Shock had set in.

Ilse was here. A starving prisoner. A witness to all he had tried to stop.

He turned toward the fence, but out of the corner of his eye, he watched Bauer herding the children in front of him like confused lambs. Only seventy meters to go until they reached safety. The last of the rescued Jews were loaded just in front of Bauer.

Then, he turned and locked eyes with his wife. He forced himself to walk in that direction, overcome with despair. He suffocated in the painful truth that his treasonous acts caused her arrest. But how? The Wehrmacht believed he was dead, so why go after his widow?

And his sons? What of them?

Gravel crunched behind him. "Halt!" a guard called.

Emotionally numb and more exhausted than he had ever been, he lurched forward. Nothing would keep him from holding his wife again.

Guards called out more commands for him to stop.

The women behind Ilse backed away, sensing the danger.

He reached the fence as Ilse approached him, tears flowing over her quivering lips as she smiled. "Wilhelm." Her voice breaking as she spoke his name.

"I'm sorry." He choked out the words and reached for her hands through the wire. They were boney, rough and cold. "What happened? Why are you here?"

"The military told us you were killed. In Italy"—her whole body shook—"We mourned. Then Pastor Theodore Graf wrote. He sent money. He said you were a hero, helping the Americans defeat Hitler."

"I tried." He gulped. He locked eyes with hers, vowing to never look away, broken by the pain but also by the love he saw in her eyes.

The crunch of footsteps drew closer behind him, and the shouting intensified for him to get away from the fence.

"I wanted them to know about the exterminations." He lifted his eyes to the barbed wire enclosure. "About this."

"Wilhelm"—she broke down and confessed—"I trusted a friend. About the information you have collected. I was proud of you."

The words he longed to hear. That she was proud of him.

He gripped both of her arms and tried pulling her to him, even as the wire caught his clothes. He needed to feel her breath, to touch her skin.

"She reported us to the Gestapo." Her face spasmed.

The shouting increased behind him. Guards were also moving in behind Ilse, commanding her to step away.

The next words were nearly impossible to form. "Hans and Dietrich. Are they...?"

"Away from the prisoner!" a guard shouted from behind as several guns cocked.

She shook her head. "Gassed."

Deep in his soul he knew the answer. His sons were gone, like Hiam, like millions of other children.

Panic gripped him. "Ilse. Turn around and step away from me." She had a chance to survive. He tried to pull himself from her arms. "Do it for me." He would be shot, but she didn't deserve it.

She pulled him closer, the wire cutting into her face, her arms tight around him.

"No. We stay together."

A cacophony of sounds surrounded him. His name shouted. Guards yelling commands behind both of them. Guns readied. He met her gaze once again.

"I love you," they both said at the same time.

Pain exploded through his body. Ilse jerked and gasped, but didn't cry out. Another shot ripped through them. He held on, refusing to let her slip to the ground. He wanted to say so much—she was his life, his world, she gave him sons. Her eyes still fixed on his, slowly lost focus, just as his grip weakened. As his world slowly came to a close, he let Hiam go and felt at peace for the first time in three years.

-56-

IZAAK TAUBER

Aboard the Red Cross Train - January 1945

Izaak flinched at the gunshots behind him. The grown-ups yelled to each other, and the man carrying him, handed him up through the bus door. Another man with red crosses on his clothes hurried him to a seat and ran back for more children. He watched out the window as the doctor who took him from Uncle Josef's building held on to a woman through a fence. To Izaak's horror, guards moved closer to the man and woman and fired their guns. They didn't fall at first but then slowly slipped to the ground on each side of the wires, facing each other.

Afterwards, everything on the bus happened in a flash. A Red Cross worker rushed to the closed door with his gun drawn. Dozens of other people were on the coach already, staring out the windows, all big-eyed. Faces marked with fear.

Izaak didn't know what was happening and the drum inside his chest pounded so loud, he thought it might break apart. Tears ran down his cheeks. He wasn't sure where he should be. Uncle Josef in the camp took good care of him. But the doctor who once stayed at his house was once a soldier and gave him candy and was also a nice man. But they shot him.

The bus rocketed out of the camp and soon the yelling stopped, and everyone calmed down. The man who spoke his language slid onto the seat next to him. "My name is Jonathan. What is yours?"

"Izaak." He studied the man's eyes. He knew that looking at a person's mouth did not always tell you the truth about someone. Mean people could smile and then do something terrible. But the eyes. They showed him if the person was good, or full of rotten juice inside. Jonathan's eyes said he was extra nice. "Is the nice doctor dead?"

Jonathan didn't answer right away. "Do you mean the man you knew, the one who brought you out of the camp?"

He nodded.

"He is. How did you know him, if you're..."—Jonathan squinted and studied him—"if you say he was a German officer?"

"He came to our house in Amsterdam before Papa left. We were still in our nice house. But back then, he did not seem happy." He remembered the man talking to himself and his cries from behind his bedroom door. "He seemed more cheerful today dressed like you." He touched the Red Cross patch on Jonathan's shirt.

Jonathan smiled and put his arm around his back and pulled him closer.

"I can imagine you've had to be very brave, haven't you?"

His lips quivered as he heard Mama's voice in his head. *You are the bravest boy, Izaak. If there comes a day when we aren't together for a while, I'll need you to stay strong.* He was suddenly very tired.

"My brave feels all worn out." He blinked hard to keep tears from storming his eyes, but they came anyway. "I want my mama and papa."

The man didn't say anything, but slowly rocked him back and forth until Izaak wasn't sure if he was asleep or awake. A little dream found its way in. He and Papa were fishing, Mama was sitting on a blanket knitting, and Papa was laughing about the fish on Izaak's hook. The dream moved like a motion picture show: Their picnic lunch of sausage and biscuits. The afternoon spent skipping stones on the lake, and finally, the evening when the stars came out as they packed to go home. Mama giggled and kissed Papa and said, "I love you." Papa passed the kiss on to Izaak and said, "I love you both more." This was a game they always played. Who could say who loved the other the most. Izaak noticed the chips of light hanging in the night sky and he had said, "I love you both to the stars and back."

His papa rubbed his hair and said, "That's the best so far."

He held on to that dream as the bus drove on and on. Even wrapped in the man's arms, he never felt so empty and alone.

-57-

IZAAK TAUBER

Regensburg, Germany - May 1945

This was Izaak's fourth month in a Displaced Persons Camp in Regensburg, Germany. As far as he could tell, everyone was looking for someone. He was still looking for two somebodies—his mama and papa.

The Red Cross bus brought him here from Auschwitz. He lived in a military barracks, but unlike the other camps he was in, this one was clean. Each night, he marveled he had a bed to himself with sheets and a pillow. The camp was near a pretty village. Once in a while, the children rode by bus to the sweet shop in town where each child was allowed to choose a candy. The storekeeper didn't seem to like children though. He stood way back until they all made their choices and then quickly took their military chaperone's money. Izaak didn't care. A candy shop was special enough not to worry about who liked him or not.

Another good thing about being at Displaced Persons was how many children were there. Hundreds! And the Catholics were back. Nuns and priests invited the children to group meetings where they all sang songs and talked about heaven. They wanted the children to remember nice things about their families as if they'd never see them again. To push away those thoughts, Izaak drew all the images he remembered from their life in Amsterdam, but most times those memories made him cry. He checked the stars every clear night and never saw any stars that looked like they might be Papa's or Mama's. That led him to believe his parents were still waiting for the next Red Cross bus.

A camp teacher saw a drawing he completed of a boy's mama from a worn-out photo the boy carried. The boy said he was sad because the picture was fading away, and he was afraid he'd forget her. Izaak sketched the woman with fresh lines, making her appear young and healthy.

Other people came forward and asked him to draw their family members, the ones they hoped to find. Papa's phrase ran through his head—"A man's true wealth is the good he does in this world"—as his hand ached on some days from gripping a pencil for hours. But it gave him a happy feeling in his chest. He'd lose himself in the scent of pencil shavings and heavy paper, the soft scraping sound of lead filling a new page with a slippery memory.

Jewish religious workers from Israel asked the adults to tell their stories of what happened to them. Those workers, busy day and night in one corner of the library room scribbling in notebooks, made sure they had their story details all correct for a book they were writing. Izaak remembered how he wrote dates in his notebook early on in the war. He would have filled a dozen books by now if he'd kept any with him.

The camp had an extra big celebration the night before. The war was over! Someone in the nearby town shot off fireworks, and cars along the road blew their horns and flashed their lights. Izaak and the children stayed up late and were allowed an extra serving of cookies.

He'd prayed for this day and even heard that the German leader, Hitler, was dead and camp prisoners were freed. Now, he only needed to wait for Mama and Papa to figure out where he was.

Today was the first time in weeks the cold rains stayed away from their camp, and everything smelled warm, green, and clean. Clean was now his favorite scent.

When the weather cleared, he and the other children were allowed onto the sports field to kick a soccer ball around. He ran alongside his three pals, boys from different countries who learned they didn't need to speak the same language to enjoy playing together. Just like back at Terezín.

One of his favorite adults walked to them across the grassy field. He played ball with them for hours. Chased them, tickled them, and showed them how to make swords and airplanes out of sticks. But no matter how much they were together, the man never smiled. His eyes looked as if they would be sad forever. When he saw the man staring at a photo one day, through a translator, he offered to draw the two children and the woman pictured there. But the man quickly put the photo away, wiped his eyes and shook his head. And before he walked away, he gave Izaak a quick hug.

The camp leaders helped search for everyone's family members. Now that he was almost ten, he learned to write letters. Every week, with the camp leaders' help, he wrote to Mama and Papa. The post office put stamps on the letters and sent them off. A mean girl named Cora, whose mama worked at the postal building, said the letters were dumped into big bags and taken to the refuse pile. But Cora also picked her nose and pulled babies' ears to make them cry, so he didn't believe her.

The sad man had a Dutch-German name—Müller. Today, he and three other men took turns lifting the children onto their backs. In the warm spring breeze, in just shirtsleeves, they chased each other around having chicken fights, or tossing a balled-up cloth at each other. Izaak liked riding on Mr. Müller's shoulders because he had a bad leg and sitting on him was like being on a real horse. They rocked side to side when he ran. The leg didn't seem to hurt him, but he noticed the man usually chose the smaller children as riders.

Just as the sun was dropping behind the big mountains in the distance, a military officer jogged onto the field. He ran up to Mr. Müller and spoke rapidly in English, a language Izaak was trying to learn. At this point, he knew polite words, but nothing more.

The military man left. Mr. Müller stood alone with his head bowed as if praying. He ran his hands through his hair, stood up straight, and crossed to Izaak and his friends.

Mr. Müller bent over and hugged each of them for a long time and said, "Goodbye," one of the English words Izaak understood. He didn't want the man to leave, although he believed sooner or later, they would all get to go home. He forced himself to smile, knowing he needed to be happy for Mr. Müller because he must have found the people in his photo. Mr. Müller looked around the camp one more time, and then shoved his hands in his pockets and walked to the gate where the lucky people going home left.

Just before he disappeared, he hesitated and turned around. His eyes found Izaak watching him with his hand raised. The man didn't move for a moment, but eventually raised his hand in return and dropped his head and left.

He sat on the grass. His drawing supplies were in his room, so he'd draw the idea he had in his head. Mr. Müller wouldn't see this drawing of himself, but he really needed to sketch his grown-up friend. Today, he drew Mr. Müller stepping from a train and looking around at the big crowd. He looked lost and then something amazing happened in his imagined picture. Mr. Müller's eyes grew big and he finally smiled.

EPILOGUE

HERBERT MÜLLER

Tulpehocken, Pennsylvania - September 1945

H erbert drove the tractor with the mower through the rows between the apple trees. Earlier that morning, he cut the grass in the peach and apple orchards. The apples hung ready for harvest, and the trucks filled with pickers would arrive in the next few days.

He left the orchard and let the machine idle at the edge of the field as he watched Jutta and Frieda hang sheets on the line. Their voices carried as they laughed about something. It was a sound he never thought he'd hear again. He vowed that if his family returned home, he would show gratitude every day. And he worked hard to do that. Inside, he carried the lasting ache of losing Otto and Alfred. Some moments, and they usually flared out of nowhere, the crushing weight of heartbreak nearly dragged him under. He had lost two people he loved but had to remember that so many had lost everyone.

His family was reunited when a return message from Jutta reached the Displaced Persons Camp, and he received permission—with the Red Cross's help—to join Jutta and Frieda in Wiesbaden.

They explained they'd traveled the final leg of their journey to Wiesbaden in a lorry filled with onion sacks. A farmer braved retribution and took pity on them. Although Elke didn't have the means to take them into her home, and had not received notification they were arriving, she welcomed them. They slept in a chilly attic but were safe. Food was sparse and simple, but they were fed. She would accept none of the money in Graf's envelope to help with expenses.

But their reunion in Wiesbaden was bittersweet. His family was wracked with deep sorrow and disbelief when he first told them of Alfred's death. To add to their profound sadness, he explained he had no choice but to have Alfred buried next to a thousand-year-old Protestant Church on the Laufen Castle grounds. Otto's ashes were to be shipped home with the help of the U.S. Embassy in France. One day, Herbert would save enough to bring Alfred home to be buried in the family plot.

He drove the mower to the barn. Overhead, white buffaloes of clouds floated across the deep-blue sky. The day warmed and the rays were infused with the sweet scent of cut grass rising off the tractor's back tires. He breathed in the intoxicating smells of turned dirt, wild flowers, and the wash flapping on the line. A gift like so many others he recognized and would never take for granted again. He'd been a broken man after Alfred died, believing he had nothing to live for. Jutta and Frieda would go on without him. He'd failed them all. Pastor Graf once encouraged him to reach out and help others to find happiness, and the good Father was right. In the Displaced Persons Camp, he put Graf's words into action. Before leaving the camp, Herbert filled out additional papers. Four sets of them.

After parking the tractor in the barn, he brushed the grass clippings from his pants and rolled the barn door shut.

It took time to obtain reissued U.S. passports and new visas, but within a month, the seven of them boarded a passenger liner bound for America. All paid for by the United States military and Pastor Graf's surprise gift.

Upon reaching Tulpehocken in June, just as the war ended, Herbert learned his property was up for sale again. The couple who bought it at auction was selling, overwhelmed by the work required to run a mill. Pastor Graf's money was used as a down payment to buy back Herbert's land holdings. The pastor had really known his way around the pony track because he had amassed $7,500.

He had no way to thank Graf though. The Red Cross notified him of the pastor's fate. Graf and a dozen U.S. airmen were to be moved to a less crowded prison. Due to the demolished rail lines, they were forced to walk through the heavily bombed city of Rüsselsheim. The prisoners were escorted by two German soldiers. In Rüsselsheim, the townspeople, assuming the fliers were the men who wiped out their town and killed their family members, quickly turned into an uncontrollable angry mob. The citizens beat them to death while the two escorts did nothing to stop the assault. And Graf did not receive a Christian burial.

He crossed the yard to Jutta and Frieda, just as they pinned the last shirt to the line.

"You've finished," Jutta said. Silver streaks showed in her hair, revealing what stress and mourning could do to a thirty-six-year-old. Her positive spirit returned, although she would never laugh as freely as she used to. "Can you round up the children for the noon meal?"

"What experiment are we trying today, Frieda?" Herbert only teased. Frieda had immersed herself in the art of creating traditional Jewish dishes, all delicious.

"Potato and cheese *bourekas*." Frieda tucked her short hair behind one ear, her pigtails long gone.

"Sounds good." His daughter's innocent view of the world was lost. She was still tenderhearted but practical. She accepted her role as a big sister with gusto. Alfred once protected her. She in turn protected her four adopted brothers.

And the new family members?

Alfred once remarked when they were walking through Germany that his family would surely take in refugees if the need ever arose. And it had. Language was still a barrier, but the adopted children picked up English quickly. School was about to start and that would certainly help.

Herbert watched the oldest boy, Mikolaj, twelve and orphaned from Poland, trying to teach their new hunting dog to fetch. The Labrador, happy to run alongside the boy, never returned with the stick and sometimes needed to be fetched himself. Emil, age ten, another child from Poland, had not yet to overcome the nightmares that woke him during the early morning hours.

Each child carried a shadow of grief, for which there would most likely be darker days, no matter what he and Jutta did. But they were safe and loved. He and Jutta would keep the boys' Jewish traditions alive, a promise they'd made to the adoption board.

The third boy, Gabek came from Prague and turned ten aboard ship. All his relatives were murdered in Auschwitz. The child had a natural penchant for music, and Frieda enjoyed the long hours she spent teaching him to play the saxophone.

As Herbert stepped out of the barn, he surveyed his land. Surprisingly, several neighbors showed up at the start of summer to help plant the gardens. Now it looked as though he would have a bumper crop, big enough to share with the war widows in the area. No apologies or explanations were given by the neighbors who originally turned against him, but he didn't need one. Their willingness to help mattered most, and he now understood war caused strange behavior patterns that echoed in ways no one could guess.

Herbert wrote to the U.S. government several times asking about restitution for their losses. No price was high enough to compensate for Otto's and Alfred's deaths, but he kept trying. He held out little hope.

He walked to the orchard and picked his favorite apple, a crisp, almost spicy variety called Fortune. He took a bite and shut his eyes, enjoying the sweetness. Someone tugged on his shirt, and he opened his eyes and smiled down at his fourth adopted son.

The boy was brought to the Displaced Persons Camp at about the same time Herbert arrived. He first spotted the child sitting on a bench, buttoned up and stiff, but alert to everyone passing by. When the child wasn't drawing everything and everyone, he seemed to desperately study the starlit sky each clear night.

He played with the boy and his other adopted sons during his confinement. The Red Cross workers told him the boy's mother and father, both Dutch, perished in Auschwitz and that no extended family had survived.

Herbert's house blossomed with drawings and paintings made by this fourth son. One picture was a fragile drawing the boy carried with him throughout the camps. It was of his father. Now framed and under glass, the image was so worn it was indecipherable. The boy's most astounding painting, however, was called "Poppy Field," modeled after a famous artist's landscape. The painting was full of greens in the background with vaguely outlined trees and fields with orange and red splotches.

Herbert rubbed the boy's curly hair, picked another apple, and handed it to him. "Never saw a child who loved apples as much as you do, Izaak."

THE END

Author's Note

As World War II raged, when Africa and Italy were retaken, Allies such as Great Britain were running short of prison space to house captured POWs. From 1942 through 1945, more than 400,000 German and Italian prisoners were shipped to the United States and detained in camps in rural areas across the country. Some five hundred POW facilities existed, mainly in areas facing a labor shortage since most American males were away, fighting the war, which meant industries struggled to fill positions.

According to the rules of the Geneva Convention, POWs were kept safe, housed, and well fed. But deaths inside the camps were a different story. Although a minority of the prisoners were Nazis, they created internal courts to accuse and convict POWs who showed disloyalty to Hitler. Dozens of prisoner "suicides" were likely murders.

The character of Wilhelm Falk is based on Kurt Gerstein, a German SS officer who witnessed mass murders in Bełżec and Treblinka, two Nazi extermination camps. Horrified and ashamed by what he witnessed, he gathered information and wrote letters to Swedish and Swiss diplomats, as well as to Pope Pius XII, hoping to alert the international public about the atrocities that were occurring. Much to his despair, the countries didn't think there was anything they could do. In 1945, Gerstein surrendered in France. He received a sympathetic reception and wrote the Gerstein Report. Later transferred to a prison in France, he was treated as a Nazi War criminal and found hanged in his cell. His "suicide" was questionable since the prison also housed other SS officers. His report helped convict many SS at the Nuremburg Trials, mainly officers who claimed they were merely unenthusiastic bystanders.

Hadamar Psychiatric Institute was one of six facilities where Nazis ran the T-4 Euthanasia Programme, which resulted in mass sterilizations and mass murder of "undesirable" German citizens, specifically those with physical and mental disabilities. In total, an estimated 200,000 people were killed at these facilities, including thousands of children. Doctors and nurses involved in the program stood trial at the end of the war and several were executed. The psychiatric hospital remains in operation today.

In addition to historic events, many of the "schemes" used by the Nazis in WHEN WE WERE BRAVE are also true. For instance, thousands of Jewish families were duped into boarding trains heading east once they received a postcard from a family member. In fact, at one time, it's been said that every store in Germany was depleted of postcards because the Wehrmacht used them in the concentration camps to flush out more Jews hiding in neighboring countries. The concentration camp prisoners were promised extra food or favors if they would notify relatives they were doing well. The postcards were mailed from nearby towns with railway stations. Then the prisoners were gassed and the addresses on the cards were used to hunt down the recipients who would then take their relative's place in camp.

Many characters in the novel were real people. In Terezín, for instance, Friedl Dicker-Brandeis, was an artist from Austria who taught hundreds of children the joy of escaping through art. She and her husband, Pavel, never had children, but while in Terezín, Friedl was finally able to give free rein to her maternal instincts. To nurture and teach hundreds of children who viewed her as a surrogate mother.

When Pavel was deported from Terezín in late September 1944, Friedl volunteered to take the next transport. Friedl and sixty of her students were sent on transport number EO 167 to Auschwitz-Birkenau, where most of them were murdered upon arrival. But before she left Terezín, Friedl packed 5,000 pieces of artwork into two suitcases and hid them. After the war, the suitcases were moved from Terezín to the Prague Jewish community. Ten years passed before the drawings were rediscovered and exhibited. In 1964, the artwork and poetry of the children of Terezín were brought to a worldwide audience with the publication of the book, *I Never Saw Another Butterfly*.

Today, two exhibits honor her. One, titled *Innovator, Activist, Healer: The Art of Friedl Dicker-Brandeis* tours Jewish Museums, and in

Czechoslovakia, the Memorial at the Terezín concentration camp has dedicated a two-story wall to the children's artwork. Although Friedl herself did not sign most of the work she created in the Upper Fortress, she made sure the children signed their creations with their name and age, a testimony to their identity, and a document of their existence.

Terezín (Theresienstadt in German) was a transit camp and then a propaganda camp. On June 23, 1944, three foreign observers—two from the Red Cross—came to Terezín to learn if the rumors of Nazi atrocities were true. They left with the impression all was well, duped by a well-planned "beautification" of the camp. The Nazis carefully choreographed every detail of the visit. The observers saw children studying in hastily built schools, and stores packed with fresh food. Children appeared happy. The prisoners were given food for weeks, so they no longer appeared emaciated. Hitler was so pleased with himself that in September 1944, he ordered the making of a film about the camp called *A Town Presented to the Jews from the Führer.* All but 4000 of the 87,000 inmates who passed through Terezín were exterminated or died before the war's end.

The visit from the Red Cross delegation, and the production of the film that followed, brought hope of liberation to the prisoners of the Ghetto. However, the Jewish elder, Dr. Paul Eppstein, asked people not to get too hopeful. A week later, on Yom Kippur, he was arrested and sent to the Lower Fortress of Terezín where he was executed. The Terezín inhabitants who performed so well for the Red Cross were loaded in trains and nearly all died in Auschwitz.

Also true. In Terezín, at the end of the war, in order to cover their actions, the Nazis ordered the ashes of 22,000 people dumped into the Ohře River from the Columbarium where they were stored. The few remaining prisoners in the fortress were forced to form a human chain to speed up the activity.

Commandant Karl Rahm fled Theresienstadt on May 5, 1945, along with the last of the SS personnel. He was captured shortly afterward by American forces in Austria and put on trial. Rahm was found guilty of crimes against humanity and executed on April 30, 1947, four hours after his guilty verdict was handed down by the Czech court.

Herbert Müller's story is also based on historical fact. During the war, 12,000 German-Americans were arrested as enemy aliens and sent to internment camps around the country, including one on Ellis Island. Of those 12,000 detainees, several thousand were repatriated to war-torn Germany, many exchanged for *more important* Americans who were trapped in Europe when the war broke out. A countless number of those German-Americans lost their lives as they were not safely chaperoned once in enemy territory, and all lost their property and assets. Some chose never to return to the United States. No one received restitution for what they lost.

The displaced persons camp that united Herbert and Izaak housed 12 million people at the war's end. In 1946, there were 200,000 inquiries for lost children. At the end of 1947 and into 1948, three years after the end of the war, the International Refugee Organization (IRO) was still in charge of 370 camps in the English, French, and American Zones in Germany containing 800,000 displaced persons.

WHEN WE WERE BRAVE

READER'S GUIDE

1. Why do you think WHEN WE WERE BRAVE is told from three different points of view?
2. At the beginning of WHEN WE WERE BRAVE, Herbert Müller is incredulous that the FBI is interested in his family, as he, his wife, and children are all flag-flying citizens of the U.S. What, if any, similarities are there today regarding the issues immigrants and their children face?
3. Hundreds of thousands of German POWs were shipped to America and lived in over 500 internment camps throughout the U.S. Did you know the United States housed German (and Italian) soldiers for three years during the war? Do you think it's possible for such an event to occur today?
4. Izaak's mother, and later his father, protect Izaak by inventing games and by shielding him from the awful truth of what was happening around them. How do you believe so many Jewish people remained brave in the face of death?
5. When we first meet SS officer, Wilhelm Falk, we learn to believe an SS officer could be sympathetic to the Jewish plight. Do you think there were more upper ranking officers who believed *The Final Solution* was horrible? Should/could they have done more to stop Hitler?
6. Pastor Theodore Graf becomes entangled in the enemy-alien roundup when a postal worker turns him in for receiving a package from Germany and writing back. How do you feel about Graf

paying with his life for his association with Falk? What would you have done if you received information like this that put you in jeopardy?

7. Herbert makes the choice to "repatriate" to Germany after Frieda is attacked at Ellis Island. If he knew what life was like in Germany, do you think he would have made the same decision?

8. In the *Author's Note*, we learn that SS officer Falk is loosely based on Kurt Gerstein, an SS officer who wrote to many dignitaries and clergy hoping for a stop to the Jewish extermination. Were you surprised that as early as 1942 these other countries were aware of the massive murders, yet did nothing? Three more years passed until the end of the war. Do you believe any of the informed leaders regretted waiting once they learned of the millions who had been killed?

9. Helen Keller said, "The welfare of each is bound up in the welfare of all." WHEN WE WERE BRAVE is filled with examples of human nature at its best and worst. Discuss the themes of good versus evil throughout the story demonstrated in Keller's words.

10. What do you believe happens in times of war and ethnic cleansing that causes so many to turn on others? If you were told your neighbors were to be rounded up, what would you be willing to do?

ACKNOWLEDGEMENTS

This story took root during a conversation with my mother-in-law who said she'd ridden a passenger train full of German POWs from Utah to Kansas in 1944. Of course, I suspected this was a false memory until I turned to Google. I threw myself into research and soon fell in love with the idea of telling a story about these POWs. I also learned of German-Americans sent to internment camps, and a propaganda scheme played out in a Czechoslovakian extermination camp. The three stories started out separately, however, in the end, the threads of war wove through each of them, and they braided together.

It nearly took an army of devoted and tireless readers before this book found its true voice. Thank you to my early readers, who truly were the champions at steering my rough draft in the right direction. Kristy Pappas, Kate Beckerman, Marla Deakins, Scott Brendel, Karen Kroll, Bill and Kate Chabala, Camille Wintch, Rick Christensen, Mark Todd, Karen Nickel, Lynda Smart-Brown, and Valerie Walsh. To my critique group, Sherri Curtis, Linda Orvis, Rich Casper, Jeff Lowder, Dave Tippetts, and Ericka Prechtel, your enthusiasm has kept me going all these years. Thanks to John Hardy and Brittani Jay, who read the book twice, and who were great at brainstorming ideas. Thank you to The Manuscript Doctor for helping me understand Deep POV. Thanks to Julia Hardy for the beautiful cover and for your creativity.

My heartfelt appreciation goes out to E. Faith Mayo for your tireless enthusiasm and enduring friendship. Thank you for pushing me and demanding the very best from each scene. You are a writer's dream.

Last, but certainly not least, thank you to my husband, John Hardy, for supporting my crazy writer's journey no matter what blockages came my way.

ABOUT THE AUTHOR

Originally from upstate New York, Karla lives with her husband, her mini-me niece, and one big dog in Salt Lake City, Utah. She owns a learning center and volunteers helping children whenever she can. When she's not writing, she can be found gardening and reading. She and her husband travel as much as possible, always in search of another story that needs to be told.

Follow Karla M. Jay

Twitter – @KarlaMJay1
Facebook – https://www.facebook.com/karla.jay.73
Email – authorkarlajay@gmail.com
Goodreads – https://www.goodreads.com/author/show/14167322.Karla_M_Jay
Amazon – https://www.amazon.com/Karla-Jay/e/B00VH17HAW?ref= dbs_p_ebk_r00_abau_000000

Made in the USA
Middletown, DE
12 December 2019